MW01124893

BE WITH THE DEAD

AN ANN KINNEAR SUSPENSE NOVEL

MATTY DALRYMPLE

WILLIAM KINGSFIELD PUBLISHERS

For Margi and Rob Eden, two of the most generous people I know, for opening their (spirit-free) "Eden Beach" home to me for the inspiration for and creation of this story.

Better be with the dead,
Whom we to gain our peace have sent to peace,
Than on the torture of the mind to lie
In restless ecstasy.

William Shakespeare, "Macbeth"

1

Darren Van Osten took a sip of tea, trying to figure out how to convince his editing client that twelve exclamation marks on one page, even in a thriller novel, were at least eleven exclamation marks too many.

It had been years since Darren had had to deal with these kinds of amateur faux pas. He had been spoiled by the fact that until the previous year, almost all his editing work had been for Jock Quine's Robert Wolfram thrillers. Jock had probably used fewer than twelve exclamation marks across the entire series—he had more sophisticated means of keeping a reader's attention.

And it wasn't only Jock's talent as a writer that had spoiled Darren; Darren had also become way too accustomed to the generous salary Jock provided. When Harrison & John had first picked up the Wolfram thrillers, Darren worked for the publishing house, and Jock Quine was one of a number of H & J authors to whom he was assigned. But after the success of the first few books in the series, Jock hired Darren away from H & J to work for him full-time. In fact, the salary Jock provided had enabled Darren to drop most of his freelance clients as well.

Now Darren was regretting having put all his financial eggs in the Jock Quine basket.

As he did periodically—but with decreasing frequency—he tapped *jock quine tamaston* into his browser and scanned the results. There was nothing within the last month, and the most recent news article had barely more information than the first articles about Jock's death, ten months earlier.

Jock Quine, author of the enormously popular Robert Wolfram thrillers, was gunned down in his Princeton home, Tamaston. It appears that Quine might have surprised a burglar, since his collection of ivory figurines, valued at several hundred thousand dollars, is missing.

At the time the break-in was estimated to have taken place, Jock Quine's son, Alec Quine, author of legal thrillers, was attending an event in New York City hosted by their mutual publisher, Harrison & John. Also in attendance at the event was Jock Quine's editor, Darren Van Osten.

H & J had been panic-stricken at the prospect of the Wolfram series cash spigot shutting off. They had appealed to Jock's son Alec, whose legal thrillers they published, to take over the series. Alec agreed, and H & J had contracted with Darren to shepherd Alec through the transition to a more action-oriented genre.

Alec wasn't a bad writer—at least he didn't try to enliven his prose with exclamation points—but Darren wasn't having much luck redirecting Alec's focus from the crafting of nuanced, if fictional, legal arguments to the gun fights, chase scenes, and seductions that Jock's readers expected. Darren's faith that the bookish Alec could hold Jock's devoted fan base was dwindling. He sensed that H & J shared his doubts, and that they placed the blame at Darren's door. Their most recent email to Darren had included a reminder that Jock's fans expected a new Robert Wolfram adventure every six months, and that the three years it had taken Alec to pen each of his legal thrillers wouldn't cut it. Couldn't Darren hurry Alec along?

Alec was not to be hurried, and if Darren didn't rebuild his client base—and quickly—it wouldn't mean just missing out on some of the perks of working on the Wolfram thrillers, such as the 1979 Ford F-150 that he had bought with the bonus Jock had given him when sales of the series hit ten million. It would mean selling that pickup and downsizing to an even more modest apartment. It might mean relocating to a place with an even lower cost of living than Wilmington, Delaware, and losing the benefit of being able to hop on the train and be in the mecca of the publishing universe, New York City, in less than two hours. Losing that access would make it even more difficult to find new clients. He was holding on to his professional standing by a thread, and it wouldn't take much to snap it.

He heaved a sigh, set his mug of tea aside, and began typing a note in the manuscript.

While I certainly agree that the scene is a thrilling one, it's best to convey that not through the use of exclamation marks but

His laptop chimed with a notification, and he clicked over to email, grateful for the distraction.

The message was from the editor of *Latent Prints* magazine, Maude Solas.

Darren, I'm so happy to inform you that Latent Prints *has nominated Lara Seaford's* Darkest Before Death *for our best debut novel award!*

His celebratory slap on his desk and pleased exclamation —"Excellent!"—set off a brief barking fit from the hypervigilant German Shepherd in the adjacent apartment.

Congratulations are in order for you as well as Ms. Seaford, since I know her first novel wouldn't have reached such levels of sophistication and polish if it hadn't been for your editorial ministrations.

Self-published novels generally don't hit our radar screens, and I might have missed this one if it hadn't been for that fabulous review by Egan Salier.

Darren smiled. He himself had brought Lara's book to Salier's attention. Then the smile faded. This ability to exert some influence in the publishing world was another thing he would lose, along with his livelihood, if he couldn't drum up some more clients. But a nomination for best debut, even from a publication as modest as *Latent Prints*, would help attract some much-needed attention to his editorial services.

I've tried to find Miss Seaford's contact information and have been unsuccessful. Might you have an email address I can use to reach her?

The two of you have certainly crafted a thrilling and compelling novel—an impressive debut indeed. I look forward to seeing what else might come from Miss Seaford's pen (and your editing pencil).

Best,

Maude

P.S. Looking forward to seeing you at GothamCon!

Lara Seaford was Darren's only client other than Alec Quine and the exclamation mark aficionado. H & J had all but said that if Darren couldn't get Alec to produce more suitable material more quickly, they'd shift their focus to promoting a more viable heir apparent to Jock Quine's dynasty. Might Lara Seaford be that heir apparent?

Her story had arrived on Darren's desk a bit meandering, her plot points too overtly borrowed from other thrillers. However, it was her first novel; some issues were to be expected. And not only did she not skimp on gun fights, chase scenes, and seductions, but she had crafted a killer ending. In Darren's few attempts at drafting a novel of his own, the endings had been his Achilles' heel.

He reached over to the bookcase next to his desk, pulled out his copy of *Darkest Before Death*, and flipped it over to the author photo on the back cover. It showed a woman from the shoulders up, her face turned away so that the camera caught only dark hair pulled back in a fashionably messy bun, an intricately patterned silver hoop earring, and a deeply tanned cheek. It was all Darren had ever seen of his client—she didn't even have a social media presence.

He put the book aside and tapped out a response to Maude.

I'm so thrilled to hear about the Latent Prints *nomination! Lara has asked me not to share her contact information with anyone—there's a true thriller novelist for you—but I'd be happy to forward your email on to her. Just let me know how you'd like me to proceed.*

He sent the email and returned his attention to Lara's author photo. She had proven to be a cooperative client—willing to heed the advice he dispensed via email—and Darren had been more pleased with the final manuscript than any save Jock's. He was proud of the role he had played in bringing *Darkest Before Death* to fruition. From a more practical point of view, even if no one ever found out that *ghostwriter* might be a more accurate representation of his involvement than *editor*, a win by his client would be a valuable addition to his résumé. *Latent Prints* might not be the biggest name in the genre, but any nomination by a well-respected publication was helpful, and it might pave the way for bigger things ... like a Best Debut nomination from GothamCon.

Darren had served as a volunteer supporting the

GothamCon board for many years, mainly acting as a liaison to the conference speakers. It would be a thrill to be one of its honorees, even if only second-hand.

And if the reception of *Darkest Before Death* continued to be this favorable, might Lara be persuaded to write a second? For all Darren knew, a sequel might be drafted and awaiting his own *editorial ministrations*, as Maude had described his contribution. If anything would draw in clients more than award nominations or even wins, it would be a follow-up novel whose enthusiastic reception and sales matched that of the first.

2

Jeanette Frobisher opened the videoconferencing app and turned on her computer's camera. Then, as she often did, she regretted not taking an extra minute to tame hair that was only partially corralled in a ponytail, or to add some mascara to accentuate eyelashes that were long but almost invisible in their paleness. But it had been years since she had bothered with makeup, and even if her hair looked tidy when the meeting started, by the end it would look just as untidy as it did now. How it got that way, she couldn't tell—it was probably just returning to its natural state.

She also noticed that she had gotten a drop of whey protein shake on her shirt. She zipped up her sweatshirt to cover it.

She tapped a message into her phone—*He's on now*—but didn't send it. She opened the meeting to the other attendees, then sat back to wait. As usual, she made a guess about when Ezra Parsons would sign on. She decided on seven minutes.

He must have been feeling magnanimous because he made her wait only four.

"Jeanette," he said.

"Hello, Ezra."

"Any sign of Marilee?"

Her phone off-screen, Jeanette tapped *Send* on the text. "I'm sure she'll be on in a minute."

Ezra raised an eyebrow. "It's funny how, no matter when I sign on, she always arrives a minute later."

"Yes. Funny."

Sure enough, almost exactly sixty seconds later, the image of the third attendee appeared on the screen. "Ezra. Jeanette. My apologies for being late. I was writing and lost track of time."

There was no question that Marilee Forsythe had checked her hair and makeup before signing on. And even in the video thumbnail, anyone could have guessed her petite stature from the fine bone structure of her face. However, rather than her usual bright pastels, Marilee was wearing a nubby aubergine sweater. Jeanette speculated that the wardrobe choice was driven by the fact that Marilee was not in her usual winter digs in Sarasota, Florida, but stuck in Ocean City, Maryland, pending an author event Ezra was requiring her to attend.

"How are you holding up in this dreary winter weather?" Ezra asked Marilee.

Jeanette's guess was bolstered by Marilee's response. "I hope Oh Buoy Books appreciates the fact that this will be the first January I've spent in Ocean City in years. Beach towns are so bleak in the winter."

Jeanette herself loved beach towns off-season—the ocean a turbulent gray, boardwalk stores shuttered, miles of almost deserted beach to walk. "I'm sure they do appreciate it," she said.

"And it has given you some time to finish up *Mulberry Murder*," said Ezra. "At least I hope it has."

"Oh, God, Ezra," groaned Marilee, "I'm starting to wonder if the world really needs another Berry Mystery. I'm running out of berries and alliterative crimes to pair them with."

Jeanette did a mental inventory of Marilee's backlist: *Blackberry Blackmail*, *Elderberry Espionage*, *Huckleberry Homicide* ... there were many others, but she couldn't think of the titles.

"If you can't come up with more names, I'm happy to propose some," said Ezra. "Or we'll come up with a different approach. The Flower Mysteries."

"I'm sure it's been done," Marilee said dismissively. "But at least it would be more enjoyable to show up at author events bringing a bouquet of flowers—or, more appropriately, *receiving* a bouquet of flowers—than some berry-laden dessert. Do you know how hard it was to find a bakery that makes huckleberry muffins?"

Jeanette couldn't help thinking that Marilee herself knew how hard it was only because Jeanette periodically had to explain why they had to drive so far out of the way to pick up the traditional offering for an author event.

"Just be happy you didn't sign a contract for, let's say, the Reptile Mysteries." Ezra chuckled. "I might have been looking for the manuscript for *Rattlesnake Ransom*, and I suspect that even the ever-helpful Jeanette might have had a hard time rustling up the party favor for that one."

Jeanette wished she could interpret Ezra's comment as a compliment, but his patronizing tone suggested it was more insult than accolade.

"Actually," countered Marilee, "the story behind *Rattlesnake Ransom* might engage my interest more than yet another story of a baker turned sleuth. It's as important to keep your writers interested as your readers."

"Actually, it's important to keep my writers *productive*.

Interested is icing on the cake ... or cupcake, as the case may be." He chuckled again.

Marilee's mouth tightened against a retort. Jeanette was always interested to see how far Ezra and Marilee would push each other. Marilee owed Ezra a debt for taking her on as a novice author, for editing—*heavily* editing, Jeanette guessed—her books, and for shepherding them to the top of the cozy best-seller lists. Ezra owed Marilee a debt for penning the books, or at least providing a beefy draft, and for being the public face of the Berry Mysteries. If Jeanette hadn't accompanied Marilee to most of her mid-Atlantic author events, she would have thought that Marilee would be as unsuited for that role as Ezra. However, Marilee's ability to subsume her prickly personality behind a saccharine-sweet facade always surprised Jeanette.

"So, *Mulberry Murder*—" began Ezra.

Marilee ignored his gambit to change the topic. "Have you ever considered branching into other genres?"

"And what other genres would you suggest a publishing house called Cozy Up Press branch into?"

"Start another imprint. You're limiting your audience with such a specific focus. What if the bottom falls out of cozies? The zeitgeist might shift to something a little edgier." Marilee laughed humorlessly. "Which leaves open pretty much every other genre. Like thrillers, for example. Have you read Lara Seaford's debut, *Darkest Before Death*? It was just nominated for an award."

"Which award?"

"Best Debut Novel."

"Whose award?"

"*Latent Prints.*"

Ezra snorted dismissively. "I know enough about thrillers

to tell you that's nothing to brag about. They're a minor player."

"They're a big enough player that even you—head of a publisher called Cozy Up Press—recognize the name."

Ezra scowled. "Have you read Seaford's book?" he asked as he tapped on his keyboard.

"As a matter of fact, I have. I might be forbidden from using sex, violence, and profanity in my own books, but it doesn't mean I don't enjoy reading about them in others' books."

He sat back from the keyboard. "*Darkest Before Death* is self-published."

"So?"

"No publisher means no gatekeeper to keep dreck from making its way to readers."

"She had an editor."

Ezra snorted again. "And who would that be?"

"Darren Van Osten."

Ezra's expression modulated toward mild surprise. "Really?"

"Yes."

"Who is Darren Van Osten?" asked Jeanette.

"He's Jock Quine's editor for the Robert Wolfram series—" Marilee began.

"*Was* Jock Quine's editor," corrected Ezra. "Jock died last year, and his son Alec picked up the series."

"My, Ezra, you seem to know quite a lot about the thriller field for someone with an imprint called—"

"Marilee," Ezra interrupted, "why are you even bringing this up?"

Marilee began massaging her wrist. Several years earlier Jeremy had been chauffeuring Marilee to an author event when a car ran a red light and broadsided them. Marilee had broken her wrist, an injury that, as she liked to remind her son and daughter-in-law, was especially inconvenient for someone who made her living at a keyboard. Jeanette wasn't sure if Marilee's wrist still ached from the injury, or if rubbing it had become merely a habit she indulged in when needing to buy time.

"If Lara Seaford can write a best-selling and award-nominated thriller with the help of Darren Van Osten," said Marilee, "I think I could write one that would at least be as financially successful with the help of an experienced editor. Like you helped me with my cozies."

Jeanette tried to keep her eyes from widening—she knew what this acknowledgement cost Marilee.

"Are you suggesting that you redirect your energies from the Berry Murders to thrillers?"

"Yes, as a matter of fact, I am."

"No."

"No?"

Ezra removed his glasses and pinched the bridge of his nose. Then he set the glasses aside, laced his fingers over his stomach, and said in what Jeanette guessed he considered a patient tone, "Marilee, I find cozy writers. I mentor cozy writers. I edit cozies. I publish cozies. I market cozies. I promote cozies. It's what I know. It's what I'm good at—as evidenced by the success of your own books. I doubt you'd have homes in Ocean City and Sarasota if it weren't for me."

"Don't you ever want to edit, publish, market, and promote something that has a little more excitement? An on-page murder? A little sex? A few swear words?"

"No, Marilee, I do not. Besides, look at you—if ever an author's appearance screamed *cozy* and not *thriller*, it would be yours." His chuckle was beginning to sound a bit forced. "I can barely restrain my urge to buy you doilies at the holidays." He reached for his glasses.

"I could buy out my contract," said Marilee.

Ezra's hand stopped for a fraction of a second, then he picked up the glasses and settled them carefully on his nose. "No."

"No? Just like that? You're not even willing to entertain offers?"

"You know as well as I do that your contract doesn't include provisions for a buy-out."

Marilee shrugged. "I didn't anticipate the direction my interests would take when I signed the contract."

"And you expect me to accommodate your lack of business savvy? You should have had an agent represent you when you came to me with your first book. In fact, if you had an agent now, I suspect he or she would advise you that only the most talented writers can make a leap between such dissimilar genres as cozies and thrillers ... although maybe you don't want to give up the fifteen percent an agent would charge. You should appreciate the deal you have, Marilee."

"I imagine if I could learn to write the fluff you publish," snapped Marilee, "I could learn to write something a little more substantial."

"Substantial, eh? You want to write something more substantial? Well, the profit Cozy Up Press is making from the Berry Mysteries is quite substantial, so I feel like a buy-out amount should be commensurately substantial." Ezra sat back and cast his eyes upward, then returned his gaze to the camera. "Half a million."

Jeanette groaned aloud, grateful that she had muted her audio. Ezra couldn't have picked a worse number.

There was a beat before Marilee responded. "Half a million?"

"Yes. Half a million."

"The Berry Mystery series is really worth half a million dollars to you?" asked Marilee.

"Of course, that wouldn't include the books that are already published," replied Ezra. "I'm assuming you don't want to buy those back, cozies being a genre that you now hold in contempt. I'm talking about the books you still owe me. You signed a contract for twenty-four books, and you haven't even delivered half of them."

Marilee was silent for a moment, and Jeanette imagined that Marilee's eyes slid from Ezra's image on her monitor to Jeanette's. "Half a million dollars. Interesting. Jeanette, please include a note of the amount Ezra just quoted in the meeting minutes."

Meeting minutes?

Jeanette temporarily unmuted her audio. "Sure thing, Marilee." She opened a Word document and tapped out a note.

"You can have Jeanette note whatever you want to, Marilee," said Ezra, "but what counts is what's in the contract you signed. And as you know, I expect my authors to comply with the terms of the contracts they sign."

Even Jeanette had heard about the steps Ezra had taken with another Cozy Up Press author who had stepped out of line: a carefully orchestrated social media smear campaign, a lawsuit, and scant hope of finding another publisher for her books.

Without giving Marilee an opening, he continued. "And speaking of the terms of your contract, let's not forget the author events. Since the one at Oh Buoy Books isn't tied to a specific title, perhaps you should provide a variety of berry snacks."

Now re-muted, Jeanette groaned again, wondering if she'd be able to find a bakery near Ocean City—or maybe near her own home in Downingtown, Pennsylvania—that could provide cakes or pies or tarts or cookies that included the requisite berries.

"I can't imagine that me showing up with a tray of desserts moves the needle much on sales," muttered Marilee.

"Au contraire," replied Ezra. "It not only moves the needle on sales at that store on that day, but it builds a relationship with all the attendees, and all the other cozy readers that the attendees talk with." Ezra's voice became fluty. "'That Marilee Forsythe—what a charming woman. Exactly what I would have expected of the woman behind the Berry Mysteries.'" He dropped his voice to its usual timbre. "The perfect cozy author persona. I even gave you a new name, since 'Frobisher' was a little ... pedestrian."

"The people at those events are insufferable—"

Ezra removed his glasses and tossed them aside, tired of the badinage. "How hard can it be? Jeanette does all the work." Ezra's eyes shifted on the screen. "She paying you anything yet, Jeanette?"

Before Jeanette had to respond, Marilee said, "She's family. She's paid in ways other than a salary."

Ezra laughed. "I wonder if she bargained for an unpaid assistant position when she married your son."

"I gave her and Jeremy the money to buy a new building for their pharmacy when the old one flooded."

"And I'm sure you never let them forget about your generous contribution."

"This isn't the last conversation we'll have about my creative direction, Ezra."

"Talk all you want, Marilee—you're not going to change my mind." He sat back again. "And I expect you to keep making those cozy readers happy." His smile was reptilian. "And once you've discharged the terms of our contract, maybe you can try your hand at the stage."

3

Ann Kinnear shrugged into her puffy red parka, a Christmas present from her brother, Mike, and stepped out onto the porch of the Curragh, the guest house of the Mahalo Winery that had been her home for several months. The vantage point offered a picturesque view across the property. Mike's beloved Audrey the Audi was the only car in the customer lot in front of the Cellar—not surprising, since the tasting room had opened only a few minutes earlier, at noon. There were several vehicles in the staff lot behind the Cellar. Ice rimmed the Tarn, the pond that lay between the Curragh and the Cellar, although the cold didn't appear to bother the raft of ducks paddling across the still-open water at the pond's center. Beyond the Tarn lay the vineyard, the barren vines brown under the gray January sky.

She shivered and zipped up the parka, then followed the path to the Cellar and stepped into the tasting room. The wide plank floors, the copper-topped tables illuminated by pendant lights, and the sparkle of light off the wine glasses hanging over the barn board bar created an ambiance that was simultaneously rustic and elegant. The bright abstract paintings by a local Chester County artist provided a welcome relief from the dreary day.

Winemaker Del Berendt was behind the bar, and Mike occupied one of the stools. From down the hall that led to the staff-only area, Ann could hear the distinctive laugh of Del's wife, Rowan Lynch, and the responding gurgle from Del and Rowan's four-month-old daughter, Rose.

"Hey, Del," Ann said as she crossed the tasting room.

"Hey, Ann, how are you doing?"

"Fine." She reached the bar and climbed onto a stool next to Mike. No one would have guessed they were siblings. Mike was only a few inches taller than the slender, reddish-blond Ann, his hair dark, his frame stocky. She gestured to the glass in front of Mike. "Sampling the wares?"

"It just seems wrong to sit at a tasting bar at a winery and drink coffee."

"I can't disagree with that."

Del took a glass down from the rack above his head, pulled a bottle of Sapele from behind the bar, and poured a glass of the ruby-red wine for Ann.

"Why does she always get the Sapele?" asked Mike.

"She earned it," said Del with a smile. "You could get Sapele, too."

"Sure," said Mike, "but I'd have to pay for it."

The previous year, Ann had helped bring to justice the person responsible for the deaths of Rowan's father, Niall, and her brother, Harkin—and had done it before Rowan and Del became victims as well. She hadn't paid for a glass, or a bottle, of Mahalo wine since.

Ann took a sip, aware of Del watching for her reaction. She suspected that, as Mahalo's winemaker, Del would always watch for her reaction to the winery's premium offering, despite all the times she had told him—truthfully—that it was the best red she had ever tasted.

She was saved from having to reassure him once again by the arrival of Rowan and baby Rose. Rose had kept the riot of strawberry blond curls she had had at birth, but she had lost her original chunkiness, and Ann guessed she would be tall like Del rather than petite like Rowan.

"I thought I heard voices." Rowan crossed to the bar and gave Ann and then Mike a kiss on the cheek.

Ann had never thought of herself as a cheek-kisser—certainly not a giver, and not even as a receiver—but she and Rowan had grown close.

"Here for business or pleasure?" Rowan asked, joggling Rose on her hip.

"Business," said Mike. "I'm giving Ann the low-down on a prospective client."

"Not exactly a client," said Ann.

"Someone who wants to tap into Ann's unique skill set," he said. "Darren Van Osten. He's a representative of the Gotham Crime Fiction Conference, and he wants Ann to give a talk on 'Making the Supernatural Super in Your Novel.'"

"Really? That's great!" exclaimed Rowan. She turned to Ann. "Have you done talks before?"

"Nope. And I haven't agreed to do this one yet."

"But this could be a whole new income stream," said Mike. "An easy gig ... speaking fees ... subsidized travel ..."

"And," Del added wryly, "not particularly dangerous."

Ann laughed. "Not unless I really piss off the audience. Especially an audience who's there to learn about crime."

"Speaking of supernatural," said Rowan, "I had Rose in the barrel room the other day, and she kept gurgling and smiling, apparently at nothing. Do you think she might be reacting to Dad?"

"I suppose so," said Ann. "There's a theory that we're all born with some sensing ability, but that it wears off quickly—in the first few years, even months. She might still have it." Ann smiled at the baby. "She might even keep it."

Del polished a wine glass and hung it on the overhead rack. "You might have a partner in your business one day."

"Sounds good to me." She shot Mike a look. "She can do the conference talks."

Rowan laughed. "Ann, would you mind stopping by the barrel room in the next couple of days? Ask Dad if he's what Rose is smiling at?"

"Sure."

Ann generally steered clear of the building they called the Ark, which housed the winery's production facility. She wasn't enthusiastic about an encounter with the irascible spirit of Niall Lynch, who still haunted the barrel room.

Del hung another glass on the rack. "I wonder if Harkin will ever come back to Mahalo."

"I don't think so," said Ann, thinking back to her last encounter with Rowan's late brother. "I'm pretty sure he was just hanging around until he could talk with his wife and son. By the way, how are Alana and Kepi doing?"

"Great," said Rowan. "They've banked the first payments I've sent for buying out the winery, and Kepi's already planning where he wants to take his scuba tour clients."

Del shook his head. "That kid's a planner—it'll be eight years before Alana lets him launch the business."

"I wouldn't mind signing up as Kepi's first clients," said Mike. "I'd love a trip to Hawaii, and Scott's been talking about learning to scuba dive." He turned to Ann. "How 'bout it?"

"I'm in."

Mike turned back to Rowan and Del. "Is the winery's

teenage owner showing any interest in his Pennsylvania-based business?"

Rowan smiled and shook her head. "Not at all."

They chatted for a few more minutes, until two couples entered the tasting room, bringing a blast of cold air with them. Rowan handed Rose over to Del, then took menus listing the wines on offer to the table where the new arrivals were shedding coats amid a flurry of laughter and conversation.

Del wrinkled his nose. "I think someone's in need of a diaper change. Need anything before I do that?"

Mike held up his half-full glass. "I'm good."

"Me, too," said Ann.

Del disappeared down the hallway to the workspace he and Rowan shared, and to which they had added a crib and changing table for Rose.

Ann and Mike carried their glasses to a table on the opposite side of the room from the chatting couples.

"So, about this speaking gig—" he began as soon as they were seated.

"I don't know why you're so hot on the speaking gig. We're making enough with the engagements to keep the lights on at Ann Kinnear Sensing, right?"

"Sure, but sensing engagements aren't scalable—" He laughed. "—at least until we bring Rose onboard. And they have their challenges. It's hard to anticipate scheduling needs since they take different amounts of time depending on the circumstances. I think we should consider diversifying."

"Into what?"

"Speaking gigs." He took a sip of wine. "Book sales."

Ann groaned. "Mike, I don't want to be an author."

"I'll ghostwrite them for you."

"I don't want to *pretend* to be an author."

"Okay, so we'll start with speaking engagements and see how it goes."

"I hate public speaking."

"When have you ever spoken publicly?"

"There was that speech class in high school—"

"Everyone hates high school speech class. But now you're a respected professional—at the top of your game and the best in the country, maybe in the world—and people want to hear about it."

"They can read the papers."

"They want to hear about it from you."

"I don't know ..."

"What's not to like? GothamCon is one of the biggest writers' conferences in the country. We make some money, have a subsidized trip to the Big Apple, and in return you give a forty-five-minute talk."

"Not an hour?"

"Fifteen minutes for Q&A."

"Oh, God," she groaned. "Q&A."

"Listen, you don't even have to decide now about the talk. Just meet with Van Osten and let him tell you more about it. It might be a tiny bit stressful—at least until you get a couple of these speaking engagements under your belt—but at least you're unlikely to land in the hospital."

"That would be refreshing." She downed a slug of wine. "Okay. I'll talk to him."

Mike grinned. "Excellent. He lives in Wilmington, so he said he could drive up if you wanted to meet with him before you made up your mind."

"Where should we meet? Your office at the townhouse?"

Mike shook his head. "I'm tired of having people come to the townhouse on business. I have an idea about an alternative. Rowan and Del are thinking of turning Niall's place into an event space, right? We could rent one of the rooms—at least temporarily—as an office. It would give us a place to meet with clients, it would be super convenient for you, and I'm sure they'd be happy to get the extra money."

Ann smiled. "I like that idea." She raised her glass. "Well done, baby brother."

He clinked his glass against hers. "Just trying to keep the boss happy."

4

The morning after the conference call with Marilee and Ezra, Jeanette was at the kitchen table, sipping a mug of rooibos tea. She tapped *ocean city* into her phone's GPS app and brightened when she saw the time estimate: two hours. Then she realized she had failed to specify Maryland rather than New Jersey. She corrected the search and sighed as she saw the estimated duration of the drive from Downingtown, Pennsylvania: three-and-a-half hours.

Jeremy brought their breakfasts over to the table: two bowls of oatmeal and a plate of turkey bacon. "And I got your favorite," he said, setting another bowl down with a flourish. "Mixed berries!"

Jeanette laughed. "I must really love berries if this whole mess with the Berry Mysteries hasn't ruined my appetite for them." Her expression became more serious. "But aren't berries in January a bit of a splurge?"

"Not too much of a splurge for my honey," Jeremy said as he lowered himself onto the other chair.

"Thanks, Jer," she said as she leaned over and gave him a kiss.

"Can't send you off on your errand of mercy on an empty stomach." He lifted the teapot and poured himself a cup, then topped up her mug.

She looked at him fondly as she took another sip of tea before tucking into the oatmeal. No one would be surprised that either of them disdained the idea of an empty stomach, and casual observers might have considered that fewer calories would benefit them both. But those observers might have changed their minds if they saw Jeremy and Jeanette Frobisher hiking, swimming, playing volleyball, or taking part in any number of other activities for which they shared a passion. Before meeting Jeremy, Jeanette had been self-conscious about her size: just a shade under six feet and what friends inevitably described as "big-boned." It helped that Jeremy was taller than she was, and just as hefty.

"There's a backup around Wilmington," she said. "I'm never going to make it there by noon. That's when Marilee wanted me there so she'd have plenty of time to sign the books and still get them to the post office before it closes." She didn't mention that she would have been on the road by now if she didn't have to drop Jeremy off at the pharmacy. Their second car hadn't passed inspection, and they were trying to postpone shelling out the money for the new brakes it needed.

"The world won't come to an end if you're a little late."

Jeanette appreciated the sentiment—after all, Marilee was Jeremy's mother—but he wasn't the one who would have to face Marilee's disapproval.

"Do you think she'll bring up the loan?" she asked.

"Probably." He sighed. "It sort of sucks that the amount Ezra quoted for Mom buying out her cozy contract is almost exactly what we owe her."

Jeremy and Jeanette owned Frobishers' Pharmacy. The original location had been on Business Route 30 in Downingtown, but the previous year the east branch of the Brandywine Creek had flooded, leaving the building a muddy mess. Insurance would cover most of the damage—at least, that's what they hoped—but they had decided that they didn't want to reopen in the same location and risk another flood.

They had bought another property, this one closer to the 30 bypass. They had borrowed a little over five hundred thousand dollars from Marilee, planning to pay her back as soon as the repairs to the original property were complete and they could sell it. But the schedule kept slipping, supply chain issues and over-extended contractors introducing unexpected delays.

"What if she asks us to pay back the loan so she can pay off Ezra?" she asked.

"We're going to pay back the loan."

"I mean, what if she wants the money right away?"

"Well," he said, marshaling a smile, "We'll just tell her she can't get blood from a stone."

Jeanette knew that, despite the confident front, Jeremy had shared her alarm when she told him about the conversation between Marilee and Ezra, and Marilee's desire to buy out her contract with Cozy Up Press. Jeanette regretted that she and Jeremy hadn't had a more formalized agreement with Marilee about the loan, but it would have never occurred to Jeanette that Marilee would need the money back in a hurry, and certainly not that she would want it to launch into a new career as a thriller writer.

They ate in silence for a few minutes, then Jeanette asked, her voice hesitant, "Could she make us sell the pharmacy?"

"She can't *make* us do anything." He chewed a piece of bacon. "Although I suppose she could make life pretty uncomfortable if she wants the money and we can't produce it." He squeezed Jeanette's hand. "We'll work it out."

She squeezed back.

As they finished up their breakfasts, Jeanette said, "I figure I'll be back from Ocean City by six and I can return any non-urgent customer voicemails from today."

"If it's not busy, I can take care of that," said Jeremy.

"But you need to handle the calls from doctors about medication orders."

"Multi-tasking!" said Jeremy. He tried for a cheerful tone, but Jeanette knew he was as tired from the twelve-hour days as she was. It was just the two of them holding down the fort. His expression sobered. "I just wish you didn't have to make the drive twice in two days. When I came up with the clever idea of earning some brownie points with Mom by surprising her at the Oh Buoy Books event, I didn't realize she'd want you to go down there the day before. Maybe you could save yourself one round-trip—spend the night there."

Jeanette groaned. "I *really* don't want to spend two full days with your mother."

"Yeah. Even I'd prefer the extra six hours on the road to that."

"Plus, surprising her is a nice idea—let's stick with that plan." Jeanette picked up her phone. "I'm going to send her an email letting her know I'm going to be held up by the Wilmington traffic."

They finished breakfast, then climbed into their CR-V hybrid for the drive to the pharmacy.

When Jeanette pulled up at the entrance, Jeremy leaned over to give her a kiss.

"Don't let her give you a hard time," he said.

She raised an eyebrow. "Ha."

"Don't let her give you *too* hard a time," he amended. He opened the door, then turned back to her. "We're going to pay back the loan as soon as we can, and once we do, I'm going to make sure you never have to kowtow to my mother again. Deal?"

She laughed tiredly. "Deal."

5

Ann walked up the drive that led from the Curragh to *the big house*, as Rowan Lynch and her family called the rambling home at the top of the hill. As Mike had expected, Rowan and Del had been enthusiastic about renting out one of the first-floor rooms as the headquarters of Ann Kinnear Sensing.

The weather continued cold and gloomy, and Ann pulled her scarf more tightly around her neck. As the house came into view among the trees that lined the curving drive, she could see Audrey the Audi parked in front.

Ann stepped into the two-story entrance hall. Gone were the aged coat rack and worn runner that, in Niall Lynch's time, had been the space's only décor. As Ann made her way through the house to the accompaniment of hammering coming from the second floor, she saw that Rowan, Del, and Rowan's Aunt Nola had already cleared out much of the outdated, uncomfortable furniture as part of the transformation into an event space.

Rowan and Del were creating an apartment on the second floor of one wing, and when it was complete, they would move there from their Unionville house. They planned to create a matching apartment in the other wing for when Rowan's sister-in-law Alana and nephew Kepi visited from their home in Hawaii.

Ann reached the room that would be the new headquarters of Ann Kinnear Sensing: Niall Lynch's former home office. It was sufficiently set apart from what would become the event spaces that Ann and Mike could meet with clients there undisturbed, even if an event was in progress.

Unlike the rest of the house, Niall's office looked much as it had the last time Ann had seen it, shortly after his death: a spacious room containing an imposing desk with two chairs facing it, a filing cabinet, and little else. No one was in the room when she arrived, and she was wondering if she would have to look elsewhere for Mike when he and Del appeared at the door carrying a scarred wooden table.

"What's that for?" she asked as she helped them maneuver it into the room.

"When we meet with clients, I don't want to be barricaded behind *that* monstrosity," Mike said, with a nod toward Niall's desk. He moved the guest chairs and desk chair to the table. "We'll get different furniture if it looks like this will be a long-term arrangement."

"I always thought Niall's set-up was a strange one for a home office," she said. "Who could he have been meeting with at the big house that he needed such a formal arrangement?"

"Me and Rowan," Del said. "And Harkin, when he was around."

Ann shook her head. "Strange set-up for a family meeting."

"Not for this family. Or, I should say, for the family under Niall's rule."

Mike stood back to assess the new seating arrangement.

"That's better." He waved toward a coffee maker on top of the filing cabinet. "Plus, I can offer caffeine."

"Homey," said Ann.

"If you want some help decorating," said Del, "I'm sure Nola would be happy to lend a hand."

Nola had designed the interior of the Curragh as well as the tasting room at the Cellar and was putting together the plan for the event space.

"That would be great," said Ann.

Ann heard the ping of an incoming text, and Mike pulled his phone from his pocket and glanced at the screen. "Darren Van Osten is down the hill at the Cellar," he said as he tapped out a response. "I'll have to figure out better directions to give visitors to get them up to the big house." He dropped his phone in his pocket. "I'll go out front to meet him."

Ann and Del followed Mike to the entrance hall, then Del headed up the stairs. "I'll ask the workers to keep the noise to a minimum during your meeting."

"Thanks, Del," Ann called after him.

She and Mike stepped outside just as a vehicle appeared on the drive. It was a classic pickup, its deep red paint scheme bisected by a narrow strip of chrome, *FORD* spelled out above the grill in chrome lettering.

"Sweet!" exclaimed Mike.

The driver parked and got out of the truck. He was in his sixties, with wire-rim glasses, a neatly trimmed beard and mustache, and receding but still thick gray hair pulled back in a stubby ponytail. He crossed the drive to where Ann and Mike stood next to the entrance.

Mike extended his hand. "Mr. Van Osten, I'm Mike Kinnear," he gestured to Ann, "and this is Ann Kinnear."

"Pleased to meet you," said Van Osten, shaking Mike's hand, then Ann's. "Please call me Darren."

Mike led them inside and to the office. "You'll have to excuse the furnishings. We're just moving in." He gestured them into seats at the table. "Coffee, anyone?"

"Sure, I'll have some," Ann said.

"That sound great—especially on a cold day like this," said Darren.

Mike filled three mugs, handed them around, then sat. "Darren, you gave me some background on your proposal, but it would be helpful for Ann to hear it directly from you."

"Of course." Darren took a sip of coffee, then turned to Ann. "I help organize the Gotham Crime Fiction Conference, the premiere conference for crime fiction in the U.S.—in fact, I think it would be fair to say, in the world. With the rising interest in paranormal fiction, we'd like to include a session that would be of particular interest to authors in that genre, and the board came up with the topic 'Making the Supernatural Super in Your Novel.'"

Ann glanced over at Mike. He was listening to Darren with what Ann referred to as his "teacher's pet" look, but she suspected that her own expression didn't reflect the enthusiasm that Darren was hoping for. She tried her best to mimic Mike's expression.

Darren was sufficiently encouraged to continue. "With your experience and reputation, the GothamCon board would love to have you speak on that topic, Ann. I would act as your liaison to the board, which is headed by this year's honorary chairperson, Alec Quine." Again the expectant look. Again, Ann was sure her response was a disappointment. "He recently picked up the Robert Wolfram thriller series from his father, Jock Quine," Darren prompted.

Relieved that Darren had mentioned a name she recognized, she said, "I've heard of Jock Quine. Didn't he die recently?"

Darren's expression sobered. "Yes, killed by an intruder in his home near Princeton. It was the night of an event hosted by his publisher, Harrison & John, in New York. If Jock had been there instead of at home, he'd still be alive."

"Jock Quine didn't rate an invite?" asked Mike.

Darren smiled. "I suspect the event wasn't targeted at H & J's A-list guests."

"A consolation event for the B list?"

Darren cleared his throat. "I was there."

"Ah," Mike said, then hurried on. "So, the son is writing the series now? I thought he wrote courtroom dramas."

"He did. Alec is a lawyer, and he brought enormous expertise to his legal thrillers. I'm helping him transition to the more action-oriented approach that fans of the Wolfram series expect. The board chose Alec as the chairperson of the conference when Jock died, and I'm serving as liaison for Alec as well, and for author Lara Seaford." This time, Darren seemed unsurprised by Ann and Mike's lack of response. "Her novel has been nominated for best debut by *Latent Prints* magazine, and I understand is being considered for a best debut nomination at GothamCon. I'm her editor as well."

"That's great," said Mike. "Congratulations to both of you."

"Yes, congratulations," said Ann.

"Do you read crime fiction?" Darren asked her hopefully.

"Not really."

"Do you read ... anything?" Darren's expression was shading toward panic.

"These days I'm reading a lot of aviation magazines."

"Ann recently got her private pilot's license," said Mike.

"Ah. Congratulations to *you*," said Darren.

"But I've read some of Jock Quine's books and really enjoyed them," said Mike.

"Really?" asked Darren, a bit cheered. "Any favorites?"

"Oh, I've enjoyed them all." Mike took a sip of coffee, which Ann suspected was a ploy to keep Darren from probing Mike's familiarity with Quine's books too deeply.

Fortunately for Mike, Darren redirected his attention back to Ann. "As I was preparing the proposal for your talk, I did a bit of research into your work. I believe that your experiences —the Philadelphia Socialite Murder, that haunted hotel in Maine, even what happened right here at the winery last year —would lend themselves perfectly to a book, either true crime or a fictional treatment. Have you considered becoming an author?"

Ann shifted in her chair. "Once an experience is behind me, I don't really have the desire to relive it by writing about it."

"But that's the beauty of fiction—you can mold the events to how they should be, not how they actually are. And you could use a ghostwriter—" He laughed. "—which would be especially appropriate, considering your area of expertise."

"Do you write as well as edit, Darren?" asked Mike.

"I've done my share of ghostwriting, but editing is really my forte." He turned back to Ann. "Even if you're not a writer of crime fiction yourself—or even a reader—I hope you might share your unique perspective at the conference with those who are."

Under the table, Mike tapped Ann's shin with his foot.

"Yes, of course," she said. "I'd be happy to."

Darren's expression relaxed. "Excellent—we're so happy to have you onboard for GothamCon."

Darren and Mike talked through some of the financial and logistical details while Ann topped off her mug from the carafe. They then segued into a discussion about Darren's pickup.

"That's a beautiful vehicle you've got," said Mike. "F-150?"

"Yes—1979 Ranger four-by-four. I bought it with a bonus Jock gave me when he sold his ten millionth Wolfram thriller."

"Jock Quine was a generous man."

"He was indeed."

Mike and Darren chatted about the truck while the three finished their coffees, then Darren stood and pulled on his coat.

"Darren," said Mike, "thanks so much for the invitation to the conference. I think Ann is going to be a big hit with the attendees."

"I have no doubt," said Darren, directing a smile toward Ann.

Mike led the way to the front door, describing to Darren the owners' plans for the space. They ran into Del in the entrance hall, and Mike made introductions.

"I understand you've invited Ann to speak at your conference," said Del. "Seems like a great addition to her business."

"Yes, I agree," said Darren. He turned to Ann. "If this is your first speaking engagement, it would be natural to be a bit nervous. Perhaps I could experience a sensing myself. If I could vouch for your skills, it could smooth the way with your audience."

"I'm afraid it's not a spectator sport," said Mike, "and most of our engagements are governed by confidentiality agreements that would preclude an observer."

"You could set up an engagement of your own," said Ann.

Darren smiled. "I did discuss that with Mike. I'm afraid the fees for Ann Kinnear Sensing services are a bit high for me."

"Ann could mediate a conversation with Niall for you," said Del.

"Niall?" asked Darren.

Ann rolled her eyes.

Del, noticing Ann's eye roll, tried to backpedal. "Just a thought, probably doesn't make much sense ..."

Ann sighed. "Niall Lynch is Del's late father-in-law. He's haunting the winery production building."

Darren's eyebrows rose. "Really?"

"Thanks for the suggestion, Del," said Mike with a grin.

"I don't mind," said Ann. "I need to talk to Niall about whether he's what's making Rose smile, and if Rowan doesn't mind, Darren could come along."

"I'll check with Rowan," said Del. "I'm sure she won't mind Darren going to the Ark." Ann just caught his rueful aside to Mike: "But I sure am going to catch hell for foisting an audience on Ann."

6

Del called Rowan and got her okay for Ann to mediate a conversation with Niall in the barrel room with Darren present. Ann guessed from his abashed expression that he also got the scolding he expected.

Del ended the call. "I'm going down that way. I can open the door of the Ark for you if it's locked."

The four stepped outside, and Del started down the drive toward the winery buildings.

"A little cold to walk, don't you think?" said Mike. He turned to Darren. "You won't need to come back to the office, and the Ark is right on your way out. Want to drive down? I could come with you and direct you to the right building."

"Sure, that would be great," said Darren. "Thanks."

Ann suppressed a smile. She was pretty sure Mike was more interested in checking out Darren's truck than in saving Darren a brisk walk or the short drive back to the big house after the demonstration at the Ark.

"I'll walk down with Del," she said. "I'll meet you there."

Darren and Mike climbed into the pickup and rolled down the drive. Ann and Del followed on foot.

"You think Niall will be at the Ark?" asked Del.

"I've been in there a couple of times since Rose was born, and he's been there both times."

"What could Niall Lynch possibly do that would make an infant smile?"

It seemed rude to agree, but Ann wondered the same thing.

When they reached the Ark, Mike and Darren were waiting outside.

"Check out the interior of Darren's car," Mike said enthusiastically, supporting Ann's belief that he was smitten with the vehicle.

She peered through the window and had to admit that the interior lived up to the promise of the exterior: immaculate bench seats of red and black leather with white piping, an analog dash with what seemed to modern eyes like a bare minimum of instrumentation, a glove box with a faux wood door. "Very nice."

Del unlocked the door to the Ark and led them into the fermentation room. Along the walls stood the stainless-steel tanks in which the Mahalo grapes were undergoing their transformation into Mahalo wine. The bottling equipment had been moved to one side until it was needed in the fall.

"You'll have the place to yourself," said Del. "Through the winter it's mainly Rowan, me, and Sam Griller, the assistant winemaker, holding down the fort, but Sam's on vacation now, taking advantage of the slow season." He pocketed his keys. "I've got some stuff I need to do in the Cellar. Just let me know when you're through and I'll come back and lock up."

"I'll head out, too," said Mike. "Generally," he said to Darren, "the bigger the party, the less likely a spirit is to make an appearance."

"Do you have to walk all the way back up to the house now?" asked Darren, embarrassed.

Mike waved a hand. "No problem—I can use the exercise."

Del and Mike departed, leaving Ann and Darren alone.

"We're most likely to find Niall in the barrel room," said Ann, gesturing toward the back of the Ark.

"Why is that?" asked Darren, following her.

"Because it was the place that was most special to him."

She led Darren through a heavy wooden door and into the barrel room.

This part of the Ark was built into the side of one of the hills that rolled across the Mahalo Winery property. The room was dimly illuminated by a fixture suspended from the ceiling and a lamp on the desk Niall Lynch had used when updating the inventory sheets. Along the back of the desk stood a row of photos: Niall's father, who had founded the winery as Lynch and Son. Niall himself. His sister, Nola. His daughter, Rowan. Niall's late son, Harkin. Harkin's teenage son, Kepi. And, at the end of the row, little Rose.

"Niall?" Ann called.

After a moment, the late winery patriarch appeared from one of the aisles formed by the rows of barrels that stretched into the hillside. He was just as gaunt as when Ann had first encountered him after his death, but he looked less ill—his eyes a bit brighter, his hands steadier. However, his always irritable expression darkened further when he saw Ann wasn't alone. "Yes?"

"Hello, Niall." She gestured to Darren. "This is Darren Van Osten. I'm working with him on a project, and he thought it would be helpful for him to experience a sensing. Del suggested we might talk with you."

Niall snorted derisively. "Of course he did."

"And Rowan said it would be okay," she added. She looked

toward Darren, who was scanning the area toward which she was directing her comments. "You'd probably like some proof that I'm not just talking to thin air."

"Well ..." he said, flustered.

"How about this—I'll stand facing away from you, you hold up some number of fingers, and I'll ask Niall to tell me how many fingers you're holding up."

"That would be interesting," said Darren, excitement replacing his discomposure.

"No," said Niall.

"No?" asked Ann.

"No."

"Jeez, Niall, it's not that big a favor to ask."

"I'm busy."

"With what?"

Niall glared at her.

She turned to Darren. "He doesn't want to do it."

"Oh, well," said Darren, his discomfiture returning, "it's certainly not absolutely necessary ..."

After a beat, she said, "That's very understanding of you. Let me show you out."

"Uh ... okay."

Ann stepped back through the door and closed it behind her and Darren.

"Listen," she said, dropping her voice slightly, "I don't think Niall is going to play along if he realizes he's playing along. Let's try this ... on your phone, look up three facts only someone familiar with winemaking would know, then we'll go back into the barrel room, and you ask me questions related to what you looked up."

Darren got out his phone and tapped for a minute, then slipped the phone back into his pocket. "Okay, I've got three questions."

"When I'm ready for a question, I'll scratch my ear."

Darren gave her a thumbs up.

They stepped back into the barrel room.

Niall emerged from an aisle, looking like he was ready to offer some reasons for his disinterest in participating in the test.

Ann raised a hand. "Darren just wanted to take another look at the barrel room. He's very interested in winemaking."

"Ah," said Niall, slightly mollified. "Very well."

Ann wandered toward an aisle, and Darren followed. She scratched her ear.

"I wonder what gives the red wine its color," he said.

"I guess they use darker grapes for red wine and lighter grapes for white wine," said Ann.

"That's ridiculous," said Niall. "It's the skins of the grapes that give red wine its color."

Ann strolled down the aisle, followed by Darren and Niall. She scratched her ear again.

"I've heard the term malolactic used to refer to the wine-making process," said Darren. "What does that mean?"

"Well, 'lactic' means milk. Not sure about 'malo.' Maybe something to do with marshmallows? Maybe it means the wine becomes milky and sweet, like a marshmallow."

Niall groaned. "For God's sake. It has nothing to do with marshmallows. Malolactic conversion refers to the bacterial process that converts malic acid, which has a crisp taste, like green apples, to lactic acid, which, as you managed to guess, refers to a softer, creamier taste."

They reached the end of the aisle and turned back. Ann scratched her ear a third time.

"I've also heard the term 'pomace,'" said Darren. "Any idea what that means?"

"No idea," said Ann.

"Pomace is the solid remains of the grapes after pressing," said Niall.

"Well, I think we've seen enough," said Ann. "Thanks for indulging us, Niall." She led Darren through the door to the fermentation room and closed it behind her.

"Grape skins, not the grapes themselves, give red wine its color," she said. "Malolactic conversion is the bacterial process that changes the crisp taste of malic acid into the creamier taste of lactic acid. Pomace is what's left after the grapes are pressed."

Darren's expression brightened. "That's right!"

Trying to avoid looking smug, Ann said, "I knew Niall Lynch couldn't resist setting me straight about anything having to do with wine."

Darren laughed. "That's an experience I'll be pleased to tell the GothamCon attendees about. Thank you for humoring me."

Ann walked Darren to the door and stood in the doorway of the Ark as he drove away. Then she went back inside and returned to the barrel room.

Niall appeared again from one of the aisles. "Now what?" he asked, exasperated.

"Rowan says Rose seems to smile at nothing when Rowan brings her here. Is it you she's smiling at?"

Niall looked uncomfortable. "Perhaps it is."

"And you can do something to make her smile?"

Niall's discomfort deepened. "Perhaps I can."

"Like what?"

Niall blushed. "I ... make faces at her."

Ann smiled. "Enjoying being a grandfather?"

The tiniest of smiles tugged up the corners of Niall's mouth. "Perhaps I am."

7

By the time Jeanette got to Wilmington, the traffic back-up had cleared, and she made it to Ocean City in the usual three hours.

She drove down the Coastal Highway, ocean to her left and Assawoman Bay to her right, on the narrow strip of land that, had she taken it to its end, would have brought her to the tip of the barrier island and the Ocean City boardwalk. When she reached Marilee's ocean-front condo building, she did a U-turn to clear the highway's median, and then turned into the entrance to Eden Beach.

During the summer, the parking garage under the building was reserved for residents, and there was always spillover into the outside lot. In January, however, the ranks of spaces were nearly empty. Jeanette could see only two cars, both parked near the entrance to the lobby. One was a Lexus sedan that Marilee had bought with the money from her first advance from Cozy Up Press. Jeanette guessed that the car had less than ten thousand miles on the odometer since she or Jeremy often drove Marilee on errands and to author events. The other vehicle was a Bondo-bespeckled Ford Taurus belonging to the Eden Beach security guard, Kenny. She pulled the CR-V in next to the Lexus.

Jeanette normally took the stairs from the ground-floor garage to the first floor and then the elevator to floor 14, where Marilee's condo was. This enabled her to bypass the security desk in the ground floor lobby and avoid the annoyance of an interaction with Kenny. However, since today's assignment required a stop at the security desk, she passed through the sliding glass doors from the garage to the lobby and crossed to the desk.

"Hello, Kenny," she said, trying for a cheerful tone.

When Jeanette had first met Kenny, she had thought he must be close to retirement age based on his dull eyes, his heavily veined hands, and a thinness close to emaciation. However, over the course of her visits to Eden Beach, and the inevitable stops at the security desk, she now guessed he was no older than fifty—maybe even forty.

"Hey, Miss Forsythe," he greeted her, his voice reedy. "How are you doing?"

She chalked up his inability to remember that she was neither a Miss nor a Forsythe to the fact that his brain must be aging as fast as his body ... or maybe just as a sign that he didn't give a damn.

"I'm fine, thank you. You have a delivery for Marilee?"

"I do—came just the other day." He rose stiffly from his chair and beckoned her to step behind the desk. He pointed to a box about the size of a copier paper box. "Wish I could help you with it, but this back of mine ..."

"It's no trouble," said Jeanette, lifting the box.

"No trouble for a big girl like you."

There were few things Jeanette hated more than being called *a big girl*.

"Plus, I'm not supposed to leave my post," he continued.

"I'm not sure why," she said, not bothering to hide her irritation. "If someone wants to get into the building, they can just take the stairs to the first floor."

She started for the elevator, Kenny trailing behind her.

"Books for Mrs. Forsythe to sign, I imagine," he said.

"Yes."

"Want me to get you a cart?"

"No."

"I could have carried that box up the stairs to fourteen before I hurt my back."

Jeanette shifted the box to her hip to free a hand to press the elevator button. "I'll bet."

The door slid open.

"Will Mrs. Forsythe be coming downstairs today, do you think?"

Jeanette stepped into the elevator. "I imagine we'll be running some errands later."

"Tell her she has a special delivery. I have it at the desk."

Jeanette glared at him. "Why didn't you tell me that when I was picking up the box? I could have picked up the special delivery at the same time."

"I have to give it right to her." He must have noticed Jeanette's offended expression because he added, "She has to sign for it."

"Fine," said Jeanette, prodding *14* with her elbow. "I'll let her know."

Jeanette propped the box against the side of the elevator as the digital display over the door counted off the floors. Ten ... eleven ... twelve ... fourteen. Jeanette thought it was quaint that Eden Beach's builders had avoided labeling Marilee's floor *13*. When the doors opened, she hefted the box and started down the walkway toward Marilee's condo.

The long side of the Eden Beach building ran parallel to

the highway and to the water, short wings at each end angling back slightly from the ocean. The entire building was only one unit deep, so each unit had an ocean-facing balcony and a bay-facing entrance off the open-air walkway. When Jeanette and Jeremy visited during the summer, they enjoyed bringing cocktails out to the walkway in the evenings and watching the sun set over the bay. Now, though, Jeanette found herself clenching her teeth against the biting wind that whistled through the walkway's railings.

As she approached Marilee's unit, located in the angled wing, the door opened and a man stepped out, his movements made awkward by the end table he was carrying. He was even more bundled up than she was, in a bulky coat, heavy gloves, a black watch cap, and a scarf pulled up around his cheeks.

As far as Jeanette knew, no one other than she and Jeremy had ever visited Marilee's condo, and for a panicky moment she wondered what to make of this unfamiliar man, and what, if anything, she should do about it. Then Marilee stepped out behind him, her coat draped over her shoulders, her arms crossed against the cold.

"I don't want the top to get scratched," she was saying, "so put a blanket over it." Marilee saw Jeanette, and her expression twisted with irritation. She turned back to the man. "That's all for today."

He nodded to Marilee and bobbed his head to Jeanette, then started down the walkway toward the elevator. The table, which rested against one of his legs, added a hitch to his gait.

"We're letting all the heat out," Marilee said impatiently, holding the door open for Jeanette.

Jeanette maneuvered herself and the box past Marilee and into the condo.

Jeanette had expected to be able to rest her burden on the bay-side guest room bed to work a kink out of her shoulder before carrying the box the rest of the way to Marilee's ocean-front study. However, the door to the bay-side room was closed. With a sigh, she continued down the tiled hallway toward the living room.

To her surprise, her options for spots to put down the box were limited there as well. Of Marilee's suite of bleached wood, wicker, and palm-patterned furniture, only the couch remained, facing an entertainment center on the opposite wall. The matching chairs that formerly flanked the couch were visible through the balcony's sliding glass doors—an odd choice, since as far as Jeanette knew, they weren't weather-proofed. The only other seats were three stools pulled up to the breakfast bar that separated the living room from the small kitchen.

Jeanette set the box down on the counter.

"It needs to go in the study," said Marilee.

Jeanette rolled her shoulder. "I'm just resting my arms for a second."

"You're earlier than I expected."

"I got through Wilmington faster than I thought. Who was that guy?"

"Someone I hire to do odd jobs for me."

Jeanette tamped down her reflexive response: that as long as she was driving down from Downingtown, she could take care of any odd jobs for Marilee. If Marilee had found someone else to serve as her lackey, Jeanette should be the last person to deter her.

"What was he doing with the table?" Jeanette asked.

"Taking it down to the storage room."

"Are you getting new living room furniture?"

"No. I've been doing some yoga, and I wanted extra space to practice."

"Really?"

"Yes, really. Why?"

"I just never thought of yoga as something you'd be interested in."

Marilee raised an eyebrow. "You might be surprised at some of the things I'm interested in."

"You could show me some yoga poses," Jeanette said gamely.

"I hardly think so."

Somewhat relieved that she wouldn't have to feign interest in Marilee's new hobby, Jeanette hefted the box. As she passed her mother-in-law, she wondered, not for the first time, how a woman as petite as Marilee—barely five feet tall, barely one hundred pounds—had produced a child as big as Jeremy.

"And can you stack the books?" Marilee called after her.

"Sure," muttered Jeanette. "Why not."

The study, like the living room, highlighted Jeanette's favorite part of Marilee's condo: a million-dollar view of the Atlantic. In fact, Marilee had wisely optimized the set-up of what was intended as the condo's master bedroom by furnishing it to use as her writing space as well. Against a side wall was a sleeper sofa, which Jeanette had never seen other than in its sofa configuration. Marilee's desk faced the floor-to-ceiling windows. Because of the angle of this section of the building, the windows provided not only a stunning view of the ocean but also a glimpse of the high-rise building next door. Jeanette often wondered if, like the James Stewart character in Hitchcock's *Rear Window*, Marilee got any of the ideas for her cozy mysteries from spying on the inhabitants.

As Jeanette unpacked the books and stacked them the way she knew Marilee preferred—unsigned books on the left, a cleared space on the right to stack the books as Marilee signed them—she wondered how long after the author event at Oh Buoy Books Marilee would leave for Sarasota. Jeanette and

Jeremy enjoyed making off-season, Marilee-free visits to the Ocean City condo ... at least they had before they opened the pharmacy.

However, even once Marilee was safely in Florida, Jeanette couldn't imagine how she and Jeremy could leave the pharmacy for even two days ... although a lack of vacation time was the least of their worries. If Marilee insisted they pay back the loan so she could buy out her Cozy Up Press contract—an amount of money Jeanette and Jeremy could only raise by selling the new building—they would have all the time in the world.

When Jeanette had the books unpacked and stacked, she returned to the living room.

Marilee was sitting on the couch, paging through a magazine, and Jeanette noticed that the absence of furniture was not the only change. Marilee was wearing a sweater that was similar to, although even darker than, the sweater she had been wearing in the video call with Ezra, and her tapered wool slacks and black leather ankle boots were similarly uncharacteristic.

"That's a new look for you."

"If I ever see another ruffle, it will be too soon." Marilee set aside the magazine and stood. "Make yourself at home while I sign the books." She disappeared into the study and shut the door.

Jeanette shrugged out of her coat and hung it over one of the kitchen stools. She'd kill for a cup of coffee, but Marilee was maniacally protective of the professional-grade Breville espresso machine in her kitchen and didn't allow anyone else to use it. Jeanette found a box of Red Rose tea in a cabinet and made herself a cup. Then she sat down on the couch and picked up the magazine Marilee had been reading: *Latent Prints*. She paged through it, past a short story with a noir-style illustration and an article describing blood spatter patterns and what they meant, until she came to the listing of the magazine's nominees for best debut novel. She recognized one of the names: Lara Seaford. Marilee had mentioned her in the conversation with Ezra. She skimmed the rest of the magazine, but none of the articles piqued her interest.

She set it aside and pulled her phone out of her pocket, then tapped open the e-reader app to *Foye's Principles of Medicinal Chemistry*. Jeanette's father had been a pharmacist, and she had planned to follow in his professional footsteps. Then he had gotten sick, and she had withdrawn from St. Joe's PharmD program to take care of him. But she still found the study fascinating and was continuing it on her own. She would have preferred perusing the well-worn hardcover copy she had inherited from her father, but at almost eight pounds, it was too cumbersome to carry around.

About twenty minutes later, Marilee emerged from the study, massaging her wrist. "All done."

Jeanette stood and gestured toward the copy of *Latent Prints*. "Reading up on thrillers?"

"If I hope to be successful in a new genre, I need to study it."

"You're still thinking about that? Even after what Ezra said?"

"I'm not just thinking about it, Jeanette. I'm planning it." She lowered herself onto the couch and arched an eyebrow at Jeanette. "Once I have the money I need."

There was no useful response to that parry. Clamping her lips over an unuseful one, Jeanette went back to the study and packed the signed books into the pre-labeled padded envelopes that Ezra had provided. She stacked the envelopes back in the box and carried it back to the living room.

"Anything else you need to do while I'm here?" Jeanette asked as she set the box down on the breakfast bar.

"Yes, there are a few errands I'd like to run," said Marilee, rising from the couch.

Jeanette didn't look forward to spending what was going to be a good portion of her day with her mother-in-law, but at least it was less irritating than making a six-hour round trip just to get the books from the security desk to Marilee's condo and then to the post office.

"Hey," she said, brightening, "maybe that guy who's helping you move the furniture could help you with the books, too."

"He doesn't have a car," said Marilee as she slipped on her coat.

"You could let him use yours."

"I hardly think so."

Jeanette donned her coat, hoisted the box, and followed Marilee out of the condo.

When they were in the elevator, Jeanette said, "Kenny told me he has a special delivery for you."

"And you're just telling me now?"

"I was busy unpacking books. Then you were busy signing them. I figured we'd be going out to run errands—I didn't realize the delivery was so special that you had to be notified immediately."

The elevator door slid open, and they stepped out.

"I'll pick up the package and meet you in the garage," said Marilee. She hurried across the lobby to the security desk.

Jeanette passed through the automatic doors into the garage. She guessed Marilee would prefer taking the CR-V since, as a nervous passenger, she usually chose the largest available vehicle. She managed to extricate her keyring from her coat pocket without dropping the box, chirped open the hatch, and dropped the box into the trunk.

She got in the driver's seat and Marilee arrived a moment later, tucking a small, padded envelope into her purse. As Jeanette expected, she climbed into the back seat. Marilee seemed to feel that the less she could see of the drive, the better. Jeanette had no objection to having a bit of space from her mother-in-law, even if it made her feel even more like hired help.

"What's the special delivery?" asked Jeanette.

"Just some letter from Ezra."

"About the contract buy-out?"

Marilee didn't respond to the note of alarm in Jeanette's voice. "I haven't had a chance to open it—I just picked it up."

"I thought it was an emergency."

"It was a *special* delivery, not an *emergency* delivery."

Jeanette started up the CR-V and backed out of the space, casting about for a topic that wouldn't be likely to provoke a rebuke from Marilee. "You'd think that Eden Beach could afford someone a little more on the ball than Kenny."

"I understand his brother owns the company that manages the building."

"Don't they give him some vacation time? I hardly ever see anyone other than him at the desk."

"He has a studio apartment right behind the desk. I think the only time he's not at the desk is when he's sleeping," said Marilee. Then she added tartly, "And sometimes, he doesn't even bother leaving the desk for that."

8

Jeanette stopped at the post office and dropped off the books while Marilee waited in the car. They made a few other stops: CVS to pick up a lipstick and the Acme for bagged salad greens and dressing. At Gold Coast, Marilee surprised Jeanette by picking up a bottle of bourbon rather than her usual sherry.

As Jeanette stowed the bottle in the trunk with the other purchases, Marilee said, “Why don’t we grab something to eat at Marco’s. My treat.”

Jeanette suppressed a groan. She and Jeremy had planned a night in with pizza and a movie. Plus, since they only had one car, it meant Jeremy would have to stay at the pharmacy past closing time, and even Jeremy was ready to put the pharmacy behind him at the end of his workday.

“That would be nice,” she said, trying to muster some enthusiasm.

Marco’s was one of the few upscale restaurants in Ocean City, a town that tended more usually toward crabs, fries, and beer, served in restaurants labeled *Grille* or *Shack*. It was also one of a handful of restaurants open year-round.

During the summer, the parking lot of the ocean-front restaurant would have been packed, and Jeanette would have dropped Marilee off at the entrance and then gone searching for a spot. Today, however, there was a place right outside the door. She pulled in, then followed Marilee inside.

Even at mid-afternoon in off-season, a dozen diners occupied the cloth-covered tables. Most sat near the wall of windows that gave a view across the beach to gray rollers under an overcast sky.

A man whom Jeanette recognized from previous visits as the owner crossed the dining room to where they stood.

"Ms. Forsythe," he said, "how lovely to see you again."

"Lovely to be here, Marco," replied Marilee. "Is my regular table available?"

"Of course." Marco picked up two faux leather-bound menus. "Please follow me."

He led them to a window-side table and pulled out the chair with the better view for Marilee. Jeanette seated herself opposite her mother-in-law and accepted a menu from Marco.

"I see that even in the middle of the winter, you're still bringing in diners," Marilee said to Marco.

"Yes—we appreciate the patronage of the locals as well as the visitors, and of course we're thrilled to be seeing you here, although I imagine you'll be heading for Sarasota soon."

"Yes, after an event at Oh Buoy Books." She made a minuscule adjustment to her salad fork. "I'll be the guest of honor."

Marilee and Marco chatted about Sarasota for a minute. Marco mentioned that he had started his restaurant career in nearby Tampa, and Marilee expressed her delight at recognizing the name of the restaurant, one she frequented when in Florida. Jeanette occupied herself by scanning the menu and wondering how Marilee could be so pleasant with a casual acquaintance when she was so unpleasant with her own family.

Marilee ordered a glass of Chardonnay, and Jeanette, thinking of the three-hour drive ahead of her, asked for water.

Marco bobbed his head and bustled away.

They continued the conversation about Florida restaurants—or, more accurately, Marilee continued it, with Jeanette as her silent audience—until Marco returned to the table with their drinks. He took their orders: *whatever Chef recommends* for Marilee and a vegan dish with eggplant and couscous for Jeanette.

When they were alone again, Marilee took a sip of her wine. "How are things going with repairs to the old pharmacy building?"

Jeanette cleared her throat. "It's dragging on a bit."

Marilee gave a little moue of disapproval. "It's taking a very long time. Certainly longer than I expected."

"Longer than we expected, too. There's a lot of work to be done. Plus, a bunch of businesses and houses in Downingtown got flooded, and they all need the same people we need: carpenters, electricians, drywall installers, painters. It's hard to line up people for the work."

"You and Jeremy should be firmer with your contractor."

Jeanette didn't remind Marilee that, to save money, she and Jeremy were working as their own contractor, and that it was difficult to be firm with the subcontractors if they didn't return Jeanette and Jeremy's calls.

"Of course, you remember the conversation with Ezra about buying out my contract," continued Marilee.

"Of course."

"It would be a great help for me to have that money."

"It would be a great help for us to have it to give it to you."

Marilee raised an eyebrow.

Jeanette flushed. She took a sip of water, then set the glass carefully back on the table. "Marilee, I realize we should have discussed this in more detail when you loaned us the money, but Jeremy and I expected to have some time to pay you back. You know how long any construction project takes, and even once all the repairs are done, it may take us a little while to sell the old building."

"I don't want to wait too long between Ezra making the offer for the buyout of my contract and when I can act on that offer."

"It didn't sound to me like he actually made an offer. In fact, he said that—"

"When I have the money in hand," Marilee interrupted, "his attitude will shift."

Jeanette changed tacks. "Are you really so sure you want to start writing a completely different kind of book? Your cozies have been so successful."

"Have you read my cozies?"

"Of course. I read the first one when Jeremy and I started dating."

"And have you read any more of them?"

"Well—"

"I'll take that to mean that you have not. Any why haven't you?"

"Well—"

"Because they're boring!" exclaimed Marilee. "You know what people want to read? Thrillers. You should check out that Lara Seaford thriller."

"I recall you said it had been nominated for an award."

"Yes—the *Latent Prints* magazine best debut novel. And I hear through the grapevine that it may be nominated for best debut at GothamCon." She sat back with a smug smile. "But you know what? I could write a better one."

Marco saved Jeanette from having to respond by arriving at the table with an appetizer of four seared scallops. "Courtesy of Chef," he said, setting it on the table between them with a flourish.

Marilee tasted one and declared it delicious.

Jeanette, who hated scallops, said it certainly looked delicious.

When Marco bustled away to seat a newly arrived party of four, Marilee asked, "If you don't like cozies or thrillers, what do you read?"

"Mostly pharmacy textbooks."

"Ah, yes, pharmacy textbooks." Marilee took another bite of scallop. "Why Jeremy wanted to become a pharmacist, I'll never know. It was to pay for his medical school tuition that I started writing the damn cozies."

Jeanette steeled herself for a recitation with which she was all too familiar.

"I would have been perfectly comfortable living off my late husband's pension and insurance money," continued Marilee, "if it hadn't been for Jeremy's plan—his *professed* plan—to become a doctor. But then, after a couple of years of medical school, he decides that his true calling is behind the counter of a pharmacy."

"Behind the counter of *our* pharmacy."

"And a naturopathic pharmacy at that. I don't believe in relying on drugs to take care of your problems."

"You took Percocet when you broke your wrist."

"Well, of course, for a broken bone it's hardly avoidable. And in that case, I needed something a little more potent than leaves and roots."

"Actually, leaves and roots—"

"But a naturopathic pharmacy is what Jeremy wanted, and I didn't stand in his way." Marilee finished the scallops and patted her lips with her napkin. "I believe the pharmacy bug runs in your family, correct?"

"Dad was a pharmacist. He's the person who inspired me to have a pharmacy of my own."

They were both silent for a few beats, then Marilee said briskly, "It's fine to have dreams, but the dreams need to pay for themselves."

Jeanette didn't share the full extent of the dream she and Jeremy had: for Jeanette formally to return to her pharmacy studies as soon as profits from the business would enable it. That dream seemed increasingly distant, especially with Marilee so eager to buy out her contract with Ezra.

As if sensing Jeanette's train of thought, Marilee heaved a sigh. "But I'm not going to be able to pay my way to *my* dream in time to avoid this event at Oh Buoy Books."

9

Darren stepped into his Wilmington apartment, tossed his keys into the basket on the hall table, and hung his coat, hat, and scarf on the coat rack. He was grateful that he had gotten home before the light snow that had started to fall had a chance to stick. The only downside of the Ford was its lack of anti-lock brakes and airbags.

He went to the kitchen to make a cup of tea, and as he waited for the water to boil, he thought about the demonstration Ann Kinnear had given in the Mahalo Winery barrel room. 'Making the Supernatural Super in Your Novel' was going to be a compelling talk, especially since he could now vouch for Ann's ability. He just wished she had a speaker reel he could have watched, as he usually did with other speakers, to see if she could hold an audience. He took his role supporting the GothamCon board seriously and didn't want one of his charges to sully the conference's reputation by providing a sub-par performance. His role as GothamCon gofer might not pay, but it was important to stay in front of the movers and shakers of the thriller world, especially with the way he feared things might go with the Wolfram series under Alec Quine's authorship.

At the previous year's conference, the board had announced Jock as this year's honorary chairperson. When Jock died a month after that announcement and H & J announced that Alec would pick up the series, the board felt that transferring the chairmanship to Alec was the path of least resistance. However, Darren suspected that no one—least of all Alec himself—believed that the board would have chosen him based on his modestly successful, tepidly reviewed, and ponderously paced legal thrillers.

The board had asked Darren to work with Alec to create a memorial video for Jock Quine to be shown at the banquet held on the last night of the conference, and Darren had sat through plenty of such videos to know what the board expected. But Jock Quine had been such a big personality that Darren felt he deserved something more ... well, more memorable. After Ann Kinnear's demonstration at Mahalo, Darren saw an opportunity to provide that—a message from beyond the grave from Jock to his colleagues and fans.

But another thought had struck him on the drive back from Kennett Square. Jock's murder, apparently by an intruder who had stolen his valuable collection of ivory figurines, was still unsolved. If Ann could contact Jock, she might find out information from him that would lead to the apprehension of the killer. Now *that* would be a story worthy of a thriller.

Darren finished making his tea, then carried the steaming mug to his office. He sat at his desk, got out his phone, and placed a video call.

Alec's image appeared against the backdrop of the office of his mid-century-modern home in Princeton. His reddish-blond hair, long on top and short on the sides and back, was combed back from a high forehead, his eyes magnified behind tortoiseshell glasses. He wore a button-down white shirt under a V-neck sweater, and if Darren had to guess, Alec would have completed the outfit with a pair of pressed khakis and shined leather loafers. Darren wondered if, as Alec's editor, he had any responsibility to suggest that a different look might be more on-brand. Jock's battered leather jackets and worn jeans—dungarees, as Jock preferred to call them—had been an effective homage to his popular protagonist. Alec's was more likely to bring to mind the protagonist's nerdy sidekick.

"Hello, Darren."

"Hey, Alec."

"What's that noise?"

For a moment, Darren didn't know what Alec was talking about, then noticed the barking from the adjacent apartment. "Oh, it's the neighbor's dog—I'm so used to it, I barely hear it anymore. Do you have a couple of minutes?"

Alec's eyes shifted, checking the time on his monitor. "A couple."

"The plans we've been discussing for Jock's memorial video, it's all been pretty standard fare: a photo montage of Jock hobnobbing with fans at various cons. A half dozen of his author colleagues saying a few heartfelt words. A tribute from the head of Harrison & John. It seems a little anemic."

"It seems like what people expect in these circumstances."

"Yes, but you know what a big personality Jock was. I'm not sure that 'expected' is what he would want." Before Alec could disagree, Darren hurried on. "I have an idea for the video, one I think would be truer to the spirit of Jock Quine. It would mean bringing in ..." Darren cast about for the right word. "... a professional, but I think the board would foot the bill. The thing is, this person—her name is Ann—would need access to Tamaston to confirm if the idea is viable." Darren thought of the rambling mansion Jock had bought just a few miles from Alec's home in order to be near his son. There could hardly be a more atmospheric location for Ann Kinnear to ply her craft.

"Professional video, eh? Scouting the location?"

Darren laughed nervously. He hadn't planned to lie to Alec about Ann's profession, but Alec's assumption seemed too good an excuse to pass up. "Something like that."

"Just the one person? In my experience, those video types always travel with a crew."

"I'd ask them to hold the number down to avoid disrupting things more than necessary. In fact, since I'll be coming up to Princeton to work on the book with you, why don't I arrange for them to come to Tamaston after you and I are done with our work for the day. That way I can show them around, but we won't disturb you."

"Will the video crew need to scout my house as well?" asked Alec.

"Oh, I don't think that will be necessary."

"You don't want video of me working on the book?" Alec asked, his voice peevish.

"Oh, of course, as long as it won't be an imposition."

Alec adopted a look of exaggerated patience. "I'll work around it."

"That's great, Alec—I really appreciate it. I'll talk with Ann and let you know what the plan is."

They ended the call, and Darren sat back and puffed out a breath. Could he pull together a fake video crew to accompany the fake video producer? Maybe Mike Kinnear would accompany Ann on the engagement. Then he rubbed his hand down his face as he realized that wasn't his biggest challenge. He'd also need to try to arrange for honorary chair Alec Quine not to run into presenter Ann Kinnear at GothamCon.

10

A few hours after seeing Darren Van Osten off on his drive back to Wilmington, Ann called Mike and his husband, Scott Pate, and invited them over for an early dinner. She got them settled in the Curragh with glasses of Mahalo wine, then drove over to Kennett Bistro to pick up takeout. When she returned with the food, she pulled in next to Audrey the Audi and tramped to the front door through a few inches of snow that had fallen that afternoon. Among the many reasons she loved living in the Curragh was the fact that the only snow removal she had to do was to sweep any accumulation off the front porch. And if she ever got snowed in, she had enough canned soup, crackers, and cheese to last a week, and a virtually limitless supply of wine just down the hill at the Cellar.

She found Scott standing at the breakfast bar, blond head bent over the jigsaw puzzle she had set out, chunky black glasses tucked into his shirt pocket. Mike was sitting on the couch scrolling on his phone and absently stroking Ursula the dachshund, who was curled up next to him.

"Dinner's served," she said.

Mike stood and relieved her of the boxes. "Smells great. You'll have to give me the recipe."

"Ha ha," she said as she shrugged out of her parka.

With the breakfast bar covered with puzzle pieces, Mike bent to put the pizza boxes on the coffee table.

"I wouldn't if I were you," said Scott, nodding meaningfully at Ursula, who had jumped down from the couch and was already sniffing at the corners of the boxes.

"You can put them on the stove," said Ann, "and we can eat at the kitchen table."

Ann got out plates and flipped open the lids of the boxes. Mike had requested *prosciutto di parma*, Scott had opted for *fungo epico*, and Ann had selected chorizo and potato, but they all took a slice of each, then settled down at the small kitchen table. Ann poured herself a glass of wine and topped up Mike's and Scott's glasses.

Mike swirled the wine and took an appreciative sip. "Darren Van Osten left me a voicemail. He might be good for a more traditional sensing engagement as well as the speaking gig. He says that the GothamCon board wants to hire you to try to contact Jock Quine. Something about a memorial video to be shown at the conference banquet."

"They want to video me talking with Jock?" asked Ann with a scowl.

"Or maybe just conveying a message from him to his fans. I'll call Darren back to get more detail and let you know what he says."

"Darren said Jock lived near Princeton, right? Is that where the engagement would be?"

"I assume so."

"I've been wanting to fly to Princeton," said Ann through a mouthful of pizza.

"I haven't been to Princeton for years," said Scott. "What a beautiful town."

They chatted about Princeton and other destinations easily reachable in one of Avondale Airport's rental planes. Then the conversation segued back to Darren Van Osten—and, more specifically, to Darren's pickup.

"You'd love it," Mike said to Scott. He got out his phone, tapped, and handed the phone to Scott. "I took a bunch of pictures. Scroll through."

"It's a beautiful vehicle," said Scott, swiping through the photos. "He's certainly taken good care of it."

Mike's phone, still in Scott's hand, pinged with a text.

"Who is it?" asked Mike.

"Craig," Scott read from the screen.

Mike reached for the phone.

Scott handed it back, but said, "Craig can wait until we're done eating."

Mike sighed and set the phone aside. "Okay, you're right."

"Who's Craig?" asked Ann.

"Buddy from back in my financial planner days," said Mike.

They resumed their discussion of the truck, but a minute later, Scott's phone pinged from his pocket.

Mike raised his eyebrows. "Coincidence?"

"I don't know," said Scott, taking a sip of wine. "I guess we'll find out after we're done with our meal."

A half minute passed, then Mike's phone rang.

"Oh, come on," Mike said, picking up the phone. "You've got to be curious." He tapped the screen. "Craig!" he said as he got up from the table and stepped into the sitting area. "What's up?" He listened for a few moments, then his tone brightened. "No kidding, that sounds great. ... Absolutely. What are the dates again? ... Damn, that's not a lot of advance notice. ... No, no, don't count us out. Let me talk to Scott and I'll get right back to you. ... Yeah, send me a link. Thanks for thinking of us."

He ended the call and returned to the table. "Craig got a last-minute deal on a ski chalet in Colorado and wants to know if we want to go."

"How last minute?" asked Scott.

"We'd leave tomorrow."

Another text came in and Mike tapped, whistled, and turned the phone toward Scott and Ann. It was a photo of a massive A-frame on a snow-covered hill surrounded by snow-bedecked pines.

"Not really what I think of when I hear 'chalet,' but very nice," said Scott.

"Really nice," said Ann. "You guys should definitely go."

"I haven't skied since high school," said Scott. "Although I've treated plenty of skiers at Bryn Mawr. Doesn't make me want to do it myself." He shuddered. "The things a person can do to a knee on a ski slope ..."

"Come on," said Mike, "you can stick to the bunny slope if you want to. Or just hang out at the chalet." He brought up another photo and turned the phone back to Scott. "Just look at that view!"

"It does look really nice," said Scott, "but I don't want to take time off from work, especially on such short notice. It would be hard to reschedule my patients to other PTs, and I don't want to interrupt their therapy schedules."

Mike knew as well as Ann did that once Scott made up his mind, argument wouldn't sway him. He sighed and turned to Ann. "How about you? Fancy a trip to Colorado?"

She raised an eyebrow. "Was I actually invited?"

"I know the guys who are going—they'd love to have you there."

"Nah. I don't want to interfere with any planned trips to the local strip club."

Mike rolled his eyes. "I'm hoping it's not that kind of ski trip."

"That kind of trip or not," said Scott, "you should go. You haven't skied since last year."

"I don't want to go without you."

"We can video chat every day. We can have virtual cocktails overlooking the gorgeous view. I can advise you and Craig and the other guys on the best way to wrap a knee for maximum flexibility."

"You sure?"

Scott patted Mike's hand. "Very sure."

"Cool!" Mike jumped up. "I'll let Craig know I'm coming." He retired again to the sitting room.

Ann took a sip of wine and turned to Scott. "We'll have to think of something to do while Mike's gone to make him jealous."

11

The day after dining with Marilee at Marco's, Jeanette was again on the road to Ocean City, this time with Jeremy. As they approached Oh Buoy Books, where Marilee's author event was to be held, Jeremy asked, "What's the berry snack for this evening? And how's Mom getting it to the bookstore? For that matter, how's she getting herself to the bookstore? She hates to drive any time, but she really hates to drive after dark."

"She's taking a taxi, and Nina—she's the owner—is picking up the snack. I ordered a vanilla sheet cake."

"The event isn't specific to a certain book, is it?" asked Jeremy. "How did you pick which berry to feature?"

"I had them put a bunch of different berries on top."

"Smart thinking."

When they got to the store, the small parking lot in front was full.

"There are a couple of spaces in back," said Jeanette.

Jeremy circled to the alley that ran behind the store and parked. They hurried to the back door and slipped through, trying to let in as little of the frigid evening air as possible.

They found Marilee chatting with a group of white-haired women clutching copies—and in a couple of cases, stacks—of Berry Mysteries. When they caught Marilee's eye, they waved.

Jeanette expected Marilee to be pleased by their surprise appearance, but her expression morphed from saccharine sweet to scowling.

"Not quite the reaction I was hoping for," whispered Jeremy.

"No kidding," muttered Jeanette, irritated that their unannounced trip to Ocean City might somehow result in a black mark against them on Marilee's emotional tally sheet. "I think I'll wait to say hello."

"Good idea." Jeremy glanced around the room. "Looks like they have punch. Want a cup?"

"Sure. If it's spiked, make it a big one." She gestured to a corner of the store, away from the crowd gathered around Marilee. "I'll be over there."

Jeremy squeezed her arm, then made his way through the crowd to the punch bowl. He ladled out a half a cup, took a sip, gave her a thumbs up, then served out two generous portions. He rejoined Jeanette and handed her a paper cup of a pinkish-orange liquid.

Jeanette downed most of her punch and gestured toward Marilee, who had thrown back her head in girlish laughter at something one of her fans had said. "How can she be so different at these events?"

"If there was an Oscar for Best Off-Screen Portrayal of a charming woman, Mom would win hands down."

Jeremy's expression didn't quite match his lighthearted tone. Marilee felt just as free to express her many disappointments in Jeremy as she did Jeanette, and it couldn't be easy for him to endure her disapproval.

The crowd was standing room only, so when Nina asked

the attendees to take their seats, Jeanette and Jeremy had an excuse to maintain their position in the corner.

Nina delivered an effusive speech about Marilee's success and her appreciation of Marilee's ongoing outreach to her enthusiastic fans. Then she turned the mic over to Marilee, who read the first chapter of the upcoming *Mulberry Murder* to the rapt audience.

During the Q&A, Jeremy snuck back to the punch bowl and refilled their cups.

When the Q&A wrapped up, Nina began directing attendees to form a line in front of the table where Marilee would be signing.

Marilee headed toward the back of the store, casting a furtive look behind her, then turned back when Nina called out, "We're ready for you, Marilee!"

Jeanette expected the signing portion of the evening would take some time, since Marilee normally chatted with each customer. Tonight, however, she seemed to just be signing the books and handing them to the customers with a distracted smile. When the line at the signing table had disappeared and reformed at the register, Marilee again headed toward the back of the store, to be waylaid again by Nina, who steered her toward a group of fans hoping for photos with the author. After the photo op, Nina bestowed a small trophy bedecked with plastic berries on Oh Buoy's favorite author.

When the applause died down and Marilee had said a few words of thanks, the customers began bundling into their coats, scarves, and gloves. Jeremy and Jeanette stood in line at the register to buy a tofu cookbook, probably the only non-Marilee book the store had sold that evening.

The customer ahead of them stepped away from the register and Jeremy handed the cookbook to the salesclerk. As he got out a credit card, Jeanette noticed that Marilee was slipping on her coat. "Is she leaving now?" Jeanette asked Jeremy. "She usually stays around until all the customers leave."

Jeremy looked toward where Marilee was once again heading for the back of the store.

"She is acting kind of weird," he said. "Maybe she was hitting that punch a little too hard. Would you mind checking on what she's up to while I pay for this?"

Jeanette sighed. "Sure."

She made her way through the thinning crowd to the back of the store. She opened the door and, in the dim illumination cast by a security light, saw Marilee standing, arms crossed against the cold, looking up and down the alley.

Jeanette was about to call out to ask Marilee if she needed anything, when a movement in the near darkness just outside the pool of light caught Jeanette's attention. A form emerged from the shadows and, as it moved into the light, she saw it was a person wearing a balaclava-type ski hat with the mask pulled down against the cold.

He was moving down the alley toward Marilee, who was looking in the other direction. As he approached her, he ducked his head and shoulders.

Suddenly Jeanette's heart was in her throat—was he going to tackle Marilee?

"Hey!" she shouted.

Marilee jumped at her shout, then saw the man. "Jeanette, stay back!" she yelled. "I'll handle this!"

Jeanette scrambled down the few stairs, but misjudged the last one and staggered, barely catching herself on the handrail. She looked up to see Marilee looping her arm over the man's lowered head and around his neck. What was she trying to do? Marilee was so much shorter than the man that if he straightened from his hunched position, he would lift her off the ground, maybe toss her over his back onto the pavement.

Jeanette ran across the alley and threw her hands around the man's waist, trying to pull him away from Marilee. He twisted and his elbow connected with Jeanette's cheek. Her vision went bright white for a moment, but she sensed that his movement had thrown Marilee free. Jeanette tried to follow the twist, to keep her hands around his waist so he wouldn't go for Marilee again.

But the twist carried her into Marilee, who reeled back with a shocked shriek. Jeanette lost her footing, and her grip on the man, and hit the asphalt with a jarring thump. Marilee went sprawling on the pavement next to her.

The man was still standing, and Jeanette sensed him reaching down toward Marilee. An image flashed through her mind of him picking up Marilee and running away with her—her mother-in-law was so petite that at that moment it didn't seem an unreasonable fear. Jeanette flung her arm up to knock his hand away as Marilee, obviously disoriented, scuttled on her hands and knees in his direction. Then the man staggered, overbalanced, and fell, and Jeanette heard the sickening thud of bone against something hard.

There was a moment during which none of them moved. Then the man dragged himself to his feet and limped down the alley, his hand to his head.

Jeanette also climbed to her feet and was just helping Marilee up when Jeremy, Nina, and half a dozen customers came spilling out into the alley.

Jeremy ran to Jeanette and Marilee, wrapping an arm around each of them. "What happened?"

"Someone attacked Marilee," gasped Jeanette. She pointed in the direction the man had run. "He went that way."

"Are you okay?" he asked.

"Yes. I think so," said Jeanette, trying to take stock of her condition.

"Are you okay, Mom?" he asked Marilee.

"Jeanette knocked me down."

"You seem fine." He shifted Marilee into Jeanette's arms. "Can you help Mom?"

"What are you doing?" quavered Marilee.

"I'm going after him," said Jeremy.

"No!" yelled Marilee. "No! Don't leave me!"

"Mom, Jeanette can help you. He's getting away!"

"No!" Marilee yelled again. She clamped her hands around Jeremy's arm.

"Jeremy, this is a job for the police," said Nina. "Everybody inside. I'm calling 911."

12

By the time the ER doctor examined Jeanette's eye, it was swelling, and it was clear she would have a shiner.

"I don't believe any bones are broken," said the doctor, pressing gently around her eye. "But we can do a CT scan if you'd like."

"No," said Jeanette, gingerly touching her puffy lid. "I'm sure it will be fine."

"We can pick up some arnica cream to bring down the swelling," said Jeremy.

"I prefer something with FDA approval," said the doctor.

Jeremy rolled his eyes.

"My wrist hurts," said Marilee, who was propped up on a stretcher in the cubicle adjoining Jeanette's, the intervening curtain drawn back. "Can I get some Percocet?"

"My mother broke her wrist quite badly in a car accident several years ago," said Jeremy to the doctor.

"They gave me Percocet at the time," said Marilee.

"The x-ray doesn't show anything that would merit Percocet," said the doctor. "Let's try something a little less high-powered first. Like ibuprofen."

"Or curcumin," suggested Jeremy.

"Sure," said the doctor with a shrug. "Or that."

Marilee rubbed her wrist with exaggerated care. "I'd prefer to get something that will provide actual pain relief," she grumbled.

A nurse popped his head through the curtain. "There's a detective here who would like to take statements from Ms. Forsythe and Ms. Frobisher."

The doctor looked questioningly at Marilee and Jeanette.

"Fine with me," said Jeanette.

"Oh, all right," said Marilee. Her words suggested reluctance, but her tone reflected some enthusiasm at the prospect of a conversation with the police.

The doctor and nurse withdrew, and the detective stepped into the cubicle. He was about thirty, with close-cropped dark hair and bushy eyebrows. He nodded to the three.

"I'm Detective Lewis Morganstein, and I'll be investigating the incident." He shook his head. "Really sorry this happened to you ladies—we usually don't have much in the way of violent crime here in Ocean City, especially in January." He pulled a small spiral-bound notepad and pen from his pocket. "The bookstore has a security camera in the back that captured the altercation, and the owner showed us the video. Ms. Frobisher, it's clear that you were completely justified in your defense of Ms. Forsythe."

"I would think so," said Jeremy, smiling at Jeanette, who felt herself blush.

"I could have taken care of it myself," grumped Marilee.

Morganstein smiled. "I think your daughter-in-law is a little better equipped to play the part of bodyguard."

Jeanette knew that her pleased blush had morphed into an irritated flush.

Morganstein clicked the pen open. "Can either of you give me any description of the attacker?"

"No," said Marilee. "It was too dark, and it all happened too quickly."

"Yes, it was pretty dark," said Jeanette. "He was wearing a balaclava. At first, I didn't think anything of it because it's so cold, but I couldn't see his features at all. He was wearing dark clothes—a heavy dark coat—but nothing distinctive."

"Gloves?"

Jeanette thought. "I think he must have been wearing gloves. I don't remember seeing his hands."

Morganstein glanced toward Marilee, who shook her head.

He turned back to Jeanette. "Definitely a man?"

"I think so."

"Tall? Short? Heavy? Thin?"

She considered, then shook her head. "Medium. Sorry I can't be more help."

Morganstein nodded. "He obviously planned his outfit to minimize the chances of being identified."

"When he ran off, I think he was limping," said Jeanette. "And he was holding his head."

"On the video, it looked like he hit his head on the curb. He probably twisted his leg in the altercation." Morganstein turned to Marilee. "Ms. Forsythe, can you think of any reason someone would attack you?"

"Of course not."

"I understand from the owner of the bookstore that you're a writer. Is it possible someone was angry about something you wrote?"

Marilee snorted contemptuously. "Not unless they have a violent aversion to berries."

"My mother writes cozy mysteries," clarified Jeremy. "They all have a reference to berries in the title."

"And none of them are interesting enough to prompt someone to attack me," added Marilee.

If Morganstein was surprised to hear an author speak so disparagingly of her own work, he managed to hide it. "It could have been an attempted purse snatching."

"Yes, that must have been it," said Marilee.

"It would have to have been a pretty unobservant purse snatcher," said Jeremy, "since she wasn't carrying a purse."

"Oh," said Morganstein, turning to Marilee, "I assumed you were leaving the event. But if you didn't have your purse with you ..."

"It was stuffy in the store," said Marilee. "I wanted to get a breath of fresh air."

"And if he was really lying in wait for Marilee," said Jeanette, "wouldn't he have assumed she would leave through the front door? Why would he have waited for her in back?"

"Maybe he was waiting for Nina to come out," suggested Jeremy. "They sold a lot of books tonight. Maybe he thought she would leave with a lot of money."

"But she wouldn't be taking it to the bank at night," said Jeanette. "And who pays with cash these days anyway? He'd probably just get a bunch of credit card receipts."

"All good ideas," said Morganstein without much enthusiasm. He flipped his notepad closed and returned it and the pen to his pocket. "We'll check other security cameras in the area, see if we can figure out where he went. We'll let you know what we find out. If you think of anything else that might be helpful, no matter how small, please give me a call."

He handed each of them a business card, nodded a farewell, and stepped back through the curtain.

"How are you feeling?" Jeremy asked Jeanette.

"My wrist hurts," said Marilee.

"Lucky that the x-ray came back okay. You probably just need to give it a rest." He rubbed his neck. "It's probably too late to find a pharmacy that would have curcumin. Do you have any ibuprofen at home?"

"I believe the only thing in my medicine cabinet is my make-up and a bottle of Chanel No. 5," Marilee replied irritably. She swung her legs off the stretcher. "But just being at home would make me feel better. I'm ready to get out of here."

"You've had quite a shock," he said. "Do you want to come back to Downingtown with me and Jeanette?"

To Jeanette's great relief, Marilee shook her head. "I'm not up for a long drive. I just want to go back to the condo."

"Do you want ..." His voice trailed off, and he shot a look toward Jeanette. "... one of us to stay with you?"

Jeanette knew which one of them it would be—if Jeremy wasn't back in Downingtown in the morning to fill prescriptions, they might as well close for the day. So she was doubly relieved when Marilee again shook her head.

"No," said Marilee, "I want to be alone."

13

Ann was browsing the cheese selection at Wegmans when her phone buzzed with a call from Mike.

"Hey, what's up?" she answered. "I thought you'd be Colorado-bound by now."

"I'm on the plane and they're just about to push back from the gate, but I finally connected with Van Osten about the sensing gig for GothamCon. He got the okay from the board to hire you to try to contact Jock Quine for the memorial video. I didn't have time to talk with him for too long. I wanted to get off the phone so I could call you before the flight leaves and see what you think about it."

"Do they just want me to convey some message from Jock from the great beyond?"

"I trust you never to use the phrase 'from the great beyond' with a client or prospect, but I think that's what he has in mind—just conveying a message, not videoing the actual contact. I'll confirm that with him. And they're in a bit of a hurry because the conference is coming right up. I proposed a slightly higher than normal daily rate for a rush job and the board didn't balk."

"Princeton's easy enough to get to, especially if I can fly. That seems fine."

In the background of Mike's call, she heard the announcement for passengers to put away their electronic devices.

"Damn," he muttered. "I was hoping to call Darren back before we took off."

"You're supposed to be on vacation. I'll call him."

"I hate to make you take care of the business side of things—"

"Just give me the number before the flight attendant has to yell at you."

He gave her the number. "Make sure you agree on the logistical details—"

Ann heard another voice in the background of Mike's call. "Sir, I'm going to have to ask you to put away your phone."

Mike said, voice aimed away from the phone, "I will, definitely—just one minute." Then back at Ann. "Talk to Darren before you go, just to make sure you're in sync about expectations."

"I'll take care of it," said Ann. "Now go have fun in Colorado."

"Thanks, I appreciate it."

"Sir—" she heard from Mike's end of the call.

"If you or Scott change your minds about Colorado—" he said hurriedly. Ann pictured the flight attendant reaching for Mike's phone.

"We won't change our minds," she said. "Have fun. Don't break a leg—we don't want Scott to have to be doing home PT on you."

She tapped to end the call.

She finished picking up the few items she needed: some yogurt, fruit, a dozen eggs, and her favorite chocolate chip cookies. When she got back to the Forester, she called Darren.

"You want me to convey a message from Jock Quine?" Ann asked.

"Yes ... among other things." Before Ann could ask about 'other things,' Darren hurried on. "But before we decide on how we might be able to use any information you get from Jock, I think we should make sure he's there to be contacted. It's not a sure thing, right?"

"Not a sure thing at all. Some people don't stay around after they're dead, and there may be spirits who stay around that I can't contact, or who don't want to be contacted. A test run is a good idea."

"And based on what you said about Niall Lynch haunting the barrel room at the winery because it was a special place to him, contacting Jock at his home seems most likely, right?"

"Yes, if it was special to him."

"Very special. He moved to Princeton to be near Alec, but it was like Tamaston was just waiting for Jock as its perfect tenant."

"And it's also the location of his death, correct?"

"Yes."

"He was killed at night?"

"Yes. Around midnight."

"That's probably going to be the most likely time to encounter him."

"Could you come tomorrow night? We're on a bit of a tight timeframe to get everything ready for the memorial event at the banquet. I'm going to be in Princeton to do some work with Alec on his manuscript, and I usually stay at Tamaston. That's a holdover from Jock's time," he added wistfully. "We used to work practically round the clock when we were on a streak." He sighed. "In any case, I can arrange to be there tomorrow night and I can show you around."

"Is the son going to want to be there? Like Mike said, the

more people in attendance, the less likely it is that I'll be able to make contact."

"He doesn't need to be there for this scouting expedition. If you wanted to meet me somewhere along 95, we could drive up together."

"Actually, if the weather's good," said Ann, "I'll probably fly into Princeton Airport. Do you know if I can get a ride share from there?"

"I can pick you up." After a moment, he said, "Actually, I just realized that if you want to be at Jock's house around midnight, it will mean we'll finish up very late. Are you going to fly home after the visit?"

"No, but I can stay over."

"The board has already authorized the fee for the engagement," he said nervously, "plus the extra charge for the short notice. I don't think they'll approve overnight accommodations. And I'm not sure how Alec would feel about other visitors staying at Tamaston. As many times as I stayed there when Jock was alive, I feel a bit like I'm imposing now that he's gone."

"That's okay—I'll cover the cost of a hotel room," she said, knowing that Mike would take her to task for that.

"Ah, that's fine, then," he said, relieved. "I appreciate that." He cleared his throat. "I understand that Mike is out of town."

"Yes. Do you need to talk to him? I could ask him to call you when he gets back. Although that won't be for a few days."

"No, no. I just thought he might want to come along."

"He just handles the business side and generally lets me handle the engagements themselves on my own."

"Yes!" said Darren with more enthusiasm than Ann thought her explanation merited. "I was impressed by what a business-like operation you run. Does Ann Kinnear Sensing have other staff?"

Ann wondered if this was a common question for a client to pose and, if yes, what Mike's answer would be. "Not really—it's mainly just me and Mike ..."

"Ah. Right," said Darren, obviously disappointed.

After a moment, she asked, "Would it help if we did have other staff?"

"Yes, I think it might. It sounds to me as if Alec expects a crew."

A crew? Ann had never heard of a senser, at least a reputable one, who worked with a crew, but Mike was always harping about the importance of accommodating client expectations. "Well, I'm not sure I can swing a whole crew, but I can probably rustle up one other person."

"An assistant, you might say," prompted Darren.

"Sure, you might say that."

"Excellent," he said, sounding far cheerier than he had until that point in the conversation. "And how should we handle the payment for the engagement?"

"I'll ask Mike to send the bill when he's back from Colorado."

They ended the call, and Ann hit an entry in her favorites list.

"Hey, Annie," answered Scott.

"Any chance you could get off work tomorrow night and the following day for a trip to Princeton?"

"As luck would have it, I work an early shift tomorrow and I'm off the next day. Is this what we're doing to make Mike jealous?"

"Actually, Ann Kinnear Sensing is looking for a fake assistant."

"A fake assistant? I'm intrigued."

"Interested in the job?"

Scott laughed. "You know I am."

14

The day after the Oh Buoy Books event, Jeanette was in the back room of the pharmacy, updating some customer records. She was self-conscious about her black eye, so Jeremy was trying to cover the register as well as fill the prescriptions.

Her phone rang, and she looked at the caller ID: Ezra. She groaned, realizing that she should have let him know about the attack on Marilee.

She hit *Accept*. "Hi, Ezra."

"Jeanette, what's going on? Is Marilee okay?"

"She's fine. Did Nina call you about what happened at the bookstore?"

"No—I have an alert set for when Marilee's name pops up online."

"It's online?"

"A couple of local news outlets picked it up, and now it's trending on social media. What happened?"

Jeanette described the event to Ezra.

"And Marilee's okay?" he asked again.

"She said her wrist hurt, but the doctor seemed to think

she just needed to take some ibuprofen. Other than that, she just seemed shaken up. We asked her if she wanted to come stay with us in Downingtown, but she just wanted to get back to the condo."

"Her wrist? Damn. I hope it doesn't interfere with her writing."

"I'll convey your concern to her," said Jeanette pointedly.

"Just considering the practicalities." After a moment, he continued. "Why in the world would someone attack Marilee?"

"We don't know."

"Not exactly in line with the persona we've developed for her," Ezra muttered. After a moment, he added, "And I see that we have you to thank for leaping to Marilee's defense."

"I thought I was better equipped to deal with the situation."

"Of course. I appreciate what you did. I'm sure Marilee does, too."

"Yes, I'm sure she does," said Jeanette, although she realized that Marilee had never expressed any appreciation—only irritation.

"Is she going to be heading down to Florida now that the Oh Buoy Books event is done? She has a couple of events near Sarasota coming up."

Jeanette felt a twist in her gut as she contemplated what it would mean if Marilee postponed her departure. Her mother-in-law's relocation to Florida was a respite for Jeanette, since even Marilee didn't expect Jeanette to drive that far to run her errands. Fortunately, the Sarasota condo community offered everything she might need within golf cart distance: a grocery store, a dry cleaner, a post office. Jeanette would sometimes pass the time when she was staffing the pharmacy register searching online for similar communities near Ocean City, imagining a scenario where Marilee could take her own packages to the post office. But Jeanette doubted Marilee would trade the fabulous ocean view of her Eden Beach condo just to save Jeanette the drive from Downingtown.

"I can't imagine why not. She'd obviously rather be in Sarasota than Ocean City in January," said Jeanette.

After a few more awkward pleasantries, and a request from Ezra that Jeanette keep him informed of Marilee's plans, they ended the call.

Jeanette pulled up Facebook on her phone.

Marilee's author page was filled with comments from fans. Some had shared the link to the security camera video that the Ocean City police had posted on their page, along with a request that anyone with information that might help identify the attacker call a tip line. Others had shared links to a few major news outlets that were carrying the story. All expressed concern for Marilee's well-being. Most directed invective against the attacker. Jeanette was shocked to see that a small but vocal contingent castigated her own role in the incident.

Too bad that woman had to knock Marilee over

That's her daughter-in-law Jean

Obviously not a blood relative—can you imagine Marilee having a child that big???

Jeanette felt her cheeks flush—did they really think she wouldn't see their posts? She fought off a brief urge to post a photo of Jeremy to illustrate that Marilee had, in fact, had a child even bigger than Jeanette.

She waited until the pharmacy was free of customers, then called Jeremy into the back room.

"The police posted the security video from Oh Buoy Books," she said.

She pulled up Facebook on the computer and they pulled up chairs to watch the video.

When it was over, Jeremy said, "That's scary, Jen. I'm so sorry you had to deal with that by yourself, but you certainly did a good job of it."

"Marilee's fans seem to think I was as much to blame as the guy in the balaclava for anything that happened to her during the attack." She clicked over to the comments on the Facebook page.

Jeremy read a few, then shook his head. "You know how idiotic people are on social media."

"Sure, I know. But it doesn't make it any more pleasant to see what they have to say." She read from the feed. "*Keystone Cop to the rescue*."

"It's real life, not some choreographed movie fight scene. Plus, he didn't get away unscathed—it looks like he hit his head pretty hard. I wonder if the cops are checking hospitals for someone with a concussion." He pushed his chair back. "How did you find out about the news coverage?"

"Ezra called me."

Jeremy pinched the bridge of his nose. "Ezra." He dropped his hand and said, trying for a wry tone, "Maybe he's expanded his tactics from social media smear campaigns to siccing goons on Cozy Up Press authors who get out of line."

Jeanette raised an eyebrow. "He wants to keep her out of the thriller world, not make her the star of one." She glanced back at the Facebook feed on her phone. "Maybe we should call Detective Morganstein and see if he has any updates."

With Jeanette's phone on speaker, they called Morganstein. After hearing that he had no news for them, they suggested the concussion angle.

"We did ask around," said the detective, "and no one checked themselves into an ER or urgent care center with the kind of injury it looks like the attacker might have sustained. And we checked all the nooks and crannies near the bookstore, so we know he didn't pass out after he ran away. We'll cast the net a little wider since he could have driven away ... or been driven away by an accomplice."

"Have you gotten any information from people who have seen the video?" asked Jeremy.

Morganstein snorted. "Lots of information. No useful leads. Having the video is a mixed blessing. It's always possible that someone will see something that will help us out, or might even recognize the perpetrator, but it also means a lot of wasted time sifting through the cranks and following up on dead ends."

They ended the call.

"We should check in on Mom," said Jeremy.

Jeanette sighed. "Yeah, I suppose so." She placed the call and again put the phone on speaker.

After asking Marilee how her wrist was doing—still painful—and how she was feeling otherwise—as well as could be expected—Jeanette said, "Ezra called me. He wants to know if you're still planning to go down to Sarasota on your original schedule."

"Well, that had been my plan, but ..." She trailed off, then resumed, sounding both irritated and abashed. "This morning I was going to go down to the lobby to pick up my mail, and I had a bit of a panic attack. Didn't even get as far as the elevator."

"It's understandable that you'd be nervous after such a scary episode," said Jeremy. "I'm sure in a day or two you'll feel better."

"How comforting," said Marilee sourly.

"Marilee, would it be helpful for me to come down to Ocean City?" asked Jeanette. "Maybe you'd feel more comfortable going out if someone was with you."

"No, I don't need you down here. We'll see if Jeremy's optimistic prognosis is correct."

It seemed clear that Marilee wasn't going to regain any semblance of good spirits, so they wrapped up the call with a promise to check in with her the following day.

"It was nice of you to offer to go down there," said Jeremy.

Jeanette summoned a rueful smile. "I'm willing to do whatever it takes to make sure your mother leaves for Florida on schedule."

"Too bad we can't use the Sarasota place while Mom is holed up in Ocean City."

"We can't close the pharmacy that long ..." began Jeanette, then added hopefully, "... can we?"

He sighed. "No. At least not until we can hire a back-up pharmacist and some staff."

She nodded. "I figured."

He took her hand. "It won't be like this forever—the two of us trying to do everything ourselves."

"When's it going to change?"

"I don't know. Soon, I hope."

But Jeanette couldn't imagine investing in staff while they still had Marilee's loan hanging over their heads—a loan that Marilee was evidently anxious to call in.

15

Ann was sitting at the Curragh's breakfast bar, planning her flight to Princeton, when she heard a knock at the front door. She looked up to see Scott waving to her through the glass-paned door, and she beckoned him in.

"How did the drop-off go?" she asked as he wiped his feet on the mat.

"Ursula was exploring the big house when I left, much to Rose's delight."

Scott had asked Del and Rowan if they could watch Ursula while he was in Princeton. The dachshund had appeared at Ann's Adirondack cabin at a time Ann desperately needed some canine companionship and had accompanied her when she moved into Mike and Scott's West Chester townhouse. Since then, Ursula had become more Scott's dog than Ann's, and had stayed at the townhouse when Ann moved to the Curragh.

"Is the snow going to interfere with our travel plans?" Scott asked as he joined Ann at the breakfast bar.

"It shouldn't. It's only an inch or two, and if we get to

Princeton and conditions aren't as reported, we'll just come home and tell Darren we need to reschedule."

"Will he be okay with that? It sounded like the board was in a hurry."

"Hurry or not, I'm not landing on a snow-covered runway, even if it's just an inch. Not yet anyway." She gestured to the coffeepot. "Coffee?"

"I don't want to hold things up ..."

"I can make it to go."

"Ah, a flight with food service! I can't say no to that."

Ann filled two thermal mugs and pulled on her red parka, then they climbed into the Forester and headed for Avondale Airport.

"So what's the plan?" asked Scott.

"Darren made it sound like Alec Quine wouldn't be wild about visitors hanging around Tamaston any longer than necessary, so we won't go there until close to the time Jock died, near midnight. Since I want to land while it's still light, we'll have some time to kill in Princeton, but I figure that won't be a chore."

"Not as far as I'm concerned. And I'm your assistant for the engagement?"

"Yeah, although I don't think you'll need to do much assisting."

"I stand ready to assist as needed. But what's the scoop behind the need for an assistant?"

"I gather that Alec Quine would look favorably on Ann Kinnear Sensing having staff."

"If you ever need a bigger staff, I'm friends with the person who's in charge of PR for Bryn Mawr—next time, we could invite him, and he could pretend to be your publicist. And if you ever need to go somewhere by car, I know someone who's restoring an old Rolls—she could pretend to be your chauffeur."

Ann laughed. "Let's hold the staff escalation in reserve until we see a need to expand the entourage."

When they got to the airport, they headed for the office to pick up the keys to the rental plane Ann had reserved. The airport's young manager, Ellis Tapscott, was staffing the desk.

"Morning, Ann. Morning, Scott. Nice day for a flight to Princeton."

After sharing some updates on the latest improvements the airport's owner, Gwen Burridge, had underway, Ellis handed over the key to the flight school's Piper Warrior.

Thirty minutes later, the Warrior's wheels left the ground, the cold temperatures and dense air giving even the modestly powered plane impressive climb performance.

They turned northeast, and Ann shifted her gaze between the instruments and the snowy landscape. As they gained altitude, the features became an abstract of light and dark: the rectangles of parking lots and the lines of roads interspersed with the more irregular brushstrokes of creeks, rivers, and ponds. The high rises of Philadelphia were visible on their right, and soon the runways of the decommissioned Willow Grove air base appeared on their left. Soon the buildings of Trenton came into view, and they crossed the Delaware River and began their descent into Princeton. The features of the landscape became more clearly defined, the trees' bare branches a filigree against the snow-dusted ground.

The plane's wheels squeaked onto the runway, and Ann taxied to the transient ramp. She ran through the shut-down checklist, then they climbed out of the plane.

"How are we getting around?" asked Scott as he helped Ann with the tie-down ropes. "It looks from the map like we could walk into town, but I don't know where Jock Quine's house is."

Ann snugged down the last rope. "Darren Van Osten is picking us up. In fact," she said, pointing to a figure standing next to the entrance to the fixed base operator building, "I think that must be him."

They crossed the ramp to the FBO. When they reached Darren, Ann made introductions.

"You're the one with the classic Ford F-150, right?" said Scott. "Mike showed me a photo. Gorgeous truck."

"Thanks," said Darren, pleased. "Although I brought a bigger vehicle so we wouldn't all have to cram onto the bench seat."

Ann left them chatting about the pickup and went inside to arrange a fueling and an overnight stay for the Warrior. When she rejoined them, Scott picked up both their overnight bags.

"I'm the assistant, remember?" he whispered to her.

Darren led them to a gigantic Range Rover.

Scott shifted the bags to free a hand, opened the front passenger door, and stepped back. "The boss sits in front."

She suppressed a grin and climbed into the vehicle.

"This was Jock's car," said Darren as he got into the driver's seat and started up the engine. "He let me use it when I visited him."

"Did you visit him a lot?" asked Scott.

"Yes. When we were in the thick of editing, I would often stay at Tamaston. In fact, he reserved a room for me, and I kept some toiletries and a couple of changes of clothes there so I could run up here on the spur of the moment if he needed me."

"That was nice of him to set aside a room for you," said Scott.

Darren laughed. "Not much of an inconvenience—wait until you see the house." He pulled out of the parking lot and onto the two-lane highway. "I thought we could stop by the hotel, you could drop your things off, then you can hang out in town and grab dinner until it's time to go to Tamaston."

"Will you be able to join us in Princeton?" asked Scott.

"Well, if you want company for checking out the town, I can show you some of my favorite places."

Darren drove them to the Nassau Inn, where Ann discovered she had accidentally booked one room with two beds rather than two rooms with one bed each. The inn was hosting a conference, and there were no extra rooms available.

She turned to Scott. "Looks like we'll be having a slumber party," she apologized.

"Okay by me," said Scott.

As she finalized the arrangement with the desk clerk, she realized it had been months, if not years, since she had booked her own accommodations—yet another thing Mike usually took care of. She was definitely looking forward to when her brother got back from his ski vacation.

16

The day after learning of Marilee's unwillingness to leave the condo, Jeanette and Jeremy called her back to check on developments. Marilee reported that the situation was unchanged.

"Are you sure you don't want to come up and stay with us in Downingtown for a little bit?" asked Jeremy, his phone on speaker.

"No, Jeremy," said Marilee peevishly, "because that would involve leaving the condo, which I just told you I can't do."

"You're going to have to leave it eventually—I just thought if we were with you, it might be okay."

"I'm not suffering here in the condo. In fact, it might prove to be a very productive period—a time I can focus on my writing." After a moment, she added, "With no distractions."

"You're sure you don't want one of us," he shot Jeanette a contrite look, "probably Jeanette, to come stay with you?"

Jeanette threw up her hands in a *what the hell?* gesture.

"I'm quite sure," said Marilee. "I'm not an invalid. And in any case, I don't have the bay-side room set up as a guest room anymore."

"You're set for groceries?" he asked.

"Yes. I'm fine."

"And if you run out of anything, you could have it delivered," he said.

Jeanette said, "The only things we've been able to get delivered right to Marilee's door have been pizza and flowers, when we can tell the delivery person to take the steps to the first floor to bypass Kenny ... and when we can promise them an extra tip. Regular deliveries go to the security desk."

"Can't Kenny bring them up?"

"He has a bad back. Plus, he says he's not allowed to leave the desk."

Jeremy snorted. "He needs to stay there so he can beat back the hordes of intruders? How much security is that man providing, anyway?"

"Seems like it's more a matter of Kenny's family providing him with a job," replied Jeanette.

Marilee cleared her throat. "Let's not start asking Kenny to do things that are beyond his job description."

"How about that guy who was moving furniture for you?" asked Jeanette. "I know you said he doesn't have a car, but if he could walk over, he could carry packages from the security desk up to the condo."

"I don't want people coming to the condo."

"You wouldn't have to let him in—" began Jeremy.

"No," snapped Marilee. "I don't want anyone coming up here."

"Ezra's going to need to know what's going on," said Jeanette. "He's concerned about your Sarasota events."

"Jeanette, I don't know how to be clearer," said Marilee, her exasperation clear. "I can't leave the condo, much less get to Sarasota. And even if I could, after what happened at Oh Buoy Books, I don't know that I'm going to want to go to another author event anytime soon. Tell him to cancel the Florida events."

Jeanette grimaced. "Marilee, I don't think Ezra's going to want to hear it from me. You need to call him."

"Fine. I'll deal with Ezra." After a pause, Marilee added, "If you two repaid the money I loaned you, I wouldn't have to worry about catering to Ezra's completely unrealistic demands."

"Mom, let's not get into that right now, okay?" said Jeremy. "In any case, let's not argue about it over the phone. If necessary, I'll drive down there one day after the pharmacy is closed so we can discuss it in person."

"If you'd rather put off that conversation, I'm not going to force you into it now. I'm going to go work on the manuscript for Ezra, since whatever he wants is evidently what's most important."

She ended the call.

"Jesus," Jeremy groaned, running his fingers through his hair. "What a mess."

"How long do you think she's going to refuse to leave the condo?"

"I have no idea."

"And for however long that is, Marilee's going to expect me to continue to make a six-hour round-trip drive to ferry supplies and packages up to the condo?" She glared at Jeremy. "Assuming she's willing to make an exception to her no-visitors rule for her errand girl."

Jeremy reached over and squeezed her hand. "We'll think of something."

They sat in silence for a few moments, then Jeremy said, "Do you remember Maury, my housemate in my first year of med school?"

"Sort of. Why?"

"He went into psychiatry. I'll call him and see if he has any suggestions."

Jeremy put in a call to Maury and, when it went to voicemail, left a message. Maury called back a few hours later, and Jeremy went to the back room to speak with him while Jeanette covered the register. She couldn't make out the words and could only speculate about what the rising and falling inflections of Jeremy's voice might mean.

When he emerged, he at least looked more optimistic than he had before the call. When Jeanette had rung up the couple of customers waiting to check out, she and Jeremy returned to the back room.

"Maury had a couple of suggestions," he said. "Let's call Mom back and see what she thinks."

Jeremy put the call through and set his phone to speaker.

"Yes?" answered Marilee, her tone ominous.

"Mom, do you remember Maury, from med school? He became a psychiatrist, and I gave him a call. He suggested—"

"I'm not interested in what he suggested."

"He felt that better understanding what triggered your discomfort with leaving the condo—"

"I know what triggered it—I got attacked."

"If that really is the trigger, and that certainly makes sense to me, then maybe getting away from Ocean City is the thing to do."

"Did Maury suggest that?"

Jeremy rolled his eyes. "No, Mom. You just told me you weren't interested in what he suggested. But I thought that if we could figure out a way to get you down to the Sarasota condo—"

"I'm not going to Florida."

"Marilee," said Jeanette, "you know Ezra's going to find

some way to punish you if you don't do the Florida author events."

"Ah yes, Ezra. If only I had the money to buy out my contract."

Jeanette took a deep breath, trying to calm her rapidly frazzling nerves. "I still don't think Ezra was serious about that buy-out offer—"

"In fact," interrupted Marilee, "I'm thinking of selling the Florida condo."

Jeremy and Jeanette exchanged shocked looks.

"Jeremy," said Jeanette, "it looks like there's a customer at the pharmacy counter. Mrs. Smith. You know she'll only talk with you."

Jeremy glanced at the security camera, which showed an empty store.

Jeanette glared at him. "Jeremy ..."

He gave her a thumbs up. "Mom, I need to take care of this. We'll call you right back."

Before Marilee could respond, he ended the call.

"Jeremy," said Jeanette, "this is serious. I mean, I suppose it was serious before, but now she's talking about selling the Florida place, and you know how much she loves it. If she plans to live out her life holed up at Eden Beach, it's just not going to be possible for me to drive down to Ocean City whenever she needs anything. Not only is it a huge pain in the ass, but you can't keep trying to cover the pharmacy all by yourself."

"Do you think ..." Jeremy trailed off.

"Do I think what?"

"Do you think we might need to ask her if she wants to stay with us?"

"We already asked her that."

"I mean permanently."

"Oh my God," groaned Jeanette.

"Maybe it would be just for a little while," Jeremy added hastily. "She's bound to venture out into the world again eventually, right?"

"If she moved in with us, where would she stay?" But Jeanette knew there was only one room they could convert to a guest room for Marilee: the room Jeanette currently used as an office and study.

Jeremy must have known this as well, but he responded, "We'd have to talk about that."

She sighed. "Well, I guess it would be better than making that drive."

"Maybe she could help out at the pharmacy."

Jeanette snorted her derision.

Casting a sympathetic look at Jeanette, Jeremy placed the call and put the phone on speaker.

Marilee answered. "Get Mrs. Smith all straightened out?" she asked, her skepticism about Jeanette's excuse clear.

"Yeah," said Jeremy. "All taken care of. So, Mom, if you're saying you can't leave home, and you don't want to go to Sarasota—in fact, might give up the Florida place—I think there's no alternative. You need to come stay with us in Downingtown, at least for a little while. We could give you a sedative for the drive. A little CBD oil would take the edge off—"

"I am not taking one of your quack medicines," Marilee snapped. "The only way you could get me to make that drive is if you knocked me out completely."

"Mom, Jeanette can't keep driving down to Ocean City every time you need something—"

"I wouldn't be too hasty making threats about what you two can and can't do for me. I might be less patient about having that loan paid back."

Jeremy's face reddened. "We'll pay you back everything we

owe you as soon as we finish the repairs on the old place and sell it."

"Or you could sell the new place."

Jeremy's face paled, and Jeanette felt the nails of her clenched fingers dig into her palm.

"Mother, if you're predicating your plan for your author career—and your suggestion that we sell our pharmacy—based on an assumption that Ezra is going to honor a comment that Jeanette and I both believe he meant as a joke, I think you're making a huge mistake. At least get Ezra's offer in writing."

"Fine," snapped Marilee. "Jeanette can set up a meeting."

Jeanette, her face flaming, opened her mouth, but Jeremy quickly said, "We'll get something set up."

Marilee ended the call.

Jeremy slumped back in his chair. "Jesus, I thought the worst that would happen would be that we'd have to keep making trips to Ocean City. Then I thought the worst that could happen would be that she'd have to move in with us. Now it looks like the worst that could happen is that we lose the pharmacy!"

Jeanette heard the ding signaling that a customer had entered the store. She pushed herself to her feet. "At least then we could stop sucking up to her," she snapped. She jerked open the door, stepped out of the back room, and slammed the door behind her.

17

Since Ann, Scott, and Darren needed to occupy themselves until the late-night engagement—and since Darren hadn't suggested hanging out at Tamaston as an option—they wandered the streets in the shopping area, Ann wrapping her scarf more tightly around her neck as the temperature dropped after sunset. When the stores began to close, they switched to exploring the paths through the campus.

Eventually Ann could no longer ignore the rumbling of her stomach. "I'm ready for dinner. Anybody else?"

"Sounds good to me," said Scott.

Ann turned to Darren. "Any recommendations?"

He looked uncomfortable. "There's a nice farm-to-table restaurant …"

"But …?"

"Dinner out really isn't in my budget," he said, embarrassed. "Or in the GothamCon budget, at least for me."

"I'll cover it," said Ann. She was really going to catch hell from Mike for her financial management, or lack thereof, of this engagement.

"That's very generous of you," said Darren sheepishly. "Thank you."

They walked back to town and to Darren's recommended restaurant. Once the server had brought them their cocktails —Ann assured Darren that cocktails had never interfered with her sensing ability—she asked, "So will Alec be at Tamaston tonight?"

"No, he and I finished up our work for the day before I picked you up at the airport. He's back at his own house now."

"He's not staying in Tamaston while you're working with him on the book?"

"No. He prefers his own house." He poked his cocktail's ice cubes with the stirrer. "I had hoped that Alec might decide to move into Tamaston—it's the house on which Jock based the home of Robert Wolfram in his series—but it's not really Alec's style. He has a very authentically furnished mid-century-modern home just a few miles away. He's going to be selling Tamaston—in fact, he's already sold off some of the contents." He took a sip of his drink. "I'll be sorry to see it go. It's a magical place. Or at least it was when Jock was still alive."

When their entrées arrived, Scott complimented Darren on his taste in restaurants. The conversation wandered pleasantly from food to farms to Darren's childhood in rural Ohio to farm machinery to Darren's classic pickup. However, as the meal wound down, Darren's mood shaded from cheerful toward pensive.

As they were finishing their coffees, he said, "The GothamCon board is very excited to find out what the outcome of this trial run is. But I'm afraid that Alec may be a bit of a skeptic. He is a lawyer, after all—he wants everything nice and logical." He dropped his eyes to his cup. "I didn't want to spend too much time trying to convince him about the authenticity of your ability if Jock isn't around to be contacted.

In fact," he glanced up at Ann, then back down, "I didn't tell him exactly what your area of expertise is."

Ann raised her eyebrows. "Alec doesn't know I'm here to contact his dead father?"

"Well ... no."

Scott sat forward. "You put Ann in a very uncomfortable position by failing to tell Alec Quine the real reason for our visit to his father's home."

"I know," said Darren, looking up at Scott, then at Ann. "I just didn't want to propose the idea to Alec unless it looked like it would pan out."

"Does he even know we're going to the house?" asked Ann.

"Oh, yes—I told him that. But he thinks you're scouting the house for a video shoot. I didn't tell him that, about you being a video crew," he added hastily. "He jumped to that conclusion on his own."

Scott raised an eyebrow. "But you didn't correct him."

"No, I didn't." After a beat, he asked Ann, "Does this mean you won't go through with the trial run?"

She pushed her coffee away. "Scott's right. This puts us in an uncomfortable situation. And by 'us,' Darren, I mean you and me. Besides, how long are we supposed to keep up the story that I'm a video producer? Alec is the honorary chair of GothamCon, right? He's going to see me at the conference and think it's pretty weird that the person who is ostensibly producing his father's memorial video also happens to be giving a talk on supernatural fiction."

Darren looked miserable. "I know, I know. I didn't think of that when I realized he thought you were a video crew. It seemed like such a great cover story." After a moment, he said hopefully, "I wouldn't be surprised if he didn't attend any of the talks." Then, more despondently, "Despite the fact that he's an author, he's really not all that interested in writing craft topics."

She glared at him for a moment, then sighed. "I don't much feel like turning around and going home. In fact, after a cocktail and wine, I couldn't fly home tonight even if I wanted to." She didn't add that she also didn't want to bail out of the first engagement she had tried to manage on her own before it even began. She turned to Scott. "How do you feel about being an assistant on a video shoot?"

She could tell he was having trouble maintaining his severe expression.

"As the official assistant of Ann Kinnear Sensing, I stand ready to do whatever is required."

18

Ann, Scott, and Darren nursed their coffees until they were the last diners in the restaurant. Then, shortly before eleven o'clock, they returned to the Range Rover and headed for Tamaston.

They left the downtown area and were soon passing palatial homes behind finely wrought metal fences or stone walls. Darren turned into one of the drives, its passage through a waist-high brick wall protected by a gate. He entered a code into a keypad next to the drive, and the gate swung open. As they entered the grounds, the home came into view: a sprawling mansion of turrets, dormers, and gables, the first floor sheathed in ivy-covered brick, the second floor half-timbered with stucco infill. Darren's pickup was parked in front.

"What a beautiful home!" exclaimed Scott, delighted.

Darren nodded. "Jock bought Tamaston when Alec set up a law practice in Princeton—moved here from out West to be near him."

They climbed out of the Range Rover, and Darren led them to the entrance and into an octagonal foyer lit by a heavy iron chandelier. A deer head gazed down at them with glassy eyes.

Darren collected their coats and hung them in a closet whose door was disguised as one of the room's wooden panels. "I thought we'd start in the turret room. It's where Jock died."

They wended their way through a maze of rooms. Some were filled with heavy furniture in which wood and leather predominated. The heft of the furnishings reminded Ann of the Niall Lynch-era chairs and tables at the big house at Mahalo Winery. However, whereas Ann guessed those had been chosen based mainly on their sturdiness and longevity, these had been meticulously selected by someone intent on creating a very specific ambiance. Jock's hulking wooden armoires and cupboards looked like they might hold intriguing treasures and memorabilia, and the cracked leather chairs and couches would have been comfortable seats in which to enjoy those treasures, especially with fires crackling in the capacious fireplaces. She expected to run into Ernest Hemingway around every corner.

The only deterrents to an enjoyable evening exploring Jock's home were the stuffed trophy animals in almost every room. In one, a gigantic black bear reared on its hind legs, long-clawed paws raised, mouth agape. In another, a wolf paused, mid-stride, to fix the observer with a canine glare.

"I take it Jock Quine was a hunter," Ann said, not bothering to hide her disapproval.

"Yes," said Darren, apologetic. "Although he scaled back on his hunting activities—both in real life and in his books—when public sentiment turned against that pastime."

The further they ventured into the house, the more sparsely furnished the rooms became. Some rooms contained only cardboard boxes stacked against walls. Others were completely empty.

Eventually, Darren gestured Ann and Scott into a room off one of the hallways. Like the foyer, it was octagonal, although larger and rising through two floors. Bookshelves holding ranks of leather-bound books lined the walls, with one empty row of shelves at about eye level. In the middle of the room, two chairs were pulled up to an octagonal table. Darren flipped a switch and a soft light suffused the ceiling twenty feet above. It was painted sky blue, with puffy white clouds decorating the periphery.

"What a stunning space," said Scott.

"Yes," said Darren. "This was Jock's writing room. It's where we would meet to review my editorial input or to brainstorm plots for new books."

"And this is where he died?" asked Ann.

"Yes. He was working in here late, as he often did, and a burglar surprised him. He had a gun in a drawer in the table, but it wasn't loaded, although there were bullets in the drawer."

"And they haven't caught the guy who did it?"

"No."

"How do they know it was a burglar?" asked Scott.

Darren gestured toward the line of empty shelves. "Jock had a collection of ivory figurines worth several hundred thousand dollars. Those were the only things that were taken."

Ann raised her eyebrows. "Jock was killed by an ivory tchotchke collector?"

"Or someone working for an organized crime syndicate. In some places, ivory is a common way to bribe officials. And some people consider it to be a good investment. They call it 'white gold.'"

"Did Jock shoot the elephants himself?" asked Ann, with some distaste.

Darren forced a smile. "I'm relieved to say he did not. As attitudes toward owning ivory changed, he started keeping his collection something of a secret, just as he did with the trophy animals."

"So the burglar had inside information about the collection?" asked Scott.

Darren shrugged. "Well, it wasn't *that* much of a secret. Years ago, when he first started collecting, he wasn't shy about telling people about his latest acquisition. It's just that he wasn't exactly issuing press releases anymore."

"Do you know what the police's theories are?" asked Ann.

"They were able to eliminate a lot of Jock's professional colleagues because Harrison & John was hosting an event in New York. I was there. Alec was there. A lot of H & J's other thriller writers—the second-tier authors—were there."

"So not someone motivated by professional jealousy?" asked Scott.

Darren shook his head. "At least not one of his fellow H & J authors."

Ann moved around the room, more out of curiosity than on a search for Jock's ghost. If he had been present, there was nowhere in the room he could hide. She stopped at a photo on one of the shelves.

It showed two men standing next to each other against a backdrop of yellow grassland and cloudless blue sky. The taller of the two had a dark tan set off by a full white beard, a neatly trimmed white mustache, and a grin revealing a mouthful of teeth that were, in fact, the color of old ivory. Aviator sunglasses hid his eyes. Apparently, Jock Quine's fascination with Hemingway extended beyond his home's décor to his own appearance.

His arm was draped over the shoulders of the shorter man, whose sunburned face was clean-shaven and whose eyes, behind tortoiseshell glasses, were squinted against the sun. Both men wore wide-brimmed hats, safari vests, khaki pants, and heavy boots, but whereas the taller one's clothes looked well worn, the shorter one's looked fresh off a rack at Orvis.

Ann nodded toward the photo. "Jock and Alec?"

Darren stepped away from the door and crossed the room to where Ann stood. "Yes, Jock took Alec on a safari several years ago."

They heard footsteps approaching from the hallway.

Darren looked toward the door with alarm. "I didn't expect Alec to be here." He dropped his voice. "Remember, you're a video crew scouting the location."

The shorter man from the photo stepped into the room. His complexion was winter-pale, and he was wearing a white button-down shirt, crewneck sweater, and carefully pressed jeans, but two spots of red highlighted his cheeks, and he looked just as irritated now as he had in the safari photo.

"Alec," said Darren, "what an unexpected pleasure to run into you here."

"It can't be that unexpected," snapped Alec. "You're the one who's always banging on about how I need to spend time at Tamaston to get the gestalt of Dad's books. But I certainly didn't expect you to be taking these people to the turret room." He turned to Scott. "Don't you think it's a little morbid to think about videoing in the room where my father died?"

Ann stepped forward. "I agree completely. We're—" She suddenly realized that she didn't know if Darren had given Alec the names of the ostensible video scouting party. She looked toward Darren, hoping he would bail her out. Unfortunately, he must not have realized what the issue was.

"Mahalo Video Productions," said Scott. "Gorgeous home, Mr. Quine. And we couldn't agree with you more—we, and Darren, I might add, believe it would be highly inappropriate to video in the location of your father's death. We were just walking by, and I couldn't help but step in to admire the architecture of the room."

Darren, who must have caught on to the name issue, came to the rescue. "Alec, this is Ann and Scott—"

Alec looked at him expectantly, evidently waiting for last names.

"—Mahalo," Darren appended.

Alec turned back to Scott. "Unusual name."

Scott laughed. "You're not the first to think that." He stepped forward and shook Alec's hand. "I handle the administrative end of things at Mahalo Productions, but my sister Ann is the creative force behind the business."

Slightly mollified, Alec redirected his attention to Ann. "So what exactly do you have in mind for this production?"

"We plan to produce a respectful homage to your father," she said.

"And how do you plan to go about that?"

"We want to use the house as a representation of the man," she improvised, "his outsized persona, his zest for life."

Ann was pretty proud of that line, but it elicited a scowl from Alec.

"Yeah, 'zest' would be one way to describe it," he said.

Scott chimed in. "The success of the video will hinge on us creating a storyline tracing the evolution of the Robert Wolfram series from Jock's first book to when the torch passed to you, Alec, with some foreshadowing of the creative stamp you will no doubt put on the story and characters."

Alec's scowl relaxed. "Yes, that's a good angle."

"It would be helpful to know what parts of the house were especially meaningful to your father," said Ann, hoping that Alec's response might help them focus their search for Jock's spirit more effectively.

The scowl returned. "Obviously, this room was *meaningful* to him, considering he died here."

"If you didn't object to a brief shot of your father's writing table," Scott put in hurriedly, "we could illuminate it with the light of a single candle, a representation of your father's spirit, then fade to you seated at your writing desk, which we would illuminate with a spot, backed with C-47-secured drapes."

"The single candle is good," said Alec, turning his attention from Ann back to Scott. "A representation of his spirit. I like it."

At that moment, to Ann's combined satisfaction and annoyance, Jock Quine appeared in the doorway.

19

Jock stood in the doorway, hands stuffed into the pockets of his jeans, his expression pensive. He was an even more imposing presence than she would have guessed from the safari photo. Although he couldn't have been much over six feet, and was broad-shouldered but not muscle-bound, he seemed to fill the doorway. Ann could imagine that in life, he would have been a force to be reckoned with.

Jock's attention was initially focused on Alec and Scott's conversation, but then his eyes drifted to Ann and his eyebrows rose, surprised that one of the visitors could meet his gaze.

"You can see me?" he asked.

She nodded.

He pulled his hands out of his pockets. "And hear me as well."

She nodded again.

Jock laughed. "I have to say I never expected to be able to talk with anyone again." His tone became more serious. "I have information about the night of the break-in. You could pass it along to the cops."

Ann considered her options. It would be hard for Darren to explain why his video producer was speaking to thin air, and it seemed clear that even before Alec had arrived at Tamaston to find them in the turret room, Darren's relationship with him was strained.

"Tomorrow might be better for a follow-up visit," Ann said. "What with us being the video scouting crew and all."

Scott's expression was carefully deadpan, but Alec's scowl returned once again.

"You want to come back tomorrow with more people?" Alec asked.

"No—actually, fewer people would be better. Probably just me. And Darren, of course."

Scott, who must have inferred from Ann's odd responses that there was an unseen presence in the room, jumped in. "Yes—I need to head back to L.A. We need to shoot some B-roll for another project. But Ann could come back tomorrow. She's the one who will best be able to craft the story you'll want to share with the Robert Wolfram fans."

"I'm going to be out of town tomorrow night," said Alec.

"Really?" asked Darren. "I thought we were going to be working on the manuscript."

"I'd rather be working on the damn manuscript," grumbled Alec, "but one of Dad's big game hunting buddies is going to be in New York, and I'm having dinner with him tomorrow—hoping I can talk him into buying some of those taxidermied monstrosities. I planned to stay overnight."

"That's perfect," said Scott. "Ann can do the final walk-through with Darren and not be a bother to you."

"I thought you needed me for some shots," said Alec. "You know, sitting at my desk, working on a Wolfram book ..."

"We'd pick up those shots at a different time," said Scott. "And we'd love to do that at your house, if you'd be willing."

"Sure, that would be fine," said Alec, mollified.

"Tomorrow ..." said Ann, taking out her phone and tapping as if checking her calendar. "I wonder how tomorrow would work ..."

Jock's laugh this time was rueful. "You don't want Alec to know I'm here, right? I'm not surprised. I'm a little more open to crazy ideas than he is, and even I would find this hard to believe. Let's talk tomorrow—same time, same place."

"... maybe earlier?" Ann asked.

"This time of night is better."

She glanced up from the phone at Alec and Darren. "Same time?"

"This late?" asked Alec.

"This time of night is better." She tried to think of other things that a video producer might say. After all, she had dated a professional filmmaker—Corey Duff—although it appeared that Scott had been paying more attention to Corey's conversations about his profession than she had. "The darkness of the night would mirror the darkness of the books ..."

She was relieved when Alec's sigh of resignation saved her from having to continue. "Okay, fine." He turned to Darren. "You'll be here anyway since you're staying in one of the guest rooms—you can show her around." He glanced at his watch. "In fact, as long as we're both awake—and assuming your scouting tour is complete—why don't we go over that chase scene. The sooner we get through this round of edits, the sooner I can get back to my own house."

"I need to get Ann and Scott back to the inn."

"They're coming back tomorrow, and I suspect you'll be heads down on the manuscript all day. Just let them use your truck," Alec turned to Scott. "You know how to drive a stick?"

"I don't," said Scott, "but Ann does."

Darren's expression suggested that he would have been happier if neither Ann nor Scott had been qualified to drive his truck.

Alec nodded and said to Darren, "You can see them out. I've been working in the kitchen. Meet up with me there." He turned and marched out of the turret room.

Ann gave Jock a surreptitious wave as she and Scott followed Alec out, and Jock bobbed his head in reply. Just before a turn in the corridor took the door to the turret room out of sight, she looked back. Jock was standing in the doorway, watching them but not following.

They reached the door to the foyer, and, with a wave of his hand over his shoulder, Alec continued on to the wing where the kitchen must be.

"Sorry about that," said Darren, his voice low. He pulled a ring of keys from his pocket.

"If Alec Quine is going to be the public face of the Robert Wolfram series as well as its new author," said Scott tartly, "you might suggest to the publisher's PR department that they give him some coaching on his interpersonal skills."

"You wouldn't be the first to suggest that," said Darren as he worked a key off the ring. "Jock was such a people person. With Alec, it's going to be ... a challenge."

Ann glanced again in the direction in which Alec had disappeared, then whispered to Darren. "I saw Jock."

Darren looked up, his eyes wide. "Really?"

"He was in the turret room. He has information he wants to give me about the night he died—that's all he said to me—but I didn't want to have that conversation with Alec around and blow the video crew story."

"I appreciate that." Lowering his voice further, Darren asked, "Do you think we should go back there now?"

"Darren," Alec called from several rooms away. "I don't want to be up until dawn."

"Jock seemed to think it would be okay to wait until tomorrow," said Ann. "After all, it's been almost a year since he died. I can't imagine one more day will make a difference. And I'd rather have the conversation with Jock when we don't have to worry about Alec popping by. When I talk to Jock, I'll get some information from him we can use to convince Alec that I really did contact his dad."

Darren looked relieved. "That sounds like a good plan." He handed the key to Ann. "There you go."

"I feel bad taking the Ford," said Ann. "Would GothamCon spring for a rental for us while we're here?"

Darren smiled wanly. "I think I've gotten as much money from them as I'm going to."

"We'll take good care of your truck," said Scott. "You're not the only one who would kill us if something happened to it. Mike was quite smitten."

"Darren?" came Alec's voice from the back of the house, his increasing irritation clear.

"We won't hold you up," said Ann. "I'll see you tomorrow back here, same time."

Ann and Scott stepped outside, and Darren closed the door behind them. They crossed the drive toward the pickup.

"We could get a rental tomorrow and return Darren's truck," said Scott. "I don't mind pitching in some money for our own set of wheels."

"I'm already going to have a hard time explaining why this engagement is costing us so much—let's not add yet another expense I'll need to explain to Mike when he gets home." She cocked an eyebrow at him. "By the way, you drive Audrey the Audi all the time, and that's a stick. Why did you tell Quine you didn't drive a stick?"

"Because he was being such a misogynistic jerk. I wonder if he would have kept directing all his comments to me if I had made a pass at him."

She laughed. "And what the hell is a C-47? You said the video crew would secure the drapes with C-47s."

"Remember when Corey needed to hang up some socks when the dryer at the townhouse broke and he asked if we had any C-47s? He told me it's what video professionals call clothespins."

Ann laughed again and shook her head. "I wish I had been paying as much attention when Corey talked shop as you obviously did."

They reached the truck and Scott ran his finger along one of the side mirrors. "It is a beauty."

"You can drive now if I can drive tomorrow," she said, dangling the key in front of her.

"Deal," he said, taking the key with a grin.

20

Jeanette was in the back room of the pharmacy, continuing her work on the customer record updates, when her phone rang: Marilee.

"Damn," Jeanette muttered. She jumped up and hurried to the door to the pharmacy. Jeremy was sweeping the floor in the otherwise empty store. "It's your mom," she said, beckoning him into the back room. "I forgot to set up the meeting with Ezra about the contract buy-out."

"That's okay," he said, leaning the broom against the counter and following her into the back room. "We can do it today."

Jeanette answered the call and put it on speaker. "Hi, Marilee. I have Jeremy on as well."

"I just got a call from Page Turner Books in Harrisburg," Marilee said, without preamble. "They sent several boxes of Berry mysteries to Eden Beach for me to sign."

"And of course they're at the security desk," said Jeanette, her voice tight.

"I didn't even realize they were sending them," retorted Marilee.

"We'll come down in the next few days," said Jeremy, "and we can bring the books up to the condo."

"It needs to be today," said Marilee. "They want to pick them up at Eden Beach tomorrow morning. They're going to have a display right inside the entrance, and they want to strike while the interest generated by the bookstore attack is high."

Jeanette thought longingly of her original plan for the day: completing the record updates, followed by inventorying the supplements. She had to admit that it was only appealing compared to another six hours on the road to and from Ocean City, and the time she'd have to spend with Marilee in between. But she wasn't about to give Marilee an excuse to press her request for the loan repayment.

"It's fine," she said, as much to Jeremy as to Marilee. Then she added gamely, "It's an indication of how much your readers love your cozies that there's such a sense of urgency about it."

"It's not the *cozies* that the readers love—it's the excitement of what happened at Oh Buoy Books. It shows how much people love *thrills*," said Marilee, "which is what I want to give them in my writing."

"Too bad you can't go to the store and sign in person," said Jeremy. "I know that's a place you and Ezra have been trying to get into for an event."

"Yes, it is too bad," said Marilee testily. "I'll expect you soon, Jeanette." She ended the call.

Jeanette sighed. "At least I won't have to pick up a damn berry snack."

Jeremy folded her in a hug. "You know how much I appreciate you doing all this, don't you?"

"I do," she said, her response muffled in his shoulder. She extracted herself from the hug and picked up her purse. "I'll get back as soon as I can. I might still be able to do the inventory."

He pulled her coat off the back of the desk chair and held it up for her. "I can take care of that. And I'll make veggie soup for dinner when you get back."

She shrugged into the coat. "That sounds good." She gave him a kiss, then headed outside for the drive to Ocean City.

~

After the inevitable delay around Wilmington, she pulled into the ground floor garage at Eden Beach and trudged across the lobby to where Kenny sat at the security desk.

"Hey, Miss Forsythe," he rasped, his eyes more bloodshot than usual, "that's quite a shiner you got there."

"Kenny, my last name is Frobisher, which is what Marilee's last name was before her publisher had her change it to Forsythe. I understand there's a box of books for me to pick up."

"Not just one." Kenny gestured Jeanette to come around to the back of the security desk.

Four boxes were piled against the wall.

Jeanette groaned. "It's going to take Marilee forever to sign all those." She sighed. "I'm going to need a cart."

"Carts are right outside the sliding doors."

She glared at him. "Yeah. I know."

Jeanette retrieved one of the hip-height carts. She loaded the boxes in, ignoring Kenny's helpful suggestions, then began wheeling the cart across the lobby to the elevator.

"Wait a minute!" Kenny called after her. "Want to take Mrs. Forsythe's mail up to her?"

Leaving the cart where it was, she trudged back to the desk.

"This is what's come in since she was last down here," he said, handing her a rubber-banded stack of mail and flyers, as well as a padded envelope with a USPS label.

She took the mail without a word and recrossed the lobby to the cart.

"Don't forget to bring the cart back," called Kenny.

Not bothering to respond, she got in the elevator, dropped Marilee's mail on top of the boxes, and pushed *14*. "It's thirteen, you superstitious idiots," she muttered. When the doors opened, she pushed the cart down the open walkway to Marilee's condo and knocked, perhaps a little harder that necessary.

"Good heavens, keep your pants on," Marilee called from inside.

Jeanette heard the rattle of locks being unfastened and the security chain drawn back, then the door opened to reveal Marilee dressed in a dark gray Angora sweater, black slacks, and maroon suede boots.

Without stepping out of the condo, Marilee stood on tiptoe to look into the cart. "How many books did they send?"

"A lot," growled Jeanette.

"You can't bring the cart into the condo. It dings up the walls."

"I'm aware of that. If you can hold the storm door, I'll carry the boxes in."

"I can't go outside—remember?"

"Then we'll have to prop it open until I get all the boxes in."

Marilee gave Jeanette a seashell-shaped doorstop to wedge under the door, and Jeanette transferred the boxes from the cart to the breakfast bar. By the time she had unloaded all the boxes from the cart and begun the second half of the process—moving them from the kitchen to Marilee's study—most of the warm air of the condo had been replaced by the bone-chilling January cold.

"I'm going to have to wear a coat until the condo warms up again," said Marilee reprovingly.

"You know what would have made it go faster?" snapped Jeanette. "If you had helped."

Marilee raised an eyebrow but didn't respond.

As Jeanette trudged toward the study with the last box, Marilee said, "There won't be room for all the books on the desk. You can unpack the overflow onto the floor."

Jeanette set the box on the desk with a bang. "Just open the boxes as you get to them." She put the stack of mail on the desk, returned to the living room, and dropped heavily onto the couch.

Marilee stepped into the study. "I'll need something to open the boxes with," she called.

"Use a knife," Jeanette called back.

Marilee stomped out to the kitchen, got a knife from a drawer, stomped back to the office, and slammed the door. Jeanette heard the sounds of boxes being moved and some exaggerated grunts of effort from Marilee.

Suppressing a satisfied smile, Jeanette pushed herself off the couch and went to the kitchen to fix herself a cup of tea. While she waited for the water to boil, she opened her e-reader to *Foye's Principles of Medicinal Chemistry*. She struggled a bit with chemistry, and if she ever hoped to return to school to become a pharmacist, she wanted to grab any opportunities to brush up.

She had just taken the kettle off the burner when she heard an uneven and barely audible *thump THUMP thump THUMP*, apparently moving from the front door, down the hallway and toward the living room.

"Hello?" she called.

The noise stopped, then retreated more rapidly back toward the front door.

She stepped out of the kitchen and looked down the hallway. It was empty.

Had the sound been coming from the neighboring condo, despite Marilee's boasts about the thorough soundproofing the building's concrete construction provided?

Was there someone right next door who might be willing to ferry packages and supplies up to Marilee?

She pressed her ear against the wall separating Marilee's condo from the neighbor's but couldn't hear anything.

She went down the hallway to the front door and stepped outside. The walkway was deserted. She stepped the few feet to the door to the neighboring condo and knocked lightly, then, after a shivering dozen seconds, a bit harder. No answer.

Disappointed, and perplexed, she returned to Marilee's condo. She went to the door to the study and knocked lightly.

"What is it?" answered Marilee.

"Can I come in?"

"Yes."

Jeanette stepped into the room and saw that Marilee was making brisk progress through the piles. Maybe she'd be able to get back to Downingtown at a reasonable hour after all.

"Did you hear something?" asked Jeanette. "A sort of uneven thumping noise?"

"No."

"Have you ever heard anything like that? Like someone walking down the hallway?"

"No."

"Maybe coming from the condo next door?"

"You know how well sound-insulated these units are. Plus, the people in the condo next door are never here during off-season." She slapped a book shut and put it on the right-hand pile. "No one is at Eden Beach during off-season. Except me." She massaged her wrist. "This is going to aggravate my injury."

Without responding, Jeanette backed out of the room and closed the door. She finished making her cup of tea, then returned to the couch and *Foye's*.

It took a couple of hours for Marilee to finish the books—not only the signing itself but also several breaks to rest her wrist, during which she made coffee for herself. Jeanette was sourly amused that even Marilee didn't use the Breville but broke out a Keurig. And that she didn't offer to make Jeanette a cup.

Regardless, Jeanette didn't find the time entirely unpleasant. She rarely had uninterrupted hours to read and, even more rarely, an opportunity to read with as gorgeous a view as she had from the condo. By the time Marilee was done, Jeanette was feeling more charitable.

Jeanette packed the books back into the boxes and loaded the boxes into the cart. She was relieved that Marilee's inability to leave the condo precluded a round of errands or a meal at Marco's, and she didn't extend an offer to run the errands solo. After a few insincere departing pleasantries, she maneuvered the cart down the walkway, into the elevator, then across the lobby to the security desk, where her luck held: Kenny was snoring away in his chair and didn't wake even when Jeanette unloaded the now-signed books back to their original location for pickup.

She climbed into the CR-V and tapped her home address into the GPS. It gave an estimated time of a little less than three hours—she would make it home in time for a leisurely dinner of veggie soup. She was about to call Jeremy with the update when her phone rang with an incoming call. Ezra. She hit *Accept*.

"Hi, Ezra."

"Jeanette, there's a bookstore that's looking for a hundred signed copies of the Berry mysteries, but they need them right away."

"We already got those done—they're at the security desk, ready to be picked up."

"That's not possible—I haven't sent them yet."

Jeanette felt a pinprick of dread pressing against her fragile balloon of good cheer. "This is for Page Turner Books?"

"No, it's for a New York store. What's this about Page Turner? I didn't know anything about that."

"Maybe I got the location wrong—"

"I've told you—all requests for signed books need to come through Cozy Up Press."

"I just assumed—"

"And where did Page Turner get their inventory? I don't remember an order from them."

"Maybe it was inventory they already had ..."

"Let's hope so. In any case, I'm sending a driver down to Ocean City with the books for the New York store tonight for her to sign tomorrow."

Jeanette's good mood burst, and she slumped back in the seat.

"Jeanette? You still there?" asked Ezra.

"I'm still here."

"The books will be ready by the end of the day tomorrow?"

"Sure."

"Great. Really appreciate it. Listen, I've got to go."

He ended the call.

Tears pricked Jeanette's eyes, and she gripped the steering wheel, white-knuckled.

She was so damned tired of having to accommodate every whim of Marilee's and Ezra's—Marilee's so she wouldn't call in the loan, Ezra so he wouldn't take some retaliatory measure that would increase Marilee's motivation to call in the loan.

The tears that she had held back through this whole sordid mess finally fell, and she fumbled a tissue out of her pocket and noisily blew her nose.

What she really wanted to do was to tell them both to go to hell.

21

By the time Jeanette arrived back in Downingtown, the pharmacy was closed. Jeremy, stranded there without a vehicle, stood in the supplement aisle, tapping inventory numbers into his laptop one-handed.

He must have noticed her red-rimmed eyes, because he put aside the laptop and folded Jeanette in his arms. "Sweetheart, what's wrong?"

His sympathy started her tears again, and he led her to the back room, pulled out the desk chair for her, and pulled another chair over to sit next to her.

"What did Mom do this time?" he asked, his voice resigned.

"She was just being her usual self, and for a while I was actually kind of enjoying having some time to read and watch the waves. By the time I left, I was in a pretty good mood." She pulled a tissue from a box on the desk and blew her nose. "But now I have to go back tomorrow. Ezra is sending down more books to be signed." She was silent for a moment, then closed her eyes. "I probably can't go back tomorrow, anyway. We're supposed to get a shipment in, and I have to stock the shelves."

Jeremy took her hand. "You're not doing either of those things. We're going to take a vacation."

She gave a hiccupping laugh. "Yeah, right."

"No, I'm serious, Jen. You deserve a vacation." He smiled. "You deserve a *grand* vacation, but I have something a little more modest in mind. Let's go down to Virginia Beach—just overnight—and visit John and Nancy. They're always asking us to come down and see their new place."

"But what about the pharmacy? What about the customers?"

"We'll implement the same plan we did when the old location flooded. Send out an email to customers letting them know the pharmacy is going to be closed for a couple of days. Leave out-of-office messages on the website and the voicemail and the door."

"We can check the refill reminder status," said Jeanette, warming to the idea, "and call anyone we think might stop by to pick up a prescription and ask them to wait a day or two."

"And provide contact information for the closest pharmacy in case they can't wait." He squeezed her hand. "This emergency might be an Act of Mom rather than an Act of God, but I'd say it merits the same measures."

Jeanette felt a glimmer of excitement she couldn't remember feeling for weeks, if not months. "Will that be okay?"

"It worked before—it'll work again. We can do all the prep work tonight so we can leave first thing in the morning. We can get to Virginia Beach in time for a late lunch, play a round of golf. Remember what good margaritas John makes? We can stay through lunch the next day, drive back, and be bright-eyed and bushy-tailed for work the next morning."

"But what about the books Marilee needs to sign?"

"Screw the books. We certainly don't owe Ezra any favors, and I can't imagine Mom will object."

Jeanette chewed a thumbnail. "I hate to make Ezra angry if we can avoid it. Maybe we could stop by Ocean City on the way to Virginia Beach—it's right on the way. We could bring the books up to the condo, then bring the signed books down to the security desk on the way back home."

He squeezed her arm. "Only if you think seeing my mother won't ruin our vacation. Are you up for it—a couple of days off?"

She gave him a watery smile. "It sounds great."

"Let's call Mom and let her know about our plans. And let *her* tell Ezra when he can pick up his books."

They called Marilee and described the plan.

"This could work well," Marilee said briskly, "because I've decided to take you up on your offer to come stay with you in Downingtown. If my unwillingness to leave the condo is really some sort of PTSD related to the attack at the bookstore, staying here in Ocean City won't help. I can come back with you on your way back from Virginia Beach."

Jeanette fought to retain her good mood as Jeremy squeezed her hand. "Good idea, Mom. I think getting out of Ocean City will help. But I think we also have to respect what you said before: that a long drive is going to be more stressful than just a trip out of the condo. I think you'd be happier if you had some sort of sedative."

"What did you have in mind?"

"Like I said before, maybe some CBD."

"Oh, good heavens," muttered Marilee. "I can't imagine that stuff actually works."

"Well, if you don't think it works," said Jeremy, keeping his temper in check with obvious effort, "and you were willing to make the trip with no sedation, then no harm in trying it."

Marilee sighed. "Fine."

"We'll drop it off along with the books when we stop by Ocean City on the way to Virginia Beach. The next day, when we're on our way back, we'll call you when we're about an hour from Eden Beach. If you take it then, you'll be relaxed for the trip by the time we arrive."

They ended the call, and Jeremy turned to Jeanette. "I'm not sure if Mom deciding to take us up on our offer to stay here is a good development or a bad one. What do you think?"

"Our lives are going to change a lot with your mother staying with us," said Jeanette.

"I know. Once things settle down, we'll talk with her about a long-term plan. If she's willing to leave Ocean City for Downingtown, she might be more willing to consider the trip to Sarasota. And after what happened at Oh Buoy Books, maybe she'll decide to stay in Florida year-round."

She gave him a wan smile. "That might be all the vacation I would ever need."

22

A little before midnight, Ann punched the passcode Darren had given her into the keypad at the Tamaston entrance and pulled the F-150 through the gate. She parked, then went to the front door and knocked, pulling her parka more closely around her against the cold.

After a moment, Darren opened the door and waved her in.

"I'd offer to take your coat," he said, "but you might want to keep it on. Alec decided to economize by turning the heat off in the wing where the turret room is."

"Alec made the planned trip to New York?"

"Yes. It's inconvenient from an editing point of view, because we were meant to be working on the latest Wolfram manuscript, but I suppose it's his best chance of finding a buyer for Jock's hunting trophies."

"If he's selling Tamaston, maybe the buyers would let him keep them here."

Darren shook his head. "There's already a prospective buyer, and they've been quite explicit that the animals have to be gone." Then, with an attempt at cheerfulness, he asked, "Did you and Scott have a nice day?"

"We wandered around the town." She didn't add that they had taken Darren's pickup for a little drive through the countryside outside of Princeton. "When I left the inn, Scott was hanging out by the fireplace with a book and a glass of wine."

"A fire sounds appealing." Darren shivered theatrically. "Back to the turret room, then?"

"Yes. I think it might be better if I spoke with Jock alone, at least about whatever he wants to tell me about the night he died. Then we can decide what we want to do for the memorial video."

"Yes, that makes sense," he said, although he was clearly disappointed he wouldn't be privy to another demonstration of Ann's skill. "Do you remember how to get to the turret room?"

Ann waved a hand. "That general direction, right?"

"Yup." Darren shivered again. "I'm going to wait in the kitchen—it's a little warmer there. Just text me when you're done, and I'll meet up with you here."

Ann wandered through the rooms and down the hallways through which Darren had led them the previous night. The packing had progressed, and Ann wondered if Alec had brought in movers or was doing any of it himself. For that matter, she wondered if he was having Darren do it.

She finally reached the hallway leading to the turret room. Jock appeared in the doorway as she approached.

"Glad you could make it back," he said, stepping aside to let her enter the room. "So, Alec is in New York trying to sell the hunting trophies. I'm not surprised—hunting was never really his thing." After a moment, he added, "Although some of those are fine specimens." He shook his head. "And I assume he's selling the house?"

"Yes. I understand there's a prospective buyer."

"I kind of hoped he'd come to love it as much as I did." He smiled ruefully. "Although I didn't expect to get stuck here permanently."

"In the house?"

"In this room—and the hallway and a couple of rooms nearby. I can't go anywhere else. And I always find myself here—awake, I guess you could say—at around this time."

"What are you doing other times of the day and night?"

He ran his fingers through his hair. "I don't know. Is that strange?"

"No, that seems pretty normal." She glanced at her watch. "If your presence this evening is limited, we should get right to what you wanted to talk to me about. If we have time after that, I could get Darren and mediate a conversation between the two of you if you'd like. As soon as we break the news to Alec that I'm not actually scouting the house for a video shoot, I'd be happy to do the same with him." If, she thought, Alec didn't kick her out of the house and lock the door behind her.

"Sure, that makes sense." He waved her into one of the chairs at the octagonal table, although he stayed standing. "What does everyone know about what happened?"

"According to Darren, the assumption is that you were shot by an intruder who then stole your ivory collection."

Jock stuffed his hands in his pockets. "I suspected as much when I came to and saw the figurines were gone. But if that was the only motive ..." He grimaced. "It's a pretty piss-poor reason for getting killed." After a moment he drew a deep breath, then said, "I was working in here on a Wolfram book. I heard a noise and looked up and there was a guy in the doorway, pointing a gun at me. I had a gun in the desk drawer. I got the drawer open, but he shot me before I could get it out."

"Even if you had been able to get it out, you probably wouldn't have had time to load it."

"That gun is always loaded. What's the good of having a weapon for self-protection if it's not loaded?"

"It wasn't loaded."

"Who did you hear that from?"

"I heard it from Darren ... but hold on." She got out her phone and tapped for a minute, then said, "The news coverage included the fact that the gun wasn't loaded." She scanned the article. "Although I see that several of your friends commented that it was uncharacteristic of you to have an unloaded weapon."

Jock dropped into the other chair at the table. "That kind of makes sense based on what I heard."

"Heard when?"

"After he shot me."

Ann leaned forward. "What did you hear?"

~

Jock became aware of his surroundings—and himself—gradually.

It was clear the intruder had shot him, and he expected pain but didn't feel any. In fact, he felt nothing at all. He couldn't see, and he wasn't sure if his eyes were closed or if they were open to a room that was pitch dark.

But he could hear.

He could hear the breath of the intruder—he was sure it was a man—coming from directly above him. The breath came closer, as if the man were bending over him, then receded. Steps moved toward the door to the hallway and then to one side of the room. The man placed something on the table and Jock heard the snap of a small latch popping open. Then footsteps moved back and forth between points along the perimeter of the room and back to the table, punctuated occasionally by the click of objects against the tabletop and the shush of something hard against something soft. It took Jock a minute to hazard a guess about what was going on: the man was gathering the ivory figurines and putting them in some sort of padded case on the table.

The footsteps completed the circuit of the room. The latch snapped into place. Then the man moved toward the chair where Jock had been sitting—toward the open drawer that contained the gun Jock might have used to defend himself, if only he had heard the man's steps in the hallway and had a couple seconds more warning.

Metal clicked delicately on metal.

"Come on ..." the man muttered.

The clicks, and accompanying scrapes, became less delicate, more forceful. "Goddammit, Poindexter," the man said, slightly louder but clearly still to himself, "you said nine-millimeter!" More clicks, fumbling. "Shit. Forget it."

Metal rattled hollowly against wood. Footsteps crossed to the door. Jock heard the squeak of the door opening and the click as it closed, then the footsteps retreated down the hall.

With his attention no longer focused on the sounds, he became aware of a slight glow—the sort of light one saw at the very beginning of the day, especially in open country, like on that safari that he and Alec had gone on. Had he been lying on the floor of the turret room for so long that the sun was rising? That made no sense—there were no windows in the turret room.

He didn't think it was the beginning of the day. But it was the beginning—or perhaps the end—of something, and Jock Quine suspected he knew what that something was.

"AND THE NEXT time I was aware of anything," concluded Jock, "I knew for sure I was dead."

Ann waited a respectful few beats, then asked, "And you never got a good look at the intruder before he shot you?"

"No. I looked up just long enough to see it was someone with a gun pointed at me, then I was trying to get the gun out of the drawer." A moment passed. "Do you think I was already dead when that man was gathering up the figurines?"

"I think so. You said you couldn't feel anything. I'm guessing that when the intruder bent over you, he was checking for a pulse. If he was a pro, and it sounds like he was if your guess is right that he came prepared with a case for the figurines, then he wouldn't have gone to work packing them up if you had been alive."

He nodded. "The way he stood, the way he held the gun—he looked like a pro." He smiled at Ann. "It's the stuff you study up on when you write the kind of books I write. The kind of books I *wrote*." He laughed sadly. "I guess Robert Wolfram won't be holding a gun anymore—professionally or otherwise."

Ann realized that if Jock couldn't move from the part of Tamaston near the turret room and was only conscious of what was going on around the time his death had occurred, there were plenty of developments since his death he wouldn't be aware of. "Alec has picked up the series."

Jock's eyebrows rose. "Alec? Picking up the Wolfram series?"

"Yup."

Jock pondered this news for a moment, then a smile broke over his face. "Why, that's fine!"

"Sort of a departure for him, I understand."

"Yes, his books are a bit more ... heady, but I'm happy he's seen the benefit of providing a little less navel-gazing and a little more action. And Darren can help him make the transition."

At that moment, Ann heard footsteps approaching from the hall and Darren appeared in the door, his expression tight. "Sorry to interrupt, but Alec is coming."

23

Ann turned to Jock. “It looks like you might have the chance to talk to your son sooner than we thought. Can you give me some piece of information that I can tell him to convince him we actually talked?”

“Like what?”

“I don’t know ...” Ann glanced around the room and her eyes fell on the photo of Jock and Alec in Africa. “How about something that happened when you two went on the safari?”

“Why, hello, Alec!” Darren said from the doorway, his voice over-cheerful.

A red-faced Alec appeared next to Darren. “And I find you *again* in the room where my father died? I cancelled dinner in the city because I started having second thoughts about letting the two of you have the run of the house unsupervised.” He turned to Ann. “In fact, I’m beginning to think that the reason I found you in here on your first visit wasn’t because your brother was intrigued by the architecture.”

Ann floundered for a moment until she remembered the story Scott had spun for Alec.

“You’re right,” she said, “but maybe not in the way you

imagine. My name's Ann Kinnear, and I'm one of the speakers at the GothamCon conference."

Alec looked from Ann to Darren and back. "The psychic?"

"That's right," said Ann.

Alec turned his full attention to Darren. "You brought a *psychic* to Tamaston?"

Ann wished she and Darren had discussed a contingency plan for dealing with Alec if he showed up unexpectedly. Based on Darren's panicked look, she wasn't going to get any help from that quarter. She realized that Darren's livelihood probably hung in the balance, whereas all that hung in the balance for her was her invitation to GothamCon. Losing that definitely wouldn't cost Ann her livelihood—or even any sleepless nights.

"Darren didn't know I was the same Ann who was speaking at the conference," she improvised. "I introduced myself as Ann Mahalo and gave him the cover story about being a video producer."

Alec's eyebrows rose. "Why?"

Ann didn't see any reason to lie about that part. "I wanted to see if I could contact your father and find out what happened the night he died."

Alec rolled his eyes. "Oh my God. You don't expect me to believe this, do you?"

She shot Jock a look. "If Jock would just tell me something that I can use to convince you that I have, in fact, spoken to him ..."

"This is ridiculous," Alec said, his face reddening. "I want you out of here."

Jock burst out laughing. "The meerkat! He and I are the only ones who know about the meerkat incident."

"Jock says that only the two of you know about the meerkat incident," Ann said to Alec.

Alec's face went white.

"Although," continued Ann, "maybe that's not as fun a memory for you as it evidently is for your dad."

Alec advanced on her, and she steeled herself not to retreat, even when he pushed his face within a foot of hers.

"Hey Alec, calm down," Jock said, trying for a soothing tone that couldn't quite disguise his surprise.

"Take a step back, Alec," Ann said, her voice steely.

After a moment, he took an infinitesimal step away from her.

She shot Jock an accusing look.

His expression was abashed. "Well, *I* thought it was funny."

"I don't know who you heard that story from—" began Alec.

"Your father—"

"—but if you think it's going to improve your standing with the GothamCon board—or of retaining your invitation as a speaker—you're sorely mistaken."

"This might come as a surprise to you, Alec," she shot back "but my business manager barely talked me into accepting the invitation to be a speaker, so keeping me off the GothamCon stage isn't much of a threat. Darren asked me to give a talk on 'Making the Supernatural Super in Your Novel,' and I figured what would be more *super* than finding out from Jock what happened the night he died." She would have thought that Alec's face couldn't have gone any paler, but she would have been wrong. "Darren had never met me in person. We only ever communicated by email, and I got in touch with him and passed myself off as a video producer so I could get access to Tamaston."

"But that man who was with you—"

"My brother-in-law. And by the way, he does know how to

drive a stick. He just claimed I was the only one who could drive the pickup because you were being such a jerk."

"You're calling me a jerk? That's a ballsy statement for a freak like you to make."

"Ah, I guess now that you know I have the manly ability to drive a stick, you can describe me as 'ballsy.'"

For a moment, Ann thought she was going to need to duck a swing from Alec Quine, but then he spun on his heel and strode to the door. He extended his arm, a trembling finger pointing toward the entrance. "I want you out of my house. Right now."

She glanced at Jock and wished—almost—that she could take back some of the insults she had thrown at Alec. Jock was obviously shocked and distressed at the course the conversation was taking.

"Jock," she asked, realizing that this would likely be the last chance she had to glean any details of the night he died, "any idea who Poindexter is?"

"No—I don't know anyone named that."

"Out!" yelled Alec.

Ann crossed to the door, then turned back to Jock. "I'll tell the police what you told me."

"What are you talking about?" sputtered Alec.

"Just freaky stuff. Nothing for you to worry about."

Ann stepped past Alec and strode down the hallway. Darren followed her. Alec brought up the rear.

When they reached the foyer, Alec said, "Darren, I think you've taken advantage of Tamaston's hospitality long enough. I'm not going to kick you out in the middle of the night, but I expect you to have your things cleared out of the guest room by tomorrow morning."

"Sure, Alec," said Darren, not meeting Alec's eyes.

"And if I see this woman or her brother-in-law on this

property again, I will call the police—and I will hold you personally responsible."

Darren nodded, miserable.

"Drop her off at her hotel. I'll lock up once you're back."

"You're not going back to your place tonight?" asked Darren.

"I think I should stick around here to keep an eye on things." Alec yanked the door open, stepped aside as Ann and Darren filed outside, then slammed the door behind them.

Ann crossed her arms. "Well, that went about as badly as it could have."

"I'm really sorry, Ann," said Darren.

She sighed. "It's not your fault."

"It sort of is, but I appreciate you saying that."

"What's the deal with Alec and meerkats?"

"I have no idea." He jammed his hands into his coat pockets. "But at least it looks like you won't have to do the GothamCon talk. I know you were never very enthusiastic about that."

"Darren," she said, "if you think that idiot is going to chase me away from GothamCon without a fight, you've got another think coming."

24

Jeanette drowsed in the passenger seat as Jeremy drove south for their stop in Ocean City before continuing on to Virginia Beach. They had been up late the previous night getting all the preparations in place for the trip.

She thought back wistfully to their first years together, before they opened the pharmacy, when they could take vacations lasting more than two days. But two days was better than nothing, and even the need to stop in Ocean City to bring the books up to the condo would be worth it if it meant one less thing intruding on her vacation mindset. Unfortunately the stop probably precluded a round of golf ... although not John's famous margaritas.

When they reached Eden Beach, they parked, retrieved a cart from the corral, and stopped at the security desk to pick up the latest supply of books. To Jeanette's relief, Kenny was on the phone, and barely spared them a wave as they loaded the boxes into the cart. As they took the elevator to 14, Jeanette said, "Remember when you brought me to Ocean City to meet your mom when we got engaged?"

Jeremy grimaced. "I do indeed."

It had been the Fourth of July, and the beach town was in full swing: sunburned families grouped at crosswalks, passing between their bay-side accommodations and the beach; clusters of ice cream-licking patrons outside Dumser's Dairyland; the drone of small planes towing banners advertising Phillips Seafood Restaurant and Old Bay. She remembered how excited she was that her prospective mother-in-law had a place right on the beach—a place that she and Jeremy might use for occasional long weekends, or maybe for a week or more at a time, when Marilee was at her winter home in Florida. Jeanette's own mother had died when Jeanette was just a child, and although a mother-in-law would never take the place of her own mother, a relationship with Marilee might fill some of the void left by her mother's death.

The first hour with Marilee disabused Jeanette of that notion. Marilee's attitude toward Jeanette had been no more maternal then than it was now.

But the visit hadn't been all bad. Late that night, after Marilee had gone to bed, Jeanette and Jeremy carried a bottle of wine, two glasses, and two of the breakfast bar stools out to the walkway to enjoy the view across the bay. Jeanette would have liked to have watched the moon shimmering off the water from the ocean-front balcony, but it was right next to Marilee's bedroom, and she liked even more having some distance from her mother-in-law-to-be.

"She wasn't always like this," Jeremy said, his voice low, as he poured the wine and handed her a glass. "She changed after the accident."

Jeremy had been driving, Marilee in the passenger seat. They stopped for a red light ... the light changed ... Jeremy pulled into the intersection—and their car was broadsided by a junker with a drunk teenager at the wheel. Jeremy was uninjured, other than generalized soreness in the following days, but Marilee had cracked her wrist on the gearshift, requiring surgery and months of physical therapy.

"She was even fine for a couple of weeks after she got out of the hospital, but then she started getting the way you see her now. Irritable. Unpleasant." He took a sip of wine. "I think she still has pain from the wrist injury."

"Even after all this time?"

He shrugged. "She doesn't complain about it, but I think so."

"Can't she take anything for the pain?"

"Early on, the doctors gave her Percocet, but it didn't agree with her, and they didn't offer any good alternatives." He shook his head. "They didn't look beyond the list of pills that their friendly drug rep recommended, probably over expensive dinners."

"That's when you left med school."

"Yeah. I didn't want to be part of a system that didn't take a holistic view of treatment options." He looked down. "Although Mom didn't approve. She was counting on having a 'real' doctor in the family. I thought I could convince her if I could alleviate her pain with more natural remedies, but she doesn't believe in ..." He recalibrated his tone to match Marilee's higher voice, "... that woo-woo stuff."

As the elevator door dinged open, Jeanette shook herself out of the memories and followed Jeremy and the cart down the walkway toward Marilee's condo. Toward a woman who couldn't be bothered to be pleasant even when meeting her son's fiancée for the first time. A woman who thought nothing of asking Jeanette to make a six-hour round trip to discharge an errand that Marilee herself could take care of in a fraction of the time. A woman who might at any moment call in her loan, requiring Jeremy and Jeanette to sell the pharmacy. A woman she and Jeremy would now be required to welcome into their home.

Marilee opened the door to Jeremy's knock. She was wearing a black dolman-sleeved top, narrow black slacks, and black leather boots. "You're later than I expected."

"Nice to see you, too, Mom," said Jeremy caustically.

"You can't bring the cart in here."

"Just show me where you want the books and I'll unload them." He reached in his pocket and pulled out a small amber bottle, which he handed to Jeanette. "Can you write out the instructions for Mom while I do that?"

Jeanette took the bottle. "Sure."

"Jeanette knows what the instructions are?" Marilee asked, skeptical.

"We discussed it during the drive," said Jeremy.

As Jeremy unloaded the boxes from the cart into the hallway, Jeanette went to the kitchen and wrote out the instructions on a notepad next to the phone. She tore the sheet off the pad and anchored it under a leg of the espresso machine. She retrieved the last remaining box from the hallway, then left Marilee instructing Jeremy on where and how to stack the books.

As she waited in the kitchen for Jeremy and Marilee to finish up, she heard the same faint *thump THUMP* noise she had heard during her last visit, this time apparently coming from the bay-side guest room. She started down the hall, toward the closed bedroom door, then stopped at Marilee's voice.

"Where are you going?"

"I heard that same thumping sound I heard last time I was here. It sounds like it's coming from the bedroom."

"It's not."

"Don't you think we should check?" asked Jeanette, reaching for the doorknob.

"Don't go in there," said Marilee sharply.

Jeanette, surprised, stepped back from the door. "Okay, fine."

"They're probably …" Marilee waved her hand toward the ceiling. "… doing something with the plumbing."

"If you say so."

Jeanette followed Marilee back to the living room. As the two stood in awkward silence, waiting for Jeremy to finish unpacking and stacking the books, Jeanette heard the sound again, coming from the condo's bay side. Was someone in the guest room? She glanced toward Marilee, but her mother-in-law's sour expression was unchanged.

The sound moved from left to right—from the vicinity of the guest room toward the front door. Jeanette couldn't see down the hallway from where she stood, but she didn't want to seem to be investigating and earn another rebuke from Marilee. Instead, she crossed the living room and dropped onto the couch, from where she could see down the hallway to the front door. There was no one there. The door to the bay-side room was still closed, and Jeanette certainly would have noticed if the front door had opened. Perhaps the sound *was* coming from the plumbing system, as Marilee had said.

When Jeremy emerged from the study, Marilee said, "As long as the two of you are here, let's make that call to Ezra to get his agreement to the contract buy-out in writing."

"Come on, Mom," said Jeremy, "Jen and I are supposed to be on vacation. Let's do it when we get back."

"You're the one who was so insistent," she replied, retrieving her phone from the charger on the kitchen counter and tapping.

"Mom—!"

"Let's just get it over with," said Jeanette, resigned. It would have been nice to avoid an encounter with Marilee, and even nicer to avoid an encounter with both Marilee and Ezra, on the way to Virginia Beach. However, if Ezra was clear with Marilee that the buy-out offer had been a joke, maybe Marilee would stop obsessing about the loan.

Marilee put the phone, set to speaker, on the breakfast bar.

The call connected, and before Marilee could say anything, they heard Ezra's voice.

"I just read through the manuscript of *Mulberry Murder*. Are you out of your mind?"

"Hello, Ezra," said Marilee primly. "I have Jeanette and Jeremy here with me."

"Have the two of you read what Marilee sent me?" Without waiting for a reply, Ezra continued. "I finally got around to reading it and it's an absolute disaster. Marilee, you cannot have the bad guy threaten to torture the protagonist—and to describe in detail what he has in mind. You cannot drop the f-bomb once, let alone two dozen times. And the sex scene ... I wouldn't publish that even if I didn't specialize in cozies."

"Mom?" exclaimed Jeremy, his eyebrows rising.

Jeanette herself was simultaneously intrigued and repelled by the idea of her mother-in-law writing an unpublishable sex scene.

"Yes," said Ezra. "It seems like your sweet, innocent mother didn't want to talk to me about her new *creative direction* before going all Stieg Larsson. This book was supposed to go into production in a couple of months, and there's no way I can fix it in time. We'll have to extend the publication date. Marilee, you'll need to send me every chapter *as you re-write it*, including the ending. And it better be a happy one."

"In view of what happened to me at the bookstore," said

Marilee, her voice icy, "I'm not sure I'm going to be able to give you anything lighthearted enough for your taste."

"Marilee—" Ezra began, then stopped. There was a long silence—Jeanette could imagine Ezra trying to get control of his anger. After all, further antagonizing Marilee wasn't going to get him the cheerful mystery novel he wanted. She heard a long intake of breath, then Ezra continued. "I'm sorry for what happened to you at the bookstore, but I need you to deliver a manuscript that bears some faint resemblance to the dozen Berry books you've already written, and I need you to go out there and sell that book to your fans."

"Perhaps you've forgotten that I'm unable to leave home."

"Ah, yes, your newly blossomed agoraphobia. Marilee, it's been four days," his temper was obviously fraying once again, "and I've never found you to be a shrinking violet. I can try to shift the schedule of your Florida events back, but—"

"I'm not going back to Florida, Ezra."

The last of Ezra's patience evaporated. "Marilee, you signed a contract for twenty-four books, and we're barely halfway through that number. You also signed up for a specified number of author events, including the ones I scheduled in Florida in the winter because it would be convenient for you. If you think you can just step away from that commitment, you might want to chat with your former Cozy Up Press colleague who similarly thought she could renege on her commitments. I'm guessing she'd advise you to rethink your position. I'd recommend you start your rewrite, draft that ending, and do some research into flights to Sarasota. I'll give you twenty-four hours to think about this."

He ended the call.

The three were silent for several long moments, then Jeanette said, keeping her voice steady with an effort, "Well, that was interesting."

"That was *ridiculous*," spat Marilee. "The man's a complete idiot."

Jeremy crossed his arms. "I guess that answers our question about whether or not Ezra was joking about the contract buy-out."

"You expect me to continue working with that man? After how he spoke to me? I'm quite sure that if I showed Ezra half a million dollars, he would be happy never to have to speak with *me* again! Don't think this lets you off the hook."

"Mom," said Jeremy, "I'm not going to talk with you about this now. We'll see you tomorrow, and we'll call you when you should take the sedative." After a moment, he muttered, "Although maybe you shouldn't wait until tomorrow."

He took Jeanette's elbow and guided her toward the front door.

"Don't walk out on me!" yelled Marilee. "You're not going to be able to walk out on me when I'm living in Downingtown with you!"

"We'll cross that bridge when we come to it," Jeremy called back.

They stepped outside, and Jeremy strode down the walkway to the elevators.

"The cart—" began Jeanette.

"Leave it," he said over his shoulder. "We'll need it when we come back."

Jeanette stood staring at the cart, then at her husband's retreating back. She drew in a long, trembling breath, trying to hold her tears at bay. Then she puffed it out.

"Fuck."

She jogged after Jeremy.

25

The morning after Alec threw Ann out of Tamaston, Darren stopped by the Nassau Inn to pick up Ann and Scott for the short drive to the Princeton airport.

"Did you find out anything from Jock before Alec showed up?" Darren asked Ann as they left the downtown area behind.

"Nothing specific," she said. She had decided she wanted to consult with the police before discussing what she had learned with anyone other than Scott, whom she had updated the previous night. "What are you going to do about the memorial video?" she asked, hoping to preempt further inquiry from Darren.

He sighed. "We'll patch together the usual thing. And about your talk ..."

"Darren, if it's going to put you in a difficult situation—an even more difficult situation than you're already in—then I don't want you trying to defend my talk to the board. But Alec gave me an idea for an interesting spin on the topic, and I'm happy to go forward with it if you think it's the best thing to do."

Darren's expression became more resolute. "I have a lot longer history, and a lot better reputation, with the board than Alec does. I'm happy to put in a good word for you."

He dropped them off at the airport, then drove away, headed home to Wilmington.

"Poor Darren," said Scott as the truck disappeared down the road.

"Yeah, he's in a bind—although one he wouldn't be in if he hadn't lied to Alec about why we were at Tamaston."

Ann and Scott had an uneventful flight back to Avondale, and by noon, they were back at the Curragh.

After Scott left to pick up Ursula from the big house and drive home to West Chester, Ann dropped her overnight bag on the couch and started a pot of coffee. Then she got out her phone and put in a call to her personal contact in law enforcement: Philadelphia Detective Joe Booth.

Ann hadn't seen Joe for a couple of months, since he had been sent on a temporary assignment to Chicago. Ann had first met Joe when, after he had exhausted more traditional attempts to solve the Philadelphia Socialite Murder, he drove up to Ann's Adirondack cabin to ask for her help, and their relationship had gradually morphed from colleagues to friends.

Ann had thought it might be morphing into something more, but then he went to Chicago, limiting their interactions to occasional emails and texts and even more occasional phone calls. She wasn't even sure whether he was still dating the old flame he had run into during one of his cases—although from the few details Joe had dropped, Ann thought the two of them sounded like a mismatch.

"Hey, what's up?" Joe answered.

"I need some professional advice."

She described what had led to her visit to Tamaston and what Jock Quine had told her about the night he had been killed: that he didn't get a good look at the man who shot him, but that he looked like a pro ... that Jock was surprised to hear that the gun in the desk drawer wasn't loaded ... that the intruder mentioned the name Poindexter, a name that was unfamiliar to Jock.

"And now," she concluded, "I'm wondering how I can pass that information on to the Princeton police without being labeled a crank."

"The Poindexter thing is interesting."

"Yeah, although it might not be a person's actual name. I looked it up afterwards. It's a nickname for someone who's bookish."

"Does that fit anyone you've run into in connection with Jock Quine?"

She laughed. "He was an author, so pretty much *everyone* connected with him might be considered bookish."

"Do you know what the Princeton PD is saying about the case?"

"They're not saying much. They were able to eliminate a bunch of Jock's colleagues because his publisher, Harrison & John, was hosting some shindig in New York. Alec Quine was there. So was Jock's editor, Darren Van Osten."

Joe was silent for a few moments, then said, "Let me see if I can rustle up a connection in the Princeton PD, maybe find out more than what they're putting out in their press releases."

"But without mentioning the Poindexter thing, right?"

"Yeah, it would be hard to explain how I knew that."

"I'll do some more research and see if I can find anyone named Poindexter who had anything to do with Jock, but I think it's a long shot."

"Sounds good. How are you doing otherwise?"

"Making a mess of trying to manage the non-sensing side of Ann Kinnear Sensing while Mike's living it up with some buddies on a ski vacation in Colorado. All this is giving me a fresh appreciation of everything he does. I'll be happy when he's back."

"He's the one who talked you into doing the presentation you emailed me about?"

"Yup. Additional stream of income ... probably wouldn't result in me going to the hospital."

Joe laughed. "Both good things. So it sounds like you're off the hook for the presentation."

"Yeah. Maybe."

"You don't sound happy about it."

"I thought I would have been, but Alec Quine is such a bastard that it made me want to do the talk just to spite him."

"Can't blame you for that."

"And he obviously doesn't believe I can do what I can do ... although he sure got mad about my mention of the meerkat incident." She sighed. "It sounds like if he were titling the presentation, it would be 'Making Skullduggery Super in Your Novel.'"

"He'll be singing a different tune if we can find a way to use what you found out from Jock to put his killer behind bars."

26

Darren had just settled down at his desk after his drive back from Princeton, and the neighbor's German Shepherd had just settled down after its welcome home round of barks, when he saw an email in his inbox from Lara Seaford. He clicked it open.

Darren, just checking in about the Latent Prints *award ceremony—if you're going to be there, and if* Darkest Before Death *wins, I'd like for you to accept on my behalf.*

Any word on when the GothamCon nominees will be announced? Not that I don't appreciate the Latent Prints *nomination, but GothamCon could really light a fire under sales.*

Darren smiled and hit *Reply*.

As a volunteer to the GothamCon board, all I can say is these types of things are impossible to predict

He examined what he had typed, then deleted the draft and began again.

Please don't share this further—I can't imagine where you'd share it, since you're nowhere to be found on social media—but I can tell you that based on the rumors I'm hearing, Darkest Before Death *is favored to win Best Debut!*

Might such recognition entice you to reveal yourself to your fans?

He sent off the email, then pretended to work on the exclamation-heavy manuscript until he heard the chime of an incoming email.

Darren, it's a deal—if I win at GothamCon, I'll announce myself at the ceremony. Now that would definitely drive some sales.

And I should be able to give you the ms for the sequel then as well.

He sat back, smiling. After months of knowing Lara Seaford only through her emails, and through the money orders he received in payment for his editorial services, he might finally meet his mysterious client. His smile faded a bit as he thought through the logistics. How would she get her ticket? The board waived the banquet fee for award nominees, but telling the organizers that she planned to attend would ruin her surprise. He assumed that if she didn't win, she'd fade away into the crowd and hold her reveal for a more propitious time.

He thought again about what a win would mean for him. Even the nominations for Best Debut from *Latent Prints* and GothamCon had borne some fruit—a few feelers from publishers and authors inquiring about his availability. He realized again what an untenable position he had put himself in by his reliance on Jock Quine for his livelihood ... but he had assumed that he and Jock had many more years, and many more books, to work through together. If Lara's novel won Best Debut at GothamCon, he had no doubt that the next day his inbox would be filled with queries from prospective clients.

His smile returned, a bit wolfish this time, as he thought about the email he would send to Alec Quine when he was ready to burn that bridge.

27

Jeanette and Jeremy were taking a walk around their hosts' Virginia Beach neighborhood to work off the effects of the first round of pre-dinner margaritas when Jeanette's phone buzzed with a text. She pulled it out of her pocket and read.

"Oh, God, what now?" she groaned.

"What is it?"

"Ezra. He wants to know if we've seen Marilee's Facebook page." She grimaced. "I wonder if her fans are finding other ways that I'm responsible for every bad thing that happens to Marilee." Jeanette tapped open the app and read, then looked up, her eyes wide. "Oh my God, Jer—she announced on Facebook that she isn't going to write any more cozies!"

"What? I thought she was going to sleep on it!"

"That's what Ezra told her to do, but obviously she had other ideas."

Jeanette turned the phone so Jeremy could see it. As she scrolled, his expression darkened. "It already has dozens of comments," he said.

"And hundreds of reactions."

"I'm calling Mom and asking her what the hell is going on."

"Wait a minute. Since Ezra texted me about the announcement, let's call him first."

She put the call through, then set the phone to speaker.

"Jeanette," said Ezra without preamble, "what the hell is going on? I tried calling Marilee, but she's not answering."

"I'm as surprised as you are, Ezra. By the way, I have Jeremy on the line."

"Hi, Ezra," said Jeremy.

"Jeremy, has your mother gone insane?"

"Ezra, that's uncalled for. She had a very traumatic experience, and it's taking her some time to recover from it."

"Based on that Facebook post, *she* obviously doesn't think it's just a matter of time before she gets back to work on the Berry mysteries. She just announced the end of her interest in her cozies to thousands of followers!"

Jeremy tried to keep his tone light. "Maybe it'll turn out it's all a PR stunt. That should sell a lot of books, right?"

"Yes, Jeremy," Ezra shot back, "I feel pretty certain that tomorrow morning, Marilee is going to be at the top of the cozy sales ranks, and that spike might last into the next day, and maybe one or two more. But you know what will happen when all her mourning fans buy up her backlist? No more books, no more fans, no more income, no more career."

"We'll talk to her, Ezra," said Jeremy.

"You can talk to her all you want, but this is a black eye for Cozy Up Press, and I don't take kindly to one of my authors—an author whose work and career are pretty much solely attributable to the time and effort *I* put into them—treating our business relationship in this way. You tell Marilee that she can't change her mind tomorrow and expect to come crawling back and have everything go back to the way it was. Not publishing any more of her books is the least of the steps I'll take."

"Ezra—"

"And I can guarantee you that any other publisher she approaches is going to turn her away as well."

Ezra ended the call.

"Holy shit," Jeremy groaned.

Forcing more confidence than she felt, Jeanette said, "They're both angry now. Maybe when their tempers cool—"

Jeremy interrupted her with a rough laugh. "Tempers cool? Mom and Ezra? They're not only both hotheads—they're stubborn as hell. What if they never change their positions? Here I was, grousing about losing access to the Florida condo, thinking that having Mom move in with us is the worst that could happen—but what if she expects us to support her financially? What if Ezra doesn't just cut her off—what if he sues her for breach of contract? Jen, we might not just lose the pharmacy. We might lose everything."

Jeanette took Jeremy's hand and smoothed her fingers soothingly across his knuckles. She knew Ezra and Marilee well enough to agree that the outcome Jeremy described was a possibility. She agreed about the danger it put them in. But she disagreed about one thing: as far as she was concerned, losing the pharmacy *was* losing everything.

28

The day after returning from Princeton, Ann got a call from Mike saying he had just landed at Philly International.

"I got a message from Del," he said. "It sounds like Nola's done some decorating for us in the new Ann Kinnear Sensing office. I thought I'd swing by Kennett Square and check it out. Care to join me?"

"Sure."

About an hour later, Mike arrived at the Curragh. Ann pulled on her parka, and they walked up the hill to the big house. The weather continued cold and gray, the Tarn now fully iced over.

"Not that I didn't appreciate you before," Ann said to Mike, "but I have a whole new appreciation of your contributions to the business. Thank God you're back."

He laughed. "It's good to be appreciated. What was the hardest part?"

"Holding down expenses."

He raised an eyebrow. "Oh?"

She waved a mittened hand. "I'll cover the overage."

When they reached the entrance, Ann saw a brass plaque affixed to the wall next to the front door: *Ann Kinnear Sensing*. Underneath that, a smaller sign gave brief instructions for how to reach the office itself.

"Nice!" she said.

"It does look nice," he said, obviously pleased. "I special ordered it and Del had one of the guys from the construction crew put it up."

They stepped inside and made their way to the office.

Niall's hulking desk was gone, as was the temporary meeting table Mike and Del had set up. On one side of the room, four leather straight-back chairs surrounded a copper-topped table. On the other side, a loveseat in a nubby maroon fabric stood behind a wicker coffee table, flanked by two small chairs upholstered in a subtle geometric pattern. Paintings of the Chester County countryside hung on the walls. A room divider with the old Lynch and Son Winery logo on it screened one corner of the room.

"Hey, this looks great," said Ann, looking around.

"It's all stuff Nola found around the big house and the Cellar or that Del and Rowan had at the Unionville house but didn't think would work in the upstairs apartment. She says you can swap out anything you don't like."

"I like it all."

"I had one idea of my own," he said, "and you can reject that as well if you don't like it."

He moved the room divider to one side, revealing a hulking wooden display cabinet.

Ann's eyebrows rose. "You're suggesting we decorate the office of Ann Kinnear Sensing with Nola Lynch's cabinet of curiosities? How did you even get it out of the basement?"

"Actually, Rowan, Nola, and Del are clearing out the basement, and a couple of the construction guys got it upstairs. Del called me and asked me if we wanted it."

"Only Del would think—"

Mike raised a hand. "Just hear me out. I think prospective clients would be pretty interested to see the cabinet, considering it got some mentions in the media coverage of Niall's death—"

"—not to mention your near death."

Mike grinned sheepishly. "Yeah, that too. But it's a conversation starter. We could put some of your smaller Adirondack paintings in there—"

She crossed her arms. "It's been years since I've done any painting."

"It doesn't mean clients won't be interested in seeing the ones you did. And we could display other things, maybe some mementos of your engagements ..." He noticed her glare and sighed. "... but I totally get it if you don't want it around."

"Why would I want—?" she began, exasperated.

Then she paused. It would be natural for her to associate the cabinet of curiosities with its builder, who had been responsible for her last trip to the ER. However, she realized she associated it more with Niall's dead son, Harkin. Harkin had led her to the cabinet, and to the clue that had saved Mike and Scott's lives. Ann had come to like Harkin very much—a liking she would never have anticipated when she had first met the prickly and sullen man when he was still alive.

"Actually ..." she said, wavering. After a few moments, she nodded. "Let's give it a try. But I get to decide what goes in it."

"You got it," he said.

29

Despite the sub-freezing temperature, Jeanette cracked the window of the CR-V and let the bracing salt-scented air whirl into the vehicle. The trip to Virginia Beach had been a much-needed break, with the added benefit that their host had suggested grilling grass-fed steaks for dinner, which were not only delicious but also saved Jeanette and Jeremy the cost of a restaurant visit. They had stretched their time away as long as they could, not leaving until almost five o'clock for the three-hour drive to Ocean City.

The trip had at least blunted Jeanette's anxiety over the argument with Marilee and the surprise retirement announcement and her trepidation about how Marilee—and they—would fare on the drive to Pennsylvania.

Jeremy, who was driving, said, "Can you give Mom a call and let her know we're about an hour away and that she should take the sedative now?"

Jeanette groaned. "Jer, I'm in such a good mood right now."

"You could send her a text."

"When have you ever known your mother to respond to a text?"

"Well, hardly ever. But if we don't get in touch with her, it might mean we'll have to spend more time at the condo waiting for it to kick in."

"You spend the time in the condo—I'm going to wait on the balcony."

"It's awfully cold for the balcony."

"I don't mind. At least it will be," she looked at him pointedly, "peaceful."

He marshaled a smile. "That's fine—I'll take care of Mom when we get there." He glanced over at her. "But let's still give her a heads up."

Jeanette sighed. "Fine." She got out her phone and tapped Marilee's landline number. After several rings, the answering machine picked up. "No answer," she said as she waited for the message to play. When she heard the beep, she said, "Marilee? Are you screening calls? It's Jeanette." She waited a few seconds, then said, "We're just calling to let you know that we're about an hour away, so you should take the sedative now. See you soon." She ended the call.

"She didn't answer my calls last night or this morning either," said Jeremy. "You think she's still mad at us?"

Jeanette shrugged. "Maybe she figured she just needed to know we were on our way and didn't feel like talking."

"Or she's feeling better and left the condo," Jeremy said hopefully.

"In which case, she doesn't need to come to Downingtown," Jeanette deadpanned, "and doesn't need me running her errands for her." She looked over at Jeremy. "Don't tease me with unlikely scenarios."

They drove in silence for a few minutes, then Jeanette asked, "Did you ever hear weird sounds at the condo?"

"Like what?"

"Like someone walking around, but uneven. *Thump THUMP. Thump THUMP.*"

He shook his head. "I don't recall hearing anything like that. Coming from the condo next door?"

"I don't think so. Marilee says there's no one over there now."

"There's barely anyone in the whole building now. I wonder if Marilee's the only person there ..."

"... other than Kenny."

Jeremy laughed. "Now that's a resident mixer I would skip."

They reached Eden Beach a little before nine o'clock. As they pulled off the Coastal Highway, Jeanette pointed up toward Marilee's floor, the walkway of which was just visible in the moonlight. "The cart's still there. At least we can bypass Kenny on the way up."

Jeremy parked in the ground-floor garage, and they took the stairs to the first floor and then the elevator to 14. When they reached the condo, Jeremy rapped lightly on the door. As they waited, shivering in the wind that seemed always to be blowing this high above the ground, Jeanette tried to distract herself with the view across the streetlights of the Coastal Highway to the few flickers of light from the canal-side houses and finally to the blackness of the bay beyond.

"Maybe she's more knocked out than we thought she'd be," said Jeremy. After a few moments, he knocked again, a bit harder. "Mom, it's Jeremy and Jeanette," he called.

"I have a key." Jeanette pulled her keyring from her pocket. "I generally don't use it because she pitches a fit if I walk in 'unannounced,' but I'm not standing out here longer than I have to." She unlocked the door and pushed it open.

The hallway from the bay-side entrance to the living room was dark, but Jeanette could see a faint light coming from the ocean-side portion of the condo.

"Mom?" called Jeremy as he walked down the hall, Jeanette following him.

When they got to the living room, she could see that the light came from Marilee's study.

Jeremy crossed the living room to the bedroom door. "Mom, are you ready to go?" He got to the door and stopped, and Jeanette heard him suck in a breath. "Mom?"

He stepped into the room, and she hurried after him.

Marilee, dressed in the same all-black outfit she had been wearing the previous day, was sitting on the sofa, her head thrown back, her hands resting in her lap, palms up.

"Oh my God," Jeremy gasped. He crossed the room in a few strides and fell to his knees in front of Marilee.

As Jeanette gaped from the doorway, Jeremy pressed his fingers to Marilee's neck.

Marilee shifted in a manner more appropriate to a mannequin than a person, and Jeremy snatched his hand back.

"What?" gasped Jeanette.

"She's stiff," he managed, his voice choked. "And cold."

Jeanette forced herself forward until she could see Marilee's face. It was gray, her eyes open but cloudy, the pupils dilated. She picked up one of Marilee's upturned hands, the palm milky white, and it was like picking up a bird that had frozen to death. She barely avoided snatching her hand back, as Jeremy had done, but forced herself to return Marilee's hand to her lap, Marilee's entire body shifting slightly as she did so.

Jeremy staggered to his feet, and they both stood staring

down at Marilee. Then Jeanette began frantically searching the pockets of her coat. "Where's my phone? I must have left it in the car."

She turned and hurried out of the room, banging her shoulder on the doorframe as she passed, and snatched the receiver of the landline phone off its hook in the kitchen.

Jeremy appeared at her side. "What are you doing?"

"I'm calling 911!"

"Jen, it's no use calling in the first responders. You saw her. She's beyond help."

"You don't know that for sure—did you check for a pulse?"

"I tried, but her jaw ... rigor has already set in. You must have felt it when you touched her hand. And her face ... her eyes ..." He choked back a sob.

Jeanette let go of the receiver and it clattered onto the kitchen countertop. She rushed back into the bedroom and grabbed Marilee's wrist. It felt just as cold and lifeless as her hand, but Jeanette forced herself to search for a pulse. Nothing. As she released Marilee's wrist and stepped back, she heard the click of Jeremy returning the receiver to the cradle, then he stepped back into the study.

After a few moments, he said, "Jen, remember when that guy down the street choked on a piece of hamburger and his wife found him hours later?"

"You think she choked on something?" quavered Jeanette, her vision wavery with tears.

"No, I'm not saying that. I have no idea how she died. But remember how we said we wouldn't want what happened to him to happen to us? Wouldn't want EMTs pretending to try to revive us just to appease a hysterical relative?"

"But maybe they could ..." her voice trailed off.

"No, they couldn't." He gestured toward Marilee. "When doctors talk about 'conditions incompatible with life,' *that's* what they're talking about. She's dead—and has been dead for a long time." He gave what was either a forced laugh or a suppressed sob. "Hell, she might have been dead when we tried calling her last night."

Jeanette realized she was wringing her hands, as if trying to force warmth into them after her contact with Marilee's body.

"Do you agree that no one can help her?" Jeremy asked, his voice teary but gentle.

Seconds ticked by, then Jeanette nodded. "What are we going to do?" she whispered.

"I don't know. Let's just take a minute to calm down and think through this."

"Think through his? With her right there?" Jeanette felt herself sway, and Jeremy put his arms around her. He turned her back toward the living room, led her to the couch, and helped her sit.

"If you're feeling faint, put your head between your knees."

Jeanette leaned forward.

"I'm going to get you a glass of water." He went to the kitchen, and she heard the sounds of cupboards opening and closing. He was back a moment later. "Drink this."

She sat up and took the glass of water from Jeremy with shaking hands. She gulped it down, trickles of water escaping from either side and running down her chin and onto her coat.

Jeremy took the empty glass from her and refilled it at the sink. He returned to the living room, sat heavily on the couch next to her, and handed her the glass. Then he dropped his elbows onto his knees and his face in his hands. "Jesus."

"Could the CBD have done ... *that*?" she asked, her voice a barely audible rasp.

"It wasn't CBD," said Jeremy into his hands.

"What was it?"

He raised his head. "You gave her the instructions?"

"Of course I gave her the instructions. What was it?"

"I thought she needed something a little stronger. Hell, *she* thought the needed something a little stronger. She said she didn't believe CBD would work."

"What did you give her?" Jeanette could hear a note of hysteria creeping into her voice.

He stood and crossed to the kitchen island, where the small amber dropper bottle stood. He picked it up and slipped it into his pocket. "Where are the instructions you wrote out?"

"I put it by the espresso maker." She stood as well. "Jeremy ..."

He stepped into the kitchen. "The note isn't here anymore."

"She must have thrown it away after she took the sedative."

Jeremy moved toward the trash can.

"Jeremy, what are you doing?" She heard her voice becoming shrill. "Why are you looking for the note?"

Ignoring her question, he slid open the cupboard that housed the garbage can. "It's not here. Nothing's here. She must have taken out the trash and put it down the garbage chute."

"But she said she couldn't leave the condo. Couldn't even step out the door."

Jeremy ran his fingers through his hair. "Maybe she was getting better." He shook his head. "It doesn't matter now."

Half a minute ticked by, then he drew in a bushel-sized breath, and puffed it out. "This puts us in ... a tricky situation."

"A tricky situation?" Jeanette said, her voice spiking again.

Jeremy looked toward the bedroom and dropped his eyes. Then he crossed to the door and, without looking at the body on the sofa, pulled the door closed. He sat on the couch and gestured Jeanette to sit next to him.

"Jen, think of the headlines. *Beloved Cozy Author Dead after Pharmacist Son Prescribes Sedative.* Remember what those people on Mom's Facebook page said about you? And you were trying to help her!"

"You were trying to help her, too." After a moment, she added, "Right?"

"Yes, of course. But that won't matter. If you think keeping the pharmacy going under the current circumstances is tough, imagine what it will be like if people believe I killed my mother with a prescription drug."

Jeanette was silent for a moment, then asked in a near whisper, "Jeremy, what did you give her?"

"I think it's better if you don't know."

"Jeremy—!" she almost shouted.

He raised his hands placatingly and cast a nervous eye toward the front door. "Okay, okay, just calm down." He heaved a sigh. "It was Lorazepam."

Her eyes widened. "Lorazepam?"

"Yes. Even *I* didn't think CBD would be enough to make the drive back to Downingtown bearable for her. Or for us."

She shifted her gaze to the closed door to the study. "And it did that to her?"

"I can't imagine how ..."

"Her doctor would have factored in any considerations like her size or health conditions ..."

"Her doctor didn't know about it." He grimaced. "Hell, I don't even know if she *has* a doctor. She's always so goddamned healthy."

She was barely able to force out her next words. "You gave her Lorazepam without a doctor's prescription?"

After a moment, he nodded.

"Jeremy ..."

"So now you see why we're in a tricky situation."

Half a minute ticked by, then Jeanette said, trying for a matter-of-fact tone. "Maybe she didn't take it. Maybe she thought she didn't need it for the drive."

Jeremy drew the bottle out of his pocket and held it up to the light. He drew his eyebrows together. "Oh, she took some." He slipped the bottle back into his pocket.

"Maybe because she's so small ..."

"I factored in her weight." He stood and crossed to the sliders to the balcony. Far off in the distance, Jeanette could see the tiny lights of a freighter crawling along the horizon. "The thing that makes this situation tricky is not just the fact that I gave her a controlled substance without a doctor's prescription. You could chalk that up to simple stupidity," he barked out a harsh laugh, "and rightly so. But we're going to profit from her death. Not needing to repay the loan is the least of it. I'll inherit her estate. People have committed murder for less."

Jeanette rose and moved to stand next to him. "So what do we do?" she asked, her voice barely audible, even to herself.

They stood in silence for a full minute, and Jeanette became aware of the shell-shaped clock ticking away on the entertainment center—a tick that seemed to get louder with each passing second.

Finally, Jeremy spoke. "She hasn't left the condo since the bookstore attack—except maybe for taking the trash to the garbage chute, assuming she did that. Even if she usually socialized with the other Eden Beach residents, there's no one around. Other than the author events, I doubt she ever talked with anyone other than you, me, and Ezra."

"What are you talking about?"

He turned to her and took her hands. "I'm suggesting we don't tell anyone that she's dead."

Jeanette stared at Jeremy. "You mean ... cover up her death?"

"She's already told Ezra that she's not writing any more cozies or going to any more events. After that last blow-up on the phone, he won't be surprised if she doesn't want to talk with him."

"What would we do with her?" asked Jeanette, her eyes sliding toward the closed study door and then back to Jeremy.

"We should bury her."

"We're going to bury your mother?" Jeanette choked out. "In secret?"

Jeremy led her back to the couch.

"That's what I'm suggesting." He took her hands. "We would do it respectfully. Think of what we've planned for ourselves. Being wrapped in some natural fabric, being laid to rest in a beautiful spot. We could do the same for her."

"It's what we wanted, but Marilee? It's not what she would have wanted for herself."

He heaved a sigh. "That is true." He was silent for a moment, and when he spoke again, his voice had an edge. "She would have wanted all the pomp and ceremony, and a casket that cost more than our car is worth. But she's dead. All that pomp and ceremony isn't for the people who are gone—it's for the people who are still living." He turned so that he faced Jeanette more fully. "Jen, if I believed in hell—which I don't—I'd probably be afraid I'd burn there for what I'm about to say, but I'll say it anyway. Mom made our lives, especially *your* life, hard enough when she was alive. I don't want to let her ruin our lives after she's dead."

She raised her hands to her face and pressed her fingertips to her eyes. She heard the clock tick off one minute, then two. She heard Jeremy's breath, rough in his throat, beside her. Then she straightened and drew a deep breath.

"You're right. Let's not let her mess with our lives anymore."

30

Jeanette and Jeremy crossed the living room to the closed door to the study. Jeremy reached for the knob, then withdrew his hand.

Jeanette reached past him, opened the door, and stepped into the study. She was relieved that the drapes in this room were closed, hiding the inky darkness—and the windows of the neighboring condo building—from view.

She forced her eyes to Marilee's body. Jeremy was right—she was clearly beyond help and had been for a long time.

"She'd fit into one of the Eden Beach carts," she said, working to keep her voice steady.

"A cart. Oh my God. How are we going to explain the cart to Kenny?" Jeremy groaned. "Lord, we forgot about Kenny. He's the other person in addition to us and Ezra that Marilee talks with."

"We'll tell him we're bringing down a bunch of signed books. That's what we were planning to do in any case. In fact, we could put a couple of boxes on top to hide ..." She gestured toward the body. "... you know."

Jeremy wiped his hand down his face. "What would Mom think?"

Jeanette pulled herself straighter. "We can't think about that. In any case, she's not around anymore, so she isn't going to care."

"Taking her out in the cart might work to get her out of Eden Beach," said Jeremy, "but eventually even Kenny's going to think it's weird that he never sees her."

Jeanette fought off a wave of anger that Jeremy's willingness to hide his mother's death and bury her body didn't extend to a willingness to figure out how they were going to get away with it. "She's been telling everyone she can't leave. That gives us time to decide what to do."

Jeremy nodded, shell-shocked.

They retrieved the cart from where they had left it on the walkway the previous day and, making sure to avoid scuffing the walls, wheeled it into the study.

"We can wrap her in that," said Jeanette, pointing to a quilt hanging over the back of the sofa behind the body.

Jeremy nodded but didn't move.

Jeanette grasped the edge of the quilt and tugged. Rather than the quilt pulling free, Marilee's entire body shifted.

"Don't pull her off the couch!" gasped Jeremy.

Jeanette tamped down her irritation again. "We'll use a spare blanket instead."

She retrieved a blanket from the linen closet. They spread it out on the floor of the study and lowered Marilee's body onto it, then used it as a sling to hoist her over the cart. Working her down into the cart was more difficult—and even more stomach-churning—than Jeanette had anticipated, Marilee's stiffened limbs fighting their efforts to force her into the space. When the body was finally resting on the bottom of the cart, they folded the edges of the blanket over it. Jeanette put a couple of boxes on top, each weighted down with a few books.

After they had wrestled the cart out of the study, Jeanette went back to examine the room. She was deeply grateful that there were no stains on the sofa where Marilee had been sitting. She couldn't think of anything else they might need to clean up—but then her mind wasn't working as clearly as she might have wished.

They wheeled the cart down the hallway and had maneuvered it over the doorsill onto the walkway when Jeremy blanched. "Wait a minute," he whispered.

"What is it?"

He looked up and down the deserted walkway, then stepped back into the condo and beckoned her to follow him.

"We're just going to leave ..." She waved at the cart. "... out here?"

He nodded vigorously and beckoned her more frantically back into the apartment. "It'll take just a second."

Jeanette also glanced up and down the walkway to make sure no one was approaching. Although, she thought, if anyone else *had* been on the walkway, he or she would have been the first person Jeanette had seen at Eden Beach recently, other than Kenny and Marilee's erstwhile errand boy. She squeezed into the hallway next to Jeremy.

"What about security cameras?" he whispered.

"Damn!" she whispered back. "I didn't think of that."

He wrung his hands. "We don't have to worry about cameras between the condo and the garage, since we have her covered up, but what about in the garage? How do we get her from the cart into the car?"

"Let's move her back inside while we think about this."

They wrestled the cart back into the hallway and shut the front door.

"We have to find out from Kenny about the cameras," she said.

"But how?"

She considered for a moment, then said, "I'll ask him. I'll tell him Marilee is nervous about security after the bookstore attack—that she's relieved that at least the police have video the event, and she wonders if Eden Beach has security video."

Jeremy nodded. "Yeah, that's good." After a pause, he added reluctantly, "Want me to go?"

Jeremy's eyes were bloodshot, his face a pasty shade not so different from Marilee's, and the tremor in his hands had gotten worse. Jeanette didn't know what she looked like, but it had to be better than Jeremy. "No, I'll go. I'm more used to dealing with him. You stay here and keep thinking about where we can take her."

It took Jeanette less than ten minutes to complete the assignment and return to the condo.

"How did it go?" asked Jeremy, who hadn't moved from right inside the front door.

"He was very helpful once I woke him up," she muttered. "He says there are cameras covering all the elevator lobbies, and the doors to the stairwells. Nothing in the garage."

"That's good."

"Then he said it was a good safeguard as long as Marilee was planning to stay through the winter. I asked him why, and he said that if a tenant is away for a while and then comes back and finds their unit has been broken into, the video usually isn't helpful because they only keep the recordings for twenty-four hours." She kneaded her hands. "If we can make it seem as if Marilee is in the condo for a few more days, then there won't be any video evidence that she didn't leave on her own."

"But what about her plan to come to Downingtown?"

Once again fighting down her frustration with Jeremy's sudden helplessness, Jeanette thought for a moment. "I'll bet she was lapping up all that sympathy on her Facebook page, and people wouldn't feel as sorry for her if they knew she was out and about. I'm guessing she wouldn't have mentioned the Downingtown plan to anyone. I didn't mention it while we were in Virginia Beach. Did you?"

"No."

"And if she—or we—did mention it to someone, we'll just say she changed her mind. That wouldn't surprise anyone, considering how weird her behavior has been lately."

Jeremy ran his fingers through his hair. "Yeah, you're right. Okay, let's do it."

They maneuvered the cart out of the condo once again and, as they wheeled it toward the elevator, Jeanette realized she hadn't heard the *thump THUMP* noise in the condo tonight. Just as well—she'd rather not run into nosy neighbors making a rare visit to Eden Beach in the dead of winter.

When they reached the ground level lobby, they wheeled the cart out of the elevator. They had almost reached the door to the parking garage when she heard Kenny's voice.

"That's quite a load you've got there!"

She turned to see Kenny coming out from behind the security desk and crossing the lobby toward them.

"More books?" called Kenny. "Mrs. Forsythe's hand must be killing her from signing all those books."

"Yeah, I'm sure she could use a rest," said Jeremy. He was obviously trying for a jovial tone, but when the words were out of his mouth, he blanched and looked toward Jeanette, panicked.

"You go ahead and take the books to the car," Jeanette said to him.

Jeremy stood rooted to the spot.

"Go," she said more forcefully.

Jeremy snapped out of his trance. He pushed the cart through the doors to the garage just as Kenny reached Jeanette.

"Kenny, can you check to make sure there's no mail for Marilee?" Anything that kept Kenny away from the glass doors to the garage seemed like a good idea.

"Just checked this morning—nothing new for her."

"She says she's missing a letter from her publisher. Let's make sure it didn't fall out of the mailbox onto the floor. Or maybe got into another tenant's mailbox."

She followed a grumbling Kenny back to the security desk. When he disappeared into the area that gave Eden Beach staff access to tenants' mailboxes, Jeanette checked out the view into the garage. She could just see the front of the CR-V, but not the back, where she hoped Jeremy was getting Marilee into the trunk.

After a few minutes, Kenny returned, still irritated. "Nothing on the floor. Nothing in the other mailboxes."

"Okay, thanks for checking," she said, and hurried across the lobby and through the doors to the garage.

When she reached the CR-V, Jeremy was standing next to the hatch, open to reveal an empty trunk. Jeanette could see a bit of quilt underneath the boxes in the cart.

"Couldn't you get her into the car?" she asked.

"I didn't know if he could see me from in there."

Jeanette grabbed the partially full box of books and dumped it into the trunk. "He can't see us from the desk. Just hurry."

As Jeanette positioned herself to lift Marilee's blanket-wrapped form out of the cart, her mouth twisted at the thought that Kenny's bad back and natural unhelpfulness might be their salvation.

31

Ann, Mike, and Scott stood around the table in the Ann Kinnear Sensing office in the big house. On top of the table were a bottle of Mahalo Sapele, three partially consumed glasses of wine, and a couple of the boxes that Ann had been storing at Mike and Scott's townhouse. One was labeled *Paintings*, the other *Misc*.

"I always loved this one," said Scott, looking down at an item from the *Paintings* box. He turned it toward Ann. "What flower is this?"

She glanced up from the *Misc* box to an oil painting, about the size of a hardcover book, of a star-shaped white flower sporting curling white tendrils on each petal. "Buckbean." She shook her head. "Man, it seems like a whole other life when I painted that." She returned her attention to the *Misc* box, her thoughts turning melancholy at the memory of scouting the woods around her Adirondack cabin with her dog Beau, looking for subjects for the paintings she sold through gift shops in the area. Beau's spirit was still back at the cabin, keeping company with another of the woods' ghostly inhabitants: an old woman Ann suspected had haunted the area for centuries. Ann was glad Beau had found a companion after his death, but her heart still ached when she thought of him.

"Let's try that one on the top shelf," said Mike of the painting.

As Scott arranged it in the cabinet of curiosities, Mike peered over Ann's shoulder into the *Misc* box. "Anything in there you want to display?"

Ann held up a brass tube. It looked like a telescope, but when she held it up to her eye, the view was a kaleidoscopic display of geometric colors and lights.

"Dad gave you that, right?" asked Mike.

"Yeah," she said, panning the view across the room.

"Not really related to your work," he said. "Maybe you'd want to have that at the Curragh."

"It would look nice next to the painting of the buckbean, though," said Scott.

"I agree," said Ann, handing him the kaleidoscope, which he arranged next to the painting.

They had returned to sifting through the contents of the boxes when Scott cocked his head and asked, "Is anyone else in the house?"

"Not that I know of," said Mike, unwrapping another painting and holding it out at arm's length to examine it. "Why?"

Scott stepped to the open door to the hallway and looked toward the front of the house. "I thought I heard something."

"Like what?" asked Ann, pulling a somewhat battered white teddy bear from the *Misc* box.

"Like a door closing. Did we lock the front door?"

Ann looked up. "I don't think so."

Mike set aside the painting he was holding. "I'll check to make sure it's locked."

"I'll come with you," said Scott.

Ann looked from Mike to Scott. "You think this is a group effort?"

Scott shrugged. "Can't hurt." He disappeared into the hall, followed by Mike.

Ann put the bear back in the box and hurried after them. Just as she stepped out of the office, she heard a thunk, and the tiny swirl of air that suggested that a door had been opened and closed.

"I heard that," she exclaimed as all three broke into a jog toward the front door.

When they reached the deserted entrance hall, Mike opened the door and stepped outside. Scott and Ann followed, and the three peered into the darkness.

"Anybody see anything?" asked Mike.

"No," said Scott. "Any chance it was Niall or Harkin?" he asked Ann.

"I don't think Niall can leave the Ark, and I think Harkin's gone for good. Plus," she added, "I don't think either of them would be playing hide-and-seek with us."

"Maybe we just didn't latch the door," suggested Scott, "and the wind pushed it open and then sucked it closed."

"Could be," said Mike, still scanning the drive.

"Well, in any case, let's not go running off into the night to investigate," said Scott. He glanced at his watch. "I have an early shift tomorrow, so we should probably head home anyway."

"Sounds good to me," said Mike.

"Me, too," said Ann.

They stepped inside, Scott locking the door behind them, and returned to the office to put on their coats.

Ann reached into the *Misc* box and retrieved the bear. "This *is* coming to the Curragh."

When they stepped outside, Scott checked that the latch

had caught and that the door was locked, then they climbed into Audrey the Audi. Although the walk from the big house to the Curragh was short, the wind was gusting and the temperature was dropping, and Ann was glad she didn't have to walk.

As they neared the darkened Curragh, Mike said, "You should leave an outside light on—you wouldn't want to trip in the dark."

"Yeah, that's a good idea."

"Did you lock *your* door?" asked Scott.

She grimaced. "Probably not."

Mike pulled Audrey into the parking area so that its headlights illuminated the path to the front door, then he and Scott insisted on accompanying her inside. The three checked the small building—sitting area, kitchen, bathroom, and bedroom—then Mike and Scott left for West Chester.

Still holding the teddy bear, she returned to the bedroom and propped it up against a pillow. She stepped back, inordinately pleased by the effect. She had rented the Curragh fully furnished and decorated by Rowan's Aunt Nola, and it had always felt like the visitor accommodation it had been before she moved in. But the bear made it seem more like home.

32

As Jeremy drove north on the nearly deserted Coastal Highway, Jeanette got out her phone, opened the GPS app, and tapped in a request for directions from Ocean City to Downingtown. Then she zoomed in and followed the route north, dragging the map down with a trembling finger.

From Ocean City north to Rehoboth, Delaware, the highway ran along a narrow strip of land that in places was barely wider than the length of a football field. A preserve near Indian River inlet attracted her attention, but a grid of what must be residential streets was too nearby. The Prime Hook Wildlife Refuge? She zoomed in. It was riddled with small ponds—perhaps not a bad resting place for Marilee, but it seemed too likely that she or Jeremy would blunder into a marshy area and not be able to make it out. She scrolled a little further and winced as Slaughter Beach came into view. The names got worse further north, where a turnoff at Little Heaven would have taken them to the North Murderkill Hundred.

She looked over at Jeremy, who was staring resolutely ahead, hands white-knuckled on the wheel.

"Did you have any ideas yet for—you know—a location?" she asked.

He shook his head.

She also turned her gaze ahead, where objects swept into the periphery of the headlights' beams and then disappeared before she could identify them. "Considering the number of times I've come down here, I don't know the area very well. Maybe we need to consider something closer to home."

After a moment, he said, "Yeah, I think you're right." He groaned. "Plus, we need equipment. A flashlight." After a pause, he added, "Shovels. Maybe even picks—the ground's going to be frozen."

"There's nowhere that will be open this late," said Jeanette, a thread of panic ratcheting up her heartbeat.

"I don't want a record of us buying shovels around the time the police might be able to tell she went missing," said Jeremy roughly. "I think we need to get that stuff from home."

She took a deep breath. "You're right. Let's do that."

They stopped at home just long enough to pull into the garage and load the needed equipment into the back seat and to replace their shoes with heavy, waterproof boots. As they drove to the spot they had agreed upon, Jeanette fashioned a screen for the flashlight using a paper takeout menu she found in the glove compartment.

The site they had chosen was only about a dozen miles from their home: a community park they had visited several times in warmer weather. It was located on a property housing the remains of an old mill, and volunteers were carving out a few dirt paths through the hilly, densely wooded ground. Not only were Jeanette and Jeremy fairly sure there wouldn't be anything as sophisticated as video surveillance of the site, but its parking lot was shared by a block of row houses, originally built for the mill workers, located across the two-lane road. The CR-V would attract no attention among the other vehicles.

The choice seemed even better when they reached the location. The only illumination was from a solitary light that stood next to the short bridge spanning the creek that had at one time provided power to the mill.

They parked in the darkest section of lot. When Jeanette climbed out of the CR-V, the wind brought tears to her eyes, the cold freezing them before they could fall.

Jeremy lifted the blanket-wrapped form carefully from the trunk, then waded across the shallow creek to stay out of the pool of light on the bridge. Jeanette followed, carrying the shovels, a pick, the flashlight, and a tarp.

By the light of the screened flashlight, they located one of the rough dirt paths sloping up steeply from the creek. They followed it for a hundred yards to where it began its loop back to the parking area. The last time she and Jeremy had been in the park had been in August, and she remembered what a pleasant relief the cool, shaded path had been on that hot day.

"How about here?" she whispered, gesturing into the woods.

"Yes, this is nice," he said between panting breaths. "Let's get off the path, just in case someone decides to take a midnight stroll. Although I can't imagine it, in this cold. Try to push the branches out of the way so we don't break them."

She nodded and led the way into the woods. Once they were screened from the path by the trees, Jeremy stayed put, still holding Marilee, while Jeanette looked around for a suitable burial spot.

A few dozen yards further on, she found a round spot free of branches or leaves, which she suspected a deer had been using as its bed. A final resting place made by a deer—she'd prefer it for herself over a manicured and sterile cemetery plot, and she thought Jeremy would prefer it for himself as well. She felt the knot in her gut tighten, knowing that Marilee would disagree.

She backtracked to where Jeremy stood and led him back to the spot.

~

JEANETTE WOULD NEVER HAVE IMAGINED that digging a hole would be the most strenuous physical activity she had ever undertaken.

Jeremy at first insisted that it be six feet deep, but by the time they hit four feet, even he seemed to rethink that goal. They settled on five and arranged Marilee in her blanket shroud on the carefully leveled and smoothed bottom. When it came time to refill the hole, Jeremy began to cry, and Jeanette suggested he return to the car and let her finish the job. He dragged the back of his dirt-grimed hand across his eyes, shook his head, and began sprinkling minute quantities of dirt into the hole. When his back was turned to collect another spoonful of dirt on his shovel, Jeanette tried to get in two heaping shovelfuls.

By the time they had filled the hole, there was a hint of dawn glimmering in the treetops. They scattered some leaves over the disturbed ground and dragged a couple of branches over it, Jeanette feeling vaguely guilty that they had ruined the deer's bed.

Then they went home, showered, and changed into clean clothes. They stuffed their soiled clothes into a garbage bag, which they dropped into the dumpster behind the pharmacy, knowing it would be emptied later that morning.

When, a few minutes after the official opening time, Jeanette went to the front entrance to open the pharmacy, she saw one of their regular customers shivering just outside the door. She ushered the woman in.

"Miriam, I'm so sorry to keep you waiting. Jeremy and I were ... a bit detained. Family matters."

Miriam unwrapped her scarf from around her face and rolled her eyes. "I know how that goes." She stuffed her gloves in her pocket. "I had a couple of questions about my prescription I was hoping you or Jeremy could answer."

"Of course," said Jeanette, leading her to the pharmacy counter at the back of the store. Through the door to the back room, she could see Jeremy sitting on the desk chair, elbows on knees, head hanging down.

"Jeremy," she called, "Miriam was waiting for us to open. She has some questions about her prescription."

Jeremy roused himself, stood, and stepped out of the back room. "Hey, Miriam, sorry about the late opening—"

"It's no problem," said Miriam, sorting through the contents of her purse. "I know it's in here," she muttered to herself, then, in a louder voice, said, "Jeanette explained. Family matters. I knew if you two were late to open, it would be for a good reason."

33

Joe Booth texted Ann that he had an update on the Princeton PD investigation of Jock Quine's death, and they opened a video call. Ann settled down on the couch in the Curragh's sitting area. Joe appeared on the screen against a background of metal file cabinets and off-screen conversation—the Chicago station where he was on temporary assignment.

"I talked with the detective in charge of the investigation," Joe began, his tone sour. "Withers. He's about a year from official retirement, and as far as I can tell, he's already retired in place. They hadn't realized that the bullets in the drawer didn't fit the gun in the drawer. The gun was a .380 ACP. Its predecessor, a Browning 1910, was very popular in the early to mid-1900s. It's the same gun Gavrilo Princip used to kill Franz Ferdinand. Al Capone and Bonnie Parker used it as well. And the nine-millimeter bullets that were in the drawer are too big for the magazine."

"Does Withers have a theory about why the wrong bullets were in the drawer?" asked Mike.

"He thinks Jock just got the wrong bullets for the gun. And

it's not an entirely outlandish theory. The .380 ACP was also called a 'nine-millimeter short.'"

"Interesting." She frowned. "If *I* were looking for bullets for a gun called a nine-millimeter short, I might buy nine-millimeter bullets, but Jock Quine wouldn't have. This is a guy who loved to hunt. He went on safaris. He shot bears. He'd know what kind of bullets to get for his gun." She considered for a moment, then continued. "I've been assuming that the sounds Jock described as metal against metal were the intruder trying to load Jock's gun with the bullets Jock had in the drawer. But maybe those weren't Jock's bullets. Maybe the intruder brought bullets, and he brought the wrong ones. Jock probably talked with people about his gun collection. What if he mentioned to someone that he had a 'nine-millimeter short' and they thought it would take nine-millimeter bullets?"

"You think he was killed by someone he knew?"

"Not necessarily someone he knew *well*. Jock didn't get a good look at the intruder, but he did hear his voice, and I think he would have recognized it if the intruder was someone he knew well. But why would the intruder come with his own bullets? And why would he be trying to fit them into Jock's gun?"

"Maybe he planned to take the gun with him and wanted it loaded for his getaway," Joe speculated. "Although it's hard to explain why he would want to take the gun with him—he already had a gun. And if he wanted a gun, why didn't he take it and leave the bullets behind? He could always get the right bullets later."

Ann sighed. "I don't know."

They were both silent for a few beats, then Ann asked, "What's the Princeton PD's theory about why the gun was unloaded? They don't have to rely on Jock telling me he never kept his guns unloaded if they were intended for protection. The news articles quote a lot of his friends saying that it would be uncharacteristic. What does Withers say about that?"

"I asked him about that. I got a lecture about the dangers of storing a loaded gun in the home."

Ann rolled her eyes. "Jeez, you're right—he doesn't sound very helpful." After a moment, she asked, "And I guess you couldn't ask about the reference to Poindexter?"

He shook his head. "I couldn't think of a reason I could give him for the question. Any further thoughts on who Poindexter could be?"

"No. I didn't get any hits on searches on *jock quine poindexter* or any of the variations I could think of. If it's a nickname and not a real name, it could be anyone. And there are at least two bookish people who might have heard Jock mention he had a gun called a 'nine-millimeter short': Jock seems to have tried to involve Alec in his interests, so it's possible he talked about guns with him. And Darren worked with Jock in that room. Hell, he helped plot out the Robert Wolfram novels there. It's more than possible that Jock talked about the gun with Darren, or even showed it to him."

"But Alec and Darren both have alibis, right? I understand they were at the Harrison & John event in New York."

"Yeah."

"Although it doesn't mean they didn't hire someone to kill Jock," said Joe.

"Maybe."

"You don't think so?"

After another moment of consideration, she said, "Darren seems to genuinely miss Jock. And why wouldn't he? He was benefitting from Jock's success. But it's always possible that things weren't going as well between them as Darren would have us believe."

"How about Alec? Maybe he wanted to hurry up his inheritance ... including, I suppose, taking over the Wolfram thrillers."

"Greed is always a good motive, but I get the impression Jock might have given Alec whatever he wanted without having to be killed for it ... and would have been happy to have taken him on as a co-author, too. Jock was pretty excited to hear Alec was taking over the series." She heaved a sigh. "And setting your dad up to get shot because you don't like his taste in home décor or don't want to go on any more safaris with him seems extreme, even for Alec Quine." She shook her head. "I have no idea, but I'll keep thinking."

34

Throughout the day following the burial of Marilee's body, Jeanette or Jeremy would occasionally beckon the other into the pharmacy's back room to whisper frantically about an aspect of the situation they had overlooked in their initial panic.

Should they do something with Marilee's car? No, they had had enough trouble deciding how to handle her body—they had no idea how to dispose of a car. They also agreed that leaving Marilee's phone in the condo, assuming it was still there, was the best idea for similar reasons. They didn't know how to guarantee it couldn't be tracked and didn't want to search for the answer online. In fact, the fewer online searches about anything related to the situation, the better.

Should they remove some of Marilee's clothes and a suitcase from the condo so that, when they eventually reported her disappearance, it looked as if Marilee's departure had been planned? Jeanette pointed out that they couldn't risk having the police get their hands on security video of one of them leaving the condo with a suitcase, and neither of them wanted to use an Eden Beach cart again to try to sneak something out to the CR-V. Maybe it would be useful if the police thought Marilee had left her condo on what she expected to be a quick outing.

That evening, Jeremy hurried into the kitchen, where Jeanette was thawing two servings of turkey chili for dinner. "We forgot about the books!"

"What books?"

"We were supposed to bring the signed books for the New York store down to the security desk for his driver to pick up."

Jeanette groaned. "Oh, no." She got her phone out of her pocket and checked her texts and email. "Nothing from Ezra about it. I'm going to call him."

"Shouldn't we let sleeping dogs lie?"

She grimaced. "Not sleeping dogs who are as vindictive as Ezra. Let's do whatever we can not to make him madder than he already is."

"What are you going to say to him?"

She thought for a moment, then said, "I'll tell him Marilee couldn't sign the books because her wrist was bothering her." After a moment, she added, "Although sending him a text might be less irritating for both of us than a phone call."

"Both good ideas."

She tapped out the message to Ezra, then slipped her phone into her pocket. "I'll let you know what I hear," she said to Jeremy.

He nodded and returned to the living room.

Jeanette's phone rang a minute later.

"Hello, Ezra," she answered.

"Good thing I checked with Eden Beach security to see if the books were ready before I sent the truck down. When I heard they weren't at the desk, I figured this was just another example of Marilee's disregard for her contractual obligations."

"It's not disregard for her contractual obligations. I told you—her wrist is bothering her. She's been signing a lot of books lately." She drew a deep breath. "She doesn't want to sign any more."

"Doesn't want to sign any more ever? Or just until her wrist recovers?"

Jeanette closed her eyes against the vision of Marilee's gray-faced body, stiff on the study sofa. "I'd say ever."

Ezra met her update with silence. Jeanette tried not to dwell on whatever legal machinations he might be contemplating.

When he finally spoke, his voice was frosty. "If she promises not to advertise this latest trauma on social media—although why I should believe any promises she makes at this point, I don't know—you can sign them for her."

Jeanette was about to protest, then realized how laughable it was for her to complain about Ezra's minor deception. "Yes, all right."

"You know how she signs them? *To a Berry special reader, with my Berry best wishes.*"

Jeanette failed to suppress a manic snort of laughter. Marilee could hardly have found a more perfect example to encapsulate everything she had objected to about the genre that had made her author career.

"The readers love it," said Ezra severely.

Jeanette cleared her throat. "I'm sure they do."

"When will they be ready?"

"I'll go down to Ocean City tomorrow."

"I don't feel like sending the truck back down. Just drop them off at the post office." He ended the call.

35

Ann was just finishing her second cup of coffee and contemplating what her plans for the day would be—maybe a quick flight out to Cape May—when Mike called.

"What's up?" she answered.

"Can you come up to the big house?"

"You're there?"

"Yeah—I came over to do some work in the office."

When he didn't offer more of an explanation for his request, she said, "Okay, I'll be there in a couple of minutes."

She pulled on her parka, climbed the drive, and made her way to the office. There she found Mike, Del, and Rowan, who had Rose propped on her hip.

"What's up?"

"We think there was a break-in last night," said Rowan, her expression worried.

"You *think* there was a break-in?"

"I came over here to get things set up for videoconferences," said Mike. "I was working in here for a little while when I realized that your painting of the buckbean and the kaleidoscope were missing from the cabinet. At first, I thought maybe Nola had second thoughts about us having the cabinet in here—after all, it is hers—and had taken the stuff out. I went to check with Rowan, and she called Nola and Nola said she wasn't responsible. Then Rowan, Del, and I were poking around, thinking maybe—I don't know—one of the construction guys had moved the stuff? Then we noticed that the lock on the back door was broken."

Ann grimaced. "So someone robbed the place? What else did they get?"

"As far as we can tell, nothing else," said Mike.

"We even checked with the construction crew," said Del. "They leave stuff here that would be worth a lot to someone, and it looks like it's all accounted for."

Ann cast her eyes toward the cabinet. "But why would anyone break in and take just those things? It's not like they're worth much." Thinking of the kaleidoscope, which had been a present from her father, she added, "Not worth much to anyone else, in any case."

"We have no idea," said Rowan.

Mike said to Ann, "Remember that Scott thought he heard someone in the house the night before last, when we were working in the office? Maybe someone showed up, thought the house was empty, and then ran away when he heard us."

"Yeah, it's possible," she said. She turned to Rowan and Del. "Was anyone at the house last night?"

"No," said Rowan. "Del and Rose and I were at the Unionville house." She adjusted Rose's tiny sweater. "We were going to get an alarm system installed here but hadn't gotten around to it yet."

Del shook his head. "You can bet that getting that done went right to the top of the list."

Del and Rowan left to make another inspection tour of the house.

"You know what this makes me think of?" said Mike.

"An overenthusiastic fan of Ann Kinnear Sensing?" asked Ann, trying for a light tone. There were always a few people who were a little more interested in Ann and her ability than she was comfortable with.

"No. It reminds me of the break-in at Jock Quine's house and the theft of his ivory collection."

Ann felt her face grow pale. "You think whoever broke into Jock's house broke into the big house and stole my painting?"

"I don't know ... but doesn't it seem weirdly similar?"

"Well, except for the fact that Jock's collection was worth hundreds of thousands of dollars and my painting is probably worth less than a hundred. And," she added, "for the fact that no one died here."

"Should we alert Joe?"

After a moment, she nodded. "Yeah, I think so."

36

When Jeanette arrived at Eden Beach to discharge the assignment from Ezra and got one of the carts out of the cart corral, she found herself hoping that it wasn't the one she and Jeremy had used to transport Marilee's body. She put the boxes they had used to hide Marilee's body into it—she might as well sign those books along with the rest—then wheeled the cart into the lobby and over to the security desk, where Kenny sat.

"Hey, Miss Forsythe," he said.

"Kenny, my name is Jeanette Frobisher. Just call me Jeanette. Please."

"Sure. Sure thing."

"Are there any special deliveries for Marilee?"

He drew his brows together. "What do you mean?"

"What do you mean, *what do I mean?*" she snapped. "I don't want to have to make a second trip up to the condo. If she has any special deliveries—or any mail at all, for that matter—I want to take it up with me now."

"There might be something." Kenny levered himself up from his chair. "Hold on. I'll check."

He disappeared behind the bank of tenant mailboxes and emerged a half minute later. He handed over a small pile of marketing fliers, business letters, and one padded envelope.

"Thanks," said Jeanette.

As she walked toward the elevator, Kenny called after her. "It would be good if Mrs. Forsythe could pick up her own mail."

"No kidding," she called back over her shoulder.

As the elevator rose, she sorted quickly through the mail. The business letters looked like utility or credit card bills. Would she and Jeremy need to cover Marilee's expenses, at least until they reported her missing? The sender's name on the padded envelope's USPS label was *KAK Novelties*. That seemed like something they could safely ignore.

The door dinged open at 14, and as Jeanette passed through the elevator lobby toward the walkway, she thought self-consciously of the video cameras recording her presence. When she reached the condo, she unlocked the door, retrieved the boxes from the cart, and stepped inside.

She stood in the hallway, from which she could see only the living room couch and, through the sliding glass doors to the balcony, a slice of gray ocean. Her stomach roiled. She didn't want to walk down the hall to the living room, where Marilee, much to Jeanette's surprise, had been practicing yoga. She wanted even less to cross the living room to the study, where Marilee had died. But she had to spend at least some time in the condo to keep up the pretense that she was visiting her mother-in-law.

Taking a deep breath, she strode down the hall to the living room. Before she could cross to the study, the blinking red light of the answering machine on Marilee's phone caught her eye, and she thought back to the message she had left as she and Jeremy approached Ocean City: *We're just calling to let you know that we're about an hour away, so you should take the sedative now.*

She deleted the message, realizing that if she had left that message on Marilee's cell phone voicemail rather than the landline answering machine, she would have had no way to access it. She and Jeremy were lucky that Marilee had insisted she keep the answering machine so she could screen calls. Jeanette's heart thudded at a possible catastrophe averted only by the chance of her noticing the blinking message light, and she wondered what other evidence she and Jeremy were leaving for the police to find once they reported Marilee missing.

She entered the study. Although it was mid-day, the curtains were drawn, as they had been when she and Jeremy discovered Marilee's body. She put the boxes down on the floor and turned on a light. She scanned the room, trying to see if there was anything she should do to disguise what had happened there. The quilt draped over the back of the couch hung slightly askew, something Marilee would never have tolerated, and Jeanette forced herself to straighten it.

The books Jeremy had unpacked were still on the desk, arranged as Marilee had directed: unsigned books on the left, a cleared space on the right to stack the signed books. Jeanette went to the desk and flipped open one of the books. It was unsigned. She felt a twinge of resentment bubble up, quickly replaced by guilt. Despite Ezra's skepticism, Marilee might have intended to sign the books before Jeanette and Jeremy returned to the condo on their way back from Virginia Beach. She might have died before she had the chance. Jeanette took a deep, shuddering breath, fighting off an image of her mother-in-law's death.

She opened the drapes, so she'd at least be able to enjoy the view, then pulled out the desk chair and sat. She pulled a black felt-tip pen from the holder on the desk, then picked up a book from a stack on her left and opened it to the title page. She wished she had a sample of Marilee's handwriting, then decided it wouldn't have made a difference. In the unlikely event that a reader identified the writing as belonging to someone other than Marilee, their complaint would go to Ezra, and he could decide how to address it.

She drew in a deep breath and wrote out the inscription.

To a Berry special reader, with my Berry best wishes.

The signature was a bit wobbly, but the happy Berry fan might assume it was due to poor Marilee Forsythe's unfortunate re-injury of her wrist during the still-unsolved bookstore attack.

Jeanette closed the book and moved it to the right side of the desk.

She imagined her dead mother-in-law's eyes boring accusingly into her back.

~

JEANETTE FINISHED MORE QUICKLY than she expected. She briefly considered spending a little more time in the condo, maybe catching up on her recently neglected study of *Foye's*, but she had no wish to stay in the condo a moment longer than was necessary.

She closed the drapes and packed up the books. She decided to stage them in the guest room next to the bay-side entrance—that would require the door to be propped open for less time than if she had to carry the boxes from the breakfast bar to the cart. She walked down the hall to the guest room, opened the door, and stepped inside.

The last time she had been in it, it had been furnished with a pair of duvet-covered twin beds, a bookshelf, a dresser topped with a spray of silk flowers, and a hooked rug depicting a beach scene. But Marilee had done some redecorating.

The bookshelf was still there, but the beds, dresser, and rug were gone. In their places were a heavy wooden desk and a worn leather swivel chair. Next to the desk was a metal file cabinet—not a flimsy modern one, but a mid-century version that looked like it could survive a bomb blast. Movie posters covered the walls: *The Maltese Falcon*, *Chinatown*, *L. A. Confidential*, *Se7en*, along with blown-up covers of thriller novels by Lee Child, Dennis Lehane, and even Lara Seaford, the author Marilee had mentioned to Ezra.

Jeanette thought back to the changes she had noticed in Marilee over the previous months: an enthusiasm for yoga so great that she had cleared her living room of most of its furniture to practice it, the adoption of uncharacteristically dark clothing, a switch of theme to the violence, profanity, and sex she could never put in her cozies. Marilee had clearly been remaking her persona long before she proposed the idea of a thriller novel to Ezra.

Jeanette backed out of the room, closing the door behind her. She didn't want to spend any more time in Marilee's condo, seeing sides of her mother-in-law's life that Marilee had obviously wanted to keep private. She'd get the books down to the car and head home. If Kenny noticed her visit was shorter than usual, it meant he was a more observant guard than she had ever given him credit for—but she didn't expect to be proven wrong on that front.

37

Darren Van Osten sat at one of the vinyl-covered tables in the VFW hall in Rahway, New Jersey, with the remains of his buffet dinner on the paper plate in front of him. He joined in the applause as Maude Solas of *Latent Prints* announced the winner in the Best Short Fiction category and then posed with the winner as a volunteer photographer took a cell phone picture. As the smiling and blushing recipient returned to his seat, Maude announced, "Next up, the award for Best Debut Novel."

As she read through the list of nominees, Darren's fingers fidgeted beneath the table, shredding his paper napkin. He was somewhat embarrassed to be this excited at the possibility that a client's book might win such a modest award, but Maude's picks often presaged the winners of more prestigious awards, such as GothamCon's.

"And the winner is ..." Maude opened the envelope. "... Lara Seaford, for *Darkest Before Death*!"

Trying to moderate his grin, Darren stood and wended his way through the tables to the podium, to the accompaniment of applause. He shook Maude's hand and took the award, then stepped to the lectern.

"Good evening. I am clearly *not* Lara Seaford." He paused for the ripple of polite laughter. "I'm Darren Van Osten, and I am fortunate to be Ms. Seaford's editor. You may already know that she is a very private person and has retained her anonymity quite successfully—even from me." The expressions of the audience members shifted from polite to attentive. "I've never met Ms. Seaford in person, and we have only communicated via email. And even the excitement of a nomination for Best Debut Novel from one of the premier magazines in the thriller genre," he nodded his acknowledgement to Maude, "was not enough to convince her to reveal her identity." He smiled. "Ms. Seaford chooses to be thrilling and mysterious even in her own life."

Light laughter from the audience.

"But I'm sure I speak for Lara Seaford, and for myself, when I say that we couldn't be more excited for *Darkest Before Death* to have achieved this recognition from *Latent Prints*. Thank you."

He stepped away from the lectern to enthusiastic applause but stopped at Maude's voice coming through the tinny speakers of the sound system.

"Darren, I would be remiss if I didn't ask the question on all our minds. Can we expect more thrilling novels from Lara Seaford?"

Darren stepped back to the microphone. "I understand from Ms. Seaford that she has a draft of the sequel to *Darkest Before Death*—" he enjoyed the stir of excitement in the audience, "—and I can assure you that I am just as anxious to get my hands on it as you are."

38

The day after her trip to Ocean City, Jeanette managed to maintain her composure as she staffed the register at the pharmacy, but as soon as Jeremy flipped the sign to *Closed* and locked the door, she burst into tears.

Jeremy led her to the back room, lowered her onto a chair, then knelt beside her and put his arm around her shoulders. "I suppose it would be silly to ask you what's wrong," he said, trying for a wan smile.

"Jer, I don't think I can keep up the charade," she managed between sobs. "This waiting to report Marilee missing—I can't stand it."

"Let's figure out the timing." He pulled a chair over and sat down beside her. "It's seven o'clock now. You got home from Ocean City around five o'clock yesterday, which means you must have left Eden Beach around two. You said Kenny told you they keep video for twenty-four hours. That means that if we called the police now, it would leave five hours between when you left the condo and the time of the earliest security video coverage. That's the time she could have left the condo on her own."

"And they probably won't check the video immediately, which will mean more time when she could have left."

He ran his fingers through his hair. "I had hoped for longer, but all this cloak-and-dagger stuff is wearing on me, too. But how do we know Kenny was telling the truth about how long they keep the video?"

Jeanette gnawed a thumbnail. "We could call Kenny and tell him we can't get in touch with Marilee and ask him to review the security video to see if she left the condo."

"I don't know, Jen. It makes sense to keep our story as simple as possible. This seems like it's introducing more complexity—"

"Jeremy!" she almost yelled. "I can't keep pretending that we think she's at the condo and still alive!"

He raised a hand placatingly. "Okay, okay. We'll call Kenny—but let's postpone it to as late as possible."

After some further consultation and refinement of the plan on their drive from the pharmacy to their house, Jeremy placed a call to Marilee's land line and then to her cell phone: just a son checking on his mother's well-being. An hour later, Jeanette made the same calls: the dutiful daughter-in-law helping her husband check on his mother. An hour after that, Jeremy made another set of calls: a son increasingly concerned about a mother who had recently been traumatized by an unexplained attack. During this time, they drank a bottle of wine as an excuse for not being able to drive down to Ocean City when Marilee was found to be missing. It had the added benefit of calming Jeanette's nerves.

Finally, Jeanette called the Eden Beach security desk.

"Kenny, Jeremy and I have been trying to get in touch with Marilee and she's not answering. I thought maybe the security video would show if she left. I left her condo yesterday around two. Could you find me leaving on the video and then check after that to see if it shows her leaving the condo?"

"No can do," said Kenny. "Like I told you, we only keep video for twenty-four hours. We wouldn't have any video before about nine last night."

Jeremy, who was listening in on the call, gave Jeanette a thumbs up and she let out the breath she had been holding.

They accepted Kenny's grudging offer to go up to Marilee's condo to knock on the door—evidently even Eden Beach management allowed a bending of rules if a resident's well-being was involved—and gave him the okay to go into the condo if he didn't get an answer.

"Please call us back as soon as you've checked," said Jeanette, earning a grumbled affirmation from Kenny.

When Kenny called them back a short time later, reporting that he had received no answer to his knock and had found the condo empty when he let himself in, Jeremy placed a call to Detective Morganstein and reported Marilee Forsythe missing.

~

THEY GOT the follow-up call from Morganstein an hour later.

"I'm at the Eden Beach condo now," said the detective. "No obvious signs of foul play. Could be she left on her own, although her purse and her phone are here. I know you're up in Pennsylvania, but could you come down and check out the condo? Let me know if anything's missing or out of the ordinary?"

Jeanette rubbed her fingers across her eyes. What was *not* out of the ordinary?

"I'm afraid we can't, at least not tonight," said Jeremy.

"We've had quite a lot of wine, and I wouldn't want to make the drive. Could we do a video call?"

They switched to video, and Morganstein made a tour of the condo. Jeanette sensed Jeremy tense when the detective reached the bay-side guest room, and she realized she had never described its transformation to him. She and Jeremy told Morganstein they saw nothing missing or out of place.

"The living room's a bit sparsely furnished," Morganstein said, "and two chairs that match the couch are out on the balcony."

"Yes, but it was like that when she was there," said Jeremy. They had agreed not to share any more information than was explicitly requested—for example, Marilee's explanation that she had cleared the room for yoga practice.

"Her disappearance puts a different spin on the bookstore attack," said the detective.

"You think the attacker might be involved in her disappearance?"

Jeanette was impressed at the bit of a tremor Jeremy introduced into his speech. Marilee wasn't the only person in the Frobisher family who had some acting chops.

"It's definitely worth looking into," said Morganstein. "We'll also put out the word to the public. We didn't get any useful leads on the bookstore attack, but maybe someone has seen Marilee—either alone or accompanied—since she left. And if the two of you could come down here tomorrow, you can take a closer look at the condo. We'll be dusting the condo for fingerprints, so it would also be helpful to get your prints for purposes of elimination. And if you don't have any objections, I'd like to take Ms. Forsythe's computer and phone—we might find something there."

"Of course," said Jeremy.

"I don't suppose you know the passwords?"

"No, sorry."

They agreed they would meet up with Morganstein in Ocean City the next day and ended the call.

"You did great, sweetheart," said Jeanette, squeezing his arm.

Jeremy downed a large swallow of wine. "What the hell is going on with the guest room? You didn't mention that to me."

"I'm sorry, I forgot. You remember how she always said her décor inspired her writing? She definitely decorated for cozies, at least until recently. I think when she started getting interested in thrillers, she wanted to do the same for that genre."

"Yeah, makes sense." He finished the glass of wine in a few swallows. "So Morganstein thinks the bookstore attacker kidnapped her."

"It seems like a logical conclusion." They sat in silence for a few moments, then Jeanette said, "In fact, what's to say that the bookstore attacker isn't involved? Not in taking her out of the condo, obviously, but for what happened to her?"

"He snuck in and ... did what?"

Jeanette shrugged, regretting that she had brought up the topic.

Jeremy stood and paced back and forth—a few steps each way in the small kitchen. "He didn't choke her—we would have seen marks on her neck. He didn't do anything that caused bleeding ..." He paused. "... at least on the areas not covered by her clothes." He stopped pacing. "We should have checked her more carefully."

"For what?"

"For wounds. For bruising on her body."

She stood and slipped her arm around his waist. "Jeremy, are you really saying that we should have examined your mother's body like some kind of amateur medical examiners before we decided what to do? That it would have been *conceivable* for us to do that in those circumstances?"

He stepped away from her. "Yes, Jeanette, I'm saying we should have examined her before we decided what to do. We just assumed ..." His voice trailed off.

"Assumed ... what?" she asked, her voice taut.

He was silent for a moment, then dropped back into his chair. "Jesus, I don't even remember what I assumed. I was in shock, I guess. All I could think about was that they would suspect we killed her to get her money, and to avoid having to repay the loan."

"And they *would* have suspected us," said Jeanette, remaining standing. "I don't think you were wrong about assuming that."

"It wasn't just me," he said, his voice strangely monotone. "I gathered you thought that as well."

Jeanette tried to keep her voice equally neutral. "It did seem like an obvious conclusion for the police to jump to."

Jeremy pressed his fingers to his eyes. "What if they find the guy from the bookstore and he can prove that he wasn't involved in Mom's disappearance? Maybe he can prove he was halfway across the country the whole time. Hell, maybe he committed some other crime, and he's been in jail."

"I suppose we still have the advantage that the longer they pursue him, the harder it will be to tie it to us. Security video gets deleted. Possible eyewitness memories get vague—"

Jeremy's expression tightened with concern. "Eyewitnesses? Who saw us?"

"No one that I know of. I wasn't thinking of anyone in particular, just the effect of time passing. Plus, just think about all the calls the police are going to get when they put out the request for information to the public. They'll be inviting a bunch of devoted mystery fans to speculate about the disappearance of their favorite author. Sorting through all those calls is going to take even more time." She sat down and squeezed Jeremy's arm again. "I think things are going as well for us as they could."

"Yeah, I guess we should feel lucky," he said bitterly.

Jeanette felt tears spring to her eyes. She clamped her lips closed against a retort.

"I suspect that this is going to result in another spike in Mom's book sales," Jeremy said morosely. "That ought to make Ezra happy."

"I don't believe that even Ezra is enough of a bastard to be happy to hear that Marilee has disappeared," Jeanette countered.

But as she said it, she realized that she could count on nothing she had believed to be true.

39

Darren had just gotten to his desk, having slept in after a late-night drive from Rahway back to Wilmington after the *Latent Prints* awards ceremony, when his phone rang: Bev Wang, an acquisitions editor at Harrison & John, the publisher of Jock's—or, he amended, Alec's—Robert Wolfram series.

"So, Darren," Bev said without preamble. "I hear congratulations are in order—you edited the Lara Seaford novel, right? I saw the photos from the *Latent Prints* awards ..." The pause was almost imperceptible. "... banquet, and you accepting for her for Best Debut. Very exciting. And Seaford mysteriously absent from the ceremony. Intriguing ... especially since Solas got you to admit that Seaford has written a follow-on."

"I think 'got me to admit' isn't quite right, but, yes, Lara told me her second book is almost ready for an edit."

"But you haven't seen it yet?"

"No."

"How much credence do you put in her claim that it's almost ready for an edit? You and I both know that authors tend to overstate the status of their manuscripts."

"She doesn't have much incentive to overstate the status. She's independently published, so she's only answerable to herself."

"Maybe she's a hard taskmaster, even to herself."

"Maybe."

"Well, you know her better than anyone, I suppose. H & J would like to talk to her about the sequel."

Darren sat forward. "Really?"

"Yes, really. But obviously the immediate challenge is finding a *way* to talk to her. Might you be able to help us with that?"

"I will certainly contact her right away and let her know of your interest."

"You could give me her email. I could try contacting her directly."

"She specifically asked me not to share her contact information with anyone. She's usually quite prompt in responding to my emails—I wouldn't be surprised if I heard back from her today, and I'll get her okay to put the two of you in touch."

"Okay, but I want to talk with her soon."

Darren suspected that Bev's hurry was fueled by her suspicion that H & J might not be the only publisher whose interest in Lara Seaford had been piqued by the *Latent Prints* award, not to mention the continuing brisk sales of *Darkest Before Death*. "I'll email her now."

They ended the call. Darren opened his last email from Lara and hit *Reply*.

Lara, exciting news—Harrison & John are interested in your follow-on to Darkest Before Death*! They seem to be in a bit of a hurry about getting in touch with you. I'd love to put you in direct touch with their acquisitions editor, Bev Wang. Might I give Bev your email address?*

Of course, if you prefer to keep your email confidential, I would be happy to act as your go-between, at least in the early stages of a negotiation (especially since I have years of experience with H & J through the Wolfram series).

He hit *Send* and sat back. If *Darkest Before Death* became a series, if H & J picked it up, and if they retained him as Lara's editor, it would go a long way to ensuring he could remain solvent ... and maybe more.

40

Jeremy emerged from the back room of the pharmacy, his phone to his ear. “Hold on, Detective Morganstein, I’ll have Jeanette on in just a moment.”

Jeanette’s heart skipped a beat. It had been two days since they had reported Marilee missing, and one day since they had driven down to Ocean City to re-confirm their report that nothing in the condo seemed to be missing and to provide their fingerprints for elimination purposes. The detective had warned them that with the lack of evidence, progress in the investigation of Marilee’s disappearance would likely be slow.

Jeremy scanned the store to confirm it was empty, then beckoned Jeanette into the back room. Tapping his phone to speaker, he put it on the counter.

“Okay, I have her here now,” he said. “Can you tell her what you told me?”

“Hello, Ms. Frobisher,” said Morganstein. “I was just telling your husband that we got the results back on the fingerprints we lifted from Ms. Forsythe’s condo. There were four sets of prints. We were able to eliminate your prints based on the samples you provided, and there's a set of prints that's all over the apartment that I think we can assume belong to Ms. Forsythe. But the fourth set belongs to a man named Randall Coombs." He paused. "Does that name ring a bell?"

"Not to me," said Jeremy.

"Not to me either," said Jeanette.

"Coombs spent some time in prison for theft and resisting arrest and got out about a year ago."

Jeanette's eyebrows shot up, and she met Jeremy's equally shocked gaze.

"We checked his apartment," continued Morganstein. "There was no one there, and the neighbors say they haven't seen him recently. We haven't been able to identify any friends or family—in the area or out of it—but we're still working to locate him. I'm going to text you his mug shot."

A moment later, a text pinged into Jeremy's phone.

Jeremy tapped the screen, then turned the phone so he and Jeanette could both see it.

"Does he look familiar to you?" asked Morganstein.

"I don't think so," said Jeanette uncertainly.

"Could it be the man who attacked Ms. Forsythe behind Oh Buoy Books?"

"I suppose it could be," she said.

"Mr. Coombs was five nine, about a hundred and sixty pounds."

"Yes, that sounds about right," she said, "but that describes a lot of people."

"Mr. Coombs suffered an injury to his leg in prison, which could explain the limp that we had initially chalked up to the scuffle outside the bookstore."

Jeanette noticed Jeremy nodding vigorously at her.

"Yes," she said, flustered, "that could explain it."

"Can you imagine any reason Ms. Forsythe would have invited Mr. Coombs into the condo? For example, I know that civilians sometimes do volunteer work at the prison where Coombs was incarcerated. Maybe Ms. Forsythe taught a writing class at the prison …?"

Jeremy's mouth twisted. "I hate to speak ill of—" Jeanette could tell by the way his face suddenly paled that he had almost said *the dead*. "—my mother, but she is not the type to be volunteering at a prison. I can't imagine that she knew this man."

"Actually," Jeanette said slowly, "there was that guy who was helping her move furniture out of the condo …"

"Oh?" said Morganstein, the excitement clear in his voice. "Might it have been Coombs?"

"I don't know. I only saw him once, on the walkway at Eden Beach. It was cold, and he was bundled up—"

"Bundled up like the man at Oh Buoy Books?"

"Yes, except the man at Eden Beach wasn't wearing a balaclava. He did have a scarf wrapped around his face. But as I said, it was cold … if I had had a scarf, I would have had it wrapped—"

Jeremy interrupted. "Was he about the right height and weight?"

"Yes, I suppose so—"

"Did he have a limp?" asked Morganstein.

"I can't be sure. He was walking a little unsteadily, but he was carrying an end table—taking it to the storage area for Marilee—so I figured that was the reason."

"And you told us there was no sign of forced entry," Jeremy said, his words directed toward the phone. "So it seems possible my mother let in someone she knew."

"Yes. I think it's quite possible the man who was helping your mother was Randall Coombs, and he could very well be the same person who attacked her at the bookstore ... and who was responsible for, or at least involved in, her disappearance."

Jeanette raised her eyebrows.

Jeremy shook his head at her.

"It's definitely a path worth pursuing," continued Morganstein. "In fact, it's our best lead, both for the bookstore attack and Ms. Forsythe's disappearance. Security at Eden Beach is a bit," Morganstein cleared his throat, "porous. It would be relatively easy for a person to get in and out without being seen. There's nothing on the Eden Beach security video, so she must have left the condo between your last visit, Ms. Frobisher, and twenty-four hours before we asked Eden Beach to provide the videos, which is as long as they're kept. We haven't been able to get into Ms. Forsythe's computer or phone yet—that might take some time—and we might find something there." His voice shifted to a mutter. "And anything's better than trying to run down all the crank calls we've gotten on the tip line. Those fans of Ms. Forsythe's sure like to speculate about whodunit." Then, in a more confident tone, "Yup, I'm feeling good about the Coombs angle. I'll let you know how that pans out. In any case, I think we've gotten everything we can at Eden Beach. You can go back in there now."

They ended the call just as the bell on the front door jingled. Jeanette stepped out of the back room.

"Good morning, Mr. Raber," she said to the elderly man making his way slowly toward the pharmacy counter.

"Good morning, Jeanette," he replied, his voice as creaky as a rusty hinge. "Here for my heart meds."

"Of course, of course," she said, sorting through the

prescription pickup bin with shaking fingers. She grabbed one and rang up the transaction.

Mr. Raber was almost at the front door when she glanced into the bin and called after him.

"Mr. Raber—I gave you the wrong one!"

He tottered back to the counter and they got it sorted out.

"What did you give him the first time?" Jeremy asked as they watched Mr. Raber's Cutlass glide out of the parking lot.

"Hannah Rosty's dog's seizure meds," Jeanette said with a shudder.

He put his arm around her shoulders. "I understand that the update from Morganstein was a shock, finding out that the guy Mom had doing work for her was an ex-con." He glanced around the store and, despite the fact that they were alone, lowered his voice. "But it's good news for us—he thinks this guy Coombs is the bookstore attacker, and that he's probably responsible for her disappearance."

Jeanette stepped out of Jeremy's embrace and into the back room.

"But he's *not* responsible for her disappearance!" she hissed when he joined her.

"We know he's not responsible for her *disappearance*, but we don't know that he's not responsible for her *death*."

"What could he have possibly done to her?"

"I don't know. Does it matter?"

"Of course it matters, Jeremy! We have no idea what happened to her, and never will—she could have had a heart attack. She could have had a stroke." She took a deep breath, trying to quiet her pounding heart. "She could have had an overdose."

"The amount I gave her shouldn't—couldn't—have caused an overdose. At least not if you gave her the right instructions for taking it." He obviously regretted it as soon as it was out of his mouth. "Jen, I didn't mean—"

He reached for her hand, and she snatched it back.

"I know exactly what you mean! That if someone made a mistake, it must be poor, stupid Jen."

"Sweetheart, that is not at all what I—"

"It couldn't possibly be that you prescribed the wrong amount. Or maybe I should say, *gave* her the wrong amount, since you're not a doctor."

"I went to medical school long enough to be able to research the correct dosage of a drug."

"But not long enough to be able to legally prescribe it."

"Jen—" he began, his voice rising. He stopped himself and drew in a deep breath. When he resumed, his voice was marginally calmer. "I can't undo what I did, but the amount I prescribed—" He clamped his lips together for a moment. "—the amount I *gave* her shouldn't have done that to her."

They were silent for a few moments, then Jeanette said, trying to control the tremble in her voice, "Anyone could have made a mistake. I could have written the instructions wrong. You could have given her the wrong amount."

Jeremy opened his mouth, but she silenced him with a wave of her hand.

"Or Marilee might have taken the wrong amount. But it doesn't matter, does it? We'll never know." After a pause, she added, "Unless we tell the police where she is and they do an autopsy."

Jeremy extended his arms toward her. When she flinched away from him, tears sprang to his eyes.

"Jen," he said, his voice unsteady, "we can't tell the police. We decided not to tell them when we found her, and it's too late to change our minds. A missing mother means no one demanding we repay a loan. If she stays missing and is eventually declared dead, we'll inherit what I've got to believe is a sizable estate, including two waterfront condos. They would have had every reason to suspect us if we had reported her death right away. What do you think their position would be if they found out we snuck her out of the condo in a luggage cart, drove her to Chester County, and buried her wrapped in a blanket?" He was crying openly now. "They'd never believe it was an accident, no matter what the autopsy said. On top of all that, I gave her a controlled substance without a doctor's prescription. Whatever the cause of death, I'd be culpable for that. I'd go to prison. Even if we managed to convince them you thought I was giving her CBD, even if we convinced them that I forced you into the plan to bury her body, even if you were in a position to take over at the pharmacy, no one is going to entrust their prescriptions to the wife of a man who might have killed his mother. We can never tell the police—we can never tell anyone—what we did."

Jeanette was vaguely aware of cars whisking by outside, the busy road being one of the features that had made this location so appealing to them. She thought she could hear the tick of the clock Jeremy kept at the counter where he prepared the prescriptions.

When Jeanette remained silent, Jeremy said, "I'm going to stick with the story we told Morganstein. Will you?"

"Yes," she said, her voice dull.

"Do you want to go home? I'm not fit to fill any more prescriptions today."

"No. I'll stay here. There are a couple of customers who will be stopping by to pick up meds."

He heaved a sigh. "Okay. Let me know when you want me to come back and get you."

She nodded.

She could sense him debating whether to kiss her good-bye, then he turned and pulled his coat off the rack next to the back door and stepped outside. A minute later, she heard the crunch of gravel as the CR-V rolled away, headed for home.

She had to admit that Jeremy's assessment of the situation was accurate—no one could fail to suspect them of foul play.

She knew it to be true based on her own deepening suspicions.

41

Twenty-four hours had passed since Darren had emailed Lara about H & J's interest in the sequel to *Darkest Before Death*, and despite a follow-up that morning, he hadn't gotten a response.

Reluctantly, he put in a call to Bev Wang.

"I haven't heard back from Lara yet," he said.

"Maybe you did something to upset the new golden child of the thriller world."

"I didn't do anything to upset her," snapped Darren as he mentally reviewed the history of his interactions with Lara Seaford to see if there had been such an instance. If there had been, he couldn't think of what it might have been.

"Well, it's a shame. We have a window of opportunity here —H & J is looking for a few new faces to add to the roster— but that window might slam shut at any moment."

Darren suspected the urgency was being driven less by H & J's need for new authors and more by the fact that Bev had had a long dry spell with no breakouts.

"No author, no deal," she continued. "I would think you'd

want the reading public to be able to enjoy another book that you helped polish."

"It was a lot more than polishing," muttered Darren.

"Pardon?"

"Nothing."

"You said it was a lot more than polishing."

"It was her first novel—you'd expect her to need more help than an experienced writer would."

"How much help did you give her?"

"Enough."

"How about the second one—did she pick up on the lessons?"

"I don't know, Bev," he said, exasperated. "I haven't seen it yet."

"Why would she disappear just when her first book is hitting big? A win, even with *Latent Prints*, would bring most debut authors out in the open, and a GothamCon nomination is even bigger."

"She's always been very insistent on maintaining her anonymity." He didn't add that Lara intended to reveal her identity at GothamCon.

Bev sighed. "It's going to be too bad for both of you if she doesn't surface while H & J is still interested in the sequel—and you know how many other shiny objects are out there that might claim our attention."

"I'll keep trying to get in touch with her ... but if I could find the manuscript, I could see what condition it's in, give it a little," he cleared his throat, "*polish* if it needs it. You could take a look at it—see if you're interested."

"How are you going to get it?"

"I'm not sure yet. Just give me a couple of days."

"Hey, if you can get it, we'll take a look at it. I expect you to give us first crack at it."

"It's not up to me, but if I talk to Lara, I'll put in a good word for H & J."

They ended the call and Darren fell back in his chair. He had worked with a lot of authors in his career, and he couldn't think of one who wouldn't make themselves known when presented with the interest of a publisher of Harrison & John's stature.

He leaned forward and opened a browser to H & J's website, curious about what other shiny objects might be vying for the publisher's attention. Coming up empty, he clicked around to a few other publishing-related websites.

He frowned when he saw the featured article on one of the sites: *Foul Play Involved in Author's Disappearance?*

Was someone trying to turn Lara's by now well-known reclusiveness into clickbait with that headline?

Curiosity getting the better of common sense, he clicked over to the article.

The article wasn't about Lara Seaford; it was about Cozy Up Press's Marilee Forsythe, author of the Berry Mysteries. He scanned the article. Forsythe had been attacked by a person, still at large, after an author event near her home in Ocean City, Maryland ... she had retreated to her condo and refused to emerge ... about a week later, she had disappeared from her condo ... there was no sign of foul play, but also no sign of Marilee Forsythe, or of any attempt by the author to contact her family or authorities.

He sat back and drummed his fingers on the arms of his chair, doing a mental calculation: he had received his last email from Lara Seaford, asking him to accept the *Latent Prints* award on her behalf, just a few days before Marilee Forsythe had been reported missing. He ran through the few facts he knew about Lara—or thought he knew. She had claimed to live in New York City, and since he made frequent visits to H &

J's Manhattan offices, their emails sometimes included references to New York. But he had been surprised when she once referred to going somewhere in "the city" and he eventually realized she meant Brooklyn. Another time, she had described taking a subway "north" rather than "uptown." And if she was a New Yorker, she was the only one Darren had ever heard refer to the E train as "the Blue Line." The terminology marked her as more likely a visitor than a resident.

And *Lara Seaford* wasn't so far from being a rough rearrangement of the letters in *Marilee Forsythe.*

Had he located his mysterious thriller author?

And if he had, did it suggest a more ominous reason for her silence than general reclusiveness?

It certainly seemed plausible that whoever had attacked Marilee Forsythe outside the Ocean City bookstore might also have abducted her from her nearby condo. And Darren had edited enough crime novels to know that if that was the case, and with no word from Marilee or an abductor, it didn't bode well for the author's wellbeing.

Had Darren located Lara Seaford, only to find that she had fallen prey to a psychotic fan? And what did all this mean for Darren's ability to get his hands on the follow-up to *Darkest Before Death*?

A few weeks earlier, he would have assumed that a dead author meant no manuscript. But since then, he had met Ann Kinnear. Even if Marilee Forsythe *was* Lara Seaford, and even if she was dead, that might not put the manuscript out of reach.

He now knew that spirits were most likely to be contacted at the site of their deaths, and it was possible Marilee Forsythe had been killed in her condo. Perhaps Ann would be willing to meet Darren in Ocean City and see if she could contact Ms. Forsythe's spirit.

Darren got his Ann Kinnear Sensing business card from his wallet and picked up his phone. Then he put them both down. He shouldn't jump to the conclusion that Marilee Forsythe was dead. And even if she was, there were ways that didn't require involving a psychic he might employ to locate the manuscript for the sequel novel, if his suspicion about Lara Seaford's real identity was true.

He turned back to his computer and typed in a search for *marilee forsythe* and found an article covering the bookstore attack that referenced Jeremy Frobisher—*Forsythe* must be a pen name—and Jeremy's wife, Jeanette. He also found a clip from the security video that had captured the attack and Jeanette's defense of her mother-in-law.

Further online searches revealed that Jeremy and Jeanette owned Frobishers' Pharmacy in Downingtown, Pennsylvania.

He picked up his phone and placed a call.

42

Jeanette had just finished ringing up a prescription for a customer when a call came in on the pharmacy phone.

"Frobishers' Pharmacy," she answered.

"Hello, may I speak with Jeremy or Jeanette Frobisher?" asked a male voice.

"Who's calling?" She and Jeremy had fielded a number of calls from reporters, both after the bookstore attack and after Marilee's disappearance.

"My name is Darren Van Osten. I'm an editor, and I believe I did some work for Marilee Forsythe."

Jeanette raised an eyebrow. "You *believe* you did editorial work for Marilee Forsythe?"

"Yes. Is this Ms. Frobisher?"

"Yes. And I don't really see how you could *believe* you did work for my mother-in-law," she said, preparing to hang up. "It seems like the kind of thing a person would be sure of. But I could certainly place a call to Ezra Parsons and find out."

"Yes, I'm sure you could," Van Osten said quickly. "I know Ezra Parsons—not personally, but I know *of* him—and I suspect he could vouch for my editing credentials. But the book I edited wasn't a cozy. It was a thriller."

"Then you have the wrong author. Plus, all you have to do is look up Marilee's photo to see that she's not your client."

"I know what Marilee Forsythe looks like," he said, "but I never met my client—I only ever worked with her via email. And she gave me a different name, but I think it was your mother-in-law."

Suddenly Jeanette remembered the arguments Marilee had had with Ezra about wanting to switch to a different genre. The thriller genre.

"What was the name of your client?"

"Lara Seaford."

The name, too, was familiar: the thriller author Marilee had mentioned to Ezra, whose poster-sized book cover was hanging in Marilee's guest room. Jeanette even had a vague memory of Marilee and Ezra mentioning Seaford's editor, and Ezra's surprise that Seaford shared an editor with Jock Quine.

"You're the person who edits the Robert Wolfram series?" she asked.

"Yes, that's me," he said, his voice more animated.

"And what makes you think Lara Seaford and my mother-in-law are the same person?"

"As I said, I only ever communicated with Lara via email, but she was usually very prompt about responding to my messages. I haven't gotten an email from her in about a week. I didn't think anything of it because she didn't have any reason to contact me—we had finished our work on her first novel, and she hadn't yet given me the manuscript for the second one. But yesterday one of the big publishers, Harrison & John, got in touch with me to tell me they may be interested in the second novel, and that they were anxious to speak with her as soon as possible. I sent her an email and I feel sure that if she had gotten it, she would have gotten in touch. But I haven't heard from her … and then when I was poking around online, I came across the news about Marilee Forsythe and the fact that she disappeared right around the time I stopped hearing from Lara. Plus, *Lara Seaford* sounds like a pen name someone named *Marilee Forsythe* might come up with if they wanted to stay anonymous—somewhat similar, but different enough not to attract attention."

"They're not *that* similar," said Jeanette, jotting *Marilee Forsythe* and *Lara Seaford* on a pad of paper next to the cash register and crossing out matching letters.

"Certainly not an anagram," said Van Osten. "More like an homage."

Jeanette tore the sheet off the pad and fed it into the shredder under the counter. "But why are you calling me? Even if she is who you think she is, I can't help you get in touch with her. We don't know where she is either."

"Yes, I know. And I'm terribly sorry—this must be an awful time for you. But I think I know of a way we can determine if Ms. Forsythe and Lara Seaford are the same person."

"Oh? How's that?"

"If what Lara told me about her work in progress was true, she has the manuscript for a follow-on to her debut novel. If we could find it in Ms. Forsythe's home, that would be pretty definitive proof that they are the same person. It could help the police in their investigation."

"You haven't told the police about your theory?"

"No, because it is just a theory—and I imagine they're already swamped with leads coming in to the tip line. I'd like to try to confirm my suspicion first."

"Does whoever published the first thriller know about your suspicions?"

"She didn't have a publisher. She published it herself."

As Jeanette tried to sort through what Darren Van Osten was suggesting, she thought back to Marilee's darker wardrobe and the redecorated bay-side room that had been more appropriate to a thriller writer than a cozy author. Maybe Marilee hadn't been *hoping* to channel Raymond Chandler to write her way to a successful thriller—maybe she had already done so.

"I suppose it's possible ..." she said hesitantly.

"I'd be so appreciative if you would be willing to take a look around Ms. Forsythe's home to see if you can find the thriller manuscript. Based on some things that Lara said to me, I believe she was in the habit of printing out hard copy of her work quite frequently."

"Yes," said Jeanette with a little thrill of excitement, "Marilee does that, too."

"Ah, the evidence mounts," said Van Osten, a smile in his voice. Then, in a more somber tone, he added, "And if you'd be willing, I'd be happy to accompany you. I live in Wilmington, Delaware, so it would be an easy drive to Ocean City, and if I was there, I could assess whether any material you found sounded like it was written by my client."

Jeanette was silent for a few moments, trying to sort through the jumble of her thoughts.

"I imagine you'll want to discuss all this with Ms. Forsythe's son ..." said Van Osten.

Glancing toward the door to the back room, as if Jeremy was there and not at home recovering from the revelations from Detective Morganstein, Jeanette said, "As you can imagine, my husband has been pretty devastated by the disappearance of his mother. I don't want to get his hopes up that we've found an important piece of information that might be helpful to the police." Or, she thought, that might bail her and Jeremy out of their financial bind, if they were to inherit an estate that included not one but two best-selling thriller novels. "I'd rather wait to tell him based on what we find—or don't find—at Marilee's condo."

"Of course," said Van Osten. "Very wise."

They agreed to meet at Eden Beach the next day, Jeanette already casting about for an excuse she could give Jeremy for being away for the day. Although, she thought bitterly, if he could decide to take the day off on the spur of the moment, she figured she could, too.

"Mr. Van Osten—"

"Please, call me Darren."

"Darren, I hate to ask this, but you're going to a lot of trouble to find a manuscript that might not even exist ... what's in it for you?"

"A perfectly valid question. One motivation is that there are a lot of readers out there who are hoping for a sequel to Lara Seaford's first novel, and I'd like to give it to them. But I must admit that I have a more selfish reason as well. I worked for Jock Quine for many years, and he put out so many books so quickly that it was practically a full-time job. I let my other editing work lapse. Now I'm supposed to be shepherding Jock's son Alec through the process of picking up the series, but I don't have any confidence that he'll be able to continue his father's success. And if that belief plays out, the publisher is likely going to put the blame on me. I badly need to build up my client base, and a second Seaford thriller—which I have no doubt would be even more successful than the first—would go a long way toward doing that." After a pause, he added, a bit abashed, "I shouldn't have said that about Alec Quine. I hope you'll hold that comment in confidence."

"Yes, of course," said Jeanette, envying Darren Van Osten for such innocent indiscretions.

43

Jeanette had asked Darren Van Osten to park in the lot of the neighboring condo building, The Capstan. It made sense that she or Jeremy would have business in Marilee's condo now that Detective Morganstein had told them that the police work there was done, but she didn't feel like having to explain the presence of an unfamiliar car—or, she saw, a classic pickup—to Kenny.

In the time since Darren's call, Jeanette had read everything she could find about him online. She figured that if the police ever felt a need to confiscate her computer or phone, then having them find *darren van osten* in her search history would be the least of her problems.

She uncovered no inconsistencies with the information he had given her on the phone. He had gone from a roster of several dozen editing clients to a roster of one: Jock Quine. In fact, there were several photos of Darren with Jock: seated next to him at a banquet, standing behind him at an author event, sharing a laugh in what looked like a hotel bar. Darren's website looked legit, and several websites that listed vetted publishing professionals included his name. She found a couple of websites that listed unscrupulous professionals, and none of them mentioned Darren Van Osten. She had even gotten in touch with one of Darren's previous clients, telling the woman that she was thinking of hiring him to edit her own work.

"If he's taking clients again, grab him," said the woman. "He's a doll."

"You don't work with him anymore?"

"I had to find someone else when he started getting too busy with the Wolfram series."

"Maybe you'll be able to go back to him someday."

The woman laughed. "I imagine he's going to be twice as busy coaching Alec to match Jock's style. And even if he isn't, I have a new editor now. Much as I love Darren, once you're 'fired' by an editor, it's not like you're going to go back to them later."

Reasonable or not, Jeanette was reassured by Darren's scholarly appearance and, when he climbed out of the vintage Ford and introduced himself, by his pleasant demeanor.

She led Darren to Eden Beach and by-passed the ground-floor lobby. "The security guard is a little ..." She cleared her throat. "... overenthusiastic. And nosy. I'd just as soon stay off his radar."

"I thought I read in the coverage of your mother-in-law's disappearance that there are security cameras," he said. "Won't he see us on those?"

"They only cover the elevator lobbies and the doors to the stairwells."

She didn't add that although Kenny would see them if he happened to look at the monitors during the few seconds they would be within range of the cameras, she had never had any indication that he exercised that level of diligence. It also seemed unlikely that anyone would be reviewing the security video, based on Morganstein's comment that the police had gotten everything they could from Eden Beach.

When they reached the condo, she led Darren down the tiled hallway to the living room. She was grateful that the police had left the condo tidy. When they stepped into the ocean-front study, she was even more grateful to see that the sofa and the quilt draped over the back looked undisturbed. The police had taken the computer, although according to Detective Morganstein, they hadn't yet been able to access its data, and the only items on the desk were a ceramic pencil holder, a wire mesh letter tray, and a row of Marilee's Berry Mysteries.

"This is where she did her writing," said Jeanette. "At least the writing I knew about."

She rifled quickly through the documents in the tray, which were mainly pending bills—she'd have to take care of those—assorted receipts, and a couple of appliance manuals.

She pointed to the end tables flanking the sofa. "Those are actually file cabinets. I know she stored some of her Berry Mysteries manuscripts there. You check the one on the right and I'll take the one on the left."

"Sounds good." Darren started to lower himself onto the right-hand side of the sofa.

"No," Jeanette said sharply. "Don't sit there."

Darren rose, looking confused.

"That's ... Marilee's special place. Let's get stools from the kitchen."

"No problem." He went to the kitchen and came back with two stools.

They found what Jeanette would have expected to find—manila folders neatly labeled with Berry Mystery titles and dates—and it didn't take them long to confirm the contents of the folders matched their labels.

As Darren slid the cabinet shut, he glanced around the office. "Is there anywhere else ...?"

"Maybe." She closed the drawer of the cabinet. "There's a second office. Come with me."

Darren followed her to the bay-side room. Jeanette opened the door and flipped on the light, illuminating the mid-century office furniture and noir posters.

Darren raised his eyebrows. "This looks more promising."

"You take the file cabinet. I'll take the desk."

Jeanette sat at the desk and opened the middle drawer, but it held only pens, pencils, paperclips, and a stapler. Another drawer held a ream of copier paper. The other drawers were empty. Her assignment done, she looked out the salt-encrusted window toward the bay.

After a couple of minutes, she became aware of the occasional rustle of paper and turned to see Darren slowly turning the sheets of a stack resting on the top of the file cabinet.

"Any luck?" she asked.

Without looking up, he said, "Oh, yes."

Darren brought a stool into the bay-side room and sat down at the desk next to Jeanette. He began flipping pages, handing the ones he had looked at to Jeanette, Jeanette reading them more slowly.

After a minute, he said, "The characters, the setting—it's obviously a continuation of the first book."

They scanned the document in silence for a quarter of an hour, Jeanette sensing Darren's growing excitement, until he turned over the last page.

"Damn!" he exclaimed.

"What?"

"It's missing the ending!"

"Really?" Jeanette took the last page from Darren and read it. "Maybe it just ... ends. I've read some books like that."

"No, no," said Darren, shuffling through the stack of papers. "It's missing the climax and denouement."

Jeanette felt the page crinkle in her grasp. "I think you're right about Marilee being Lara Seaford."

"Why?"

"Because Marilee would do this to her cozy editor. She wouldn't actually commit the ending to paper until the very last minute. It drove him crazy, but her endings never needed any editing—he said they were the only part of the book that was publishable as written—so he let it go."

"But when she gave me the manuscript for her first novel, it included the ending. The ending of *Darkest Before Death* was what everyone loved the most."

"She gave you the ending for the first book because it was a new genre for her and she wasn't confident yet. She did the same thing with her first cozy." She dropped the paper onto the desk, next to the rest of the manuscript. "I guess a thriller manuscript without an ending isn't going to be much of a blockbuster."

"Not necessarily. I told you I edited the first thriller novel, but I actually did a lot more than that. I was more of a ghostwriter."

She scowled. "That's a convenient revelation to make now that we've found the manuscript with no ending."

He raised a hand. "I know, I know. I'd be suspicious in your position, too. But I think I can supply the ending. I'm as anxious for this book to get into readers' hands as Lara—sorry, as Marilee—was, and as anxious as I imagine you and your husband are. Or at least as anxious as he will be when you feel confident enough about what we've found, and what we can do with it, to tell him."

She scooted her chair back a few inches. "You say, 'as

anxious as Marilee *was*'—does that mean you think she's dead?"

Darren flushed. "I'm sorry, that was thoughtless of me, but ... it's a possibility. I think that she would have returned my email about H & J's interest in the second book if she could."

Jeanette realized she was wringing her hands and forced them to be still.

"If you wrote the ending and then she showed up—if it turned out she had just been hiding as some kind of publicity stunt—what then?"

"That would be the best outcome of all. I'd be happy to have a complete manuscript, all written by the author of *Darkest Before Death*, to edit."

"And if she doesn't show up to finish the book, what would that cost—you writing the ending and editing the rest of it?"

Darren quoted a fee. "It's my regular editing fee, plus twenty-five percent for providing the ending. If Marilee shows up, we'd drop that extra percentage."

She turned back to the almost opaque window. "I don't know ..."

Half a minute ticked by as she tried to sort through her options.

Finally, Darren said, "Jeanette, you know why I'm interested in this book: because I need to rebuild my client list and editing the sequel to *Darkest Before Death* would be a huge help. But even if you decide to go ahead with the manuscript we've found using another editor, it would still help me out. A standalone novel, no matter how successful, will fade from memories—and from the bookshelves—pretty quickly. But a follow-on—maybe even a series, if that comes about—will keep the first book on the radar of readers, and of authors who are looking for an editor. That scenario wouldn't be quite as helpful to me as editing the second book, but it couldn't hurt. If you'd like, I'll give you the names of some other editors you could contact, or agents who could find someone to do it for you."

She drew in a lungful of air and blew it out slowly. "All this would be a little hard to explain to someone else. I'd rather keep this between the two of us—and Jeremy, once we understand where this is going." She turned back to him. "But I don't have that kind of money lying around."

"I'm confident enough about how successful this book is going to be that I'm willing to wait for my payment until you have an advance, or royalties coming in."

"Do we need to sign a contract?"

"Do you have a couple of pieces of paper?"

Jeanette got some paper and a pen from the desk and handed them to Darren.

"We can draft our agreement," he said, "sign the draft, then formalize it later. How does that sound?"

Jeanette nodded. "That sounds all right."

Darren wrote for a few minutes, then handed the paper to Jeanette. She had a few questions, and Darren modified the draft to address them. When they agreed on the terms, he wrote out a clean version, then they made a copy on the printer-copier in Marilee's study and signed it.

"The electronic version of the manuscript must be on Ms. Forsythe's computer," he said.

"Maybe—but the police have that."

"Why don't we make a copy of the manuscript as well, so we both have one. You could mail it to yourself but leave it unopened to prove that you were in possession of it on the date the envelope is postmarked."

She smiled wanly. "Something an editor of thrillers would think of."

"I just want to make sure you feel completely comfortable turning this over to me."

She nodded. "It's a good idea. Let's do that."

"So ..." Darren paused, and when he continued, his voice was tentative, "... do we go to the police with the information that Marilee and Lara are most likely the same person?"

Fiddling with the paper in her hands, she said, "I know we had originally said we would let the police know, but I'm having second thoughts. If they really are the same person, then we don't need to worry about Lara Seaford having friends and family that are worried about her. If they aren't the same person, then there's no need to contact the police—and, in fact, contacting them might distract them from the investigation of Marilee's disappearance." Her voice gained confidence as she spoke. "And we still don't know what the outcome of all this will be. You might read the draft and find it's a mess—not even worth pursuing." Jeanette sighed. "Telling the police will obviously mean telling Jeremy, and I still don't feel ready to do that until we understand better what this will mean for us."

She glanced up, ready to backpedal if Darren objected, but he looked as relieved by this plan as she was.

"Yes, that makes sense to me," he said. "I'll read through the manuscript and let you know what I find. And if Marilee makes a dramatic reappearance, then of course we will honor her wishes regarding what she wants done with the novel."

Jeanette picked up the pages of the manuscript and tapped them straight. "Yes, of course. If she reappears."

"I do have a favor to ask."

"What's that?" asked Jeanette, immediately wary.

"Although the story isn't set in Ocean City, the gestalt is the same: a location that would usually be lively and vibrant, made bleak and ominous by the lack of people." He waved his hand to take in the noir-ish room décor. "You can see how much surrounding herself with the right atmosphere was important to Lara—sorry, to Marilee. I'd love to spend some time hanging around Eden Beach. According to the building's website, there are some rooms on the top floor that are available to residents and their guests. I could work up there. If that's okay with you, could you let the security guard know that I have your permission to do that? I imagine he'd accept your approval as a representative of Ms. Forsythe."

"And you'd be driving back and forth from Wilmington?" she asked. "It's not as far as Downingtown, but it's still a good two-and-a-half hours."

"That's just a normal commute for some people who work in the city," said Darren, although his good humor seemed a bit forced.

Jeanette thought back to the blemish-free profile she had assembled before meeting Darren in Ocean City. "I suppose there's no harm in you staying at the condo."

"Really?" he said, obviously enthused. "That would be great."

"You can make up the couch in the living room. It seems ..." her voice faded, then she continued. "... wrong for someone to stay on the sofa bed in the study. Like I said, that was Marilee's special place."

44

It was eight o'clock when Darren finished reading the last police update on the Forsythe disappearance, leaned back in the desk chair in the bay-side room in Marilee Forsythe's Eden Beach condo, and downed a generous swallow from his glass of whiskey. He had run out for a bottle shortly after Jeanette left for home. If he was to be enjoying the ambiance of Lara Seaford's writing room, he figured he should drink an ambiance-appropriate beverage.

He had read and edited enough crime fiction to know how to read between the lines of these official communiques, and he sensed that the Ocean City police had made little progress in the three days since Jeanette and Jeremy Frobisher had reported Marilee missing.

He had finished his second skim of the manuscript, and would start a third, more in-depth, read in the morning. But he had wanted to get through the document before it was too late to call Mike Kinnear.

He had wondered if he would find in the manuscript some authorial Easter egg that would support the idea that its author was playing out an elaborate PR charade through a manufactured disappearance. He had not. If the Ocean City police department thought Marilee Forsythe was dead, he had to agree with them—he could imagine no other explanation for her disappearance. And, like them, he believed that the man who had attacked her outside Oh Buoy Books was involved. It was hard to imagine how Marilee's inoffensive books could have triggered such an action, since as far as he knew, no one other than Jeanette and himself knew of her alternate identity. But as the Marilee Forsythe a.k.a. Lara Seaford situation proved, one never knew everything going on in another person's life.

He had hoped his second read might suggest options for filling in the missing ending. He had struck out here as well.

He downed another swallow of whiskey, got out his phone, and tapped a number.

"Ann Kinnear Sensing, Mike Kinnear speaking."

"Hello, Mike, this is Darren Van Osten."

"Hey, Darren, how are you doing?"

"I'm doing well. I wanted to ask you about the possibility of hiring Ann for a sensing engagement."

"Oh?"

"Have you heard about the cozy mystery author from Ocean City, Maryland, who disappeared? Marilee Forsythe?"

"Can't say I have."

"Well, Ms. Forsythe was almost done with her latest novel when she disappeared. Her family has hired me to finish it for her. I have to say that I'm a bit stumped about how to manage the ending to do justice to the rest of the book."

"And you think Ann can help?"

"The police aren't sure what happened to Ms. Forsythe. For all we know, she may be sipping mai-tais on a distant beach under an assumed name. I certainly hope she is. But I —and, I think, the authorities—believe it's more probable that she's dead. If she is, Ann might be able to contact her and find out what happened to her, like she did with Jock."

"And find out the ending of the book."

"It would help Ms. Forsythe's family out. And me too, of course."

"If anyone can contact Marilee Forsythe, it would be Ann, but the last time you spoke with me about a possible engagement, you said you weren't in a position to pay the fee. And our prices haven't dropped since then."

"I feel strongly enough about this opportunity that I'm planning on selling the pickup to cover the cost."

After a pause, Mike said, "Selling the Ford?"

"Yes." Darren heaved a sigh, perhaps a little more dramatic than it needed to be. "Desperate times call for desperate measures."

"Who are you going to sell it to?"

"I have a few interested buyers."

After another pause, Mike said, "I might be interested."

Darren tried to keep the smile out of his voice. "Oh? Would you consider a straight trade—the truck for the engagement?"

Darren heard some tapping over the call—probably Mike quickly researching the value of the truck—then Mike said, "Yes, I think that would work. You could sign the truck over to me and I'd pay that amount into the AKS account. But we're getting a little ahead of ourselves. I need some more details, and then I need to check with Ann—she has the final say about what engagements we take. I'll let you know as soon as I speak with her. And if we do take the engagement, I imagine Ann will need access to Ms. Forsythe's home."

"I'm sure I can arrange that."

Mike called him back within half an hour with the news

that Ann had agreed to take the engagement and would drive down to Ocean City the following morning.

"That's great news," said Darren.

"If she's able to contact Marilee, do you want to be there when Marilee reveals the end of the latest cozy?"

"Yes, that would be best. I might have some follow-up questions for her." After a pause, Darren cleared his throat and said, "The family is anxious to find out the ending of the book, but they don't want word to get out that they've hired Ann. And to maintain some distance from the engagement, they've asked that I act as the liaison between them and you and Ann."

"That's not a problem," said Mike. "Our services are completely confidential. But do you mind if I ask why?"

"It's one thing for the news outlets to imply that Ms. Forsythe is dead. It's quite another for word to get out that the family is taking action that suggests they believe it as well."

45

Ann had gotten so used to looking for any opportunity to fly to a destination that she had forgotten that she quite enjoyed road trips. She had decided driving to Ocean City was more practical than flying—she might need to stay a day or two and would need a way to get around, especially if there were places other than the Eden Beach condo building she needed to check out. The day was cold, but finally sunny after a long gray stretch, and she especially enjoyed the drive south from Rehoboth Beach, with tantalizing glimpses of water through dunes and vacation homes on both sides of the highway.

She was also a bit relieved to have an excuse to spend some time away from Mahalo Winery. There had been no signs of any additional incursions on the property, but according to Joe Booth, who had contacted the investigating officer, there were no leads related to the break-in at the big house, or about the suspicious sounds Scott, Mike, and she had heard when working in Niall's old office. A security system was now in place at the big house, and Ann was being diligent about locking the door of the Curragh, even when she was home.

She had spoken to Mike twice the previous night. The first call had been to get her okay for the Van Osten engagement.

"Sure, sounds good," she said. "I like Darren ... but I thought you said he couldn't afford an engagement of his own."

"I proposed covering the engagement fee in exchange for the Ford."

She laughed. "You're bartering the services of Ann Kinnear Sensing?"

"If it's okay with you."

"Sure ... but I thought Audrey the Audi was your girl forever."

"She is. The Ford would be for Scott. You said he really seemed to like it when you were in Princeton, right?"

"He loved it. I'm okay with that arrangement."

Mike had called back later to provide more details about the engagement, and to convey Darren's request that she park in the lot at The Capstan, the building next to Eden Beach. "Since the family wants to keep this quiet, they don't want Eden Beach's 'overenthusiastic' security guard to see people trooping in and out of Marilee's condo."

"The overenthusiastic security guard won't mind that we're sneaking in the back way?"

"It's unlikely he'll notice. Darren told me that the security cameras cover only the elevator lobbies and the doors to the stairwells."

When Ann reached The Capstan's nearly empty lot, she parked next to Darren's Ford. She briefly considered whether to bring her overnight bag with her, but keeping a happy thought that she might be able to discharge the engagement and head back to Kennett Square the same day, she left it in the car.

Darren led her to the Eden Beach property and up a flight of steps to the first floor, where they took the elevator to *14*. Ann's mouth quirked up when she noticed that there was no *13*. They left the semi-enclosed elevator lobby and followed an open-air walkway past metal screen doors roughened and pocked by the salty Atlantic air to the angled portion of the building. Darren unlocked the door and led her inside, down a tiled hallway from the bay-side to the ocean-side of the condo.

"Holy cow," she said when she reached the living room. Except for a bit of the neighboring building, the entire view was clear blue sky and indigo ocean.

"Yes," agreed Darren. "Gorgeous, isn't it?"

The living room was oddly empty. Against one wall was an entertainment center, against the opposite wall a couch that had been made up as a bed. Three stools were pulled up to the breakfast bar that separated the living room from the kitchen. Through the glass sliders leading to the balcony, she could see two chairs that were a match to the couch—odd, since they didn't appear to be appropriate for outdoor use.

"Anything?" Darren asked hopefully. "You know—spirit-wise?"

"Not yet."

"Her study is through here," he said, leading her across the living room. "This is where she worked on her cozy mysteries."

The view from this room, unimpeded by an intervening balcony, was even more stunning than the one from the living room. End tables flanked a sofa, across the back of which was draped a quilt in shades of blue and green. A desk faced the floor-to-ceiling windows. A row of books—Marilee's Berry

Mysteries—ran along the back of the desk, held up by a pair of shell-shaped brass bookends.

Ann noticed Darren looking at her expectantly. "Nope. Not here either." She stepped out of the study and popped her head into the bathroom, which also proved to be spirit-free. "Any other rooms?"

"There is one other room," said Darren. "Follow me."

They retraced their steps up the hallway, and Darren opened a door next to the entrance.

"Wow, this is pretty different," she said as she stepped in, looking around at the posters on the walls and the mid-century office furniture.

"Yes." He cleared his throat. "Her son is a big fan of noir movies. She fitted it out for his visits."

"Where does the son sleep? For that matter, where does anyone sleep? I didn't see any beds—just the couch in the living room made up as a bed."

"That's where I slept last night. I washed the sheets and remade the bed in case you have to stay overnight. The sofa in the study folds out into a bed, and that's where Marilee sleeps. Her family asked that no one sleep there—you can imagine that if Marilee does reappear, she might not be happy to learn that someone was using her bed." After a pause, he said, "Maybe the son sleeps on an air mattress when he visits."

"If I were him, I'd rather have a real bed than this recreation of Sam Spade's office."

"I guess nothing here, either?" asked Darren.

"No." Ann considered. "I read that Marilee was suffering some form of agoraphobia, so the condo seems like the most likely place to find her. I might have better luck at another time of day. But we should check the rest of the building, just to be thorough. Let's take the elevator to the top floor and work our way down. If we still haven't encountered her, we can check out the beach as well."

She didn't add that she wouldn't mind stretching her legs after the drive from Kennett Square.

From a hook next to the front door, Darren retrieved a key that, he explained, would unlock the entrance to the resident facilities on the top floor, and they headed out.

They took the elevator to the top floor. In one wing, the smell of chlorine announced the presence of an indoor pool, uninhabited and with a candy bar wrapper floating on its surface. Off the pool were locker rooms—Ann checked the women's and men's rooms—and a game room with three pinball machines, electrical cords draped over their glass tops. In the other wing was a coat check room and banquet room, the glass door to which was locked. A wooden door labeled *Eden Beach Management - Employees Only* was also locked.

They descended one floor via the stairs and stepped out at one end of the open-air bay-side walkway. Walking from one end of the building to the other, they took the stairway down another flight, and walked back.

It took them almost thirty minutes to traverse the walkway on all levels. Their survey of the building not only failed to turn up Marilee but failed even to turn up any living residents. The only movement they encountered was an unlatched screen door banging open and shut in the gusty ocean breezes. Darren pushed it closed.

When they reached the first floor, Darren asked, "What now?"

"Let's check the beach. If I had lived here, that's where I'd be."

They left the building on the ocean side and crossed a large deck area, which currently held only stacks of chairs and a shuttered tiki bar and took a path through the dunes to the beach. They slogged through the loose, dry sand to the hard-packed sand by the water. It was mid-afternoon, and the shadows of the high rises were encroaching on the beach. Ann shivered.

"Still nothing?" asked Darren.

"No. I read up on the bookstore attack—we should probably check there. After people die, they don't only go back to the places that they loved. Sometimes they go back to places that played an important part in their lives for bad reasons."

They made their way to The Capstan parking lot and Darren drove them to Oh Buoy Books. Although Ann's search of the bookstore was no more fruitful than her search of Eden Beach had been, it was certainly more enjoyable. She picked up a smoker cookbook for Mike and a history of Fenwick Island pirates for Scott. After some consideration, she selected a critical analysis of Clint Eastwood's filmography for Joe Booth.

As Darren drove them back to Eden Beach, Ann asked, "Can you think of any other locations we should check?"

"No. I really didn't know her that well." After a moment, he added, "But I can ask her family."

"Okay. I'll spend at least one night at the condo in case it's a matter of the timing of her appearance rather than the location."

"Does that mean you'll need to revisit all the places we've already been?"

"I hope not, but I will if she doesn't show up at the condo. And if I can't find her, it may be that she's not there to be found—not all dead people stick around. And based on what I read about her online, it's also possible she's not dead."

"Yes, of course. We can hope for that."

Darren pulled into The Capstan parking lot. "Want me to come up to the condo with you?"

"No, that's okay."

Darren handed over the key to the condo. "I just realized we didn't check the Eden Beach parking garage."

She scrunched up her nose. "It would be really unusual for someone to haunt a parking garage, but I'll do a walk-through just in case."

"Want me to wait while you do that?"

"No. I don't have high hopes, and if I do encounter her—there or elsewhere—I'll call you, and you can come back and I'll mediate a discussion about the end of the novel." She climbed out of the pickup and gave Darren a wave as he rolled away.

She retrieved her overnight bag from the Forester, then crossed to Eden Beach and walked up and down the two aisles of the parking garage, which was as spirit-free as she had anticipated.

She had expected that the overenthusiastic security guard might emerge from the lobby and ask her what she was doing wandering around the garage. Perhaps there was no one on duty and she could seize the opportunity to check the lobby as well.

She stepped through the sliding glass doors and sighed when she saw that a security guard was, in fact, on duty, although she suspected from his bleary expression that the whoosh of the opening doors had woken him.

"Didn't expect you until after dark," he said in an aggrieved voice.

As she crossed to the desk, she wondered how she could take advantage of this misidentification—and how much trouble she would get into should she try—when he saved her from having to make the decision.

His eyes narrowed, and he said, "You're not the regular girl."

"Uh, no. I'm not anyone's girl ..." She glanced at his name badge. "... Kenny."

"My mistake. What can I do for you?"

"I've been admiring Eden Beach for years. My brother and I just came into some money, and we'd love to get a place here. Do you have any brochures about the amenities, or contact information for a real estate agent?"

"Sure. Hold on a sec."

While he shuffled through the contents of a drawer, she scanned the lobby. As expected, there was no sign of Marilee. Ann supposed that being forced to haunt the lobby of Eden Beach in the company of Kenny might be a fitting punishment for some minor transgression in life.

When Kenny had produced a wrinkled brochure from the drawer, Ann asked, "This is where that famous author lives, right?"

Kenny grimaced. "You a fan?"

Ann shrugged. "A bit. The berry theme is clever." When Kenny was silent, she prompted, "I heard she left without telling anyone where she was going." She thought that suggesting that Marilee had left on her own would be more palatable to Kenny than that the author had been abducted during his watch.

He rewarded her with a slight relaxation of his features. "Yeah, did a runner, looks like. Probably freaked out by that attack at Oh Buoy Books."

"I heard about that. Terrible."

Kenny jotted the name and number of a real estate agent on a stained piece of notepad paper and handed it to her. "Anything else I can do for you?" he asked, clearly implying that the correct answer was *no*.

"I did have one more question. My brother is quite the security freak. Do you guys have security video coverage of the building?" She figured there was no harm in confirming what Darren had told Mike.

"Sure."

"What does it cover?"

"Elevator lobbies and the doorways to the stairwells on all the floors."

Since she and Darren had used the doors to the stairwells on every floor and had passed every elevator lobby on the search of Eden Beach, Ann suspected that the nap Kenny had been taking when she entered the lobby was not his first of the day. "Overenthusiastic" was not a term she would have thought to apply to the security guard.

"Okay. Thanks for the information."

Tucking the materials that Kenny had given her into the knapsack she used as a purse, she left the lobby. Figuring that even the recently awoken Kenny might notice her on the security monitors if she headed directly for Marilee's condo, she took a quick walk up and down the beach. Then, hoping that the guard might had resumed his nap, and figuring that she'd be visible for a shorter period of time entering the stairwell than waiting for the elevator, she trudged up the stairs to 14.

46

Ann decided to postpone another sweep of the Eden Beach walkways, since even a guard as seemingly unenthusiastic as Kenny would notice if the woman who had stopped by his desk earlier, professing an interest in buying a unit, entered the stairwell or wandered by the elevator lobby on each one of Eden Beach's almost two dozen floors.

Instead, she assessed which seat in the condo would offer the best view while she waited for the possible arrival of Marilee Forsythe. The sun was setting over the bay, but the window in the noir-ish bay-side room was small and so crusted with grit that it was almost opaque. She stepped briefly out onto the ocean-facing balcony, thinking that she might enjoy the view from one of the two chairs, but the biting cold of the wind drove her back inside.

Finally, she settled onto the sofa in the study, which offered a magnificent view of the darkening ocean. She passed the time watching aviation safety awareness videos on her phone and occasionally checking through the condo's other rooms. When she got hungry, she took the stairs down to the ground level, crossed to The Capstan's parking lot, and headed out to pick up groceries, a bottle of sake, and takeout sushi.

When she had her early dinner laid out on the kitchen island, she got out her phone and tapped open a video call to Mike.

"Howdy," he answered. "How's it going?"

She propped the phone against the sake bottle and began mixing some wasabi into her soy sauce. "I checked the condo, the rest of the Eden Beach building, the beach, and the bookstore. No luck so far. I'm going to walk up and down the beach before it gets too dark."

"Might be easier to spot a spirit when it's full dark."

"Yeah, but I don't want it to be so dark that I can't see other things that I need to see. Like a drop-off in the sand."

"Smart."

"Remember you told me Darren mentioned an overenthusiastic security guard?"

"Yes." Mike frowned. "Is he giving you trouble?"

"No. In fact, I suspect he's not giving anyone trouble. I'd say narcoleptic would be a better way to describe him."

"Good for us, if not for the residents, I guess. I suppose that makes it more likely that Forsythe might have been abducted from her condo."

"Yes. And, sorry to be morbid, but if she was abducted alive and killed somewhere else, it does lower my chances of finding her."

Scott got on the call long enough to say hi to Ann. After wishing Mike and Scott good night, Ann tapped out a text to Darren while she finished the sushi: *Nothing new at the condo. Will check beach next.*

She put on her parka, stepped out onto the walkway, and locked the door behind her. Deciding to stick with taking the stairs to minimize her on-camera time, she trudged down to the first floor.

She exited the building on the beach side. The sun had set about half an hour earlier, and the temperature was dropping rapidly. She crossed the deserted back deck and the dunes, pulling on mittens and a wool cap as she went, then crossed the beach to the hard-packed sand near the water. She looked up and down the shoreline. Not another soul—living or dead—was in sight. She turned south and, hands shoved deep in her pockets, began walking. She'd give it half an hour, then cover the same distance to the north of Eden Beach.

She passed only two other walkers—both alive—before she turned around.

She had almost reached Eden Beach when she saw a walker approaching from the other direction: a man toiling through the dry sand near the dunes and dressed in summer clothing. Just looking at him made her shiver, although it was clear he was a spirit and therefore, she supposed, immune to the cold.

But she herself was not immune, and when she reached Eden Beach, she decided that what she really needed was a warming glass of sake. She'd check the area north of Eden Beach in the morning.

After climbing the stairs to *14*, she let herself back into Marilee Forsythe's condo, poured herself a glass of sake, and settled down at the breakfast bar with one of the aviation magazines she had brought with her. However, the ocean view was irresistible. She turned out the lights so she could see out more easily and took her glass to the study, whose view was even more expansive than the living room's.

Ann finished the glass of sake, then decided that she'd make an early evening of it, hoping that Marilee would be gracious enough to reveal her presence if she arrived in the middle of the night. Ann brushed her teeth, changed into a long-sleeved T-shirt and sweats, then slipped under the covers that Darren had used to make up a bed on the living room couch. She had hoped to be able to catch a glimpse of the water from the couch, but it was too low and too far from the window.

It seemed a shame to be in an ocean-front location and not take advantage of the view. She climbed out of the makeshift bed, went to the study, and settled onto the sofa. To comply with Marilee's family's request, she wouldn't sleep there—she'd just enjoy the view until she got sleepy, then return to the living room. She pulled the quilt from the back of the couch and draped it over her legs.

In the darkness outside, there was no way to tell where the ocean ended and the sky began. The lights of cargo ships, miles offshore, drifted slowly across her field of vision. They might have been zeppelins ... or spaceships ... or a flotilla of ghost ships, hovering above the waves. If she flew the Avondale flight school Warrior out over the ocean, would she be able to reach them? Would she be able to see their ghostly crew? Would Marilee Forsythe be among them?

The moan of the wind outside the window became the moan of wind through the lines of those ships, and she slipped into sleep.

47

Ann woke the next morning with a crick in her neck and a vague sense of guilt that she had complied with neither the letter nor the spirit of Darren's directive not to sleep in the study.

Not wanting to use more of the facilities in Marilee's condo than was absolutely necessary, she decided to forgo a shower. After all, assuming she could avoid running into Kenny, she didn't expect to be close enough to anyone for it to make a difference.

She was too intimidated to make coffee in the complicated coffee maker, so she made do with a breakfast of a banana and a plain, and now somewhat stale, donut she had picked up on her supply run the previous day. Then she re-checked the Eden Beach resident facilities on the top floor and the walkways, hoping no one in the canal-side houses across the Coastal Highway was watching her trekking back and forth like the inhabitant of an ant colony.

When she reached the first floor, she exited the building, went to The Capstan parking lot where she had parked the Forester, and headed south on the Coastal Highway toward the Ocean City boardwalk. Although she had little expectation of encountering Marilee Forsythe there, it seemed a shame to make a drive to the shore and not visit the boardwalk. She stopped for coffee on the way. Then, with hardly any traffic on the multi-lane road, and what traffic there was barely reaching the thirty miles per hour speed limit, she took in the sights.

This stretch of the Coastal Highway was gratifyingly free of chains. Except for the occasional Quality Inn or Best Western, the hotel names suggested a different era: Shangri La, Bonita Beach, Kokomo, Surf Inn. The facades of the hotels and condos, painted in bright pastels or decorated with stylized fronds of seaweed, wouldn't have been out of place in Miami. Restaurant names highlighted the local specialty—crabs—or played on the double entendres that seemed to be popular in any town catering to summer tourists. Statues of animals were popular, providing a photo op for visitors. Ann was surprised to see an elevator repair company occupying what must be prime real estate, although its proximity to the high-rises would give it a strategic advantage over less centrally located competitors.

She parked in a vast and nearly deserted lot between the immobile Ferris wheel of the shuttered amusement park and the inlet that separated Ocean City from Assateague Island. She walked a few blocks north on the boardwalk, her wool hat pulled down over her ears, her mittened hands jammed deep in the pockets of her parka. A few stores were open, and she briefly thought about stopping to get T-shirts for Mike and Scott, but whereas she had found the solitude on the beach relaxing, she found the same solitude on the boardwalk dispiriting.

She turned around and started back toward the parking lot, passing one lone fellow walker of the boards: a man, underdressed for the weather, looking into the window of a closed souvenir shop. When she reached the Forester, the lot was nearly as deserted as it had been when she set out, the only addition a light-colored sedan. If it belonged to the underdressed window-shopper, he had extended his chilly walk even more by parking on the far side of the lot.

She climbed into the Forester, turned the heat to high, and headed back to Eden Beach.

Back in Marilee's condo, puffing a bit from the climb up the stairs, she stepped out onto the balcony while she decided what to do next. Thirteen stories below, she saw the tiny figure of a man throwing a tennis ball, and the even tinier figure of a dog racing after it, the sound of its enthusiastic yelps reaching her faintly on the balcony. Ann thought perhaps she, Mike, Scott, and Ursula should come back to Ocean City after the engagement for Darren was done, although Ann wasn't convinced that Ursula would be as enthusiastic about the beach as this dog was.

She leaned against the balcony railing, watching the man and dog move down the beach. She also spotted the lightly clothed spirit she had seen the previous night, now toiling along in the opposite direction. Ann wondered why he didn't stick to the hard packed sand near the water, and then contemplated the phenomenon of a spirit toiling at all.

As the living man and the dog moved out of sight, Ann's eyes drifted to The Capstan. The curtains were drawn in most of the units, but she noticed that in one, a woman sat in a chair drawn up to a window, looking ocean-ward through a pair of binoculars. Ann turned in that direction, wondering what the woman saw. When Ann looked back, the woman had the binoculars trained on Eden Beach. Any doubt about which part of Eden Beach the woman was viewing was erased by the start she gave when Ann's gaze met hers. She rose laboriously to her feet and retreated out of view.

Might one of the only January inhabitants of The Capstan —especially an inhabitant with binoculars—have been keeping track of one of the only inhabitants of Eden Beach? Might she have any information about Marilee that would help Ann locate the woman's spirit?

She counted the floors to the occupied unit, stepped back into the condo, grabbed her knapsack, and headed for the stairwell.

48

Ann stepped into the lobby of The Capstan and crossed to a security desk staffed by a man who might have played football as a lineman a decade or two earlier. Like Kenny, he wore a name tag—Deegan—but the uniform to which it was pinned was a good deal neater than that of the Eden Beach security guard.

"Help you, miss?" he asked, his voice a deep rumble.

"My name's Ann Kinnear, and I'm working for the family of a resident of Eden Beach who has gone missing: Marilee Forsythe."

His expression sobered. "I heard about that—the same lady who was attacked outside Oh Buoy Books, right?"

"That's right. I noticed that one of the residents at The Capstan, in a unit around the thirteenth floor, was keeping an eye on things with a pair of binoculars ... I thought she might have seen something."

Deegan tried to suppress a smile. "Yeah, I know who you mean."

"Could you put a call in to her, ask her if I could talk with her?"

"You're not police, right?"

"No. A private investigator, you might say."

He raised an eyebrow. "I *might* say?"

She dug an Ann Kinnear Sensing business card out of her knapsack and handed it to him.

He examined it skeptically. "Sensing?"

"I've been featured in articles in the *Philadelphia Register*."

Usually the reference to the *Register* was enough to assuage people's suspicions about profession, but Deegan turned to the computer at his desk and tapped and read. After a minute, he raised his eyebrows. "You were involved with that crazy case at the Philly speakeasy?"

"Yup."

He shook his head. "That was one to write home about. And now Marilee Forsythe's family has hired you to try to find her?"

"That's right."

He cocked an eyebrow at her. "And if the family has hired you, they must think she's dead."

She suppressed a sigh. She wouldn't have mentioned the family if she had thought another excuse would get her past Deegan. Maybe she should have Mike get some cards made up that said *Ann Kinnear Investigations*, although then she wouldn't be able to use the *Register* articles as testimonials. "I think even the Ocean City police think it's a possibility."

He nodded. "Yeah, I suppose so." He leaned back in his chair and regarded her. "I'm not accustomed to letting strangers into the building—even strangers who have been featured in the *Register*—but I suspect the tenant would enjoy a visitor." He regarded Ann for another few seconds, then shrugged. "Let me see what she says."

He picked up the desk phone, tapped a number, and after

a moment said, "Hello, Ms. Telford. I have a young lady down here who'd like to speak with you. Her name's Ann Kinnear." He conveyed the information Ann had given him and what he had found on his review of the *Register* articles. He listened for half a minute, laughed, and said, "Yes, ma'am. I'll send her up." He hung up the phone. "Edith Telford." He gave Ann the floor and unit number.

"Thanks."

When Ann emerged from the elevator on Edith Telford's floor, she was glad Deegan had provided the unit number. The Capstan hallways ran through the interior of the building, and she would have had trouble orienting herself sufficiently to guess which was the one in which she had seen the woman with the binoculars. Most of the doors she passed were featureless, and she wondered how often one tenant wandered into another's unit. Others had tired-looking, summer-themed wreaths or hangings on the door. Then she noticed one decorated with a jaunty snowman.

She knocked lightly, and after a moment she heard slow steps approaching from the other side.

"Miss Kinnear?"

"Yes, ma'am."

"Hold on one minute—let me get this chain off."

Ann heard the rattle of the chain and the thunk of a deadbolt, then the door opened to reveal a stout woman with a puff of white hair and light blue eyes behind cat's-eye glasses. She was wearing an enormous hand-knit sweater and leaning on a cane. "My name's Edith Telford. Come on in."

Ann stepped inside. "Pleased to meet you, Ms. Telford."

"You can call me Edith if I can call you Ann." She gestured Ann into the apartment.

The space could hardly have been less like Marilee

Forsythe's sparsely furnished condo. It was packed with over-large furniture, probably transplanted from a previous home. Along one wall stood a massive oak bookcase jammed with tattered paperbacks. A plastic laundry basket full of toys stood in a corner, no doubt for the grandchildren whose photos crammed the walls.

"I was just going to make some coffee for myself," said Edith. "Can I get you some?"

"If it's not too much trouble."

"It's no trouble. It's instant. If you can grab an extra chair from the bedroom, we can both sit at the table by the window."

In a bedroom that was as tightly packed with furniture as the living room, Ann found half a dozen folding metal chairs and brought one to the table. Then she looked out the window toward Eden Beach.

The two chairs from the living room suite that were on Marilee's balcony made it easy to pick out her unit, and Edith's window, at about the same height as Marilee's, gave a view into much of the condo's living room and the study. Details were difficult to pick out with the naked eye, especially with the sun shining and the lights inside the condo out, but with binoculars, at night, and with the lights on, it would be like a diorama.

The rattle of china drew Ann's attention back to the kitchen, where Edith was loading up a tray.

"Can I help you with that?" Ann asked.

"Well, I hate to make the guest do all the work, but I wouldn't say no to you carrying this to the table. It might save us a mess to clean up."

Ann carried the tray to the living room and transferred its contents to the table: two coffee mugs decorated with Minnie and Mickey Mouse and a plate featuring the Cookie Monster, on top of which Edith had arranged a pyramid of Nilla wafers.

"The guest gets the comfy chair," said Edith, taking the empty tray from Ann and leaning it against the wall. She lowered herself onto the folding chair.

Ann sat. "I didn't expect to be entertained when I came by."

Edith waved a hand. "You're indulging me—I don't get many visitors. And definitely not many ghost-hunting visitors who have made the *Philadelphia Register*. I remember that story."

They chatted about the Philadelphia Socialite Murder for a few minutes, and Ann shared a few behind-the-scenes tidbits, hoping to pave the way for Edith to do the same. Eventually, Ann steered the conversation to her intended topic.

"I'm hoping you can help me with some questions I have about the woman who owns the condo where you saw me."

"I'll do what I can."

"Do you check out what's going on outside often?" She thought this sounded better than *spy on your neighbors*.

Edith laughed. "I do love seeing what's going on." She patted her leg. "I don't get around as well as I used to, and a couple of years ago, my son got me those binoculars. Good ones, too. Some people think it's just sand, water, and sky, but there's a lot to look at. Those little banner-towing planes. Sometimes military planes. Boats. Birds. Dolphins—that's my favorite. And, boy, I could write a book about what I see going on down on the beach in the middle of the summer."

Ann leaned forward conspiratorially. "And maybe at Eden Beach as well?"

Edith laughed again and blushed. "I have to admit I'm not above taking a peek—I'm an old busy-body at heart."

"I know it's a long shot, but I wonder if you've seen anything going on in the condo where you saw me."

Edith sipped her coffee. "Actually, not such a long shot. There aren't many of us who stay year-round, so I notice those who do." She shook her head. "Knowing how much these condos cost—my son helped me buy this place—I can't imagine anyone using it for just part of the year." She nibbled a Nilla wafer. "I've lived here for a number of years, and I don't recall that unit being used in the winter before, but the woman I assume is the owner was there late this year."

"How late?"

Edith shrugged. "Until at least about a week ago. I don't remember seeing her since then."

Ann got out her phone and searched for a photo of Marilee. She turned the phone toward Edith. "Was it that woman?"

Edit peered at the phone. "Can you make that picture bigger?"

Ann took the phone, enlarged the photo, and handed it back to Edith.

"Yes," Edith said slowly. "I think so." She nodded. "Yes, I'm pretty sure that was her." She returned the phone to Ann. "Who is she?"

"Have you ever heard of Marilee Forsythe?"

Edith's eyebrows rose. "The author?"

"Yes."

"Of course I've heard of Marilee Forsythe." She pushed herself out of her seat and went to the bookcase. She pulled out a book, returned to the table, and handed the book to Ann. "That's the first of the Berry Mysteries—*Blackberry Blackmail*. I have them all."

The cover showed a finely rendered drawing of a blackberry bush. A slip of paper hung from one of the branches, its words, like a ransom note, cut from a newspaper.

Ann expected Edith to sit back down. Instead she went to where, as in Marilee's apartment, a breakfast bar separated the living room from the kitchen and a land line phone hung on the wall—although, Ann noticed, the receiver lay on the counter. Edith picked up the receiver. "Deegan, I think we can hang up now. Ann and I are having a nice chat." She listened for a moment, nodded, and said, "Bye-bye—and thank you." She returned the phone to the cradle and turned back to Ann. Her expression was a bit abashed. "Deegan called me back after you got on the elevator. He said better safe than sorry."

Ann smiled. "Smart move."

Edith, looking relieved, returned to the table and lowered herself back onto her chair. "So that woman I saw was Marilee Forsythe? I knew she lived in Ocean City, but I never realized she was a neighbor."

"You never went to any of her author events?"

"No." Edith patted her leg again. "Like I said, I don't get around as well as I used to."

"You heard that she disappeared?"

"I heard the news coverage on the radio. And right after that terrible incident at the bookstore." She shook her head. "I used to love going there."

"And you say you saw her up until about a week ago?"

"Yes. In fact ... there's a little notebook in a pocket on the side of your chair. Can you hand it to me?"

Ann looked down and saw a spiral-bound notebook with a ballpoint pen slipped into the ring. She handed it to Edith.

Edith removed the pen, paged through the notebook, then turned it toward Ann and tapped the last entry.

It showed the current date, then, *EB 13 Balcony - Woman puffy red parka*

"That's you," said Edith.

"*EB 13* means the thirteenth floor of Eden Beach?"

"Yes."

Ann glanced at some of the other entries on the page.

Coast Guard boats - rescue? practice?

6 dolph! south to north

"You have other entries for *EB 13*?" Ann asked.

Edith held out her hand for the notebook and Ann handed it over. Edith flipped back a few pages, then turned the notebook back to Ann.

"That's the last note I have, from a little more than a week ago. It's not a guarantee that she wasn't there after that and I didn't see her. Or that I saw her but didn't bother to make a note."

EB 13 Little woman fit to be tied

"*Little woman* is Marilee Forsythe?"

"I think so, based on the picture you showed me."

"And she looked mad?"

"Yeah. Stomping around the living room, looked like she was talking to herself."

"What does this one mean?" asked Ann, pointing to an entry a few lines above.

EB 13 Little + big woman with boxes

"There was a bigger woman who would visit her pretty regularly," said Edith.

"And they were carrying boxes? Like Marilee was getting ready to move out?"

"I don't think so—a lot of times the big woman would take the boxes into the room with the desk and then take them out later."

Ann got out her phone again and found a photo of Jeanette Frobisher from the coverage of the attack at Oh Buoy

Books. She enlarged the photo and handed the phone to Edith. "Was it this woman?"

Edith examined the photo for a few moments. "It could have been—I can't be sure." She reached across the table and flipped a few pages in the notebook and pointed to an entry. "Sometimes it was just the big woman in the condo."

EB 13 Big woman at desk

"Usually it was the little woman sitting at the desk," said Edith, "but that time it was the bigger one."

"Could I take pictures of the pages that reference *EB 13*?"

Edith considered, then said, "I wouldn't feel right having you take a picture of the pages since some of them have notes to do with other people I've seen, but I'll copy out the entries about *EB 13* for you."

"That would be great—thanks." Ann took a sip of coffee and suppressed a shudder. There were few beverages she disliked more than instant coffee. "What else did you see going on over on *EB 13*?"

Edith's chair squeaked as she leaned back. "Most of the time I saw that little woman—Marilee Forsythe, I suppose—at the desk in what is probably the master bedroom. I thought it made a lot of sense to set that room up like an office so she could enjoy the view during the day. I thought she must have one of those work-from-home jobs. And she had that sofa bed in there, too, so she could enjoy the view when she was falling asleep and when she woke up. I'm sure the view from the living room is very nice, but I'll bet it's a little bit blocked by the cut-out for the balcony."

"Yes," agreed Ann. "The view from the bedroom is more expansive."

"She always folded up the bed in the morning and put the bedclothes away. Very tidy, from what I could see." Edith took a sip of coffee. "And then, a while ago—I'll try to mark it in the copy of my notes—I noticed that she had put two of the chairs from the living room out on the balcony, and some of the other furniture was disappearing, or at least disappearing from the part of the condo I could see. I thought maybe she was moving out, but I kept seeing her over there, so I guessed she just liked it better that way. Seemed pretty bare to me—" She laughed and waved her hand to take in her own living room. "—but you can see that, as far as I'm concerned, more is more."

Edith's smile faded, and she picked up the notebook and paged through it, then tapped an entry. "But the weirdest thing was that one day I looked over and thought I saw her being attacked by a man. I was just about to call 911 when they stepped apart and started talking—it all looked very friendly—and then started wrestling with each other again. The woman didn't seem in any distress, and I watched for a couple more minutes and finally decided that they were practicing judo or karate or something like that, although without that bowing part at the end. Pretty soon they stopped the wrestling and went further back in the apartment where I couldn't see them anymore. Then she showed up in that bedroom-office. A few minutes later, I saw the man leave the building and walk away down the beach."

"Walking? Not in a car?"

"That's right."

"What did this man look like?"

Edith shrugged. "Average height. Average weight."

"How old was he?"

"I don't know—maybe thirties?"

"Hair color? Beard or mustache?"

"Dark hair, I think. I don't recall a beard or mustache. Why? Do you think he had something to do with her disappearance?"

"I don't know." Ann was silent for a moment, then asked, "Did you ever see anyone else at the condo?"

"Once in a while, the big woman showed up with a guy. A big guy. I thought maybe they were sister and brother, but they acted more like a couple. Holding hands and such."

"Yeah, that was probably Marilee's son." Ann didn't recall having seen a photo of Jeanette Frobisher's son online and decided not to bother taking the time to look for one to show Edith. "That's it?"

"As far as I can remember. I'll mark anything I forgot to tell you when I'm copying out the notes."

"And you saw the big woman at the condo more recently than the little woman."

"That's right."

"How about the big man?"

"I don't think so—I think the big woman has been in the condo more recently than the big man. *But*," said Edith, flipping through the notebook, "he did come back—in fact, a whole bunch of people were milling around over there. At first, I thought they were having a party—it was pretty late at night—but it seemed too business-like for that. Then I thought maybe she was moving after all and that these were movers, but that didn't seem quite right either. Then they closed the drapes." Edith raised her eyebrows. "I'll bet that was the police investigating Marilee Forsythe's disappearance."

"Yes, I think you're right," said Ann.

Edith flipped back and forth through the notebook, glancing through the entries. "I think those are the highlights, but I'll look through my notebook to make sure I find all the ones related to *EB 13*. Just write down your phone number—you can put it there on the last page of my notes, next to the entry about the woman in the puffy red parka—and I'll call you once I have the notes copied out for you."

Ann jotted her cell number in the notebook, then carried the tray back to the kitchen for Edith.

Edith escorted her to the door.

"I really appreciate all your help," said Ann.

"It's my pleasure." Edith smiled. "I haven't had this much fun since the last time the grandkids were here."

49

When Ann got back to The Capstan's lobby, she stopped at the security desk.

"Thanks again for arranging for me to speak to Ms. Telford," she said to Deegan.

"No problem. I figured she'd enjoy a visit."

"By the way, is it okay that I have my car in The Capstan parking lot?" She waved toward where her Forester was just visible through the lobby doors in the largely deserted lot. "I was told that the guard at Eden Beach doesn't like non-resident cars parked there."

Deegan shook his head. "That man's a piece of work." He shrugged. "It's okay with me. Not like you're keeping a resident from getting a space."

Ann returned to Eden Beach, pondering what she had learned from Edith as she climbed the stairs to *14*. The *big woman* and *big man* were almost certainly Jeanette and Jeremy Frobisher, and the fact that Edith had seen Jeanette at the condo after her last sighting of Marilee didn't necessarily mean anything—Marilee might have been working in the bay-side room, where Edith couldn't see her. And nothing Edith had said gave Ann a clue about how or where she might be most likely to contact Marilee's spirit, if the author was, in fact, dead.

But who was the man who had apparently been practicing some kind of martial art with Marilee in the living room? There were only two people unaccounted for in Ann's limited knowledge of Marilee Forsythe. One was Darren, who not only had a beard and mustache, but was thin enough that Ann would have been surprised to have someone describe him as medium weight. The other was the bookstore attacker, who, according to news reports, had been so bundled up that even the gender wasn't entirely certain.

Should she tell Darren what she had found so he could convey the information to Marilee's family? And if the family didn't want to reveal that they had hired Ann to try to contact Marilee, how would they explain to the police how they had found out about Edith Telford and her notes about what she observed from her window? Ann decided she'd wait to get the copy of Edith's notes and review them before deciding what to do.

As she let herself into the condo, she thought back to the copy of Marilee's book that Edith had shown her and figured that it couldn't hurt to page through some of the Berry Mysteries she had seen on the desk in the study. Maybe she'd find something that would give her a hint about where she might find Marilee.

She went to the study, draped her parka over the back of the desk chair, pulled the first book out of the set on the desk, and sat down on the sofa.

She had expected the books to be pristine—a trophy wall of sorts—but they were obviously practical tools of Marilee's trade, marked up with notes about details that would need to be synced across books and ideas that might form the basis of future stories. With a sigh, she settled back on the sofa, pulling the quilt across her legs.

A FEW HOURS LATER, with the shadow of Eden Beach stretching far across the beach, Ann returned the last book to the row on Marilee's desk. She had made a note of every place a body was found in the books, which suggested that she should take a swing through all the bakeries, florists, and yarn stores in the Ocean City area. But if Marilee's body was really in one of those locations, it would have been discovered long before.

Was this the full Berry Mysteries collection? There were no other books in the study, and no bookshelf in the living room. However, she recalled that there had been a few books in the bay-side room. She'd check them out just to be thorough.

Just as the books in the study matched that room's cozy decor, the books on the shelf in the bay-side room matched that room's noir-ish ambiance. They were thrillers, most by authors whose names Ann recognized, including the book by Lara Seaford. She recalled that Darren was not only Seaford's liaison for GothamCon but had also edited her book. She pulled it off the shelf, carried it to the study, and settled down again on the sofa.

The story certainly started out with a bang—with two bangs, in fact. A man and woman had just concluded a mutually satisfactory encounter in the back of a limousine when an explosion rocked the exclusive nightclub outside of which the limo was parked.

Ann flipped through the pages, past a gruesome description of the carnage inside of the nightclub, the woman's profanity-laced tirade against the perpetrators of the attack, and more sex between the woman—the protagonist of the story—and the man—her ostensible opponent—in a variety of inventive locations.

But what surprised her more than the fact that cozy mystery author Marilee Forsythe had a copy of Lara Seaford's thriller in her meager library were the notes Ann found in the book. *Remind DVO about this for #2* next to a flashback to the protagonist's childhood. *This is good! :)* next to a particularly action-packed chase scene. Ann was momentarily startled by *Good SM fodder*—the indicated passage was definitely sadistic, although not obviously masochistic—until she realized that *SM* probably referred to social media.

She flipped the book shut. One explanation for the notes was that Marilee Forsythe and Lara Seaford were friends—such close friends that Lara had given Marilee a marked-up copy of her book. But Ann thought there was a more plausible explanation.

She got out her phone and hit Darren's number.

"Hi, Ann," he answered. "Any luck?"

"Are Marilee Forsythe and Lara Seaford the same person?"

There was a long pause, then Darren said, "I believe so."

"You *believe* so?"

"Yes." He sighed. "I suspected the editing client I knew as Lara Seaford—knew only through our email correspondence, I might add—was really Marilee Forsythe. My suspicions were largely confirmed when her family found a manuscript which was obviously the follow on to *Darkest Before Death* in Marilee's condo. But it was missing the ending—that part of what I told you was true—and they agreed to let me take a shot at completing it."

"But you couldn't finish it."

"No. I need Marilee's help. That's why we hired you."

"Which suggests that you know she's dead."

"I don't *know* she's dead, but I believe she is. She had attracted the interest of a major publisher, and I was the only one who could connect the two of them. She never responded to my email about it. She had her own reasons for keeping her identity a secret from the rest of the world, but she had no incentive to cut off communications with me."

"What do you think happened to her?"

"I think the most likely explanation is that the man who attacked her at the bookstore got her out of her condo. I believe that's what the police think as well."

"Why didn't you just tell me all this to begin with?"

"Because if you weren't able to get in touch with Marilee, or if you were able to get in touch with her and it turned out that she wasn't Lara Seaford or that she herself didn't know what the ending of the second thriller novel was, I wouldn't have had to tell you my crazy theory."

"And if Marilee *is* dead and if I *can* contact her and she *does* have an ending for the second thriller, what happens to the money from that book?"

"All the royalties will go to Marilee or her heirs."

"How do I know that? How do I know that you're not bilking the family out of their money? Or Marilee out of hers, if she reappears, alive and well?"

"I have a contract with the family."

"Would you show it to me—with their okay, of course?"

"Yes, of course—I'll ask them about that."

"So why are you doing all this?"

"Because I have no confidence Alec Quine will be able to continue the success of the Wolfram series—there's only so much I can do as the editor—and at the moment, that's almost my only source of income. A second Seaford thriller, especially if it's successful as the first, will be a nice calling card for me to build up my client list again. And," he added grimly, "as you've seen yourself, Alec is not the easiest person to work with. I'd like to extract myself from that relationship, if at all possible."

"Yeah, I can understand that." After a pause, she asked, not bothering to hide her irritation, "Are there any other secrets you need to tell me about?"

"No, there's nothing I need to tell you."

"And you'll send me that copy of the contract?"

"I'll email you a copy as soon as I get the family's approval to share it with you."

She sighed. "Okay, do that. Until then, I'll keep looking for Marilee."

50

Ann ended the call with Darren and flopped back on the sofa. She would have felt better with a copy of the contract between Darren and Marilee Forsythe's family in hand, but it seemed unlikely he was lying about that —she assumed that at some point the signatories of an agreement for a second Lara Seaford thriller would become public knowledge.

And while she waited to get the copy of the contract, where else could she look for Marilee? Darren obviously didn't know her well enough to offer suggestions for where her spirit might appear—in fact, he hadn't even known her real identity until after Marilee had disappeared. Edith Telford had offered some interesting insights into what went on in Marilee's condo, but if Marilee's spirit was in the condo, Ann believed she would have seen or at least heard her by now. Who else might suggest other locations where she could look for the author?

Then she thought of the spirits she had seen walking the beach. Maybe one of them had seen Marilee after her death.

Ann slipped into her parka and went out onto the balcony.

She scanned the windows of The Capstan, wondering if Edith was on watch, but except for one light on the first floor and a few on the top floors, the windows of The Capstan were dark.

She turned her attention to the beach. She saw what she guessed was the light from a flashlight carried by a living walker who was unlikely to be able to help her with her search. But as her eyes adjusted to the dark, she picked out two dimmer lights that could be spirits. She stepped inside, grabbed her phone, hat, and mittens, and hurried downstairs.

When she got to the beach, she realized that there were more spirits than she had been able to see from the balcony: at least six within a few hundred yards of Eden Beach. Most strolled across the hard-packed sand by the gently lapping waves. One stood gazing out over the water.

She crossed the sand to this one, who turned out to be a deeply tanned older man wearing a Speedo and a swim cap, a pair of swim goggles dangling from his fingers. Even though Ann's parka, hat, and gloves were keeping her quite warm, she gave a sympathetic shiver.

Once she had explained to the man why she could see and speak with him, she showed him a photo of Marilee on her phone. The man peered at it and shook his head—no, he hadn't seen anyone who looked like that, living or dead.

Ann was worried that she might have to stay and chat with the man as a thank you for the information, but he turned placidly back to the water and resumed his contemplative pose.

She took up a position near the water and questioned the spirit walkers as they passed. The conversations were all the same: she explained about her ability and showed them Marilee's photo. They looked at the photo, shook their heads, then continued on their way.

After half an hour, she was considering going in—even the

parka couldn't fend off the effect of the dropping temperatures forever—when she saw another spirit approaching, one she had seen on her earlier reconnaissance of the beach. Like many of the others, he was dressed for warm weather, although not as skimpily as the older man. He seemed more vivid than the other spirits, suggesting that he might have died fairly recently. As on Ann's earlier sighting of him, he was toiling through the unpacked sand above the waterline. And he was headed in her direction.

He was about thirty, medium height and weight, with dark hair combed back from a high forehead, dark eyebrows, and thin lips covering prominent teeth.

"Hello," said Ann.

His eyebrows rose in surprise. He looked her up and down. "Are you ...?"

"Not dead." She explained again about her sensing ability. "My name's Ann."

"Son of a gun." After a moment, he continued. "I've seen you before—well, I've seen that red coat. On the beach." He gestured toward the upper floors of Eden Beach. "And on that balcony."

Ann looked up toward Marilee's condo, identifiable by the chairs on the balcony that were silhouetted against the light she had left on in the living room.

"You staying there?" he asked.

She returned her eyes to the man. "Yes."

"Friend of the owner?"

Ann felt a little jolt of excitement. "You're talking about Marilee Forsythe, right?

"You tell me."

"That's her condo, but I don't know her myself. Do you?"

He shrugged. "I did odd jobs for her now and then."

"Do you know what happened to her?"

His eyes narrowed. "How so?"

"She's missing."

"Missing?"

"Yes. Her family hired me to try to contact her."

After a pause, he said, "If they hired you, they must figure she's dead."

Ann's heartbeat raised a notch. "They don't know for sure, but they suspect she may be."

"What do they think happened to her?"

"I don't know what the police think, but ... did you know Marilee had been attacked after an author event at Oh Buoy Books?"

"Yeah."

"The person who attacked her got away and some people think that he—or she, I suppose—was responsible for Marilee's disappearance." When the man didn't respond, she continued. "It would help to have a timeline of her whereabouts—for example, when she was last at the condo."

Still no response.

She switched tacks. "Do you walk the beach a lot?"

"Yes." He turned to face the water. "I spent a lot of time here when I was alive. I loved it when I was a kid. Playing in the sand, body surfing on the waves. Loved the boardwalk, too—didn't matter the season. I could always get some Thrasher's fries and walk the boards, summer or winter." His gaze dropped to the sand. "Some not so good memories, too. When money got tight, I used to take wallets from the beach bags. You wouldn't believe how careless people get about leaving their stuff unattended." He met her gaze again. "You know what the trick is?"

"Can't say that I do."

"Don't take the stuff and then head off down the beach. Take something and then walk down to the water—other people think you're just some guy who went to his own bag to get something." His laugh was tinged with bitterness. "Although I shouldn't be giving advice—I did get nabbed eventually."

She waited to see if he would elaborate. Spirits were often quite willing to chat about things they probably never would have discussed in life. And why not? They usually had nothing left to lose. But when he was silent, she asked, "How did you end up doing odd jobs for Marilee Forsythe?"

He shook his head. "After I got nabbed, I was going to stick to the straight-and-narrow. But it's hard to get a job with a record, and when money got tight, I went back to lifting some wallets." He gestured toward the Eden Beach balcony. "She saw me. She took a video of me doing it, then confronted me."

Ann raised her eyebrows.

"She told me her name was Lara Seaford, and she offered me a deal. She was writing crime books, and she had a lot of questions about criminal life." He smiled sardonically. "She obviously wasn't the type of woman who would know about that from her own experience. She said she'd pay me money—good money—to help her out. If not, she'd show the police a video she had taken of me lifting wallets."

Ann couldn't help taking a step back. The threat of blackmail seemed all too likely a reason for the man to want Marilee out of the way.

He must have sensed her concern and raised a placating hand. "I was pissed at first, but it worked out fine. She did pay me good money—got me out of most of my financial troubles—and it was actually pretty fun work."

"And how did you find out that the woman you knew as Lara Seaford was actually Marilee Forsythe?"

"She eventually had to tell me. I guess she decided that even I was smart enough to figure out that if she was the guest of honor at a shindig for Marilee Forsythe, she must be Marilee Forsythe."

"She invited you to one of her author events?"

"She needed me to come to Oh Buoy Books."

"The event where she got attacked?"

"Yup. By me." Before Ann had a chance to take another step back, he hurried on. "She had arranged it all. It was supposed to be a publicity stunt. You know, Agatha Christie turns out to be Bruce Lee. We watched a bunch of videos on YouTube. We even practiced in her condo. We picked a choke hold."

Ann thought back to what Edith had told her about Marilee and a younger man seeming to be practicing martial arts in her living room.

"You were going to put Marilee Forsythe in a choke hold?"

He frowned. "No, of course not. She was going to put *me* in a choke hold. She said there would be witnesses, that she'd make sure that a few of the people at the event came outside with her and saw the whole thing go down so they could describe it on social media or to reporters."

"You guys weren't worried that they might try to interfere?"

"She said *the old biddies who show up at those events won't do anything other than squawk.*" He blushed. "Her words."

"And, I guess, capture everything on their phones for social media."

"No. Before they had time to get out their phones, I'd act like I had thrown her off—not hard to imagine, since she's so tiny—and run away. I didn't want video. Too likely someone might be able to identify me."

"What about the bookstore's security video?"

His eyebrows rose. "The bookstore had video? That wasn't part of the plan."

"So Marilee Forsythe wasn't following the plan as you understood it."

"Not if she knew the camera was there."

"Was Marilee's daughter-in-law, Jeanette Frobisher, the only person from the event she could persuade to come outside with her?"

He grimaced. "Not exactly an *old biddy*, is she? And she sure did more than squawk. I don't think Marilee expected her to be there. It was just such a mess—not ... what's the word ..."

"Choreographed?"

"That's right—not choreographed. I don't think Ms. Forsythe expected Ms. Frobisher to jump in." He shook his head. "It was pretty gutsy. For all Ms. Frobisher knew, I might have had a knife or a gun. Ms. Forsythe was plenty careful to make sure she didn't get hurt herself, but her daughter-in-law wasn't being careful of her own safety." After a pause, he asked, "Was she okay?"

"I read in the news that she got a black eye."

"I'm sorry to hear that. I think I hit her with my elbow, but it was an accident. And Ms. Forsythe falling like that wasn't planned either. In fact, when she fell I figured the whole thing had gone so off the rails it wasn't worth trying to stick with the script. I reached out to help her up, but then I fell."

"What caused the fall? It's hard to tell on the video."

"I'm not even sure."

"How about you? Did you get hurt?"

"Yeah. I hit my head when I fell. I managed to get away, but I felt pretty woozy by the time I got to where I was going. I fell asleep." He tried for a laugh. "Not just asleep, I guess. Never woke up."

"Did you go home?"

"No. My house was too far. Before I went to prison, I could

have run all the way, but then my leg got hurt and my running days were over."

"What happened in prison?"

"Stuck my nose in where it didn't belong and got my kneecap busted as a lesson."

Ann winced. "Ouch."

"You got that right. That's why I walk in the loose sand—free physical therapy. Anyhow, I had a bolt hole for after the bookstore."

"Where?"

"Rather not say."

"Why not? It doesn't matter to you anymore, right?"

"Not to me, but it might inconvenience other people." He laughed ruefully. "If there's one thing my little 'accident' in prison taught me, it's the importance of not inconveniencing other people and of minding my own business."

"What do you think happened to Marilee?"

He shrugged. "Have no idea."

A movement near the path through the dunes to The Capstan caught Ann's attention. Another night-time walker emerged onto the beach. She guessed it was a man, and one whom, at least from a distance, looked underdressed for the weather. He looked up and down the beach, then began making his way across the sand toward the water, near where Ann stood.

At the same time she noticed a pair of lights approaching and became aware of the low grumble of an engine.

"What's that?" she asked, gesturing toward the lights.

"Beach cleaner."

"They run it even in the winter?"

"I guess it's easier to keep up with whatever the waves throw up on the beach than to let it pile up all winter." He shook his head. "A necessary evil, I guess, but I steer clear of them—they make quite a racket." He gestured toward the path. "Looks like it's not what that guy's in the mood for, either."

Ann followed his gesture and saw that the man was headed back toward The Capstan. "Or maybe he just decided that tonight wasn't the night for a stroll on the beach." She turned back to the man. "I really need to get inside—I can barely feel my fingers. Can you keep an eye out for Marilee on the beach for me?"

"Why should I?" Despite his words, his tone was more curious than truculent.

"It would help me do what Marilee's family hired me to do."

He didn't look convinced. Was he asking her to do him a favor? "I could take a message to someone for you. Or get a message to you from someone."

"Don't know who I'd have a message for. My mom and dad are dead. No sisters or brothers. The friends I had before I went to prison didn't want to hang out with me once I got out, and the 'friends' I made in prison aren't ones I wanted to stay in touch with." He was silent for a moment, then continued. "But I do want to know what happened at the bookstore. If she knew there was a security camera behind the bookstore, she lied to me. And if she didn't tell Ms. Frobisher what was going to happen, she risked her getting an injury a lot worse than a black eye. Not sure I have a message for her, but I wouldn't mind hearing her side of the story. You might have more luck than I did."

"Than you *did*?"

"Yeah. Actually, I did see her after she died."

Ann's eyebrows shot up.

"But she wasn't talking to anyone—even me."

"Where was she?"

"In her condo."

"Could you tell what had happened?"

"No. No blood. Maybe a stroke? She was just sitting in her writing room."

"The bay-side guest room or the ocean-side study?" asked Ann with a sinking feeling.

"Ocean-side."

She shuddered, thinking of all the time she had spent on that sofa, wrapped in the quilt.

"Was her spirit there?" she asked.

"No. I went to the condo a couple of times after I died. She was still alive. She didn't see me, and when I tried to talk to her, she didn't hear me, although I think maybe she sensed something because she acted a little nervous. A couple of visits later, she was dead. I went one more time, but her body was gone."

"Do you remember the days of your visits?"

He squinted. "No. Time seems ... different since I died."

"Do you have any idea what happened to her body?"

He shrugged, then shook his head.

It seemed clear he was holding something back, but Ann couldn't think of how she could convince him to share it, and she was becoming increasingly anxious to get back to the warmth of the condo. "Can you give me any ideas of where I could look for her? Any place that would be meaningful to her. Maybe some place you took her to as part of you helping her with her thriller novels?"

He shook his head again. "No. I offered to take her to some places around Ocean City that I thought might be good for that kind of book, but she said that she wasn't going to write any more books set at the shore."

"Okay," Ann said with a sigh. She made a mental note to

switch her research from the Berry Mysteries to Lara Seaford's *Darkest Before Death*.

"Maybe you'll still find her," he said, "even without my help. If you do, can you let me know?"

"Sure—" She realized she didn't know his name.

"Randall," he supplied.

"Sure, Randall—I'll let you know."

51

The next morning, Edith called to tell Ann that the copy of the notes was ready. Deegan gave Ann a wave from The Capstan security desk as she passed through the lobby, and when she got to the condo, Edith got her settled at the table by the window.

"I looked through all my notebooks and copied out what I had about *EB 13*," said Edith. "I don't think there's more there than I already told you, but why don't you take a look while you're here. Maybe you'll have some questions I can answer."

Edith served her another cup of the odious instant coffee and a quite tasty Danish. When Edith excused herself to use the bathroom, Ann poured the coffee down the kitchen drain.

When Edith joined her at the table, Ann said, "Yeah, I think you already told me the most important parts."

"I'm sorry the notes aren't more of a help."

"They're a big help—I really appreciate you sharing these with me," said Ann, slipping the copy into her knapsack. "By the way, I met someone who might be the man who was wrestling with Marilee Forsythe in her condo." She described

Randall: medium height, medium weight, no beard or mustache.

Edith shrugged. "It could be—but then again, that could be a lot of men."

Ann finished the Danish and took the mugs and plates to the sink. After promising to keep Edith apprised of developments, she headed downstairs.

Getting the copy of Edith's notes reminded her that Darren still owed her the copy of his contract with Marilee's family. Standing outside the entrance to The Capstan, she got out her phone and tapped his number.

"Hey, Ann," he answered, sounding distracted. "How's it going?"

"No luck yet. Did you get the okay from Marilee's family to send me a copy of the contract?"

"Damn. No, sorry, I forgot. I got a call from the Princeton PD—Detective Withers—about the bullets they found in the drawer with Jock's gun in the turret room. It turns out that they were the wrong bullets. Nine-millimeter bullets for a gun that uses nine-millimeter short ammunition. You'd think they would fit, but oddly enough, nine-millimeter bullets are actually longer than the nine-millimeter shorts."

"I didn't know you were knowledgeable about guns."

"I've never handled a gun in my life," said Darren with a laugh, "but you learn these things if you edit thrillers. And you certainly learn these things if you *write* thrillers—at least if you're Jock Quine. That's not a mistake Jock would have made. I told Withers that."

Ann was gratified that the information that she and Joe had shared with the Princeton PD had lit a fire under the unofficially retired investigating detective. "I hope that will prove to be a useful lead for them."

"Me, too. And I'll call Marilee's family now about the contract."

"While you're at it, can you ask them if they have any ideas for where Marilee's spirit might hang out? The more specific the information, the better—not just 'on the beach,' but near a specific landmark, for example."

"Sure, sure. I'll see what I can find out."

To save herself a trip back up the stairs, Ann settled down on a bench outside The Capstan to wait for Darren's return call. Her vantage point overlooked the parking lot, empty except for her Forester.

She decided to call Joe with what she had learned from Darren about the Quine investigation. As the call rang, a light-colored sedan pulled off the Coastal Highway and into the lot.

Her call went to voicemail. "This is Joe's voicemail," intoned the recording. "Leave a message and I'll get back to you as soon as possible."

As she relayed the information Darren had given her about his interaction with the Princeton PD, the sedan slowed, circled the Forester, then headed back to the exit.

She tapped to end the call and watched the sedan disappear down the highway.

She thought back to her trip to the boardwalk the previous day and the light-colored sedan she had seen on the far side of the parking lot when she returned to her car. She thought, too, of the underdressed man peering in the window of a closed store. Was this the same car, driven by the same man? There was no way to tell—the car was so nondescript that it was only memorable in an environment as relatively devoid of vehicles as Ocean City in January.

Then she thought with a start of the man, also underdressed, who had appeared the previous night on the beach while she was talking with Randall. Was this man following her? And, if yes, wouldn't *nondescript* be exactly the kind of car he would choose?

52

Jeanette was at the pharmacy counter, reviewing on her phone's browser the website of a new supplier she and Jeremy were considering using for some of their naturopathic offerings. She jumped when the phone rang: Darren Van Osten. The call was conveniently timed—there were no customers in the store, and Jeremy had run out to pick up some takeout for their lunch.

"Hello, Darren," she answered.

"Hey, Jeanette. How are you doing?"

"Okay. How are things there?"

"Very productive, very productive. I want to thank you again for being generous enough to let me stay here at the condo. But I thought it would be nice to get out of here for a little while, and I might as well go somewhere that Marilee enjoyed—more inspiration for channeling her muse. Are there places in Ocean City that were especially meaningful to her?"

"Sure. Of course. Well, let's see ... there's Oh Buoy Books ..."

"Yes, I'll check that out. Anywhere else?"

"She enjoyed Marco's. It's a restaurant on the beach."

"Another good suggestion. I don't want to use up any of Marilee's groceries while I'm here. Does Marilee have a favorite table at Marco's? I'd love to sit where she sits."

"She has a regular table by the window. And I'll let you know if I think of any other places that were special haunts." She felt her face flush. "So to speak." Jeanette heard from Darren's side of the call the faint sound of a dog barking. "Well," she said, flustered by her faux pas, "I'll let you get back to work."

They ended the call.

Jeanette began chastising herself—she had to be more careful about slip-ups like referring to Marilee's *haunts*—but then she realized that Marilee being dead was a possibility she had discussed with Darren, not a secret. She grimaced. She was having trouble remembering to whom she had lied, with whom she had to exercise extra care. She returned to her research.

Then she set the phone aside.

Darren had implied that he was in Marilee's condo: he had said *here at the condo* and *nice to get out of here*. The condo was over a dozen stories up, and Marilee hadn't been wrong when she bragged about how well sound-insulated the units were.

So how could she have heard a dog barking in the background?

She stared at the phone for a minute, then picked it up and tapped Darren's number.

"Hello, Jeanette," he answered.

"You're still at Marilee's condo? You haven't left for Marco's yet, have you?"

"No, not yet."

"You said that you didn't want to use any of Marilee's groceries, but we can easily replace anything you use. You could tell me what's there, and I'll let you know if any of it is off-limits."

Darren's laugh sounded forced. "Oh, no need. Thank you, but a trip to Marco's sounds like just the break I need."

"Getting cabin fever?"

"A bit. Or," he said with another strained laugh, "in this case, condo fever."

The front door of the pharmacy opened, and a moment later Jeremy appeared from one of the aisles with the takeout.

"Lunch is served!" he announced.

"Jeremy's back with lunch," she said to Darren. "Got to go." She ended the call.

"Who was that?" asked Jeremy as she followed him into the back room.

"Just an acquaintance."

"You didn't need to cut your call short."

"That's okay. I didn't really have anything left to say to him." She drew a deep breath. "I want to talk with you."

53

Ann had almost decided to duck back inside The Capstan—to enjoy both the warmth of the lobby and Deegan's reassuring presence—when her phone rang.

"It's me," said Darren. "The only ideas that the family had were Oh Buoy Books, which we already checked, and Marilee's favorite restaurant, Marco's. She liked to sit by the window."

"Okay, I'll check out the restaurant. And how about the contract?"

"Oh, right. Yes, the family is fine with me sharing a copy of that. I'll scan it and send it over to you. And you know," he said, his tone brighter, "if we can locate Marilee, it will make great fodder for your talk at GothamCon."

Ann went to the Forester, tapped *Marco's* into her GPS, and pulled out of The Capstan parking lot onto the Coastal Highway. As she drove, she kept an eye on the rearview mirror for nondescript light-colored sedans.

Ann arrived at the restaurant, located on the ground floor of a beachfront hotel, not having spotted any tails. She found a spot near the entrance, next to a truck with the name and logo of an HVAC repair service. Inside, a man stood at the host station, dressed in a suit and tie, a fine wool scarf draped around his neck. Ann felt him assessing her wardrobe of puffy red parka, jeans, and hiking boots without his eyes ever leaving her face.

"May I help you, miss?"

"I was wondering—" Ann looked past the man into a virtually deserted dining room … and saw Marilee Forsythe seated at a table next to the window. "—if I could get a table for one."

Although Ann's wardrobe might not have been what the man hoped for from his clientele, he could hardly afford to turn her away if the empty dining room was any indication.

"Yes, certainly." He pulled a menu from under the station. "Please follow me."

Ann followed the man across the dining room, noticing that, despite the flames flickering in a gas fireplace near the bar, the room was quite cold.

Marilee Forsythe turned her gaze from the glass wall overlooking the beach toward Ann and the host. She was dressed in a black dolman-sleeved top, narrow black slacks, and black leather boots. Although the discrepancy between the clothing and the temperature wasn't as extreme as it had been in the case of the Speedo-clad man on the frigid beach, the restaurant was chilly enough that a living woman would have been shivering.

"I'd love to sit by the window," Ann said to the host.

"Of course." He veered toward a table near a server station —and, Ann thought, out of the line of sight of any other, more poshly dressed diners who might arrive.

"How about that one?" asked Ann, pointing to the table where Marilee sat.

Marilee's eyebrows rose.

The host looked toward Marilee's table. "That particular table?" He glanced around a room inhabited only by himself, Ann, and, unbeknownst to him, a dead woman. "There are plenty of other tables to choose from."

"It has sentimental value. My parents got engaged at that table." Realizing that she had no idea how long the restaurant had been open, she amended, "My mother and stepfather. I'd love to sit where they sat, maybe send them a photo."

"We normally reserve that table for one of our most loyal customers. Marilee Forsythe. A well-known local author. Perhaps you've heard of her?"

"I believe I have."

"Then perhaps you also know that Ms. Forsythe has been missing for some time. We here at Marco's are quite concerned."

"Yes, I can imagine you would be."

"Of course, Ms. Forsythe enjoyed sitting in the chair that had the better view of the water."

"Who can blame her—it's a lovely view."

"But perhaps you would be willing to sit in the other chair? Out of respect for Ms. Forsythe?"

"Yes, I think that would be best."

He led her to the table, the temperature dropping still further as they approached. Ann noticed a shiver shake his hand as he set the menu down at the place opposite Marilee.

"Normally I would offer to take your coat, miss," he said, "but you may wish to leave it on."

"Good idea."

"I do apologize. We have been having some trouble with the climate control."

He pulled out the chair for Ann and she sat.

Marilee glared at her with a combination of anger and surprise.

"Is that why there aren't more diners?" Ann asked.

"I suspect so." He marshaled a smile. "Not all our guests are as hardy as you."

"So, Marilee Forsythe was a regular?"

His smile became somewhat warmer. "Oh, yes. Ms. Forsythe has been coming to Marco's for many years. We've been honored to have her as a frequent guest."

Ann glanced at Marilee. The host's words had moderated her glare somewhat, although she looked haggard in a way Ann wasn't used to, even among the dead.

The conversation about Marco's favorite guest seemed to have cheered up the host as well. "Anything to drink, miss? Perhaps a hot coffee drink?"

"I'll have a Macallan, two rocks. That always warms me up."

"Very good." He crossed the restaurant and stepped behind the bar.

Ann glanced at the menu, then set it aside. "I understand you're a regular," she said, sotto voce, to Marilee. "What would you recommend I order?"

Marilee's glare returned. "So you *can* see me."

"Yes." Ann got an Ann Kinnear Sensing card out of her knapsack and put it on the service plate in front of Marilee. "I do it for a living."

Without looking at the card, Marilee said, "It's going to be a bit of a challenge for you to hold a conversation with a ghost without looking crazy."

"I stopped worrying about looking crazy years ago." Ann cast her eyes over the deserted dining room. "Plus, who's going to hear me?"

"Marco. And the dinner crowd will show up soon."

"Not if you keep freezing out the dining room."

"What?"

"You're what's making the room so cold."

"It doesn't seem cold to me."

"Of course it doesn't."

Marilee also looked across the dining room. "I just thought the heating system was being fluky."

"Nope. It's you."

Marilee rallied. "Still, someone will show up and wonder why you're talking to thin air."

"As I said, not a problem as far as I'm concerned." She pulled a pair of earbuds from her knapsack and slipped them in. "But if it *was* a problem, modern technology means that nobody thinks it's weird if someone is talking to thin air."

Marilee's expression darkened. She glanced at the card. "So someone hired you to contact me? Who was it—Ezra? Jeremy?"

"No. Darren Van Osten, who's hoping that you can help him with the ending of the second Lara Seaford thriller."

Much to Ann's annoyance, the man who had seated her—evidently Marco himself—chose that moment to deliver her drink to the table.

"Have you decided what you would like, miss?"

"What are Ms. Forsythe's favorites?"

Marilee rolled her eyes, but the question seemed to please the host.

"Ms. Forsythe enjoys the salmon and, of course, the Maryland crab cakes with the house salad."

"Crab cakes seems like the right dish to order in Ocean City—I'll have that. And a glass of whatever kind of wine you think would go well with it."

"I recommend our Oregon Pinot Blanc. Not overly acidic, and I think the hint of citrus will go well with the crab."

"Sounds good." Ann handed him the menu, and he crossed the dining room and disappeared through a swinging door to the kitchen. She took a sip of Scotch. "So, you wrote *Darkest Before Death*."

After a moment, Marilee said, her voice haughty, "I did." She was trying to look disapproving, but Ann suspected she was gratified that someone other than her editor knew that she was the author of the popular book. Marilee gestured to the business card. "And how did Darren know about your services?"

"I'm going to be at GothamCon, and he's my handler."

"Handler?"

"You know, like he was doing for you as Lara."

"I think you mean *liaison*."

"Sure. Liaison."

"And what is your role at GothamCon?"

"I'm giving a talk."

Marilee pursed her lips. "I didn't realize they allowed people not associated with the writing or publishing industries to present at GothamCon."

"They must be lowering their standards." Ann took another sip of Scotch, then asked, "How did you end up here at Marco's?"

A look of confusion flickered across Marilee's face, and she shifted her gaze out the window, toward where waves crashed against the shore. "I don't know. One minute I was in my condo at Eden Beach and the next minute ..." Seconds ticked by, then she turned back to Ann. "Are you aware that I was the victim of an attack at an author event?"

"Yes."

"I was supposed to travel to stay with Jeremy and Jeanette —my son and daughter-in-law—in Pennsylvania."

Ann raised an eyebrow. "I hadn't heard that. I thought you couldn't leave your apartment."

"Jeremy prescribed some woo-woo drug that was supposed to make the trip easier for me. I took it … and I don't remember anything between then and sitting here at Marco's."

"What did he give you?"

"CBD."

"I hadn't heard about the CBD either." Ann got out her phone and tapped. After a couple of minutes, during which Marilee fidgeted vigorously, Ann said, "I thought maybe you OD'd, but it seems as if it would be hard to OD on CBD."

"Well, I only have his word for it that that's what it was."

"Why would he give you something other than what he claimed he was giving you?"

"I have no idea. Maybe he had decided it was preferable to having to pay back the loan I had given them."

Ann sat forward. "That's also news to me. Your son and daughter-in-law owed you money?"

"Yes. I loaned them half a million dollars so they could buy a new building for their pharmacy when the old one flooded."

"Are you suggesting that your son gave you an intentional overdose of CBD, or of something else he claimed was CBD, to avoid having to repay the loan?"

Marilee shrugged. "I suppose it's possible."

Ann sat back and examined Marilee. "So, none of this has anything to do with the bookstore attack?"

"Who knows?"

Ann took another sip of Scotch. "I think *I* know, since it sounds like you and your accomplice Randall were buddies—or at least colleagues."

Marilee's eyes narrowed. "You talked to Randall? When?"

"I talked to him yesterday."

Marilee's eyes drifted to the business card then back to Ann. "And what did he tell you?"

Marco's next arrival at the table, this time with Ann's salad, was welcome. As he arranged the plate in front of her and regaled her with the provenance of the ingredients, she was able to think through what Marilee had told her.

When Marco stepped away, Ann said, "Randall told me you two arranged the attack at the bookstore. He told me he was surprised when Jeanette showed up. And he was surprised when I told him there was a security camera behind the bookstore—he thought that 'no cameras' was part of the plan."

"There was no point in staging the attack if no one saw it."

"How about Jeanette coming to your rescue? That wasn't part of the plan as he understood it. He's wondering if that was a surprise to you, too."

"Of course it was a surprise to me. I thought she was in the store." After a moment, she added, her voice sullen, "Lucky for me, I suppose."

"It wasn't lucky for Randall. He died."

After a beat, Marilee said, "Oh?"

"Probably as a result of hitting his head when he fell."

"Certainly an unfortunate—and entirely unanticipated —outcome."

"You know what I think?"

"No," said Marilee irritably, "but I feel sure I'm about to find out."

"I think you knew about the security camera behind the bookstore—you were counting on it capturing the fake attack so you could use it for publicity—but you didn't tell Randall because you knew he wouldn't go along with the plan if he knew. I think you didn't expect Jeanette to come to your rescue, because you wouldn't want to share the spotlight with anyone."

"And why did I go to all this trouble?"

"To pave the way for revealing that you were really Lara Seaford. Like Randall said: Agatha Christie turns out to be Bruce Lee."

"So what if I did? No one was supposed to get hurt. It would have worked perfectly if Jeanette hadn't interfered."

"And then you couldn't leave the condo because you were so traumatized by what happened at the bookstore?"

"I *chose* not to leave the condo," snapped Marilee, "because I was tired of being expected to ask, 'how high?' every time Ezra Parsons told me to jump."

"And Jeremy and Jeanette were playing along with that?"

"No," Marilee said reluctantly. "They didn't know it wasn't for real."

"You were keeping them in the dark about quite a lot."

"It sounds like *they* were keeping *me* in the dark about whatever was in that prescription Jeremy gave me."

They glared at each other across the table.

Finally, Marilee said, trying for a conversational tone, "Did Jeremy and Jeanette at least have a nice memorial service for me?"

"No one knows for sure that you're dead. Your body wasn't in the condo."

Marilee's eyebrows shot up. "What? How could that be?"

"Someone must have moved it."

"But who? And where?"

"I don't know. No one knows."

Marilee sat forward. "You need to find my body. It might provide some evidence of what happened to me. You can't resolve a mystery without a body."

"Where would I look? It could be anywhere. It could be floating in the Atlantic somewhere."

"Bodies dumped at sea wash up, eventually. That happens in *Darkest Before Death*."

"Maybe, but there's not much I can do to make that happen faster. Besides, my engagement is to contact you to find out what you planned for the ending of your second thriller novel, not to help the police find out how you died and what happened to your body."

"But if they think I might just be missing, you can tell them I'm dead. That I died in the condo after taking whatever Jeremy gave me."

"Me going to the police and telling them you died in your condo and that somebody moved your body is, at best, going to result in them thinking I'm crazy or, at worst, adding me to their suspect list."

"You'll just have to find a way to convince them."

"I'm telling you, I can't—"

"Otherwise, I won't tell you what I had planned for the ending of the sequel to *Darkest Before Death*." Marilee gave Ann a Cheshire Cat smile. "And it's spectacular."

Ann groaned. "Please don't do this."

Marilee sat back and folded her hands on the table. "Those are my conditions. You find my body or help the police find it. When the police have the body, they'll be able to figure out what happened. Even an amateur sleuth knows that."

Ann glared at her.

"If Jeremy or Jeanette hid my body, I can't imagine it could be anywhere that would be all that difficult to locate. They have no gift for subterfuge." She brightened. "In fact, they might have used one of the locations referenced in my cozies."

Ann sighed. "Okay, I'll check those out. But if I don't find your body hidden in the back of some muffin bakery—"

Ann started as she realized Marco was standing by her chair with her meal and a glass of wine.

"Your crab cakes, miss," said Marco starchily, placing them in front of her and removing the Scotch glass.

Ann could tell by his expression that he not only disapproved of people talking on their cell phones in the restaurant, but thought it was bad taste to be talking about finding a body in a muffin bakery while sitting at the table usually frequented by Marco's favorite cozy mystery author.

"Thanks," she said. "This looks great."

"Bon appétit." He stalked back to the kitchen.

"If you don't find my body," said Marilee, "then Darren is just going to have to come up with the ending on his own."

Ann considered what she had heard while she ate a bite of crab cake. "So why had you decided to leave the condo and go stay with Jeremy and Jeanette in Downingtown?"

Ann had assumed that with their relationship on a somewhat rocky footing, Marilee wouldn't answer, but the author's need to share her plans must have trumped her desire to speak with Ann as little as possible.

"I needed to get to GothamCon, and I could easily get a train into the city from near their house. And then, if *Darkest before Dawn* won Best Debut, I was going to reveal my identity at the award ceremony." Marilee cast a wistful gaze back to the beach and the white-capped ocean beyond. "It would have been marvelous."

54

Ann spent the afternoon visiting some of the places she had noted as the locations of bodies in Marilee's cozy mysteries, with no sign of Marilee herself at any of them.

By the time she returned to The Capstan parking lot, the sun had long since set, and the moon cast a faint illumination when not obscured by the clouds scudding across the sky. The radar on her phone's weather app showed a line of freezing precipitation moving in from the east—spits of wet flakes were already evident in the gusty wind—but she figured she had time for a quick trip to the beach before returning to Marilee's condo. She wanted to update Randall on the events of the day and see if he had any other suggestions for locations she could search for Marilee's body. Keeping an eye out for nondescript sedans and underdressed beach walkers, she made her way from the parking lot to the beach.

She found Randall standing near the water, barely out of the freezing spray from the crashing waves, his warm-weather clothing looking even more incongruous than before.

He turned as she approached. "Any luck?"

"Yes, indeed. I ran into Marilee at Marco's. She did know about the camera behind the bookstore."

He shook his head. "I should have known."

"She also said that Jeanette showing up was a surprise to her, and I don't have any reason not to believe her."

Ann relayed to Randall the rest of the discussion with Marilee.

When she was done, Randall asked, "And she wants you to find her body because she thinks an autopsy will show that her son gave her an overdose?"

"If it really was CBD, it seems unlikely that would have killed her ... but I suppose he might have told her it was CBD and given her something else."

"Maybe if the CBD was mixed with something else ..." Randall said slowly.

"Like what?"

"I don't know. Maybe painkillers."

"Why would her son give her painkillers?"

"Maybe he didn't give them to her. Maybe she took them herself."

"Marilee was taking painkillers?"

"I don't know for certain—I'm just guessing." He scuffed his foot in the sand. "She told me she was writing a scene for her thriller where a character hides a supply of painkillers. She said she had read about stash boxes and asked if I could get her one to check out."

"Did you get one for her?"

"I told her I could, but that if I was trying to hide drugs, I wouldn't use one of those. I told her I'd use some everyday object that no one would think twice about."

"Interesting." After a moment, Ann asked, "Can you come back to the condo with me and help me poke around?"

Randall nodded. "You bet." He smiled sadly. "Nothing much else to do."

~

ANN DECIDED ONCE AGAIN to take the stairs to the condo as the option least likely to attract Kenny's attention. As she puffed up flight after flight, she could hear the uneven *thump THUMP* of Randall's steps behind her and realized she should have asked him if he preferred the elevator. She wasn't surprised that this lasting reminder of his time in prison, an injury inflicted on him for failing to mind his own business, had deterred him from delving too deeply into the mystery of Lara Seaford and Marilee Forsythe's shifting identities.

As winded as Ann was, she pulled ahead of Randall during the climb to 14. She stepped out of the stairwell and almost fell as her foot slipped on a walkway made icy by the increasingly heavy sleet. Although she was anxious to get into the warmth of the condo, she proceeded more gingerly along the walkway to Marilee's condo.

She pulled open the storm door, slipped off her mittens, and pulled the key out of her pocket. She hadn't thought to leave the outside light on, and she was fumbling to try to get the key in the lock when the door swung open, revealing the imposing figure of a woman Ann recognized from the news coverage of the bookstore attack as Jeanette Frobisher.

Startled, Ann took a step back.

Jeanette's eyes widened. "You?" she gasped. She lunged out the door.

Ann let out a squawk, some part of her mind registering that even if Jeanette hadn't known that Ann had access to Marilee's condo, the response seemed extreme.

But Jeanette barreled past Ann—and toward Randall, who was approaching the condo on the open walkway.

Ann pictured the outcome a fraction of a second before it happened: Jeanette, expecting to be tackling a living person, passed through Randall and slammed into the walkway's railing so hard her torso pitched over the top.

Ann dived for Jeanette, momentarily experiencing an even more bone-chilling cold than the freezing rain would explain as she, too, passed through Randall. She tried to grab Jeanette's waist, but Jeanette had already tilted too far over the railing for Ann to get any purchase. She grabbed the back of Jeanette's sweater and felt her fingernails bend and tear as the fabric pulled through her fingers.

Jeanette screamed as her hands flailed for an anchor. Ann reached out, intending to guide Jeanette's hand to the railing. Instead, Jeanette clamped her hand onto Ann's wrist. Ann strained back against Jeanette's momentum, but Jeanette outweighed her by fifty pounds, and now they were both being dragged inexorably over the railing.

Ann felt that spectral chill again. She realized that Randall had joined the fray, his arms passing through them both as he reached for Jeanette. He was trying to help, but Ann knew there was nothing he could do.

Now Ann's head and shoulders were over the railing as well, and in the shimmer of the streetlights along the Coastal Highway she could see the swirls of snow on the concrete parking lot a dozen stories below.

Jeanette's whimpers grew more desperate, and Ann was despairing of being able to pull her back. If she hit Jeanette's hand with her free fist, would it be enough to loosen the grip?

And even if it would, could Ann bring herself to do it?

Then Jeanette twisted her head back and her eyes locked on Ann's ... and she released her grip on Ann's wrist.

"No!" Ann shouted.

Jeanette's body tilted further over the railing, and Ann threw her arms around Jeanette's legs.

For a moment, everything stopped. Jeanette hung over the railing from the hips up, her legs wrapped in Ann's arms. Then Jeanette reached back again, obviously trying again to grab the railing, and the movement disrupted whatever tenuous equilibrium they had achieved. Ann felt Jeanette's legs sliding through her arms. She squeezed her eyes shut, her feet scrabbling for a firmer purchase on the icy walkway.

She heard a man's shout—"Jen!"—and then there was another person by the railing, not Randall's amorphous presence but a form of gratifying solidity, height, and weight.

The man reached over the railing, grabbed Jeanette's shoulders, and hauled her up, sending all three of them tumbling back onto the walkway.

55

Jeanette hauled herself into a sitting position on the walkway and buried her face in her hands. "Oh my God ... oh my God ... oh my God ..."

The man—Ann assumed he was Jeremy Frobisher—knelt beside her and wrapped his arms around her. "Jenny, sweetheart, are you okay?"

Randall hovered to one side, switching his wide-eyed gaze from Ann to Jeanette and Jeremy and back to Ann.

Ann made a shooing gesture at Randall. If Jeanette had seen him, as events suggested she had, Ann didn't want her launching another attack on him. Randall nodded and limped rapidly down the walkway, the slight glow of his form disappearing into the stairwell.

Jeremy looked up at Ann. "Who ...? What ...?"

"I'm Ann Kinnear," she said, through teeth chattering with a combination of cold and adrenaline. "Your mother's editor hired me to help him finish Marilee's book. Can we go inside?"

A still-stunned Jeremy nodded, helped Jeanette up, and led her into the condo. Ann managed to get to her feet on her second attempt and followed them. When they got to the living room, Jeanette lowered herself onto the couch. Jeremy sat next to her and wrapped his arm around her shoulders. Ann pulled out one of the kitchen stools and dropped onto it.

"Ezra hired you?" Jeremy asked Ann.

"No, not Marilee's cozy editor. She was writing thrillers as well, and the editor of her thriller novels hired me."

"Darren," said Jeanette dully.

"The guy you hired to finish the second thriller novel?" Jeremy asked Jeanette.

Jeanette nodded.

"Darren told me you wanted me to get in touch with Marilee to see if she was really Lara Seaford," said Ann, "and to find out the end of the novel. In fact, he was supposed to send me a copy of the contract to prove he wasn't trying to bilk you guys out of the money the second book would make."

Jeremy was rubbing Jeanette's back. "Jeanette signed the contract with Darren—" he said to Ann, then he turned to his wife, "—but just with Darren, right? Not with—" He waved his hand toward Ann.

"Ann Kinnear," Ann supplied.

Jeanette nodded again.

"Jeanette told me about it today," said Jeremy. "She explained that she hadn't told me earlier because she didn't know if it would pan out. But then she called Darren, and it was clear he wasn't at the condo, although that's where he claimed he was. But what are you doing here?"

Ann grimaced. "I guess Darren wasn't keeping you in the loop after all."

She explained about her sensing ability, giving them an Ann Kinnear Sensing business card and pulling up on her phone the article about her in the *Philadelphia Register* that she had shown Deegan.

"And you've been staying in the condo?" asked Jeremy, mounting confusion trumping his anger.

"Yes."

He glanced at Jeanette, then back at Ann. "Where?"

"Well, I intended to sleep out here on the couch ..."

"But?" asked Jeanette, her voice unsteady.

"I did fall asleep in the study one night."

"You make yourself at home in my mother's condo—," said Jeremy, anger now getting the upper hand, "illegally, I might add—"

"Darren told me he had your permission for me to be here," said Ann.

"And who was that man on the balcony?" Jeanette said, seeming not to have heard Ann.

"What man?" asked Jeremy.

"That man in the T-shirt and shorts," said Jeanette. "I think ..." She hiccupped back a sob. "I think it was the man Detective Morganstein showed us the mug shot of: Randall Coombs. And I think Morganstein is right that he might be the man who attacked Marilee at Oh Buoy Books. And he was coming after Ann just like he came after Marilee!"

Ann sat back against the breakfast bar and gave a shaky laugh. "Well, I'll be damned."

"It's not funny," said Jeanette, although she sounded more uncertain than angry.

"Sorry," said Ann. "He wasn't trying to attack me, although his name *is* Randall, and he *is* the man at the bookstore. Marilee enlisted him to fake the attack. She wanted the publicity as a lead-in to announcing herself as Lara Seaford."

"Wait, who are you guys talking about?" asked Jeremy, looking from one woman to the other. "And how do you know all this?" He glanced down at Ann's business card, which he still held in his hand. "Did you find that out ... from my mother?"

"No, I found out from Randall that she got him to help her stage the attack. I met him on the beach, and he was coming back to the condo to help me with something." She turned to Jeanette. "Randall didn't expect you to be involved in what happened at the bookstore. He feels bad that you got hurt. In fact, he was impressed with how you were willing to come to Marilee's defense."

Jeanette looked suddenly alarmed. "But if you know that he was involved in the bookstore attack, even assuming it's true that he thought it was going to be a charade, we have to tell the police." She gestured toward the bay-side door that led to the open air walkway where she had tried to tackle Randall. "He might have killed Marilee."

"Now, Jen—" began Jeremy.

"No, Jer," said Jeanette firmly. "We have to let the police know. He might be a danger to someone else."

"Not anymore," said Ann, "if he ever was—which I doubt. Randall is dead. He hit his head when he fell, and he died later."

Jeanette gaped at her. "But I saw him!"

Ann summoned a tired smile. "Sounds like maybe Darren didn't have to hire me after all."

~

ANN TOLD THEM, as succinctly as she could, what had led up to her apparently unauthorized visit to Marilee's condo. When she was done, Jeanette and Jeremy both looked more, not less, confused.

"So ... what are you doing here?" asked Jeanette. "I thought you must be here to find out what happened to Marilee."

"Not exactly," said Ann. "Once Darren guessed that Marilee was Lara, he wanted me to find her so that she would tell me the ending to the second thriller novel."

"I guess you haven't had any luck on the assignment from Darren."

"Actually," said Ann, "I have had luck. I located Marilee."

Jeanette's and Jeremy's eyes shot up. "Where?" gasped Jeanette.

"At Marco's restaurant."

"But how could she get—" Jeanette clamped her lips shut and looked toward Jeremy, then back to Ann. After a few moments, she asked, "Did Marilee tell you what the ending of the book was?"

"No. She said she would only tell me if I found her body." Ann didn't add that Marilee's primary motive in wanting her body found had been to find evidence implicating Jeremy and Jeanette in her death.

Almost half a minute ticked by, and Ann imagined Jeanette and Jeremy trying to wrap their brains around the story she had told them.

Finally, Jeanette turned to her husband. "Jer, we need to talk."

Jeremy cast a nervous glanced toward Ann. "Not right now —right, sweetheart?"

"Yes, I think we need to talk right now."

"But not in front of ..." Jeremy waved his hand toward Ann.

Jeanette looked up at Ann, then dropped her eyes back to her hands. "No, probably not."

Ann stood. "I can give you guys some time alone." She went to the kitchen island, where she had seen a pad of paper and pencil. She wrote down her cell number, tore off the sheet of paper, and put it on the breakfast bar. "Call me when you've talked."

"But where will you go?" Jeremy asked.

"I'm going to see if I can find Randall and tell him Jeanette is okay. He seemed concerned."

She started for the door, then turned at Jeanette's voice.

"Wait, you said that man—Randall—died because he hit his head?"

"That's right."

"During the bookstore attack?"

"Yes."

"I knocked him over when I thought he was trying to grab Marilee." She looked between Ann and Jeremy, her eyes wild. "He's dead because of me!"

Ann took a step toward where the couple sat. "Anything that happened to Randall is down to Marilee involving him in her crazy scheme, and to him agreeing to it. What you did behind the bookstore was nothing but noble."

Jeanette drew in a deep breath, and Ann thought she was going to dissolve in tears again. Instead, when Jeanette spoke, her voice was calmer. "I wish I could think of myself as noble, but I can't—not with all the things that have happened."

Ann waited a moment to see if Jeanette would say more, but the woman's eyes were on her fingers twisted in her lap.

"Let me know when you're ready for me to come back," Ann said, and stepped outside.

The sleet had tapered off, but the temperature had dropped further. The faint glow from Randall's spirit was visible in the covered area of the walkway outside the stairwell. Ann made her way gingerly toward him.

"How's she doing?" Randall asked when she reached him.

"Physically, fine," said Ann. "Mentally, freaked out. She recognized you from a mug shot the police showed her."

"How did they know to show her my mug shot?"

"Since you were in Marilee's apartment before you died,

I'm guessing you left fingerprints that they found when they investigated her disappearance, and the prints would be on file since you were in prison."

Randall sighed. "Yeah, makes sense. But, wait, how did Jeanette see me just now?"

"Lots of people have some sensing ability. Think about all the people who have seen ghosts—they're not all cranks. It's just that most people can't do it as consistently or clearly as I can." After a moment, she continued, "Maybe Jeanette can see you because she has a connection with you."

"What connection is that? Marilee?"

"Jeanette thinks she was responsible for your fall, and so she thinks she was responsible for your death. And other than saving someone's life, I imagine that being responsible for their death is about as strong a connection as it's possible to have."

"If Jeanette was responsible—and I honestly don't know if it was her or Marilee who knocked me off balance—I know it was an accident. And she's a brave woman. She had no way of knowing that Marilee wasn't in any danger, but she was willing to throw herself into the fight when she thought I was attacking Marilee. She was even willing to defend you, and she doesn't even know you. I haven't known many people like that in my life."

They were silent, Ann shivering in her parka, Randall bending and straightening his bad leg. A minute ticked by, then he continued. "I wish I had known someone like her when I was alive. If I had had a friend like that, my life might have turned out a lot different." He smiled ruefully. "I guess if I had had a friend like that, I might still *be* alive."

Ann nodded. She thought back to those interminable seconds when she hung over the railing of the walkway, the concrete of the parking lot a dozen stories below. She shuddered as she remembered the slide toward what had felt like an inevitable outcome. And she thought of Jeanette releasing her wrist, speeding her own slide toward what had seemed like certain death but saving Ann.

"If I didn't have a friend—or at least an acquaintance—like that," she said, "I might be dead."

They were silent for another minute, then Randall asked, "So, did you find any drugs in the condo?"

"Damn," sighed Ann. "I sort of lost track of that in all the excitement."

56

Ann's phone pinged with a text: *You can come back*

"They want to continue our conversation," Ann said as she sent Jeremy a thumbs-up emoji.

"What do they want to talk about?" asked Randall.

"I don't know. There's obviously something Jeanette wants to tell me that Jeremy was balking at sharing."

Randall glanced toward the door of the condo. "Do you think they killed her?"

Ann grimaced. "I certainly hope not."

"Do you think you're safe?"

She considered. She didn't get a sense of Jeanette being a danger—after all, Jeanette had demonstrated her willingness to sacrifice her own life to save Ann's. Ann knew nothing about Jeremy, but he did seem even less enthusiastic than Jeanette about Ann's involvement in their affairs.

"I could come in with you," said Randall.

"And do what? Scare them silly if they do anything threatening?"

Randall stuffed his hands into his pockets and shrugged, abashed.

"Sorry, Randall. I didn't mean to be a jerk. You have a good point, but I'm afraid that seeing you again would rattle Jeanette, and I think she's rattled enough as it is."

She pulled her phone out of her pocket and considered who she could have on the line when she went back into the condo. Mike? Scott? Joe? She wished she could know in advance how the conversation with Jeremy and Jeanette Frobisher was going to go before she made her decision.

Then she realized she had another option.

She sent Jeremy a text: *I'll be there in just a minute*

~

A FEW MINUTES LATER, Ann stepped into the condo and followed the tiled hallway to the living room. Jeremy and Jeanette were still seated on the couch, Jeanette's hands folded between Jeremy's, as if he was trying to warm them.

"We agreed," said Jeremy, his face pale. "It's time to tell someone what really happened."

Ann crossed the living room and looked out through the sleet-streaked windows, then turned back to the couple, her hands deep in the pockets of her parka. "Okay, let's hear it."

Jeremy turned to Jeanette. "Do you want to tell her?"

Jeanette nodded and drew a deep breath. "Marilee was traumatized by the attack outside Oh Buoy Books and couldn't leave the condo. It was an impossible position—we couldn't get stuff delivered to the condo, and I just couldn't keep coming down here every time she needed something. We finally convinced her to come stay with us. She was a difficult person to travel with at the best of times, and if she was reluctant to leave the condo, we figured that the drive from Ocean City to Downingtown with her was going to be ..." She hitched a breath. "... unpleasant." She twisted her fingers in her lap.

"We stopped here on our way to Virginia Beach to visit friends and dropped off a sedative for her to take, to calm her down for the trip. When we got to Eden Beach on the way back to pick her up, we found her in the study. She was dead."

"What had happened?" Ann asked.

Jeanette looked at Jeremy, then back at Ann. "You don't sound surprised."

"Randall saw Marilee's body in the study."

Jeanette's eyebrows shot up, and she and Jeremy exchanged alarmed glances. "And he didn't report it?" she asked.

"He was dead," said Ann.

"Oh." Jeanette squeezed the bridge of her nose. "Right."

"So what happened to Marilee's body?" Ann asked.

Jeanette's hand dropped, limp, into her lap. "We took it."

Ann remained silent.

After a moment, Jeremy said, "We were afraid that the police would suspect us. We stood to benefit from her death—not having to repay some money she had loaned us, and probably eventually inheriting her estate."

"That sounds like a pretty plausible motive to me," said Ann.

"Plausible, maybe—for someone else," he said, his tone defensive. "But there's a big difference between being upset with your mother because she's being unpleasant and killing her."

"What did you do with the body?" asked Ann.

"We wrapped her in a blanket," said Jeanette. "It was all very respectful." She sounded as if it was important to convince Ann of this. "We took her downstairs ..."

"You just carried her downstairs?"

"We used one of the luggage carts."

"And then what?"

Jeanette pressed her hand to her mouth.

"We buried her," said Jeremy. "Not very far from our home in Chester County." After a moment, he added, his voice carrying a hint of anger, "And what Jeanette says about us treating my mother's body with respect is true. We buried her exactly as we would like to be buried: in a beautiful spot, wrapped in fabric that we had used in our lives, returning to the natural environment. Not laid out in some thousand-dollar box that will be the next generation's responsibility to deal with."

"So you got rid of her body," said Ann. "But what killed her?"

"I guess we'll never know." said Jeremy

"What sedative did you give her?"

After a pause, Jeremy said, "Lorazepam."

"That's pretty heavy-duty stuff, isn't it?" Asked Ann.

"She had taken Percocet before and didn't have any trouble with it," said Jeanette. "Her doctor prescribed it when she broke her wrist in a car accident several years ago."

"Well, I suppose if the doctor thought Lorazepam was appropriate ..."

Jeremy and Jeanette exchanged a look, then Jeremy dropped his eyes.

Ann groaned. "A doctor didn't prescribe it?"

"No." Jeremy's voice was almost a whisper. "But I did every check that a doctor would do. The amount I gave her—it shouldn't have killed her. It *shouldn't* have."

Ann thought back to her original goal in returning to Eden Beach with Randall, before meeting up in dramatic fashion with Jeremy and Jeanette on the walkway: to search the condo for a possible hiding place for drugs.

"What if the Lorazepam wasn't the only drug she was taking?" asked Ann.

"The Percocet my mother took when she hurt her wrist was the only drug I've ever known her to take, and that was only because the injury was so painful and the doctor insisted. She thought pharmaceuticals were for weaklings, and she thought naturopathic remedies were a scam." He rubbed his eyes. "Which, as you can imagine, was a point of disagreement between us, considering that Jeanette and I own a pharmacy."

"You may have thought Marilee was only taking the Percocet as long as her surgeon prescribed it," said Ann, "but maybe she never stopped. I understand it's easy to get addicted to it. And if she was taking Percocet and took Lorazepam on top of that ..." She shook her head. "Although it's hard to imagine anyone thinking that combining those would be a good idea."

"I never told her it was Lorazepam," said Jeremy. "She assumed it was CBD oil, and I let her believe that."

"I certainly believed it," whispered Jeanette.

"The reason I came back to the condo," said Ann, "was something Randall told me. She asked him where someone might hide drugs—she told him it was research for her book, but maybe it was for her own information. He told her the best place to hide drugs would be in plain sight. We came back to see if we could find anything that would suggest that Marilee might have been taking something on the sly."

Jeremy and Jeanette didn't look at each other for confirmation, but kept their eyes on Ann, and Ann was surprised to see in their expressions not dread, but a sort of desperate hope.

"Should we look for that now?" asked Ann.

Jeanette gave an almost imperceptible nod.

Jeremy said, "Okay, let's do it."

"I'm going to ask you two to make the search," said Ann. "I'm leaning toward believing that you didn't kill Marilee in cold blood—although having met her, I can imagine it might have been a temptation—but I don't want to be naïve." She waved toward the window overlooking The Capstan. "I met a woman who lives in the condo building next door. She's watching us through binoculars, and she's ready to call the police if needed. I also have a call open to her on my cell phone," she drew her hand out of her pocket, and Jeanette and Jeremy's eyes widened. "It's on mute, so she hasn't heard anything you've said. But I can take it off mute anytime I might need to have her hear what's going on."

Jeremy's face reddened, and Jeanette put a hand on his arm. "It's smart of her, Jer. She doesn't know us."

After a moment, he nodded. "You're right. It's a sensible precaution."

"In fact," said Ann, "I'm going to give her a quick update, so don't say anything you don't want her to hear." She pulled her phone out of her pocket and unmuted the audio. "Hi, it's Ann. Everything's fine here. Practically like sitting around eating Nilla wafers." It was the first of several phrases they had agreed on to indicate that all was, in fact, well.

"Glad to hear it," said Edith.

"But I think it's going to be a long evening. You okay staying on the line?"

"Sure thing," Edith responded, her voice cheerful.

"Okay, I'm going to mute the phone again."

Jeremy stood and helped Jeanette up. "So, hiding in plain sight?"

Ann nodded. "That's the theory."

57

With Ann stationed by the window, Jeanette and Jeremy began their search. They started with the medicine cabinet in the bathroom, since what could be more appropriate to *hiding in plain sight*, but they found nothing there. Although the condo was hardly over-furnished, it took the two of them almost an hour to search the study and the bay-side room, with similar results. The kitchen took another half-hour, with the couple searching behind canned goods in the cupboards and peering into boxes of cereal and crackers. When it was time to search the living room, Ann moved away from the window but unmuted the call to Edith. They chatted while the search proceeded in silence, Edith sounding much less tired than Ann felt. The search of the living room also proved unfruitful.

Ann moved back to the window and re-muted the phone as Jeremy and Jeanette sank onto stools at the breakfast bar.

"It's hard to know where she would have hidden something she didn't want us to find," said Jeanette. "I spent quite a bit of time here, and at one time or another, I'd be in all the rooms. I unpacked books for Marilee in the study. Before she turned the bay-side room into what I guess was her thriller writing space, Jeremy and I used to sleep there when we stayed overnight. When I was here waiting for Marilee to sign books, I'd sometimes open kitchen cupboards or drawers—to make myself tea, for example. The living room has so few pieces of furniture now that there's barely any place to hide anything. I don't know where she could have hidden something where she wouldn't have been worried we would find it."

"There wasn't anywhere she warned you away from?" asked Ann. "Like, *Whatever you do, don't look on the top shelf in the closet because that's where the Christmas presents are*—that sort of thing?"

Jeremy laughed tiredly. "I can't recall that she ever warned us away from Christmas present stashes. Can't recall that she ever had presents to warn us away from."

Ann noticed that Jeanette's eyes had drifted toward the kitchen. "Jeanette? Any ideas?"

"The coffee maker," said Jeanette slowly. "She was always telling me not to use the coffee maker because I'd make a mess."

"It *is* in plain sight," said Ann.

Jeanette rose and went to the counter, and Jeremy followed her. Ann, after a quick message to Edith, left the window and stood on the other side of the breakfast bar.

Jeanette checked in the bean hopper, the filter, the water reservoir, and the drip tray.

From Ann's vantage point, she had a better view into the innards of the machine. As Jeanette was about to replace the tray, Ann said, "There's something behind there."

Jeanette reached in and pulled out another tray that Ann guessed was intended to store machine accessories. Jeanette's eyes widened. "Oh my God."

Curiosity trumping caution, Ann abandoned her position on the other side of the breakfast bar and moved into the kitchen to peer into the tray. It was filled with oblong yellow pills, some with the *PERCOCET* imprint clearly visible.

Jeremy put his hands on the kitchen counter and let his head fall forward. After a few moments, he straightened, his face haggard. "It would explain a lot." He got out his phone, tapped, and read. "Anger. Agitation. Aggression." He choked out a laugh. "Poor decision-making."

"What are you reading?" asked Jeanette.

"Symptoms of Percocet addiction." He groaned. "I never thought to ask her if she was taking anything when decided to give her the Lorazepam. She was so against drugs of any kind —or at least that's what she let us believe—that it didn't occur to me."

"Even if she was taking the Percocet at the same time, would one dose of Lorazepam result in an overdose?" asked Ann.

"Not at normal dosages," said Jeremy, his eyes on his hands.

Jeanette's face paled. "What do you mean, Jer?" she asked, her voice trembling.

Jeremy looked up, his eyes rimmed with red. He looked between Jeanette and Ann, as if weighing a decision, then sighed. "Well, I already admitted to failing to report my mother's death and burying her illegally. In for a penny, in for a pound, I suppose." He made his way to the couch and dropped onto it. Jeanette followed him and sat down next to him.

"I knew the drive from Ocean City to Downingtown was going to be painful," he said. "Her making 'helpful' comments from the back seat about the speed limit, gasping every time she saw brake lights ahead of us." He rubbed his eyes. "I know she was traumatized by the accident where she broke her wrist, but, Jesus, that was years ago. She should have gotten over it by now." He dropped his hand to his thigh. "Anyway ... I figured maybe we could extend the vacation vibe just a little bit, at least until we got her home." He met Jeanette's wide-eyed gaze. "The dosing information I told her to write down—it was more than she needed just to calm her for the trip. Quite a bit more."

Seconds ticked by, then Jeanette groaned, "Oh my God."

Jeremy leaned forward. "Jen, I'm so sorry I didn't tell you earlier. At first, I panicked and thought the Lorazepam alone had killed her—that was why I didn't want to report her death." He shook his head. "One of the reasons. Then as time went on and the panic wore off, I started thinking just what Ann thought—could the dose I gave her really have killed her? But by then we had buried her. What were we supposed to do—dig her back up, wash her off, and bring her back to the condo?" His voice trembled. "I figured that the only thing we could do—that I could do—was stick to the plan. But I saw what it was doing to you." He reached out and took her hand. "Jen, I'm so, so sorry I kept this secret from you."

Jeanette dropped her eyes to their interlaced fingers. A half minute ticked by, then she gave a sad, weak laugh. "You weren't the only one."

"The only one ... what?" asked Jeremy, confused.

"Keeping a secret." She met his gaze. "I thought the same thing—that we were going to get back from our nice trip to Virginia Beach and it was all going to be ruined by Marilee being ... well, being Marilee."

Jeremy's eyes widened. "What do you mean?"

"I did the same thing you did. I raised the dosage, too, in the instructions I wrote out for her."

They stared into each other's eyes. Then a noise came

from Jeremy that Ann thought at first was a sob, then perhaps a cough, but as it grew, she recognized it as an unhinged laugh.

Jeanette looked at him, shocked, but then a smile crept onto her face and a minute later, she too was trying to choke back laughter.

Ann wondered if she was going to need to suggest they both sample the wares they had found in the coffee maker.

After another minute, their laughter began to die down.

"Oh my God," gasped Jeremy. "This whole time, we each thought we were responsible for her death."

When Jeremy and Jeanette were somewhat calmer, both looking abashed at their outburst, Jeremy said, "If she was taking Percocet and then took a large dose of Lorazepam, it's possible that it depressed her respiratory system. That could be fatal."

"Jeanette," asked Ann, "did you throw away the instructions you wrote out?"

"No. When we got to the condo on the way back from Virginia Beach, the instructions were gone. We figured Marilee had thrown them away and put the trash down the garbage chute. Since she had decided she could leave the condo to go to Downingtown, and if she was getting ready for that trip, it made sense that she would have thrown out the trash."

"But where did she get the Percocet?" asked Jeremy. He gestured toward the pile of pills. "That's not a quantity she'd get from her friendly neighborhood drugstore."

"No ideas?" asked Ann. "You never saw people around the condo you didn't recognize?"

"Just that man—Randall," said Jeanette.

"I suppose it's possible he supplied her with the drugs," said Ann, "but based on what I know about him—although admittedly it's not a lot—I don't think so. For the moment, let's assume it wasn't him. Maybe someone posing as a delivery person or a handyman who could come to the condos and not attract attention?"

Jeremy snorted. "I don't know about handymen, but delivery people could never get past—"

"Kenny," the three said simultaneously.

"He could have put it in an envelope, and then put the envelope in the mailbox," said Jeanette. "I remember Marilee getting a couple of things Kenny described as 'special deliveries.' In fact, I picked up an envelope for her after ... you know."

Jeanette stood and Ann and Jeremy followed her into the study. She took a padded envelope out of the wire mesh letter tray and held it out so they could see the label.

"*KAK Novelties*?" asked Jeremy. He looked up at Jeanette. "What's Kenny's last name?"

"I don't know," she replied, "but I wouldn't be surprised if it started with K. "Should I open it?"

Jeremy nodded.

Jeanette opened the package. Inside was a metal tin that had originally contained mints, but that now contained a few dozen of the same pills they had found in the coffee maker, padded with cotton balls to dampen any rattle. "*Novelties* is right," murmured Jeanette.

"It would be a pretty neat set-up," said Ann. "He wouldn't even have to hand it to her. He could just put it in her mailbox in the lobby. Assuming he doesn't know that Marilee's dead, and he really is her supplier, there might be a package in there now."

"But how can we check?" asked Jeanette. "Marilee told me that Kenny has an apartment behind the security desk, but he seems to be at that desk twenty-four seven."

"Even if he is at the desk," said Jeremy, "it wouldn't be unusual for him to be asleep, especially at this time of night."

"But we're not going to be able to get past him to the mailboxes without waking him up," protested Jeanette.

A slow smile formed on Ann's face. "I think I know someone who can help."

58

Ann found Randall still lingering on the walkway near the stairwell door and brought him into the condo for introductions. That went about as well as it could have. Jeanette was still a little freaked out by the idea that she was seeing—although not hearing—a man whose death she believed she might have caused. Ann did her best to convey Randall's lack of blame for Jeanette's actions.

Based on Jeremy's pallor and trembling hands, he was completely freaked out by the whole situation.

After Ann explained the plan to Randall, the four left the condo and took the elevator to the lobby. As they descended, Ann unmuted the still-open call with Edith and told her she could take the rest of the night off. Ann gathered that Edith, who still sounded quite chipper despite the time of night, was a little disappointed that her part in the drama was over.

The four exited at the lobby and crossed to the security desk and a snoring Kenny. Randall disappeared behind the partition that separated the lobby from the employees-only area behind the security desk.

"Good evening, Kenny," Jeanette said loudly.

Kenny started awake and looked blearily at his watch. "Hardly evening, Miss Forsythe. It's the middle of the night."

"Jeanette's my wife," snapped Jeremy, "and her last name is Frobisher."

"Right, right, sorry about that," said Kenny.

"I want to introduce you to someone," Jeremy said to Kenny, gesturing to Ann. "This is Ann. She got in touch with us because she's interested in buying the condo. We explained to her we can't do anything while Marilee's missing, but we agreed to show her the condo. She likes it a lot, and we've agreed to let her stay there. I just wanted you to know that we, as Marilee's representatives, have given her permission to be there."

"I guess if you're willing to speak for Mrs. Forsythe."

"I am."

There was a long pause, Jeremy looking to Ann and Jeanette for some indication that Randall was back.

Ann wondered what the hold-up was. How long could it take Randall to peek into Marilee's mailbox? As far as she knew, it wasn't as if he could take the mail out and sort through it.

"It's a great place," she said. "And that view—extraordinary."

Jeremy and Jeanette nodded over-enthusiastically. Kenny didn't respond.

"And it's so nice to know there's someone in the lobby keeping an eye on things," Ann continued.

More nodding from Jeanette and Jeremy, more lack of response from Kenny.

"Well, I guess we can head back up now that introductions have been made," she said a little more loudly, hoping to be heard in the mailbox area.

"Yes, that's a good idea," said Jeremy heartily.

The three trooped across the lobby, took the elevator up to 14, and made their way carefully along the walkway to the condo. Jeanette stayed far from the railing.

When they were inside, Jeremy glanced around the condo. "Did Randall come back with us?" he asked uncertainly.

"No," said Ann, "he didn't come out from behind the desk. Let's give him a couple of minutes."

Jeanette and Jeremy sat on the couch, while Ann sat on a stool at the breakfast bar. She considered opening the line to Edith again but decided that she'd just hit *Emergency* on her phone if things went awry.

Randall arrived about ten minutes later and relayed what he had found, with Ann conveying the information to Jeanette and Jeremy.

"I couldn't see anything in Marilee's mailbox other than what looked like a bunch of junk mail," he said. "I also checked out a table where they must put packages that are too big to put in the mailboxes. Nothing for Marilee there."

"Damn," said Ann.

"But there was a door next to the mailboxes and it led to an apartment—Kenny's apartment, I'm guessing. There were a bunch of those mint tins on the kitchen table, like you told me you found in the envelope Kenny gave to Marilee."

"I guess you couldn't tell what was in them," said Ann.

"No, but there was a bowl next to them that was filled with mints, like he was emptying out the tins."

"And I don't picture Kenny planning to play host to a whole bunch of people who would need an after-dinner palate cleanser."

"So Kenny is my mother's dealer?" asked Jeremy, who was apparently having a little trouble keeping up with the incoming revelations.

"It looks that way," said Jeanette. She turned to Ann. "How

do we let the police know it looks like Kenny is dealing drugs?" She looked apologetically toward where Randall stood next to Ann. "We can't really tell them who our source is."

"Yeah," said Ann, "telling a cop you found out important information from a dead person almost never goes well."

"Plus, even if they agree that he is responsible for supplying the Percocet," said Jeanette, "and even if they can somehow prove that an overdose of Lorazepam alone didn't kill her, we still need to explain about her body disappearing. They'll still suspect us of killing her for her money, and to avoid repaying the loan."

Ann sighed. "Let's worry about that later. And let's hold off on telling the police what happened to Marilee's body. After all this time, another day isn't going to make a difference. There's someone I want to talk with before you do that. Someone I think we all need to talk with." She turned to Randall. "If we went to another building that's on the beach, do you think you could come with us?"

"I think so."

"Good. I think it's time we all made a visit to Marco's."

59

Ann stood at the host station with Jeanette, Jeremy, and Randall, watching Marco himself approach from across the dining room. It was noon, and Ann imagined that under normal circumstances the restaurant would have held at least some diners, but it was as empty as it had been on her previous visit.

Marco's eyebrows rose as he recognized those of the party he could discern. Marilee sat at her regular table—and Ann could see her look of shock from across the room.

"Why, if it isn't Ms. Forsythe's son and daughter-in-law," said Marco. "And," he turned to Ann, "the woman who told me that her mother and stepfather got engaged at Ms. Forsythe's regular table. What a coincidence."

Jeanette stepped forward. "Ann was so interested in what you told her about my mother that she got in touch with me and Jeremy and we agreed to meet up at Marilee's favorite restaurant."

"Oh," said Marco, abashed. "Of course. I was concerned that perhaps the young lady was a member of the press. Table for three?"

"Actually, we'd like to sit at Ms. Forsythe's table," said Ann.

"I'm afraid Ms. Forsythe's table can only accommodate two comfortably."

Not pointing out that Ms. Forsythe's table could, in fact, accommodate only one additional diner comfortably, Ann said, "Let's leave her regular place empty as a mark of respect and pull over another table."

The four followed Marco to the table, Marilee glaring at them as they approached. Whether she stayed at the table because she was unwilling to retreat or because she wasn't able to leave, Ann wasn't sure.

"Can you see her?" Ann whispered to Jeanette, although she guessed the answer based on Jeanette's chalky pallor.

Jeanette nodded.

When they reached the table, Marco pulled another two-top next to Marilee's table, then asked, his tone resigned, "May I take your coats?" The room was even colder than it had been on Ann's previous visit, and Ann had noticed a second, larger, and more extensively outfitted HVAC service truck in the parking lot.

"I think we'll keep them on," said Ann.

Marco pulled out the chair opposite Marilee and looked expectantly at Jeanette.

"Jeremy, why don't you sit there," said Jeanette, her voice choked.

Jeremy glanced back and forth between Jeanette and Ann, then lowered himself onto the chair. Ann and Jeanette took seats at the other table, Jeanette next to Jeremy, Ann next to Marilee. Randall remained standing, positioning himself behind Jeremy and opposite Marilee.

"Still pretty quiet, I see," Ann said to Marco.

"Yes. Despite our best efforts, we've been unable to repair the heating system. May I get you something to drink?" He turned to Ann. "Macallan, two rocks, if I remember correctly?"

"Yes, thanks."

"I'll have that as well," said Jeremy.

Marco turned to Jeanette, who was still staring at Marilee with a look of revulsion.

"Same for Ms. Frobisher," said Ann.

Marco nodded and headed toward the bar.

"If you keep hanging out here and dropping the temperature," Ann said to Marilee, "you're at risk of closing down your favorite restaurant. Where are you going to hang out if Marco's closes?"

A flicker of concern crossed Marilee's features, morphing to confusion as she met Jeanette's gaze.

"Wait ... can she see me?" Marilee asked Ann, alarmed.

Ann looked at Jeanette, who was still staring at Marilee. "Looks that way to me."

"Can she hear me?" asked Marilee, dropping her voice.

Jeanette's expression didn't change.

"No, I don't think she can hear you," said Ann.

Jeanette confirmed Ann's guess with a shake of her head.

Jeremy was alternately looking at Ann and scanning the space across the table.

"But she *can* see me," said Marilee. "How is that possible?"

"It seems Jeanette has a bit of the sensing ability, at least when it comes to important people in her life," said Ann, giving a sardonic twist to *important*. "She can see you ... and Randall."

Marilee's eyes jumped to Ann. "Randall?"

"You don't see him?"

Marilee looked frantically around the dining room. "He's here?"

"He is. He's standing right behind Jeremy. And I'm guessing he can see you."

Randall nodded. "And hear her, too."

"Maybe you don't consider that he played an important part in your life," Ann said to Marilee. "Although you certainly played an important part in his life—or at least its ending."

"I don't know what you're talking about," said Marilee.

Marco arrived at the table with three Macallans and placed them in front of Ann, Jeanette, and Jeremy.

Jeremy downed his in a gulp.

"Another, sir?" asked Marco.

"I better not," mumbled Jeremy.

"Are you ready to order?" Marco asked the three.

"I think it will just be the drinks," said Ann.

Marco nodded dispiritedly and returned to the host station.

The interruption had given Marilee some time to compose herself. "And have your new friends helped you locate my body?" she asked Ann.

"Yes, in fact, they have."

"And what have you found out?"

"You're buried in a lovely spot in Chester County."

Marilee's eyebrows rose. "Really? And how did I get there?"

"Jeanette and Jeremy took you there. After they found you dead in the condo."

Marilee sat forward. "They told you they *found* me dead? And you believe them?"

"I do."

"And they buried my body?"

"Yes."

"Why in the world would they have done that if they weren't responsible for my death?"

"Because they believed—quite rightly, I think—that they would be suspected of killing you for financial gain."

"What financial gain?"

"Not having to repay the loan you gave them. And they assume that Jeremy is your heir."

Marilee snorted. "They would be disappointed."

"Really? He's not your heir?" She glanced over at Jeremy, who seemed too stunned to be making sense of Ann's side of the conversation.

"I thought other recipients were more deserving of benefiting from my earnings as an author."

"Oh, yes? And who might they be?"

Marilee drew herself up straight. "I wanted to benefit the genre which had given me a renewed creative spark. I wanted to help my fellow thriller writers—and, of course, law enforcement—in their work. I left my estate to ..." Her voice trailed off, then she flushed and clamped her lips shut.

"Left it to ..." Ann prompted.

"It's none of your business," snapped Marilee. "But if they did think Jeremy was my heir, what makes you think they didn't kill me for my money?"

"Because I think it's more likely that you died from an overdose of Percocet that you got from Kenny."

Marilee's eyes widened, and she looked from Ann to Jeremy to Jeanette and back to Ann. "What are you talking about?"

"We found your stash of Percocet in the coffee maker—thanks to Randall remembering his advice to you that the best place to hide pills would be in plain sight—and found some emptied-out mint tins in Kenny's apartment. Tins that match the *KAK Novelties* package that he gave you."

Marilee clamped her lips shut and glared at Ann. Then, in a motion that looked a little too well-rehearsed to be spontaneous, her hand drifted to her wrist. "I was trying to relieve the considerable pain I was suffering from a wrist injury."

"And trying to relieve the withdrawal symptoms as well, I'm guessing—assuming you ever tried to stop taking the Percocet. Did you take some to calm you down for the drive to Downingtown?"

Marilee folded her hand in her lap. "I took some of whatever woo-woo medicine Jeremy gave me for the drive."

"The woo-woo medicine was Lorazepam."

"What?" Marilee's eyes flashed to Jeremy and back to Ann. "He gave me Lorazepam? I thought it was CBD oil."

"He and Jeanette hoped that something a little more high-powered would provide a calmer trip for everyone."

She folded her hands in her lap and said primly, "Well, I certainly wasn't looking forward to that drive."

"And you took the Lorazepam Jeremy gave you?"

"Yes."

"In the amount Jeanette wrote in the instructions?"

Marilee glanced down at her hands, then back up at Ann. "I upped the dose a little. I figured what could it matter? I thought it was CBD."

Ann's eyebrows rose. "You took more than you were told to take?"

"Yes."

"How much more?"

"Quite a bit more."

Ann shook her head. "I guess no one was looking forward to that trip."

"What do you mean?"

"Jeremy gave you enough not just to sedate you but probably to knock you out for the trip, and Jeanette upped it a little more."

Marilee sat forward. "You see, they *were* responsible for my death."

Ann also sat forward. "You know, Marilee, this is why I believe Jeanette and Jeremy have come clean with me about what happened and you haven't—because they were willing to accept responsibility, whereas you are doing nothing but trying to shift the blame to others, even though you were the one secretly taking the Percocet. And you not only didn't tell Jeremy that you were still taking the drug—I suppose that's understandable—but you let your pharmacist son think you weren't taking any drug—in fact, that you disapproved of people who took any prescription drugs. That was the only reason it didn't occur to him to check for adverse reactions before he gave you the Lorazepam."

Marilee sat back and shifted her glare from Ann to Jeremy to Jeanette and back to Ann.

Ann continued. "So I found out that your body is buried in Chester County, and I imagine I could convince Jeremy and Jeanette to show me where, if necessary." She ignored Jeremy as he shifted in his seat.

"But the requirement was to lead the police to my body so they could perform an autopsy," Marilee spat. "You haven't done that."

"So you really want me to tell the authorities where they can find your body," Ann noticed Marilee's wince, "so that they can assess to what extent you killed yourself with Percocet?"

Marilee's angry gaze once again swept over the other three seated at the table. "No. I suppose not."

"So will you tell me the ending of the sequel to *Darkest Before Death* so I can tell Darren?"

"Tell Darren he can make up his own damn ending."

Ann crossed her arms and met Marilee's glare. There was nothing she could say that would convince Marilee to give her the information Darren had hired her to find out—and at this point, finding out the ending of a thriller novel seemed unimportant in view of the other things she'd learned. She uncrossed her arms, pushed back her chair and stood.

"What's happening?" asked Jeremy, still looking shell-shocked.

"I think we've found out all we're going to from Marilee," said Ann.

Jeremy tried to rise but fell back in his chair. Jeanette jumped up, grasped his arm, and helped him to his feet.

"She's sitting there?" he whispered to Ann, gesturing toward the opposite chair.

"Yes," she replied. "If you want to say something to her, I think she can hear you. If she has something to say to you, I could tell you what it is."

Marilee's expression was frozen as she stared at her son.

"Maybe ..." Jeremy began. He fell silent, and after a moment he shook his head. "No, I have nothing to say to her."

Supported by Jeanette, he turned and made his unsteady way across the dining room, followed by Randall. Ann turned away from the table as well, to see Marco approaching the table with the check.

"Wait," Marilee said to Ann. "I have a question for you."

Ann was eager to be out of Marco's, but perhaps Marilee had changed her mind about revealing the ending of the second thriller. With a sigh, she sat in the chair across from Marilee that Jeremy had vacated.

Marco, shaking his head, stalked back to the host station.

Marilee glanced around the room. "Is Randall still here?"

"No, he left."

"Will he keep coming back here?"

"I don't know. And I'm certainly not going to hang around Ocean City to report back to you on his activities."

"Has he been to Eden Beach?"

"Yes."

She hesitated. "After he died?"

"Yes."

Marilee shook her head. "I thought there was something strange going on there after he died."

"How do you know when he died?"

Marilee started. "Well, sometime after the bookstore attack, right? The blow to his head?"

"How do you know he died from a blow to the head?"

"He did hit his head, right? You could see it happen in the security camera video."

"Yes, but not all blows to the head are fatal."

Marilee looked at Ann through narrowed eyes, then said, "Did he take you to Stu's house?"

"No. Who's Stu?"

"A friend of his from prison." She waved a hand. "Maybe not a friend, but an acquaintance. He has a house close to the bookstore. He's back in prison and Randall had access to the house, so we decided he'd go there after the attack."

"Randall didn't take me there. Is that where his body is?"

Marilee looked uncomfortable. "It stands to reason, right?"

"Maybe. He didn't tell me where Stu's house was—he said he didn't want to get Stu in trouble." She arched an eyebrow. "Looking out for a friend."

Marilee shrugged, adopting an air of nonchalance. "It's no business of mine."

"Of course it's your business," snapped Ann, losing her last remaining bit of patience with Marilee. "But I can't make you care about it if you don't already." She turned her gaze out the window. "Someone named Stu with a home in Ocean City who was in prison with Randall. Even if Randall doesn't want to tell me, I can imagine it would be possible to find out where the house is ..."

Marilee rolled her eyes. "Oh, good heavens." She gave Ann an address.

Ann got out her phone and tapped in a note. "And Randall's body is there?"

Marilee's mouth was pressed in a thin line. "Yes."

"Have you been there?"

"Randall took me there once to interview Stu for *Darkest Before Death*."

"And that was the only time you were there? You didn't go there after the attack to meet up with Randall?"

Marilee scowled. "Yes. Fine. I went there the day after the attack to meet up with Randall."

"You weren't afraid of being seen?"

"I parked a few blocks away. I knocked, but there was no answer. The door was unlocked, and I went in. He was there, sitting in a recliner in the living room." Marilee's voice was becoming more animated, whether from anxiety or excitement, Ann couldn't tell. "He was beyond help. First responders couldn't have done anything. I was wearing gloves, so I knew I hadn't left any fingerprints. The neighbors probably know that Stu is in prison, so they wouldn't think anything was amiss if the drive wasn't shoveled or if the yard wasn't tended. I turned the heat off to slow decomposition so as not to attract attention by the smell—I used that in the sequel to *Darkest Before Death*. The balaclava was there on the kitchen table. The inside was stained with blood. I thought about taking it since it might tie him to the bookstore attack, but then I decided that it didn't matter if they identified him as the attacker." She must have noticed Ann's look of revulsion, because she added, somewhat sulkily, "It's not like Randall had any family or friends who were going to care."

"There are people now who would care about what happened to him."

"Who?"

"Jeanette, because she thinks she might have been the one to knock Randall over and so she feels responsible for his death. I think Jeremy, too. There was a little incident at Eden Beach, and Randall tried to help."

Marilee shrugged. "I couldn't have known that at the time, could I?"

Ann shook her head. "I can't tell if you really think you're free of blame in this whole mess, or if you're just trying to convince yourself. Either way, I don't feel like being your audience."

She rose and started toward the door, where Marco was standing by the host station, check in hand, then turned back to Marilee.

"What did you mean by 'he was beyond help'?"

Marilee shrugged again. She wouldn't meet Ann's gaze. "Just that."

Ann examined Marilee, her eyes narrowing, then said, "He wasn't dead when you found him, was he?"

"I told you, he was beyond help," said Marilee, her voice shrill.

"He was alive ... and you just left him there?" Ann hissed, trying to keep her voice low enough that Marco wouldn't hear what she was saying.

"If he was going to wake up, he was going to wake up—and if he did, he could call 911 himself."

After a long pause, Ann said, not caring if her voice carried across the dining room, "You disgust me."

She fumbled three twenties out of her knapsack as she crossed the dining room and handed them to a wide-eyed Marco. "Good luck with the climate control," she said as she walked out the door.

60

Ann found Jeanette, Jeremy, and Randall outside, looking across the beach toward the water. The day was sunny, although a brisk breeze was whipping up whitecaps on the water.

"I know it sounds like an odd thing to say about a dead person," said Jeanette, "but she looks ill. She didn't look like that right before she died."

"Postmortem opiate withdrawal?" asked Jeremy, looking at Ann.

She shrugged. "I suppose it's possible."

Ann noticed the spirit in the Speedo strolling down the beach. She pointed. "Do you see him?" she asked Jeanette.

Jeanette strained her eyes, clearly focused on a spot far beyond where the man was. "No. Who should I be seeing?"

"A dead guy in a Speedo."

Jeanette scanned the beach again. "No, I don't see anyone."

"That supports the theory that you're seeing Marilee and Randall because they played important roles in your life, but you probably won't be seeing spirits elsewhere."

"Job security for Ann," said Jeremy, trying for a joking tone.

Ann wasn't sure if Jeanette would be disappointed by this prediction, but instead she looked relieved. "Thank heavens. That's not a skill I would want to deal with day in and day out."

"Sometimes *I* don't want to deal with it day in and day out," said Ann. She jammed her hands deeper into the pockets of her parka. "Let's get somewhere warm and talk."

~

THEY ENDED up back at the condo, Jeanette making tea for the three of them. Then she, Jeremy, and Ann sat down at the breakfast bar, while Randall remained standing.

"Here's what I'm thinking," said Ann, her hands cupped around her mug. "Randall's body is going to be found at some point." She turned to him. "Do you want the authorities to find your body as soon as possible?"

Randall shrugged. "Doesn't matter to me one way or the other, except so far as it inconveniences the person who owns the house."

"Marilee told me the house belongs to a guy named Stu—"

"Of course she did," muttered Randall.

"—and although I feel bad for him, I don't see how things will work out better for him if someone contacts the authorities about your body being in his house. Someone's bound to find your body, eventually. Seems like it might be better for Stu to just let things play out. The authorities might assume that a buddy of Stu's broke in without his permission."

"That's what happened, all right." Randall thought for a moment, then said, "Yeah, that makes sense. Let's do that."

Ann nodded. She had already decided there was no need

for Jeanette, Jeremy, and especially Randall to hear that Marilee had left him in Stu's house to die.

"When they do find the body," she continued, "with the bloody balaclava from the fake bookstore attack in the kitchen, the obvious conclusion will be that you were the attacker, but not necessarily that it was a fake attack. Do you care if the authorities find out you were the bookstore attacker and assume the attack was for real?"

Randall considered, longer this time, then said, "I'm never going back to prison again, and that was my main worry. There's no one around whose opinion I care about ..." His gaze moved from Ann to Jeanette and back. "...outside this room. No, I don't care if folks know it was me and think it was for real."

Ann smiled gratefully at him, then turned to Jeanette and Jeremy. "I'm pretty sure I'm not going to be able to convince Marilee to tell me how the sequel to *Darkest Before Death* ends, so I'm not going to be able to discharge my engagement for Darren."

"Maybe if you go back to Marco's alone—" began Jeanette, although without much enthusiasm.

Ann shook her head. "I think I've burned that bridge."

Jeanette nodded. "It doesn't seem so important anymore, anyway."

"That's for sure," agreed Jeremy.

"Although I'm not so sure Darren would agree," Jeanette added.

"I think we can tell him enough to convince him that his need to build up his client base doesn't justify what we'd need to do to accomplish that," said Ann. "Next consideration ... we can probably figure out a way we can alert the police anonymously that Kenny is dealing out of his Eden Beach apartment, without necessarily revealing that Marilee was a customer."

Jeremy grimaced. "I certainly wouldn't mind ensuring that the non-using residents of Eden Beach have better security than Kenny's providing."

Jeanette nodded.

"Okay," said Ann, "we'll figure out a way to get a tip to the cops." She sighed. "And I suppose you're off the hook for repaying the loan Marilee gave you."

Jeanette blushed. "I suppose so, but—"

Ann raised a hand. "Just bear with me for minute."

Jeanette, confused, nodded.

"Marilee told me Jeremy isn't the beneficiary of her will," said Ann.

Jeremy raised his eyebrows. "Really?" His expression was more shocked than angry. "Who is the beneficiary?"

"She wouldn't say. And it doesn't take money off the table as a motive since you believed you would inherit, but it does mean that you won't benefit from her death beyond not having to repay the loan."

Jeanette and Jeremy exchanged a cautiously hopeful glance.

"And finally," Ann continued, "how likely is it that Marilee would have OD'd if she had taken the twice-increased doses of Lorazepam you two were responsible for—not the third increase she made herself—and had not been taking Percocet?"

Jeremy's expression fell. "I don't know. I don't think it's possible to know—I'm not even sure an autopsy would help at this point." He paused, then said, "But I think it would be highly unlikely."

"So the chances are good that she bears the brunt of the

responsibility for her death." Ann drew a deep breath. "So that leaves what happened to Marilee's body."

Jeremy reached over and took Jeanette's hand.

"I've been willing to believe you when you say that you buried Marilee in the same way you would want to be buried," said Ann. "If you showed me a copy of your wills, would it reflect that?"

"Yes," said Jeremy. "Obviously not in a park," he tried for a feeble laugh, "but as close as it's legally possible to get."

Ann arched an eyebrow. "I don't want to seem to condone the idea of burying bodies of relatives—of anyone, for that matter—in community parks and failing to report their deaths to the authorities." She turned her gaze out the window, to where lines of rollers formed, built, then curled onto the beach. "At the same time, I feel like Marilee is the real culprit here, and like you two have suffered enough. And from a selfish point of view, even if you went to the police and told them exactly what happened, I'm afraid I'd get hauled into the fray."

"What are you suggesting?" asked Jeremy.

She returned her gaze to Jeremy and Jeanette. "I'm suggesting that you go home and keep your heads down and let things play out. And if the facts about what happened to Marilee come out, I'm suggesting that you not mention that you both increased the recommended dosage of Lorazepam. Plus," she added pointedly, "I'm suggesting you do everything you can to keep me out of it."

They sat in silence for several long moments, then Jeremy turned to Jeanette. "Jen, I know lying about what happened has been wearing you down. Do you still think it's better if we come clean?" It was clear he hoped the answer was no, but Ann appreciated that he was trying to put a willing face on his question.

"If I'm not hiding things from *you*," said Jeanette, "then it will be much less stressful. I would be willing not to tell Detective Morganstein what happened to Marilee's body and 'let things play out.'"

Jeremy's features relaxed in relief. "Yes, I—" His voice caught, and he cleared his throat. "Yes."

Jeanette turned to Ann. "But I still don't know why you're willing to do this."

Ann gave a wry smile. "As I said, it's partly to save myself the trouble that your confession might cause me." After a pause, she added, "But it's mainly because you let go of my wrist out there on the walkway."

Jeanette blushed. "I couldn't take you over the railing with me."

"Maybe *you* couldn't, but there's at least one person who would have been only too happy to hold on if there was the slightest chance it might save her."

61

Ann was back at Mahalo Winery, lying in her bed in the Curragh and listening to Joe Booth's breath a few feet away, when she heard, very faintly, the crunch of footsteps on the gravel of the parking area outside her window. A few seconds later, she heard a scrabbling sound from the back porch, which was separated from the bedroom by sliding glass doors and drawn drapes—she pictured someone pulling themselves up and over the railing—then the barely audible rattle of the handle of the doors.

"Joe?" she whispered.

"I hear it," he whispered back.

After a few moments, she heard the scraping sound again—someone climbing back off the porch—then sensed as much as heard someone moving along the side of the house toward the front door.

Joe rose from the chair where he had been sitting. She heard a creak of leather—she guessed he had unholstered his gun—then his tread moved slowly toward the closed door to the short hallway that led to the living room. He unlocked the door and cracked it open, his form barely perceptible against the faint illumination the moonlight cast in the kitchen and sitting area.

Everything was still and silent for a minute—it couldn't be another false alarm, could it?—and then, from beyond where Joe stood, she heard a shout from the living room.

"Police! Hands in the air!"

Ann threw back the covers and jumped out of bed, dressed in sweatpants, a sweatshirt, and socks, and hurried toward the bedroom door.

Joe grasped her arm. "Stay here. Let them do their job."

There were scuffling sounds from the living room, a few more shouted commands, then the noise moderated to only panting breaths and someone reading out Miranda rights.

"All clear!" came a male voice from the living room.

Joe and Ann hurried down the hall.

In the kitchen, the low stool on which Detective Bruce Denninger of the Lenape Police Department had been hunkered down for the last several hours—and for the last few nights—was overturned. Denninger stood in the living room with his partner, Brady Plott. Between them, biceps grasped in the two detectives' hands, wrists handcuffed behind him, was a man dressed all in black, his expression a combination of shock and rage.

Den asked Ann, "Is this who you were expecting?"

"Sort of," she said, a bit breathless from adrenaline, "although I didn't expect him to be doing his own dirty work. That's Alec Quine."

"Was he armed?" asked Joe.

Brady held up a gun, extended with what to Ann's untrained eye looked like a silencer, then turned to Alec. "So, Mr. Quine, what brings you to Mahalo Winery so late at night? Hankering for some Chester County wine?"

Alec glared at Ann but remained silent.

"Looking for some valuable bric-à-brac?" asked Brady, as Den spoke into his radio. "Like when you broke into the home at the top of the hill? Did you think Ann lived there?"

No response.

"Seems like you're a big fan of objets d'art," Brady continued. "Ann's painting, a brass kaleidoscope." He paused. "Ivory figurines."

"I was at an event in New York City when my father was killed," spat Alec. "Dozens of people can verify that."

"Oh, we know *you* were at the New York shindig," said Brady, "but I imagine that as a former defense lawyer, you have plenty of former clients you might be able to pay to make a trip to Princeton to pay your father a midnight visit."

"I'm saying nothing more until I talk with my attorney," said Alec, and clamped his lips shut in a tight line as if to emphasize his intentions.

Brady shrugged. "You don't need to tell me now, but you and your lawyer will have plenty of time to chat with me and Detective Denninger back at the station."

Ann saw the strobe of police lights coming down the hill from the big house, where two uniformed officers had parked.

Brady and Den guided Alec to the front door as the cruiser pulled up next to the Curragh. When they had gotten him settled in the back seat and the cruiser had disappeared down the drive, the detectives returned to the Curragh.

"Thanks for letting us use your place for the stakeout, Miss Kinnear," said Den.

"Thanks for being willing to set it up here," she replied. "You think he'll give up whoever he hired to kill his father?"

"Brady reviewed all the clients Alec Quine defended when he was still practicing law." Den turned to Brady. "Any ideas?"

"My money would be on Leon Fryall," said Brady. "Quine got him off a murder charge a couple of years ago, and we picked out Fryall in a rental car in Princeton on some traffic cam video."

"A nondescript, light-colored rental car?" Ann asked.

"Yup," confirmed Brady.

"Do you think that's who was following me in Ocean City?" asked Ann. "Or do you think it was Alec?"

"We can place Alec in Princeton at least one of the times you saw the guy you thought was following you in Ocean City, so my guess is that it was his hired hand."

"So why would Alec come to Kennett Square himself?"

"Maybe he wasn't happy with the hired hand's work." After a pause, Brady added, more soberly, "Maybe he didn't expect you to be coming back from Ocean City."

Ann shuddered.

"Plus," added Joe, "if it was the hired hand who broke into the big house thinking that it was where you live, Ann, then Alec might already have been unhappy with his performance."

"But how will we ever know?" asked Ann.

"If it *was* Fryall," said Brady, "it will be lucky for us. He has a track record of ratting out colleagues in exchange for leniency. I think we can strike a deal to get him to testify against Alec."

Ann grimaced. "I don't know if I want him to get much leniency if he really is a killer for hire."

Den nodded. "Whoever pulled the trigger at Tamaston will go away for a long time, but he knows we could make his time in prison a lot less comfortable if he doesn't cooperate."

Ann shivered and crossed her arms, her nerves still rattled. "So Alec hired someone to break into Tamaston, shoot Jock, and steal the ivory collection?" She sighed. "I supposed that getting Jock out of the way was the real goal, and stealing the ivory collection was just intended to divert attention from that goal."

"Which it did," said Brady. "I talked to Detective Withers from the Princeton PD. If you hadn't suggested that Alec might have been behind the break-in at Tamaston, I doubt it would have occurred to him."

She smiled wanly. "I doubt it would have occurred to *me* if I hadn't seen someone in Ocean City who I thought might be following me ... and if it hadn't been for the break-in at the big house. Who else would have it in for me *and* for Jock Quine?"

"I guess you made a believer of Alec," Joe said to Ann, "if he was alarmed enough about your conversation with Jock to want you out of the way."

"Well, whatever the reason," said Brady, not entirely hiding his cheerful skepticism about Ann's ability, "looks like you were right." He grinned. "Wish I could be in the room with Withers when we tell him we've arrested a fellow Princetonian."

Den's return smile was wolfish. "No reason we can't. We'll go to the station, get Quine processed, start the interview once his lawyer arrives, and if we think he might need a couple of hours to consider his options, we'll drive out to Princeton and tell Withers in person." He turned to Ann and Joe. "We'll keep you apprised of what we learn from Fryall. And thanks for the assist, Detective Booth. We're glad he decided to come through the front door, but we wanted someone with Ann in case he came in the back."

"No problem," said Joe.

Den and Brady left to hike down the hill to where their cruiser was parked behind the Cellar.

Ann picked up a half-full bottle of Sapele from the kitchen counter and pulled out the cork with a still-shaking hand. "As far as I'm concerned, there's never been a better time for a glass—or three—of wine. You?"

"Sounds good to me—although I'll stick with one. I'll need to hit the road soon."

She got out two glasses and poured. "I'll call Rowan and Del in the morning and let them know that the Lenape PD has the guy who was likely responsible for the break-in at the big house."

"So, 'Poindexter' was Alec Quine," said Joe.

"The name fits—he is bookish. I'm guessing he's the one who gave the hit man the wrong information about the nine-millimeter bullets ... and he probably removed the bullets that were in the gun ahead of time so Jock wouldn't be able to shoot back at Alec's former client." She downed half the glass and topped up her drink. "I'm not looking forward to having to tell Jock who was responsible for his death if the cops can prove that Alec hired the hitman."

"I agree it will be hard for him to hear. But Jock should know that you were responsible for bringing his killer to justice."

Ann took a more moderate sip of wine. "I started thinking about Marilee Forsythe hiring Randall Coombs to tap into his expertise, and it made me think that Alec, with his legal background, had a whole pool of experts to choose from."

"Why do you think he did it?"

"I guess his resentment of his father—for wanting Alec to be someone so different from who he wanted to be himself—ran a lot deeper than anyone realized. And I'm guessing that Alec hoped that Jock's publisher would ask him to take over the Robert Wolfram series—and why not, with Darren right there to keep him on track—and that Alec could mold it into something he thought had more literary merit." She took another sip. "I guess there's no telling what people will do for an audience," she said morosely.

She topped up Joe's glass even though he had only taken a few sips. "And thank you again for coming back here for this. I suppose Brady could have kept me company in the bedroom —" She blushed and took another swallow of wine.

"No problem," said Joe, graciously ignoring her blush. "It's been pretty much all paperwork in Chicago. A stakeout was nice change of pace. Plus, I was getting pretty tired of calling a hotel home and living out of a suitcase—it was nice to sleep in my own bed for a couple of nights."

"I can imagine." She glanced at her watch. "Will you be okay driving home this late?"

"Yup."

"When are you heading back to Chicago?"

"I'll see if I can get a flight tomorrow—" He glanced at his watch. "—actually today—or the next day."

"Have you had a chance to catch up with your high school squeeze while you've been back in Philly?" she said, trying to sound casual.

"Nah. Not really much to catch up with there." He took another sip of wine, then put his still nearly full glass down on the counter. "You'll be okay here by yourself tonight?"

"Yup ... it's hard to imagine Alec would have had a backup henchman waiting in the wings just in case he got nabbed."

"Yeah, seems unlikely." He went back to the bedroom to get his coat, which he had hung over the chair, as well as the Clint Eastwood filmography book she had gotten for him at Oh Buoy Books. The two of them had passed the time paging through it together, at least until it was time to turn off the light to convince their prey that Ann had gone to bed. He returned to the kitchen and, as he shrugged into his coat, said, "But I'd keep the doors locked anyway."

"Yeah, that's definitely the new policy." She followed him to the front door. "Thanks again, Joe—I really appreciate it. When you get back, I'll buy you dinner at Kennett Bistro."

"It's a deal." He bent down and kissed her cheek, then stepped outside and started down the path to the Cellar. He, too, had parked in the Mahalo staff lot so that Ann's Forester was the only vehicle parked next to the Curragh.

Ann watched until he disappeared into the shadows, then flipped the lock. She retrieved her laptop from the bedroom, poured the remains of Joe's wine into her glass, and settled down at the kitchen table. She opened the browser to YouTube and typed in *tailwheel landing techniques*.

She wasn't likely to be able to fall asleep again tonight.

62

A few weeks later, Ann sat next to Darren Van Osten at a table near the front of a Manhattan hotel ballroom, a cup of coffee and the remains of her chocolate mousse dessert in front of her.

On a stage festooned with black and gold bunting, the head of the GothamCon board—a woman who bore a striking resemblance to Angelica Huston's Morticia—stepped to the lectern. "Good evening. I'm honored this evening to be presenting the award for Best Debut Novel. The story behind one of this year's nominees is one any GothamCon author would be happy to borrow for a thriller novel: a cozy mystery author, Marilee Forsythe, secretly writes a thriller as Lara Seaford, before disappearing from her Ocean City, Maryland home, and that novel, *Darkest Before Death*, grabs the attention of readers and critics."

She glanced down at the lectern, and then back out at the audience. "And that isn't the only thriller-worthy event related to the conference. As you know, the story behind this year's honorary chair is just as thrilling—if more tragic—than the story behind *Darkest Before Death*. Last year, the board named

Jock Quine as chair of this year's conference, but when Jock died, we passed the position to his son, Alec. But once the Princeton, New Jersey, police arrested Alec for Jock's death, as well as for the break-in at a winery guest house in Chester County, Pennsylvania, we felt we needed to name a new chair. The board thought it was only appropriate to bestow that honor on the man who not only edited *Darkest Before Death*, but has now been named by Harrison & John as the new author of the Robert Wolfram series: Darren Van Osten."

She gestured toward Darren's table, and a wave of applause swept the ballroom.

A blushing Darren stood, raised his hand in acknowledgement, and resumed his seat.

The presenter continued. "I am especially glad that we've been able to honor Darren in this way, since, with Ms. Forsythe still missing, her family has asked that *Darkest Before Death* be withdrawn as a nominee for Best Debut Novel."

Ann glanced over at Darren. The other attendees might have admired his ability to maintain his equanimity in the face of this disappointment. However, Ann knew that Darren's original goal of a win at GothamCon—to build up his roster of editing clients—was moot in view of his assignment as the heir to Jock's Wolfram franchise. In fact, with his advance from H & J in hand, Darren had asked to reimburse Ann Kinnear Sensing for his engagement and keep the Ford F-150. Mike had balked at first, but Ann eventually convinced him—rightly as it turned out—that Scott would be just as pleased to hear the story of Mike's attempt to obtain the truck for him as he would be to actually own the truck.

And the Ford wasn't the only benefit of his association with Jock Quine that Darren had retained. He had arranged with the new owners of Tamaston to rent a room from them and to have access to the turret room. He had contracted with

Ann to make periodic visits to Princeton to mediate plot brainstorming sessions with Jock—especially for those pesky endings. Ann had no doubt that if Darren could hang onto Jock's faithful fan base, it wouldn't be long before he might be in a position to make an offer to purchase Jock's former estate.

Two days after Alec's break-in at the Curragh, Brady Plott and Bruce Denninger arrested Alec Quine's accomplice, Leon Fryall. As Brady anticipated, Leon quickly confirmed Alec's role in setting up Jock's murder. Ann flew the Avondale flight school's Piper Warrior to Princeton and, with Darren's help, obtained access to Tamaston to break the news to Jock.

He had at first refused to believe her, but eventually accepted that his son had been responsible for his death.

"I knew it irritated him when I tried to involve him in the things I loved. I thought I might win him over, but it sounds like I just made the situation worse."

"You can't blame yourself for what Alec did. They say that the apple doesn't fall far from the tree, but in this case, I think it rolled down a hill and took root in a ditch."

"Hey, that's good," said Jock with the ghost of a smile. "Can I use that?"

She returned his smile. "Sure. By the way, what was the deal with the meerkat incident you mentioned when we were trying to convince Alec that I was really in contact with you?"

Jock laughed sadly. "When we were in Botswana, we stayed at a camp where the meerkats were habituated to humans. A guide took us to one of their dens, although I didn't tell Alec what it was—I wanted it to be a surprise for him. I told him to sit down on the ground, and the little critters piled out of their burrows and ran right over to him. One of them got up on his shoulder—looking for high ground—before he swatted it away." He shook his head. "He was so damn freaked out, but I have to admit, I thought it was pretty funny. He called me a *perennial adolescent* and stormed off." His smile faded. "Guess it wasn't very nice of me to laugh."

"Maybe not—but there are a lot of kids that would have loved to have that experience with their fathers."

A few days after the trip to Princeton, Ann flew to Ocean City, rented a car, and drove to Marco's. She peered through the glass doors into the dining room and was greeted by the sight of a dozen diners, none wearing coats. Marco was holding out a bottle of wine for inspection by a couple seated at Marilee's table. There was no sign of Marilee herself.

Ann found Randall walking the beach, his summer clothing looking not quite as incongruous on a cold but at least sunny day. She blamed the brightness of the day for the fact that she didn't see him until he was quite close to her.

"Hey, Randall," she said. "How's it going?"

"Not bad," he replied. His voice was hard for her to hear over the sound of the waves. Perhaps it wasn't the brightness of the day that was lessening his presence after all.

"I went to Marco's," she said, "and Marilee's not there. I don't suppose you've seen her?"

"Nope. But then I hardly ever leave the beach, and I wouldn't expect to run into her here. That first time I met her —when she blackmailed me into working for her—was the only time I saw her on the beach."

They stood in companionable silence for a minute, looking out at the water, then Randall asked, "Are you going to keep coming back to Ocean City to see if she's still around?"

"I doubt it. Darren Van Osten doesn't need me to find out the ending of her second thriller novel anymore, and I suspect Jeanette and Jeremy aren't going to be interested in trying to contact her again." She glanced over at him. "How about you? Would you like me to come back to visit you? It wouldn't be a chore for me to fly down here periodically for a stroll on the beach."

"Oh, no," he said vaguely. "You don't need to do that."

She nodded and turned back to the water. She suspected that if she did come back in a week or two, Randall Coombs would no longer be walking the Ocean City beach. She hoped he was headed for a different—and better—destination than wherever Marilee had gone.

Applause brought Ann back to the Manhattan ballroom. The presenter had announced the winner of the Best Debut award, and the smiling recipient was making his way to the stage.

Ann had wondered if Jeremy and Jeanette might attend the conference, but she was relieved that they were laying low, as planned. Ann had gotten a handwritten letter from Jeanette the previous day.

Ann, just a quick note to let you know that Jeremy is holding down the fort at Frobishers' Pharmacy while I focus on expediting the repairs to our former location. It's almost ready to put on the market, and a couple of potential buyers have already contacted us.

Ann shook her head. If Marilee had just left Jeanette and Jeremy alone, they might have been able to repay the loan faster then any of them had expected.

Now that we have a little more free time, Jeremy's helping me to study to qualify to become a pharmacist. I wish my father was still here—he'd be so proud.

Ann suspected that the progress Jeanette and Jeremy were making was due not just to the time freed up because they no longer had to make those drives between Downingtown and Ocean City, but to the mental energy freed up by the fact that Marilee had, willingly or unwillingly, carried the knowledge of their outstanding loan to the grave with her.

I've enclosed a few documents that I thought would be of interest to you.

All the best,

Jeanette

The letter contained three folded sheets of paper. Two were copies of the pages from Jeanette and Jeremy's wills that confirmed their requests for natural burials for themselves. The third was a page from Marilee's will, a sealed copy of which Marilee had given Jeremy, that named her heir: a body farm in Tennessee, where her money would be used to study the effect on a body of an unofficial burial.

63

The morning after the GothamCon banquet, Ann stood on the ballroom stage, shuffling her notes nervously. Darren had told her that the sessions held on the last morning of the conference were usually sparsely attended—participation limited by attendees' travel plans and hangovers. But the board had moved her session from a small breakout room to the ballroom and it was nearly as full as it had been during the award ceremony.

Darren stepped to the lectern and tapped the mic. The room quieted.

"I'm very pleased to announce one of our most anxiously awaited speakers. Many of you know that I hired Ann Kinnear to help me create a memorial video to celebrate Jock Quine's life. Based on the video shown at last night's banquet, you know that Ann was able to contact Jock and convey his messages to his colleagues and fans." Darren had been disappointed that Ann didn't want the session with Jock videotaped, but had gratefully accepted the second-hand messages, which he had read in the video. "You may or may not believe in Ann's ability, but I can tell you I believe in it unequivocally, and it was a great comfort to me to hear a message from Jock to me." He paused for a moment, gathering his thoughts, then continued. "As I pick up the torch of the Robert Wolfram series," he arched a playful brow, "you can decide for yourselves how much of the stories are my own invention, and how many might be coming to me via Ann from Jock."

He paused for the friendly laughter to die down.

"And now, it's my pleasure to introduce one of our most intriguing speakers, who will share her thoughts on 'Making the Supernatural Super in Your Novel.' Please welcome Ann Kinnear."

Ann walked to the lectern to enthusiastic applause.

"I'd like to thank the GothamCon board for inviting me to speak to you," she said, "and to thank Darren for acting as my liaison—and for giving me a chance to meet Jock Quine, who, I can attest, is bigger than life, even in death."

As Mike had predicted, that got a laugh, although there was a tinge of uncertainty about it.

"My skill is not unique. I know a baby who can apparently see and respond to the spirit of her dead grandfather. I know a woman who can see the spirits of people who have played significant roles in her life." She cleared her throat. "I've been called a freak by some, and a liar by others. I've been thought crazy by people who see me speaking with a spirit and assume I'm talking to myself. But I am not a freak or a liar or crazy, and neither are the others who share my ability. The ability to sense and even communicate with a spirit doesn't involve burning incense or consulting a Ouija board. It may be unusual, but it's not supernatural." She paused to take a sip of water.

"I know that according to your programs, I'm supposed to be talking about 'Making the Supernatural Super in Your

Novel,' but I'd like to discuss something a little different: 'Making the Supernatural *Natural* in Your Novel.'"

The attendees exchanged looks, then she saw a few smiles, a few nods. Coffee cups were placed on tables, notebooks and laptops opened. She saw someone in the back videoing on his phone. No doubt it would find its way to her unauthorized YouTube channel.

"They say that dead men tell no tales ... but they are wrong. The tales that spirits have told me and my fellow sensers have enabled them to provide a sense of closure to those still living, to share knowledge, even to solve crimes. These spirits are accessible to those of us with the sensing ability because they retain some connection to the world of the living. Sometimes they have unanswered questions ..." like Randall, so present when he asked Ann to find out from Marilee what had gone wrong in the alley behind Oh Buoy Books, fading now that he knew the answer. "Sometimes there is something too precious for them to leave behind ..." like Niall Lynch, haunting the barrel room at Mahalo Winery and making faces at baby Rose. "Sometimes their zest for life is so great that it takes them time to let it go ..." like Jock Quine, shocked by the knowledge of Alec's role in his death but enthusiastic about continuing his work with Darren.

"For much of my life, I regretted having the ability to sense the dead, especially when people called me a freak or a liar or crazy. Then I came to terms with the idea that my ability was natural, if unusual, and I learned to appreciate what it meant for me, an ordinary woman, to be able to speak with the extraordinary people from beyond the grave whom I have met." She set her notes aside.

"Let me tell you about some of them ..."

THE END

ACKNOWLEDGMENTS

Many thanks to all those who contributed their time and expertise to the creation of this story ...

Michael Briggs Pharm.D., owner of Lionville Natural Pharmacy, for advice on the profession and the practice.

David Fried and Eileen Scott, for their medical insights and advice.

Rodger Ollis, for his expertise in all things police-related.

Chris Grall, for knowing that a nine-millimeter short bullet would never fit a nine-millimeter gun.

Harold Strawbridge, for his expertise at inventing fictional names that aren't already used in the real world for books, author conferences, and publishing imprints.

Sherry Knowlton, for sharing the meerkat story from her travels in Africa.

R. G. Belsky, for suggesting ways Ann, Scott, and Darren might occupy themselves on a wintry evening in Princeton, New Jersey.

Lisa Regan, for her service as plotting first responder par excellence.

Jon McGoran, for casting his eagle editorial eye over the story.

Wade Walton and Mary Dalrymple, for lending their unqualified support to my creative endeavors.

Any deviations from strict accuracy—intentional or unintentional—are solely the responsibility of the author.

ALSO BY MATTY DALRYMPLE

The Lizzy Ballard Thrillers

Rock Paper Scissors (Book 1)

Snakes and Ladders (Book 2)

The Iron Ring (Book 3)

The Lizzy Ballard Thrillers Ebook Box Set

The Ann Kinnear Suspense Novels

The Sense of Death (Book 1)

The Sense of Reckoning (Book 2)

The Falcon and the Owl (Book 3)

A Furnace for Your Foe (Book 4)

A Serpent's Tooth (Book 5)

Be with the Dead (Book 6)

The Ann Kinnear Suspense Novels Ebook Box Set - Books 1-3

The Ann Kinnear Suspense Shorts

All Deaths Endure

Close These Eyes

May Violets Spring

Sea of Troubles

Stage of Fools

Write in Water

Non-Fiction

Taking the Short Tack: Creating Income and Connecting with Readers Using Short Fiction (with Mark Leslie Lefebvre)

The Indy Author's Guide to Podcasting for Authors: Creating Connections, Community, and Income

ABOUT THE AUTHOR

Matty Dalrymple is the author of the Ann Kinnear Suspense Novels *The Sense of Death*, *The Sense of Reckoning*, *The Falcon and the Owl, A Furnace for Your Foe, A Serpent's Tooth*, and *Be with the Dead*; the Ann Kinnear Suspense Shorts, including *Close These Eyes* and *Sea of Troubles*; and the Lizzy Ballard Thrillers *Rock Paper Scissors, Snakes and Ladders*, and *The Iron Ring*. Matty and her husband, Wade Walton, live in Chester County, Pennsylvania, and enjoy vacationing on Mt. Desert Island, Maine, and in Sedona, Arizona, locations that serve as settings for Matty's stories.

Matty is a member of International Thriller Writers and Sisters in Crime.

Go to www.mattydalrymple.com > About & Contact for more information and to sign up for Matty's occasional email newsletter.

facebook.com/matty.dalrymple
twitter.com/mattydalrymple
instagram.com/matty.dalrymple

Cover design: Lindsay Heider Diamond

ISBN-13: 978-1-959882-01-5 (Paperback edition)

ISBN-13: 978-1-959882-02-2 (Large print edition)